Also available from Selina R. Gonzalez:

Prince of Shadow and Ash (The Mercenary and the Mage book 1)

Servant, Mercenary, Brother:
A Dresden Jakobs Vignette Collection Volume 1

Coming Autumn 2020:
Servant, Mercenary, Brother:
A Dresden Jakobs Vignette Collection Volume 2

Staff of Nightfall

THE MERCENARY AND THE MAGE BOOK 2

Staff of Nightfall

SELINA R. GONZALEZ

All characters in this book are fictional. Any resemblance to persons living or dead, events, or locales is purely coincidental.

Copyright © 2020 Selina R. Gonzalez.
All rights reserved.

This book or any portion thereof may not be reproduced or used in any manner whatsoever without the express written permission of the publisher except for the use of brief quotations in a book review. Please contact me with merchandizing questions or requests—I don't bite.

Cover Design by Deranged Doctor Design

Paperback ISBN 978-1-7344676-3-5
Kindle ISBN 978-1-7344676-4-2

Published by Wyvern Wing Press
www.WyvernWingPress.com
www.SelinaRGonzalez.com

To everyone who ever wanted to give up
but persevered anyway.

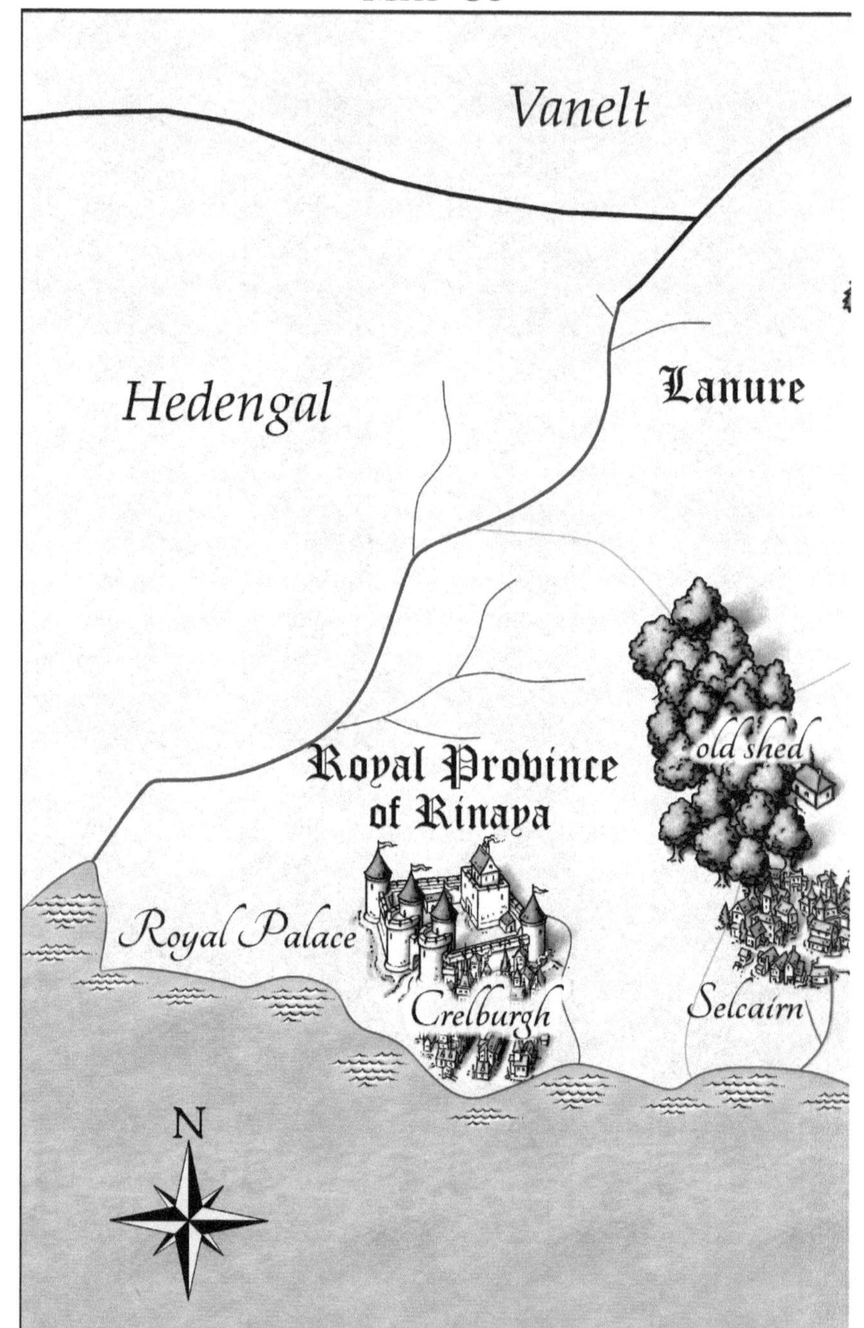

Vanelt
Hedengal
Lanure
old shed
Royal Province
of Rinaya
Royal Palace
Crelburgh
Selcairn
N

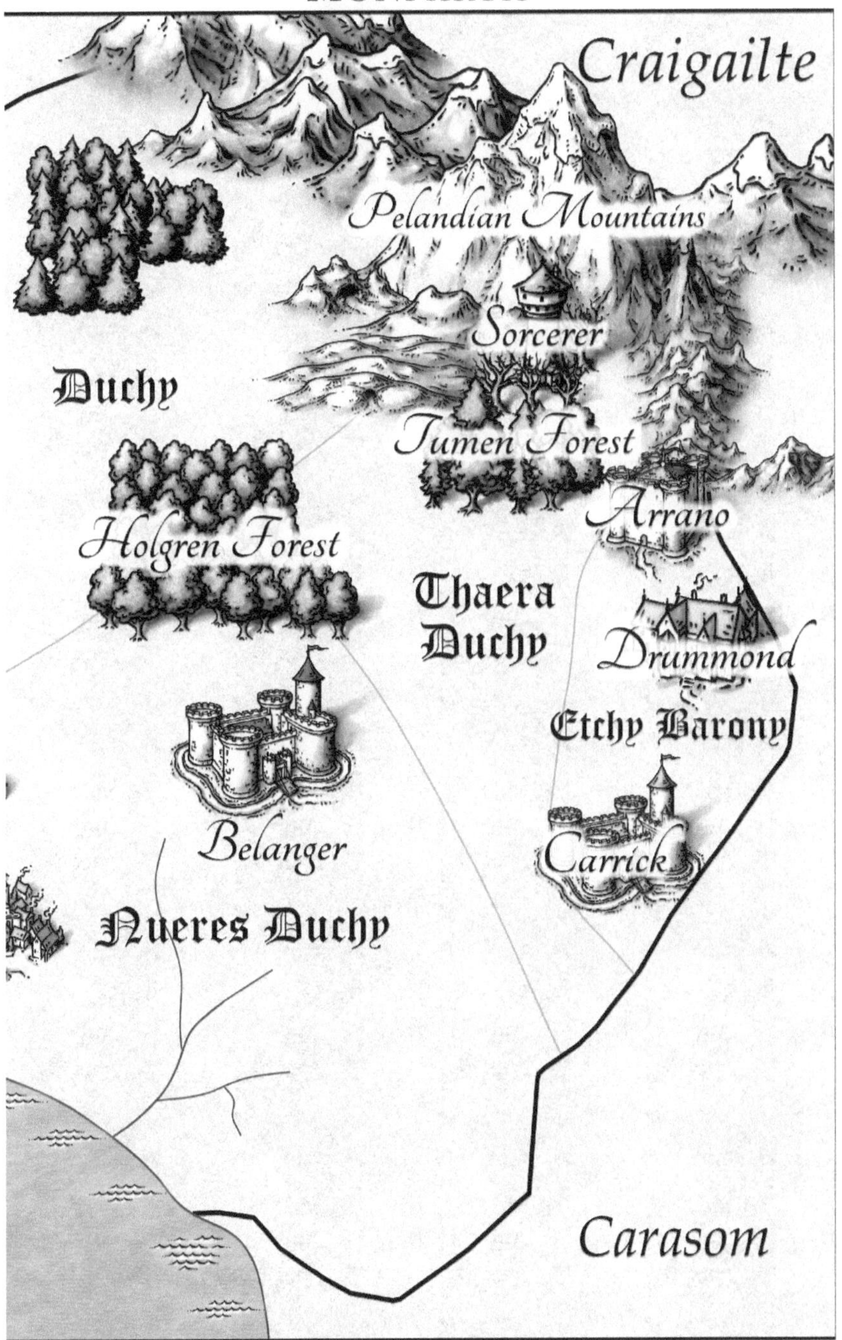
Craigailte
Pelandian Mountains
Sorcerer
Tumen Forest
Arrano
Duchy
Holgren Forest
Thaera Duchy
Drummond
Etchy Barony
Belanger
Carrick
Nueres Duchy
Carasom

CHAPTER 1

REGULUS CLUTCHED ADELAIDE TIGHTER. HIS HEART THUDDED against his ribs. Every hoof beat as Sieger galloped through the woods sent a jolt through his body. Adelaide's gelding Zephyr raced behind them. The light from the window in the top of the sorcerer's accursed tower flashed through the forest, growing fainter as the trees transitioned from dead and blackened to healthy pines and birches.

His tongue stuck to the roof of his mouth as Adelaide's words echoed in his mind. *"He took it. My magic. It's gone."* Her hair flew in his eyes, his mouth. He pulled the hair away and placed his cheek next to her head, wrapping his hand back over hers. *"Gone. He took it."*

As the scene flashed through his mind again, he closed his eyes and tried to will it away but couldn't. Couldn't stop the scene replaying. Adelaide falling to her knees before the sorcerer, her head thrown back in a silent scream. Her eyes glazed over, rolling back in her head until almost all that was visible were the whites.

Regulus opened his eyes. *My fault. My fault. My fault.* The words hammered through his head in time with the pounding of his heart. He should have been right next to her; should have pushed the sorcerer away before he wound his hand around her wrist. He shouldn't have taken her in the first place. Two years ago he shouldn't have agreed to serve the sorcerer.

But that was foolishness, and he knew it. Even had he been closer, he might not have been able to stop the sorcerer. And he hated to admit it, but he would make the same choices all over again. Because Dresden and Harold and the others were still alive. Because, even with her magic stolen, Adelaide was still alive. But would she ever forgive him?

They rode until the horses panted, their chests heaving, and necks drenched with sweat. Sieger snorted as he slowed, tired by the fast pace and the weight of two riders. Regulus pulled back on the reins, bringing the stallion to a halt. Zephyr snorted, following Sieger's lead and stopping as well. Regulus shifted Adelaide forward and dismounted, then picked her up and carried her off the saddle.

"I'm fine." But her voice sounded weak, and she didn't fight him.

He set her on a mossy patch of ground under a beech tree. She slumped against the trunk as he knelt in front of her and tossed aside the oversized black sword—the last piece of the Black Knight ensemble the sorcerer had given him. He was free, he didn't need it now. He pushed her hair out of her face. In the pale moonlight, tears glistened on Adelaide's cheeks. What could he say? *I'm sorry* felt hollow. Crass.

She turned away and pressed against the tree trunk, curled in on herself, staring at the ground. Regulus ducked his head, trying to catch her eyes. *Etiros, help me.* "I'm—"

"Don't." She lunged forward and wrapped her arms around him, her fists clenching his shirt and her breath hot on his neck. "Don't you dare apologize."

"I don't know what to do," he whispered. He pulled her onto his lap and stroked her hair, his fingers brushing against her back.

"Just..." She turned and rested her head on his shoulder. "Don't let go. Please. Don't let go."

"I—"

Zephyr snorted and pawed the ground, startling Regulus. Sieger sniffed the air, then whinnied. Regulus looked around, still stroking

Adelaide's hair. Shadows moved in the trees. He couldn't tell if it was just the light, a trick of his tired eyes. Or if something actually— a glint of yellow. He stiffened and watched the same spot. There. Two eyes, a dull, reflective yellow-green in the moonlight. They vanished. A growl reverberated nearby. Adelaide jumped away. Sieger reared; Zephyr kicked his back legs. The horses took off. Regulus leapt to his feet and grabbed the oversized sword.

"What is it?" Adelaide whispered as she stood, her dagger glinting in her hand.

Regulus scanned the shadows. His newly non-enhanced muscles strained against the unwieldy sword's weight. "Not sure."

More growling and snarling sounded from the darkness on all sides. Adelaide only had a dagger. She hadn't retrieved her throwing knives from the bear. Why would she need to? She had magic. *Had.* Regulus gulped back the rising panic. They stood beneath the beech tree, surrounded by unknown creatures. An average woman and an average man. No immortality. No magically enhanced strength or speed. No magic.

Adelaide crouched, her feet spread and planted, her hands raised in front of her face, her dagger in her right hand. A good defensive stance. Protecting her torso and keeping a strong center of balance. Some measure of calm settled over his nerves.

No. Not an average man and woman. Adelaide was anything but average. And there were those who said the name Regulus Hargreaves with equal parts admiration and fear long before he met the sorcerer. He'd killed plenty of men and monsters. And Adelaide had killed a troll. He squared his shoulders and adjusted his own stance, confidence growing. *Grant us mercy, Etiros. Give us victory.* The same prayer he'd prayed as a mercenary.

The beasts still hadn't moved from the shadows. As if they were sizing them up, trying to decide if they were worth the trouble. Maybe they would give up—movement to the right drew his attention. Yellow-green eyes flashed low in the darkness. Something shifted forward.

The canine was thin, built like a racing hound, but as tall as Regulus' middle. Shaggy gray fur hung from its lithe frame, except along its neck and underbelly, which were covered with segmented bone plating. Its black lips pulled back in a snarl over long, yellowed fangs.

"What…" Adelaide breathed.

"Kanadosus," he murmured. "Pack hunters. Armored underbelly, except for just under its jaw." He didn't mention he'd seen three men ripped limb from limb by kanadosi back in his early days as a mercenary, but he recalled their screams.

Two more kanadosi crept out of the brush. Rustling and growling sounded behind them. Adelaide turned. He'd have to trust her to deal with the ones behind him.

The kanadosi growled and surged forward together. One jumped at his chest. He raised his sword and swung at the kanadosus' neck. The swing was awkward, but the beast fell, its neck half severed. Another kanadosus sunk its teeth into his right arm and he groaned. He hit the pommel on the beast's head, and it released his arm and fell back with a yelp. He swung but aimed poorly. The blade cut into its shoulder at the base of its neck and lodged fast in the armor plating on its chest. The kanadosus thrashed, and the sword ripped out of Regulus' grip. Adelaide cried out, and Regulus spun toward her. A kanadosus lay dead between them, another limped away with blood flowing down its shoulder.

But his eyes snapped up to Adelaide, pinned against the tree, a snarling kanadosus clawing and snapping at her. She held the beast at arm's length, gripping its shoulders. He ran, his heart plummeting as her elbows buckled. She jerked her head away from its bite, her scream chilling. He grabbed the kanadosus and threw it aside as another beast jumped on his back. Its claws dug into him, slicing through his shirt. He staggered and tried to reach up to grab the writhing creature. It bit his left shoulder, and he yelled.

Adelaide ran forward, bending to snatch up her dagger as she went. Regulus ducked as she stabbed at the kanadosus on his back. It collapsed with a strangled whimper. He threw it off his back and looked about wildly. Adelaide stood at the ready, her hands empty. She must not have been able to pull her dagger free. He saw one of the kanadosi disappear into the shadows. The rustling quieted as the remaining kanadosi fled. His pulse hammered in his ears as he scanned the darkness for any sign of movement, any shadow out of place.

Nothing. They were alone with the corpses of kanadosi and no horses. As the adrenaline wore off, he winced, light-headed. He stumbled toward Adelaide, frowning as he pointed at her right arm. Her sleeve hung in tatters, and blood dripped from her hand.

"You're hurt." He tripped, and she steadied him. His right arm and left shoulder burned and ached. She frowned.

"Not as badly as you are." She guided him to the ground. "Hang on." She fetched her dagger from the jaw of the last kanadosus, limping as she walked.

"Your leg…?"

"My foot." She sat next to him, cutting strips from her dress. "Just got twisted." She kept wincing as she worked with her left foot out to the side. The leather of her boot was mangled, but he didn't see any blood on her foot. Only on her arm. She moved to wrap his arm, but he stopped her.

"You first."

"It's just some scratches. You're bleeding more. I…" Her voice cracked. "Let me do what I still can."

Guilt pricked him as she tightly bound his forearm. "Thank you."

She nodded and wrapped wide strips of cloth over his shoulder, across his chest, and under his arm. The pressure made the wounds ache but would help stem the bleeding. When she finished, Regulus wrapped the last strip around her forearm. His tired hands struggled. A cloud drifted over the moon, making it difficult to tell where the cuts began and ended, so he wrapped as much of her arm as he could. The memory of the lights Adelaide had conjured before brought another stab of guilt.

"I'm sorry I didn't stop him," he said in a strained whisper. He cleared his throat. "I should have—"

"What, Reg?"

He blinked at her use of his nickname. His hands hovered over the knot he had tied on her wrist as he met her eyes.

"Should have, could have." She pulled her arm to her torso and looked away. "It doesn't change anything."

The bitterness in her voice made him wince. He wanted to ask how to fix this, how to fix them, what she wanted from him. Wanted to beg her for forgiveness. But the words stuck in his throat. Too painful to speak aloud. Too afraid to find out the answer.

"We should look for the horses. And find a place to rest, away from the…" He gestured toward the dead kanadosi.

His heart fell further as she stood without looking at him. He followed her in the direction the horses had bolted, leaving the now difficult-to-wield sword of the Black Knight behind. The horses' rapid pace had left an obvious trail in the moss, pine needles, and dirt, even in the dim moonlight. They followed the tracks, calling to their horses.

The space Adelaide maintained between them stung more than the bites on his arm and shoulder. Her limp worsened as they walked, but with the way she wouldn't meet his eyes, he didn't dare offer to let her lean on him. He was about to suggest they halt their search until morning when a whinny caught his attention. He scanned the woods to his right.

"Sieger?"

"Zephyr?" Adelaide called.

Hoof beats, then Sieger trotted around a tree toward them. Zephyr trailed behind, still tied to Sieger's saddle. Regulus sighed with relief and caught Sieger's bridle.

"Hey. There's my boy." He patted Sieger's neck, and his hand came away sticky with sweat. "Sorry you had such a fright."

He glanced around Sieger's neck at Adelaide rubbing Zephyr's forehead. She murmured something he couldn't hear. He gave her a moment before finding a nearby pine suitable for both tying up the horses and taking shelter. He fetched his knife from the saddlebag, then ducked under the branches where Adelaide had already curled onto her side. With a suppressed sigh, he laid down a couple feet away from her, his knife close at hand. The soft sounds of the horses and the background noise of insects filled the air as he drifted to sleep.

Regulus awoke to find Adelaide curled against him, her injured arm crossed in front of her chest between them, her other arm thrown over his torso. His bandaged right arm wrapped up and around her shoulders. The sun had already risen high into the sky, but in the shade of the pine, the air felt cool. The heat of her body against his, the way she fit against his side, her face tucked into his shoulder, healed him and broke him all at once. His shoulder felt stiff and sore around the bite, and his right arm ached. The longer he lay there, the more aware he became of the stinging in his back from where the wolf's claws had scratched him. He needed to move. He *should* move. She probably had drifted next to him in her sleep. But he kept still, treasuring the moment.

Afraid when she woke, she would resent him for what had happened to her.

Afraid to lose her.

CHAPTER 2

ADELAIDE SHIFTED AND WOKE UP. HER RIGHT FOREARM STUNG. Worse was the dead emptiness, deep in her soul, a hollow carved out when the sorcerer ripped away her magic. Instead of a gentle thrum of energy in her veins, she felt only silence. Months of practice, honing her ability in secret, and just when she was getting a strong grasp on her gift, it was stolen. *Etiros, why?* She shifted, squeezing her eyes against tears, and pushed against something soft and warm. She forced her eyes open to shaded daylight. Regulus lay on his back, his right arm curved around her. He moved away and sat up, stretching. The sudden departure of his body felt like a blanket being ripped away.

"Sorry." His voice, gravelly and deep, reverberated down her spine. "I didn't want to wake you. I wasn't…I didn't mean to…" He glanced away, prodding the bite on his shoulder.

"Oh." Her heart twisted. She stood and turned away, hiding the heat that rose to her cheeks and the tears that pricked at her eyes. After his odd behavior last night, the way he wouldn't meet her eyes now…

Was that really all it took? Having her magic taken? Was it that she was weak? Or broken? She touched the gray cloth strip dotted with dried blood wrapped around her forearm. Regulus hadn't always known she had magic. But it wasn't just going back to how things were before. She had been drained. Damaged. She swallowed a sob. The ache of her missing magic made her feel incomplete. Losing Regulus, too…

Regulus cleared his throat. "Adelaide?"

"Hm?" She didn't trust herself to face him.

"I don't know how to convince you I'm sorry. I failed you. I'm sorry I couldn't protect you. I don't know how to make it up to you. I probably can't."

She turned around in surprise. Regulus stood with his hands clasped behind his back, staring at his feet.

"I know this is my fault. I won't pretend I don't deserve your blame—"

"What?" she gasped. "Blame?"

"I only wanted to protect the people I love." He looked up, the desperation in his eyes wringing out her emotions. "If I could put this right, I would. I understand if you're…if we're…" He swallowed and dropped his head. "Done. I want you to know—"

"You think I'm angry with you?" Adelaide bit her lip and wrapped her arms over her stomach. "I thought—you were acting like I was broken. Different. I thought you didn't want me anymore."

For an awful moment, Regulus was silent. Then he laughed. Her face heated.

"I blamed myself and thought you did, too. I thought you didn't want *me*." Regulus strode over in the space of a heartbeat and placed one hand on her hip, the other on her cheek. Her breath caught. "There is nothing, no magic, no sorcery, no pain or pleasure, nothing on this earth that can make me stop loving you. I want you and will love none other."

His warm palm pressed against her cheek. She stared into his eyes. Those eyes, intense like molten silver yet gentle. Her lips parted, but she couldn't piece together a coherent thought.

"I am yours, Adelaide." The huskiness in his voice made her heart tremble. "You have all of me, now and forever. If you want me."

She reached up, touching the stubble growing along his jaw. She ran her thumb over his lips. "And I am yours. Heart and soul."

A smirking half-smile warned her just before he pulled her in and kissed her. She leaned into his kiss, melting against him. Regulus' fingers curled against her back and she quivered with joy, not even caring about the scratchiness of his coarse stubble.

"Marry me," he whispered.

She chuckled, breathless. "I already asked you, remember?"

"I'll take that as a yes." He kissed the hollow between her collarbones, then her neck, moving agonizingly slowly up to her mouth. She sighed as his lips found hers and wrapped her arms around his neck. He flinched with a grunt as her arm bumped his wounded shoulder.

"Sorry." She leaned back, concern conquering her desire to kiss him until she could no longer stand. "We should get going. Those bites need tended."

Regulus nodded, although he sighed with obvious disappointment as he looked around. Deciduous trees surrounded them, spaced far apart. The tallest peaks of the Pelandian Mountains glinted white between the trees behind Regulus.

"If we're about where I think we are," he said, "there should be a path nearby. If I'm right, we should reach the Drummonds' by the end of the day."

"No!" She clutched his shirt and forced herself to sound less panicked. "We can't go there."

"What? Why—"

"Nolan might be waiting there. I can't..." She rested her head against his shoulder. "We need a plan before we face him. And even if he's not there, Lord and Lady Drummond believe we're engaged." And Lady Drummond didn't like Regulus, but she wasn't about to say that.

"Oh. So, Arrano, then?"

"Also no good." She sighed, a headache forming in the middle of her forehead. "If Nolan found out I was there, he would accuse you of kidnapping me or something. I was thinking…" She chewed on her lip. The idea had occurred to her as she fell asleep last night, but she wasn't sure what Regulus would think. "We need help. I think we need to talk to my father."

"Your…oh." She could practically hear his mind churning as he spoke. "And tell him…?"

"Everything."

He pulled away and looked into her face, holding her shoulders. "Everything… Everything?"

Adelaide knew it wouldn't be easy for him. He'd barely been able to tell her the truth. She didn't relish telling her parents what had happened to her or what she had done, either. But she was out of ideas. Maybe it was childish, but she trusted Father to protect them from Nolan.

"My father is wise. And has powerful connections. He'll know what to do. But…he's astute. He won't trust you if he suspects any dishonesty or omission." She sighed. "We'll have to tell him the full truth. Is that…all right?"

After a moment, Regulus nodded. "If that's what you want to do, that's what I'll do. You won't let him kill me, right?"

She smiled. "That's what we're trying to avoid, remember?"

After a brief detour to catch and cook a rabbit, they set out. They kept up a trot as long as possible, giving their horses walking breaks before hurrying onward. The sun dipped low and Adelaide's stomach rumbled, but still they rode on. They followed the roads, but cut across fields for speed's sake. Their ragged, bloodied appearance drew plenty of stares. She was beyond caring. They made do with a meager meal of berries and a very chewy squirrel for supper, then spent the night hidden in a copse of trees and bushes, curled against each other.

The next morning, they crossed a stream and caught a couple fish. Cooking them on a stick wasn't ideal, but it tasted infinitely better than squirrel. Shortly after noon they spied a group approaching, so they moved into the tall grass alongside the rough dirt road. Sunlight glinted on helms and chainmail. There looked to be ten mounted knights and several servants on palfreys weighed down with baggage. She watched the unusual group move at a surprising pace.

"What do you make of that?"

"Nothing good results in a group like that." Regulus furrowed his brow, looking over his shoulder at the knights. "Certainly trouble somewhere."

"Hm." She halted Zephyr and raised her hand to shield her eyes from the sun. It was a curious sight. She squinted at the lead knight. The bright blue of the caparison on that lead horse… Decorated with something white…

"It can't be." She wheeled Zephyr around and took off toward the road.

She heard Regulus calling her name and following her, but the heraldry on the leader's horse consumed her focus. A rearing white unicorn was embroidered on the blue caparison over the horse's flank—the Belanger crest. The knight wore a helm, and the raised visor cast his face in shadow, but the horse she recognized. A large dappled gray destrier with a dark mane and tail.

"Father?" She urged Zephyr into a gallop, her heart leaping. "Father!"

The man slowed his horse and turned toward her. She grinned as his features came into focus. The shadow of a beard. The deep laugh lines around his mouth. His defined nose. His wide, deep-set green eyes.

"Father!"

Father reined in his horse and held up his hand, halting his knights behind him. "Adelaide?"

She jumped off Zephyr's back at the edge of the road and regretted it as her ankle smarted, but she ignored the pain and ran toward her father as fast as her throbbing foot allowed. Father dismounted and tossed his helm down as he ran to her. She registered that he was crying moments before he enveloped her in a crushing embrace.

"You're here," Father said into her hair. "How are you here? Are you all right?" He held her at arm's length, looking her over. Tears rolled down his smiling face. He grabbed her hand to look at her wrapped forearm. "What happened? How bad is it?" Without waiting for an answer, he hugged her again, his hand clutching the back of her head.

She relaxed against him, all her stress and worry melting away as she rested her forehead on his shoulder. *Everything's all right now.* She didn't even mind the chainmail under his tunic pushing into her skin.

"I was afraid I'd lost you," Father whispered.

"What?" She leaned back to look up into his eyes.

"How did you escape?" Worry lined Father's usually joyful face. He pushed her tangled hair over her shoulder. "No, no, actually, we have to get you home. Your mother is worried sick. You can tell us everything after you've gotten cleaned up and rested."

"I don't understand." She smiled despite her confusion. "Where are you going? How did you know I was in trouble? Did Minerva send word?"

"We were going to look for you." Father rubbed her shoulder, his laugh lines crinkling into a familiar smile that warmed her very soul. "And Minerva did send word, but her messenger was followed very shortly by someone else." His smile wavered as his brows knit together. "I must admit…I am confused you agreed to a marriage before I'd even met the young man in question."

Her stomach fell like a rock. *No. Etiros, please. No, no, no…*

"Hello, love." The world swayed as she turned from her father toward Nolan's voice. Nolan smiled broadly, looking relieved as he swept her into an embrace. Her whole body went stiff as one of her throwing knives, her arms plastered to her sides.

"Get the hell *away* from her!" Boots pounded dirt as Regulus ran up behind Adelaide. He grabbed her shoulder and pulled her back, shoving Nolan's shoulder with his free hand as he drew her in close. "You don't touch her."

"Hargreaves." Nolan's eyes narrowed. "I'm very interested to hear how you ended up wandering around *alone* with *my* betrothed. Seize him."

Panic turned her limbs to stone. Had Nolan already turned Father against Regulus? But Father's knights made no move to dismount.

"I give the orders here, Sir Carrick." Father held his left hand out to her, his right grasping his sheathed sword. "Adelaide, what's going on?"

She reached for his hand, like a little girl who wanted her father to keep her safe. *No. Wait.* Father needed to know she trusted Regulus, not Nolan. She shook her head and pressed against Regulus' chest.

"This is my betrothed, Lord Regulus Hargreaves."

Regulus gave her shoulder a gentle squeeze.

"Ha!" Nolan drew his sword. "I had my suspicions. The Black Knight rode a large, black horse. That's what that witless Sir

Hostland said." He pointed the sword at Sieger. "You have a large, black horse. You were missing when Adelaide went missing. And you tried to challenge me to a duel when you learned of our engagement. *You're* the Black Knight who kidnapped *my* betrothed."

"You and I are not engaged, Nolan!" Adelaide glared as she wound her fingers between Regulus'. She glanced at the knights, waiting in the road a little behind Father. She recognized all of them, although Sir Ruddard and others were absent. Sir Charing looked relieved and happy to see her. Most watched impassively.

She couldn't admit Nolan had forced her into agreeing to his marriage proposal, not in front of knights who knew she always had a blade on her. So many had mocked the Khastallander tradition behind her back, but her training had earned begrudging respect from most of them. She wouldn't appear weak and afraid, or give them reason to think they were right to doubt her.

"Adelaide, love." Nolan's look of pity and tenderness made bile rise in her throat. "Whatever this mercenary did, whatever threats he made, you're safe now. I don't care what happened. I still love you." He pointed his sword at Regulus. "But if you kidnapped and despoiled her to try to force her into marrying you, I'll have your head."

"Enough!" Father's authoritative bellow rang out like a command on a battlefield. Nolan actually shrank back. Father's iron grip latched onto Adelaide's arm, and he led her away. With reluctance, she let her hand slip out of Regulus'. She felt the tension in Father's body as he put his arm around her and led her several paces from Regulus, Nolan, and the knights. His eyes flashed as he turned toward her. Crimson flooded his strained face.

"Did this man…harm you?" Fury laced Father's clipped whisper.

"No! He saved me."

"Is that the truth?" Father cradled the side of her face in his hand. "It wouldn't be your fault. You should know that. No one will ever know. Sir Nolan seems sincere, and I would hold him to his word. But if this…Hargreaves hurt you, if he touched you—"

"Father, no." She pulled his hand down and held it between hers. She shuffled her feet and glanced toward Nolan and Regulus. They glared at each other, Nolan in chainmail and still holding his sword at the ready while Regulus stood unarmed and without armor. She gulped. The knights looked down at them from their horses. Would they be able to stop Nolan in time if he attacked? She couldn't risk provoking him. "I promise we will explain everything. But for now, trust that Regulus isn't a threat. He would never hurt me."

Father sighed, then looked over her shoulder. "I don't know what's going on here, but I agree that you have a lot to explain, Lord Hargreaves." He looked at Nolan. "You all do."

After sending a knight to the Drummonds to inform them of Adelaide's safe return, they headed home. Father insisted he ride next to her as they returned to his castle. She didn't mind. She'd missed him more than she had realized. To her relief, Father also insisted Regulus and Nolan ride on opposite sides of the group where neither could harm the other.

It was almost midnight when they arrived at the castle. Even in the dark, with hardly any moonlight thanks to the clouds, she recognized every angle and curve of the immense crenellated walls and towers. The northern part of the wall to the left of the main gate was whole again after being knocked down to accommodate adding a one-level expansion of five rooms and a second hall for Father's eldest, Landon, and his wife and infant. In the dim light, she made out the shadowy outline of scaffolding and piles of unfinished stone.

Father left the men with instructions to keep Regulus and Nolan separate and to tell the steward to put them in guest rooms. He led her to his own suite, but Mother greeted them in the hall before they even neared the door. Her black hair hung over her shoulder in a loose braid. The light of Father's candle reflected off Mother's tears, making her brown skin glisten. Her silk robes swished as she ran to Adelaide, sobbing.

"I couldn't sleep. Then when I saw your father had returned, I thought…" She cried into Adelaide's shoulder and squeezed so tight, Adelaide could hardly breathe. "*Meana sohka keh ton ner suche oh, mareh piahry ledekah.*" *I thought you were dead, my darling girl.*

"I'm all right." It was only half true, and her voice broke on a sob. "I'm alive."

Mother finally pulled back and looked her over. She wiped away Adelaide's tears and then her own. "What's this?" She brushed her fingertips against Adelaide's bandaged arm. "Are you hurt?"

"Just some scratches." She shrugged. "We were attacked by kanadosi."

Mother looked around, then lowered her voice. "You didn't heal it? I don't want you using your abilities, but this doesn't look good."

"I can't." Adelaide looked at her feet sinking into the plush red carpet in the hallway and held her arm against her chest. She took a deep breath to steady herself. The words lodged in her throat. Father placed a comforting hand on her back. "I don't have my magic anymore."

Mother gasped and Father's fingers tightened against her back.

"It's a long story. I'm too tired to tell it now."

"Right." Mother took her hand. "Come, I'll have a servant draw a bath—"

"I just want to sleep."

"Of course. Sleep well, Adelaide." Father kissed the top of her head. "We'll talk tomorrow."

CHAPTER 3

BEFORE COLLAPSING ONTO THE PLUSH BED IN A COZY GUEST room, Regulus locked the door and wedged a wood chair under the handle. He wasn't about to risk Carrick sneaking in to cut his throat in the middle of the night. He wished he knew for certain Adelaide was safe, but he would have to trust the castle was secure enough to keep Carrick from getting to her. Dreams of prowling through the castle to relieve Carrick of his head wove through his sleep.

The next morning, a short, portly servant with a balding head knocked on his door and brought in a tub, followed by several servants bearing buckets of heated water. As they filled the tub, another servant brought in a silver tray piled with eggs, ham, and potatoes. Regulus devoured the food. The balding man left and then reappeared with clothes, which he laid on the chair. He told Regulus he would wait outside to escort him to Lord Belanger after his bath.

The bath water turned repulsive, filling with dirt and blood. His bites and scratches burned. The wound on his upper arm wasn't bad, but the one on his shoulder started bleeding afresh. He had to hold his soiled shirt on it for several minutes before the bite stopped bleeding, covered by a thin layer of clotted blood. He scrubbed himself clean then put on the clothes, a pair of brown trousers, and a dark blue shirt. They fit him well enough, if a little tight across the shoulders.

Once he'd pulled on his boots, he met the balding servant in the hallway. The man led him down several hallways and two staircases. Regulus marveled at the decorative weapons, massive tapestries, and oil paintings on the walls. He knew Lord Belanger was wealthy, but…this was impressive. The man had to be nearly as wealthy as Baron Carrick himself. Not that Regulus had ever been inside the baron's castle. Still, Carrick hadn't been wrong. Arrano needed some beautifying to deserve Adelaide.

The servant opened a door and motioned for Regulus to enter. He walked into a spacious room with tall, open windows, bookshelf-lined walls, a few cushioned armchairs, and a couch. Lord Alfred Belanger stood looking out a window, his hands clasped behind his back. He turned as the servant closed the door.

Lord Belanger wasn't as tall as Regulus, but taller than average. Short, gray hair framed his square face and broad forehead. He had to be in his late fifties. Wrinkles around his eyes and mouth hinted at a playful personality, but he wasn't smiling now. In fact, he looked murderous. He stood tall, his spine straight as a lance. His shoulders back, feet planted. A stance that conveyed authority and anticipated respect. The stance of a warrior. Of a commander.

"Lord Hargreaves." His rich baritone was icy.

"Lord Belanger." Regulus bowed. "Thank you for your hosp—"

"I have neither time nor patience for niceties, Hargreaves." Belanger rubbed his temple. "I want to know your story. I've heard Nolan Carrick's. I know his father, and he seems a sincere young man. He made some serious accusations against you." Belanger's right hand twitched like he longed to grasp a sword. "But there are many things that do not add up and he cannot explain. My daughter is…" He worked his jaw and clasped his hands behind his back again. "Hurt. I want to know how and why. So tell me your story."

Regulus shifted. "First, Lord Belanger, I want you to know I love your daughter. I only want to protect her."

"Sir Carrick said the same thing."

"Carrick is a liar and villain!" He bit his tongue and tried to rein in his temper. To display proper decorum. He was starting behind, and he needed to give a favorable impression.

"Again," Belanger said dryly, "Carrick said the same of you."

"Of course he did." Regulus rubbed the back of his neck, his shoulders drawing together. "My lord, where *is* Adelaide?"

"That's not your concern at this moment."

"With all due respect, it's my *only* concern at this moment." Regulus glanced behind him at the door. "I need to know she's safe. Where's Carrick?"

"Are you implying Sir Carrick is a threat to my daughter's safety?"

"No, my lord. I'm telling you plainly that he is." Regulus crossed his arms. "I swear I will tell you the full truth. I promised Adelaide I would. But not until I know she is safe."

Belanger frowned, his gaze cold as steel. "You dare insult me by suggesting my daughter is not safe in my own home?" Before Regulus could answer, the door banged open.

"Oh, thank Etiros!" Adelaide ran in, still limping, followed by her mother. She hugged Regulus, her damp hair smelling of lavender. "I couldn't sit still for fear of Carrick and you running across each other alone. And I wanted—"

"Adelaide!" Lady Belanger's voice held both warning and disapproval, and her accent thickened. "I told you, your father wishes to speak to Lord Hargreaves alone."

Adelaide laced her fingers between Regulus' and turned to face her father. Her shoulder pressed against his. "I'm not leaving him to face Father alone." She smiled up at Regulus and some of the tension in his shoulders eased. He smiled back. She looked at her father. "And I'm not being apart from him while Nolan Carrick is here. Where is he?"

"If he's where I sent him, waiting in his guest room." Belanger tapped his foot, his frown deepening. "Why?" He gestured toward them. "Why do you throw yourself at this man you claim is your betrothed, then ask about another man who tells me *he* is your betrothed? Why do you both seem to think Carrick a threat?" Belanger's voice rose to a shout. "And why does everyone think you can be betrothed when I haven't agreed to anything?"

Regulus squeezed Adelaide's hand, hoping she sensed his support for whatever she chose to say. He wanted to defend her. But honestly, he had no idea where to start. And Belanger seemed distrustful of him already.

"I'm not throwing myself at anyone," Adelaide said, her tone irritated. "And I love Regulus." She squeezed his hand in return. His spirit gave a little leap of joy, and he couldn't stop his grin. Belanger squinted at him, lips pursed.

"Nolan was trying to court me," Adelaide continued. "He needs to marry, or his parents will disown him." Regulus raised his brows. She had left out that detail, but things suddenly made more sense. "Technically, I *did* agree to marry him—"

"You shouldn't be agreeing to marry anyone without consulting your mother and me, and you've promised yourself to two men?" Belanger sounded equal parts bewildered and furious. "I would never have expected such dishonorable—"

"Nolan was threatening to have Regulus arrested and hanged for treason against the king!" Adelaide's shoulder rubbed against his as she took a deep breath. "Among other threats. He threatened and blackmailed me into an engagement."

Belanger's jaw went slack. He took a few steps to a nearby armchair and leaned against its back as his face turned ashen. "Did he hurt you?"

"No—well…I'm fine."

Sensing her hesitation, Regulus looked down at her with a frown. She shuffled her feet, a look of indecision reflected in her brown eyes. Hot rage flamed over his skin.

"You didn't tell me he hurt you."

She fiddled with her hair. "It was nothing."

"Did he hurt you or not?" Belanger asked softly.

"I…" She licked her lips. "Fine, yes."

"What? When?" Regulus shifted to see her face better. "That night at Arrano?"

"No." She didn't meet his eyes. "After the tournament. The morning after Harold and Sieger. I shouldn't have wandered so far off; been so secluded."

Regulus clenched his free hand. "As if being alone excuses him?"

"Well, no—"

"What. Did. He. Do." His chest heaved with each word. *When I see Carrick next…*

Adelaide kept her gaze on the floor. "He threatened to reveal I was a mage if I didn't marry him. I told him to tell whoever he wanted. He got too close and I drew my dagger. I nicked his cheek, but he was too quick. Too strong. He broke my wrist and took my—" she glanced up at him apologetically, "your dagger."

Regulus worked his jaw. So that was the real reason Carrick had the dagger Regulus had won in the joust and given to Adelaide as a courtship gift. Carrick had realized she could heal her wrist so he could get away with hurting her. And that monster was somewhere in this castle. Worse than Regulus' anger was his guilt. She had agreed to marry Nolan, knowing if he had hurt her once, he might again. All to save his pathetic life.

"I was going to tell you. After dinner. But then he was there, and after he agreed to leave you alone if I married him, I couldn't…" Adelaide gripped her skirt and stared at the floor. "He told me there would be consequences for not agreeing to marry him. I didn't think he would move so quickly. If I hadn't been there…"

"He'd have killed me," Regulus finished. "Or tried, anyway."

Adelaide looked up with watery eyes. "This is why I didn't tell you. I didn't want to see the look in your eyes that you have now."

Regulus unclenched his fist and tried to relax. He knew what she must be seeing. The fury and violent intent. The stony determination he wore into battle like a second set of armor. All the darkest parts of himself. The parts that didn't deserve her.

"Nolan Carrick will pay for his crimes," Lord Belanger said, drawing their attention. A vein in Belanger's temple throbbed and his white-knuckled hands gripped the back of the armchair. "But that doesn't clarify what has happened since Adelaide disappeared. So…what?" He massaged his forehead with the palm of his hand. "You two ran away? Were you captured by a Black Knight and Hargreaves saved you, or was Carrick correct in his assessment that Hargreaves *is* the Black Knight and he kidnapped you?"

"No!" Adelaide exclaimed. "I mean, that is—well…sort of. It wasn't…uh…"

All right, Regulus. The truth. However painful. He breathed in, his shoulders rising and falling as he gathered his resolve. "Carrick wasn't lying about everything. I did take Adelaide. And his guess wasn't wrong. I am—was—the Black Knight."

Behind them, Lady Belanger gasped. Lord Belanger stepped around the chair toward him, rage in his eyes. Adelaide stepped in front of him, blocking her father from attacking.

"Wait! He didn't exactly *take* me." Adelaide cast a chastising glare at Regulus that made his cheeks burn. All right, perhaps he might have been more tactful. She looked back at her father. "I agreed to help him." She turned around and placed a hand on his chest. Looked into his eyes. "Tell him. Tell him exactly what you told me." His gut clenched, but he took courage from the love in her gaze.

"It all started two years ago."

He told the entire story. The forest. The sorcerer's demand that Regulus serve him or watch his men die. They moved to the seats. Lord and Lady Belanger took a couple of the armchairs. Regulus and Adelaide sat with their thighs touching and held each other's hands on the couch. He didn't have the mark anymore, but he showed them the scars from his attempts to remove it.

He told them about the sorcerer admitting he was the Shadow that had hunted down all the mages in Monparth twenty-two years ago. About the sorcerer demanding he deliver Adelaide. Together they told the rest. Nolan showing up at Arrano. Adelaide visiting him the next day and agreeing to go to the sorcerer. The mark the sorcerer put on her arm. Their trek up the mountains, the crying statue predicting death and destruction, everything. Whenever his throat tightened with shame over what he had done, Adelaide filled in the details, somehow making him seem less at fault than he felt. Sometimes they had to go back and clarify something out of chronological order. A few times Lord Belanger looked on the verge of leaping across the room and strangling him.

"I could scarcely believe my eyes when the mark was gone," Regulus said. "And then he removed Adelaide's. I was finally free. *We* were free. But then…" He bit his cheek. "It happened too fast. I didn't know what was happening, but he was hurting her. He said if I intervened, he'd kill her."

"It's not your fault," Adelaide murmured.

"What's not his fault?" Lord Belanger demanded.

Lady Belanger said something in Khast, her eyes wide and tone breathless.

"Yes. The sorcerer took my magic." Adelaide shuddered, and Regulus squeezed her hand. "But look. This is why I was looking for you." She beamed at Regulus, then held her free hand in front of her. After a moment, her palm glowed faintly blue, then brighter.

Regulus gasped. "It's…back?"

The light died out and she sighed, her shoulders sagging. "A little. I can feel a tiny spark of energy for the first time since he took it, but…it's weak, and more exhausting to summon."

Relief and hope surged through Regulus. "Maybe you just need time."

"Maybe." She shrugged, but he saw the fear in her eyes.

"What happened next?" Belanger coaxed. "Your injuries?"

"We left while the sorcerer repaired the staff," Regulus said. "The injuries were from kanadosi."

"Then we came here." Adelaide looked to her parents. "To ask for help with Nolan."

There was one other reason why Regulus had both supported and dreaded going to the Belanger's. He wanted her father's blessing. But perhaps they should allow her parents to process everything else, first, before he added marriage to the list.

"We thought we would be safe here," Regulus added. "Thought we could avoid Carrick until we had a plan."

Lord Belanger steepled his fingers, his elbows resting on the arms of his chair. But when he spoke, it wasn't what Regulus was expecting. "This…sorcerer. What did you say he called himself again?"

"The Prince of Shadow and Ash." Regulus hated saying the ridiculous title after two years of only saying it under compulsion. "He fancies himself royalty."

"And he *is* the Shadow? He killed the mages?" Regulus nodded, and Belanger rested his chin on his fingers. "And ash…" Belanger shook his head, deep wrinkles lining his forehead. "What does he look like?"

Regulus and Adelaide exchanged a confused glance. "Short," he said. "Built like a baker, or a scholar, I suppose. A bit tubby."

"Graying brown beard," Adelaide added. "Maybe in his early fifties. Very pale. Narrow nose. Deep-set eyes."

"Usually his face is partly hidden under a hood. But he has long graying brown hair and wiry eyebrows. Black eyes." He looked at Lord Belanger, suspicious. "Is this a test? Do you think we're lying?"

"I wish you were." Belanger stood, his eyebrows knitting together. He left without another word. Regulus looked to Adelaide, but she shook her head. So he looked to Lady Belanger, but she was staring at the open doorway, looking equally bewildered. She must have felt him looking, because her gaze cut to him. Regulus' chest tightened. That look was not promising. She muttered something under her breath in Khast.

"Mother!" Adelaide's eyes widened. She responded in Khast, her words rushed and offended. He looked desperately between them, trying to determine what they had said. Based on the ruddy tone in Adelaide's cheeks and the shock in her eyes, plus the judgmental scowl Lady Belanger was giving him, something unfavorable toward him.

Lord Belanger returned carrying a framed canvas as big as his torso with the back toward them. He set it on an armchair and stepped aside. Regulus' blood froze and his mouth fell open. Adelaide's grip on his hand tightened. He blinked at the painting.

A man who at first glance might have been the sorcerer, except he wore a black doublet, a red cape, and a gold crown. And on closer inspection, he didn't look that much like him. This man was kinder and younger, with a wider nose and blue eyes. But the man in the painting and the sorcerer could be…no.

"Please tell me that's not what I think it is," Adelaide said. Her fingers dug into his palm.

"It's the portrait I had commissioned of His Royal Majesty King Gawain a few months ago." Belanger sighed. "And your faces answer my question. He bears a resemblance to this sorcerer."

Regulus' mind spun. The sorcerer prince. The king's elder brother, born a mage. As per Monparth's laws in agreement with an ancient treaty with the surrounding kingdoms, his magic prohibited him from inheriting the throne. The prince who, as the story went, disappeared before returning as a sorcerer and trying to murder his own parents. What was his name?

"The sorcerer prince was killed," Adelaide breathed. "King Olfan said he died."

"And King Gawain told me in confidence that the mages sent after his brother wounded him, but he escaped. He doesn't know if his brother is dead. King Olfan often wondered if his son was behind the Shadow. But he couldn't very well admit that." Belanger looked at the painting and tapped his hand against his leg.

Regulus wanted to look away from the portrait, but his horror left him frozen, staring at this kinder version of the monster he had served.

"I assured the king it seemed unlikely. Years without so much as a whisper, surely he was dead," Belanger continued. "But a sorcerer of the correct age, claiming to be a prince, who you both clearly think bears at least a passing resemblance to the king…" He sighed and shook his head. "And there's more."

Regulus glanced at Adelaide, his nervousness and discomfort rising. Her eyes mirrored his panic.

"When Kirven tried to kill King Olfan and Queen Gwyneth, may they rest in peace, he told them he would take Monparth if he had to burn it to the ground. Even if it meant he would be a king of nothing but ash." He drew his lips into a hard, thin line.

His words hung in the air like smoke trapped in a room without a chimney. *Shadow and Ash. Death and destruction.* Regulus pushed off the couch as the world swayed. He leaned on the arm of the couch as his stomach seized and his hands shook.

"No. No, it can't be." Regulus shook his head. He pushed his sleeves up over his elbows, trying to cool down. The fireplace still stood empty, but he could have sworn he was standing near a raging inferno. "He can't be…that would mean…"

Treason. He'd aided a man who had tried to kill the king. And if he had tried once, now that he had a weapon designed to destroy… Words failed him, and he dropped to his knees with a strangled cry of anguish and rested his feverish face against the side of the couch.

"Oh, Etiros. What have I done?"

"The Staff…" Adelaide's voice resounded in his head like a gong as he fought the panic strangling him. "He said he searched for the pieces for decades. That's all he was waiting for. He wants to kill the king. He is going to take Monparth by force."

"We have to warn the king." Regulus stood, even though his legs shook. "I have to. He gathered all the pieces because of me."

"Hm." The new voice startled him, and Regulus spun toward the sound. Carrick stood in the doorway, arms crossed, leaning his shoulder against the frame. "Aren't you all—"

Regulus didn't wait for him to finish his thought. His anger from earlier returned full force, shocking him out of his stupor.

"You!" He charged at Carrick, angling his shoulder to slam into Carrick's chest. Carrick straightened and braced his hands against Regulus' shoulders. Regulus squinted in confusion as Carrick pushed back like Regulus was a weak, unruly child. With force that threatened to snap his clavicles, Carrick shoved. Regulus' heel caught on the rug and he teetered. Had he really lost this much strength and stamina when the sorcerer removed the mark? He straightened as Carrick kicked him in the ribs. The impact felt more like a battering ram than a boot.

Pain exploded across his ribs and he fell onto his back. The back of his head slammed onto the floor, the rug doing little to cushion the blow. Adelaide shouted his name. He couldn't suck in a breath. His right lung ached behind his injured ribs. The tightness and pain likely meant one thing. They were cracked.

"As I was *saying*." Carrick closed the door and pulled down the bookshelf next to it to barricade the door. "Aren't you all clever. Well done, Lord Belanger." He applauded sarcastically as Regulus finally drew in a full breath. "But I can't let you warn His Majesty."

CHAPTER 4

ADELAIDE GASPED, SNAPPING OUT OF THE SHOCK THAT ROOTED her in place. She rounded the couch. "Nolan, what are you doing?"

Something wasn't right. Nolan shouldn't have been able to get Regulus down that effortlessly.

"Really. This could have been simple." Nolan rolled his eyes. "I'd stay there if I were you, Lord Belanger."

Father strode past, his face pinched with fury. Before his hand found Nolan's throat, Nolan stepped forward and grabbed Father's shirt with both hands. Her heart stopped as Nolan picked Father up and threw him across the room. Father hit the stone next to the fireplace and crashed to the ground. Adelaide screamed. Mother ran to him, crying out for the guards. Adelaide's throat constricted as Mother knelt beside Father, his body looking like a discarded rag doll. He raised his head, then moaned and let his head fall back to the carpet.

Regulus stood, bent over and clearly in pain. As Nolan turned back, Regulus threw a wild punch. His fist made contact with Nolan's jaw with a crack. He drew back for another punch, but Nolan shoved against Regulus' chest while moving his foot behind Regulus' leg. Regulus stumbled backward and fell to the ground with a groan.

"Regulus!" She darted forward as Nolan grabbed Regulus' right arm and yanked it backward against his leg. The snap of bone nearly made her vomit. Regulus yelled in agony.

Adelaide pulled her dagger out of her boot and sliced at Nolan's chest, but he evaded her blade. She stood next to Regulus, dagger held in front of her and at the ready. Nolan took another step back, and she risked a glance down. Below Regulus' rolled-up sleeve, the sharp edge of a bone pushed against the skin in his forearm, like the bone wanted to break through but couldn't. She gagged. His face looked deathly pale, and huge drops of sweat beaded on his forehead.

Nolan adjusted his belt and smoothed his shirt. "I must admit, I didn't expect the mercenary to tell the truth. I hoped if he did, the good lord and lady wouldn't believe it. A sorcerer living in the woods, forcing your obedience? How unrealistic compared to a tale of kidnapping and seduction and dishonorable behavior. I didn't think he would, but I'd hoped Belanger would kill you, Hargreaves. He looked ready to after I spun my tale this morning. Alas, no. But I *really* wasn't prepared for you to figure out the sorcerer is Prince Kirven. Well done."

She stared, her hands going cold. Her heart raced. None of this made sense. "How do *you* know about the sorcerer?"

"Oh, Adelaide. If you had paid more attention to me instead of Lord Half-Breed, you'd know I'm an expert hunter." Nolan flashed her a smile with all the warmth of knives. "That was clever, making it look like the Black Knight kidnapped you and telling that knight to tell both Hargreaves and me in order to turn suspicion away from Hargreaves. He rode straight to Arrano, where I was tearing the place apart looking for you. I had my suspicions about the authenticity of your supposed kidnapping, so I went after you with only my men. I tracked you. Right to the prince's tower. What an interesting conversation we had."

Her lungs felt leaden, like she had forgotten how to breathe. Dread grew in the pit of her stomach. "About what?"

"Oh, you know. Power, politics, revenge, mutual goals and annoyances." Nolan looked pointedly at Regulus. "Plans for overthrowing the king. Normal treason things."

No. Please, no. She gulped, horrified at her rising suspicion.

"I made a nice deal with the prince." Nolan rolled up his sleeve, and the sight of the mark on the interior of his right forearm—two hollow black diamonds and a half diamond open toward his wrist—made her shudder. "I serve him when he calls, and I get strength, speed, and agility beyond belief…and immortality." He pulled his sleeve back down. "I don't understand why you were in such a hurry to get rid of it, mercenary. If you didn't have a martyr complex, you wouldn't have had to deal with the pain. But don't worry." He reached behind him and drew a dagger.

He tossed the dagger in the air and caught it, and Adelaide's grip on her own dagger tightened as she recognized the flash of swirling ivory. Regulus' dagger from the tournament.

"You can't feel pain when you're dead." Nolan moved forward, eyes fixed on Regulus.

"No!" She lunged toward Nolan and aimed a cut at his stomach. He dodged, as she knew he would, but she was already coming around with a stab aimed at his heart. Nolan hit her arm away with his forearm, and her blade sliced across the side of his arm. He hissed and grabbed her neck. Before she could react, he threw her backward. She coughed as she hit the ground beside Regulus. Her dagger slipped out of her hand and spun across the floor.

Panting, she turned and threw herself over Regulus. She wrapped her arms around his head, shielding his torso and head, but careful not to lie on his broken arm. Her entire body shook as she looked up at Nolan. She needed to distract him.

"Why would the sorcerer want you? Why would he need you?"

Nolan paused and shrugged. "Because he gave his word he would free Hargreaves. And, for whatever reason, his word is important to him. He wanted a new assistant to help him put his plans of conquering and domination into effect."

"He told you his plans?" Regulus asked, his voice weak and tight. He coughed and groaned. She wished he would shut up instead of drawing attention to himself.

"See, if you had been thankful for the gifts he gave you for one moment instead of fighting him all the time, he might have let you in, too. But, no. I'm certainly not going to tell you all his secrets." Nolan knelt near Regulus' head and met Adelaide's eyes. She leaned lower over Regulus and held Nolan's gaze, silently daring him to go through her to get to him.

Nolan balanced Regulus' dagger on the tips of his fingers. "But I *will* tell you this—the sorcerer has promised me that he will spare anyone who is with me when he takes over. Conversely, though, I'll be in a position to see that anyone…undesirable…dies. So it might be a good idea to curry my favor before we welcome the new king."

"You're not his partner." Adelaide shook her head. "You're his slave!"

"The contract I signed with him that promises me a duchy says otherwise." He gave her a self-satisfied smile. "You didn't think His Highness would seize the throne without thinking about how he would rule Monparth once he had it, did you? Even sorcerers need loyal nobles to rule successfully. Unfortunately, that falls apart if anyone alerts the king. I'll kill anyone necessary to prevent that." He leaned closer to her, and she shivered. "But not you, Adelaide. That's not what I want. I want you at my side as my duchess."

Regulus tried to push her away with his good arm, but Adelaide didn't budge. "You're out of your mind," she spat.

"You don't even love her, do you?" Mother shouted. She still knelt next to Father, who appeared to be regaining his breath.

"You'd all already be dead if I didn't love her." Nolan reached for Adelaide. Still shielding Regulus, she couldn't pull back.

"If you love me, you'll leave." Adelaide met his eyes, determined not to flinch.

"Maybe we have different definitions of love." He ran the back of his fingers down her cheek. "I *want* you, though." His voice dropped to a husky murmur. "By my sword, do I want you." She gulped against the fear strangling her and drying up her tongue.

"Adelaide—" Regulus coughed, the sound wet and concerning. "Move!" He pushed against her side. But she stayed frozen, as if Nolan's touch had turned her to stone.

"I've set my mind on having you, and now I can't get you out of my head," Nolan said, his eyes tracing the contours of her face. He returned Regulus' dagger to the back of his belt. "And so many people, including my parents—*especially* my parents—believe we're engaged." He seized her arm. "I won't be shamed by you marrying that mongrel instead."

CHAPTER 5

"WE MADE A DEAL, ADELAIDE." NOLAN YANKED ADELAIDE TO her feet, nearly pulling her arm out of its socket. Her knee hit Regulus' side as Nolan pulled her up. Regulus moaned. Nolan pulled her away, and she stumbled after him, her left ankle aching in protest. "By denying me and accepting *his* proposal, you've broken our deal." He pushed her against the side of the couch, still gripping her wrist painfully tight. The back of her legs pressed into the couch arm. "Therefore, his life is mine to end."

Adelaide trembled. She looked to her left at Regulus panting on the floor and tried to pull her wrist free. Nolan clicked his tongue. "Can you heal your wrist if it breaks again?"

She stilled, unsure. And any magic she had, she wanted to use to heal Regulus. She couldn't agree to marry Nolan. But she couldn't watch Regulus die, either.

Nolan smiled. "I do hope you're right about your magic coming back. I was disappointed to hear while eavesdropping that the prince took it. Ah, well. That was just an extra perk. Magic or no, I desire you." He moved closer, his eyes fixed on her lips.

Adelaide stiffened and leaned away. Only Nolan's legs against hers and his grip on her wrist kept her from falling over the side of the couch onto the cushions. "You repulse me."

She bit her tongue. Hurt flickered in Nolan's eyes, but he chuckled.

"I'll change your mind." He looked at Regulus, who had managed to sit up and was holding his broken arm against his chest. "Not only is my inheritance, my family name, my home, and my pride at stake, but also sweet revenge. The chance to put a no-account bastard back in his place." He looked back at her, and the greed in his eyes turned her blood cold. "And prove I'm more of a man."

How did one defend against an immortal? How could she save herself and Regulus? With Regulus and Father injured, did they have a hope of restraining Nolan? Her mind seemed a frozen river, the thoughts moving too slow, too slow. She stared past Nolan at a bookshelf, unwilling to meet his eyes. *Etiros, help us, please!*

"Look at me, love." Nolan's voice was sickeningly gentle.

"Adelaide." Mother's voice. "Move!"

Adelaide reacted without thinking. She ducked toward the middle of the room. A fleshy thunk and then Nolan yelled. He dropped her wrist and backed away. The handle of a throwing knife protruded from Nolan's shoulder.

Nolan cursed and yanked the knife out. Blood soaked into his shirt. He gasped and fell to his knees as Mother threw another knife into his heart.

"I don't care if you're supposedly immortal," Mother said as she readied another throwing knife. "I'll kill you if you touch my daughter again!" She threw the knife, but Nolan jumped aside and it bounced off the bookshelf behind him.

Someone banged against the door and men shouted. The guards were trying to get in. Nolan looked toward the door, knife still stuck in his chest.

Adelaide spotted her dagger on the ground and dove for it, but Nolan grabbed her hair as she shot past him and pulled her back. She fell to her knees and her eyes watered from the strain on her scalp. The bookshelf blocking the door teetered as the guards tried to break down the door. She twisted around, yanked the knife out of Nolan's chest, and stabbed at his throat. He held up a hand, and the blade went straight through his palm. He looked at his hand with wide, wild eyes, and pulled away. Blood ran off the knife still in her hand and streamed out of his palm, filling the air with a sharp metallic scent. Nolan yelled and released her hair as he stumbled away.

The door rattled and thumped against the bookshelf. Adelaide pulled on the bookshelf, straining to move it away from the door. *Come on!* Why wouldn't it move faster? Nolan half walked, half fell toward the windows.

"You'll all regret this!" Nolan pointed at her with a bloody hand. "I'll be back for you. You're *mine*. You hear me, Hargreaves? MINE!" He turned and leapt through a window with a crash and a cascade of falling glass.

As three guards burst into the parlor, Nolan ran across the courtyard. One guard hurried to Father and Mother. The second asked her if she was all right. She nodded, and he went to Regulus. The third guard paused only for a moment before heading after Nolan.

Adelaide stared at Nolan and the shouting guard. She scarcely believed how fast Nolan was running for the stables with the blood he'd lost. The guard would never catch him. If he got to his horse, the only way to keep him from escaping would be to make sure the gate was closed before he reached it. She looked at Father, his face pinched as the guard and Mother helped him sit up. Regulus sat against the back of the couch, staring at his broken arm as the guard left him to pursue Nolan. She couldn't decide which would be worse—if Nolan escaped, or if the guards caught him. Nolan might tear them apart.

Adelaide tried to control her violent shaking as she walked over to Father and Mother. "How bad is it?"

Father straightened with a groan and put a hand to his back. "I don't think anything is broken. Just blacked out for a minute there. There's definitely bruising and something is out of place." He smiled bitterly. "Were I twenty years younger, I'd be unfazed."

Mother grasped Father's face in her hands and kissed him. "Don't you scare me like that, *mareh piahre.*"

Father tapped her under the chin. "You don't have enough faith in me. It'll take more than a traitor under the influence of dark magic to kill this legend, *piahre cha mareh gehvam.*"

Love of my life. Adelaide smiled and walked back to Regulus as her parents kissed again. But as her gaze fell on the jagged bone pressing against his skin, her smile dropped. She sat next to Regulus. "How are you?"

"Nothing's bleeding, so there's that." He smiled, but the tightness around his eyes spoke to his pain as a cough rattled in his lungs. "Your father speaks Khast, then?"

"A little. Basically all he knows is curse words, terms of endearment, and some flirtatious phrases that make my mother blush."

"How do you know about that?" Father demanded.

Adelaide smirked. "Because you're so used to no one knowing what you're saying, you forget I speak Khast, too!" She rolled her eyes and turned back to Regulus.

"What phrases? Dresden says my flirting needs help." Regulus coughed and grunted, his face twisting. "Any…good ones?"

Her brows pulled together. "What are you doing?"

"What do you mean?"

"You seem…oddly calm." Her own hands still had a slight shake.

"Distracting myself." He closed his eyes and leaned his head back on the couch. "It's how I helped my men through bad injuries. Get them to think and talk about anything else." He coughed and moaned. "Just…talk to me?"

She opened her mouth to ask what hurt the most but jumped when her half-brother's shout interrupted her.

"Fath—what happened!" Landon stood in the doorway, face pinched and eyes bulging as he took in the chaos in the parlor. "I heard shouting, and a guard said a guest attacked…" He gestured at Regulus. "Who's this?"

"This is Lord Regulus Hargreaves of Arrano." Adelaide ground her teeth. "Nice to see you too, brother."

"Oh. Adelaide. I was glad to learn you're alive and well." Landon crossed to Father without a second glance at her.

She clenched her jaw and turned away. Eleven years her senior, Father's second child and eldest son had never paid her much attention—but neither had any of her other half siblings. Of course, disappearing with little explanation with her mother for several years hadn't helped.

Questioning concern reflected in Regulus' eyes. She shook her head and took his broken right arm as Father told Landon that Nolan was a liar and a traitor to the crown. "Maybe I can try—"

"Don't worry about it." Regulus shook his head. "What if you use what you have and then it's gone for good?" He coughed and a bit of blood leaked over his bottom lip.

"I'll take that risk." She held her hand over the jutting bone, hoping that would be easier and faster than his ribs, which based on his coughing, might have punctured his lung. If she healed the ribs first, she might not have enough magic left for his arm.

She dug deep for the spark of magical energy flickering in the carved-out place in her soul. Rather than removing a cork from a full flask like when she used her magic before, this felt like squeezing the last drop of water out of an empty wineskin. The familiar warmth spread across her hand, and she perspired from the exertion. Regulus relaxed as the pale-blue light spread over his arm. The bone straightened, no longer threatening to break through the skin. She focused on his arm. In the energy flowing out of her and into him, she sensed the bones and muscles and tendons pulling back together. Healing.

She could feel his arm was healed, so she moved her hand to his ribs. White spots danced in her vision, and she blinked them away. But she detected four broken ribs and internal bleeding. She focused on the bleeding first—healed the puncture and collapsing lung and forced the blood to reabsorb, then worked on maneuvering the ribs back together. Her hand shook.

Regulus placed a hand on her shoulder. "Hey, perhaps you should take a breather—"

"Shh. Concentrating." Black circled the edges of her sight. She swayed and her hand bumped Regulus' ribs. "Sorry." She shook herself. *A bit more. Come on. Give me a little more, Etiros.*

"Adelaide, stop!" Regulus sounded panicked.

The conversation behind her died as Landon exclaimed, "What in creation?"

Her eyes drifted shut as she sank into unconsciousness.

CHAPTER 6

THE LIGHT ON ADELAIDE'S PALM VANISHED AS SHE SLUMPED forward, and Regulus caught her shoulders. "Adelaide?" When she didn't respond, he pushed her hair away from her face. Her eyes were closed, and her head lolled to the side.

"Adelaide!" Lord Belanger shoved Regulus aside and pulled his daughter into his arms. She slumped against him, limp and unmoving, her eyes still closed. Belanger rested the back of her head in the crook of his arm. "Ad, wake up." He glared at Regulus. "What happened?"

"She healed my arm, then started healing my ribs." Regulus touched his ribs. He suspected they were still cracked, but as usual, her magic had numbed the area. "She started looking ashen, and her eyes went all unfocused, and then she swayed and she…passed out." Tendrils of dread threaded through Regulus' heart.

"She shouldn't be using her magic at all!" Lady Belanger crouched between him and Adelaide and took Adelaide's hand.

"Wait, wait, Adelaide is a *mage?*" The wiry man with mousy brown hair Adelaide had called brother crossed his arms. "Since *when?*"

"Mages are born, so forever," Lady Belanger said, her voice rising. "We kept it a secret for her protection." She gave Regulus a look that could kill. "To prevent things like this! Like everything that has happened since she met *you!*"

He ducked his head. "The sorcerer would have found her whether she met me or not. Whether she kept her magic secret or not."

"I've half a mind to have you thrown in the dungeon, you—" She added several words in Khast that were clearly not complimentary.

Lord Belanger cleared his throat. "Tamina, this anger isn't helping."

"There's a *sorcerer* now?" the brother shouted.

They all ignored him. Regulus sat up and shifted to see around Adelaide's mother. Adelaide's lips were parted, and her chest rose and fell in gentle, rhythmic breathing. She looked peaceful, if exhausted. *Please be okay.*

A guard walked in and saluted Lord Belanger. "My lord, Nolan Carrick has escaped."

Regulus leaned back against the couch, dread replacing his relief. Their best chance had been to take Carrick while he was weakened. He remembered the fury and precision with which Adelaide's mother had thrown those knives and felt a growing discomfort about her current disposition toward him.

Lord Belanger nodded. "Double the guards. Make sure everyone knows what Nolan Carrick looks like. If he approaches the castle, attack to kill, but proceed with caution. He is a monster, not a man." The guard bowed and departed, but Belanger's last words cut Regulus to his core.

He had also born that mark. He had also benefited from strength, speed, and immortality granted by sorcery. Was that how Adelaide's parents saw him? A monster, not a man?

"She needs taken to her room," Lady Belanger said.

Belanger moved to stand, still holding Adelaide. He grimaced and dropped back down. "My back... I can't lift her. Landon, give me a hand."

The brother's eyebrows lifted. "Me?"

"No, I'll carry her." Regulus knelt next to Lord Belanger and moved his arms under Adelaide's legs and back. Something metal and sharp pressed under his chin and he froze. He looked at Lady Belanger out of the corner of his eye. She held her dagger to his throat, her mouth curled down. "Tell me why I should trust you."

"Because Adelaide trusts me."

"Tamina," Belanger said gently. She looked at her husband without lowering her blade. "Adelaide intends to marry him." His expression was unreadable. "I haven't decided if I'll allow that, but he's right. She trusts him. Maybe don't kill the man your daughter wants to marry just yet."

The tip of the dagger pressed into Regulus' skin and he tried to control his breathing. After a moment, she lowered the dagger. "All right. But if I determine you have tricked or hurt my daughter in any way, if you are anything less than the man Adelaide deserves, I will slit your throat without a second thought."

"I understand." He picked up Adelaide. Thanks to Adelaide's magic, his ribs didn't hurt, but they would doubtless complain about this later. Her head rolled onto his shoulder. "Which way?"

Lord Belanger stayed behind to talk to his son while Lady Belanger led Regulus to Adelaide's room. He hadn't been thinking about how large the castle was when he decided to carry her, but he wasn't about to let her out of his sight. And he disliked the idea of Landon, who appeared to hold little affection for his sister, carrying her.

The pain in his ribs returned faster than he had hoped, although not as bad as before Adelaide started healing them. She must have undone at least some of the damage. Still, to his irritation, his lungs soon burned, but he pressed on. He had done fine before his bond to the sorcerer, he could manage fine now. Besides, he was used to pain.

Lady Belanger pulled back the thick blanket on Adelaide's four-poster bed and Regulus laid Adelaide down as gently as possible. She didn't even stir as he moved her head onto her pillow and brushed her hair away from her face. He kissed her forehead, then winced at the hissing intake of breath from Lady Belanger. He kept his heated face turned away from her by pulling the covers over Adelaide.

"All right, that's enough," Lady Belanger said. "Out." With a sigh, he turned away from the bed.

"Reg…" He spun back, bending over Adelaide. Her eyes fluttered as she tried to keep them open. "Regulus."

"I'm here." He pulled her hand out from under the covers and clasped it in his own. She wrapped her fingers around his hand and shifted, moving over on the bed.

"Don't leave me."

"I won't." He rubbed her hand. "I promise."

Adelaide's eyes drifted shut and her breathing deepened. She still clung to him. He sat on the edge of the bed, unwilling to extricate his hand.

Lady Belanger cleared her throat. "You can't stay here."

He bit back his initial response. *I've spent the last several days and nights with your daughter unattended, I'm not going to do anything untoward now.* Might not help his case much. "She asked me to stay."

The door opened with a quiet squeak of the hinges, and Lord Belanger peeked in. He frowned at Regulus before stepping inside and closing the door behind him. Lady Belanger crossed her arms.

"He won't leave."

"She asked me not to," he repeated.

Lord Belanger raised a brow.

"She was half asleep," Lady Belanger protested.

Lord Belanger continued to survey them without speaking. Regulus focused on Adelaide. She looked serene. Unworried. And beautiful as ever.

"He's in love with her; of course he won't leave." Regulus looked up. Adelaide's father looked resigned.

"Hmph." Lady Belanger gripped her braid. "I always feared she'd fall for someone like you. All stubbornness and passion with a warrior soul and a stupidly self-sacrificial heart."

"I'm very unsure if you're insulting me or complimenting Lord Hargreaves," Belanger responded with a grin.

"Both." She sighed and cut a disgruntled glower toward Regulus. "She needs someone to tame her wild spirit, not encourage her recklessness and put her in more danger."

Regulus frowned. "With all due respect, my lady, Adelaide doesn't need tamed. She's as dangerous as the nickname *you* gave her." He combed his fingers through her hair spread across her pillow. "She's a *shiraa*. Like a tigress, she shouldn't be caged. She's perfect as she is." He looked back at Adelaide's parents. "And I love her. I'm going to marry her."

"The last man who said that viciously attacked us in our own home," Lady Belanger said, but most of the venom had vanished from her tone.

Regulus clenched his free fist against his leg. "I would never hurt Adelaide or anyone she loves of my own free will. I would gladly die for her."

Belanger tilted his head, regarding Regulus with a thoughtful expression. "What if I challenged you to a duel?"

"What? Why?" The ache in his ribs increased as he tensed.

"For getting my daughter enslaved to a sorcerer, even temporarily." Belanger folded his arms and narrowed his eyes. "For putting her in a situation where she suffered pain and could have died. For letting a sorcerer take her magic. For calling her reputation into question by appearing with her after several days, alone." Belanger shrugged. "Take your pick. I have more reasons to challenge you than not to at this point."

"Please." Regulus swallowed back the knot in his throat. "Don't."

He couldn't argue. Even though he did everything under compulsion, even though he had tried to keep Adelaide as safe as he could when he didn't have the choice of saying no, he *had* still done all those things. His shoulders sagged.

"Whatever punishment or recompense you see fit, I will do it. Put me in the stocks, order me lashed, tell me what payment you want. But don't challenge me." He let his head fall. His chin rested against his chest. Exhaustion weighed him down. "Because I will accept, but I won't fight you. I won't harm my love's father."

"I won't give you my blessing."

"Then I'll have to earn it." He met Belanger's stare and squared his shoulders. They stared at each other for what felt like a small eternity, but Regulus refused to be the first to look away.

Lord Belanger's expression eased into a smile. "I like him, Mina." Regulus let himself relax and shifted to ease the growing pain in his ribs.

"Of course you do." Lady Belanger flung her hands out to her sides. "He's too much like you!"

"You like me well enough." Belanger moved behind his wife and wrapped his arms around her, leaning forward so his head was next to hers. "Come on, *piahre*. Leave them be."

"But—"

"You'll send for us when she wakes?" Belanger asked. Regulus nodded. "See?" He led his protesting wife out of the room and closed the door behind them.

Regulus waited only a couple minutes before he laid on top of the comforter next to Adelaide, careful of his ribs. Adelaide burrowed into his side in her sleep.

CHAPTER 7

REGULUS DIDN'T REMEMBER FALLING ASLEEP, BUT AS THE SOUND of voices cut through the darkness, he pried open his heavy eyes. He moved and clutched his side, biting back a moan as a stab of rippling pain spread over his ribs. It had been awhile since he'd had to deal with lingering severe injuries. Adelaide leaned over him, her concerned face filling his field of vision.

"Easy there. The physician's on her way." She bit her lip. "I can't muster enough power to heal you again. There's something there, but…I can't reach it."

"It's really not that bad." He smiled as convincingly as possible. "Help me sit up?"

She moved back and helped him sit. He had to clench his teeth to keep from crying out as his ribs pinched. Carrying Adelaide had been a bad idea. But he would have done it again. Now upright, he noticed Lord and Lady Belanger sat in wooden chairs on the other side of the bed, near Adelaide. They watched silently as he moved back to lean against the wall at the head of the bed.

"I have good news." Adelaide beamed, her eyes twinkling. "Mother has agreed not to blame you." She winked at Regulus and he laughed, then clutched at his ribs again. Her smile faded.

"I'm fine." A lie he was used to telling. He smiled and shook his head. "Maybe a kiss would help, though."

Lord Belanger cleared his throat and Regulus' face burned. He'd been so focused on Adelaide he'd already forgotten they were there. But Adelaide grabbed the sides of his face and kissed him full on the mouth. He closed his eyes, put his hands on her waist and kissed her, not caring that her parents were watching. It took every ounce of his self-control not to pull her back in when their lips parted.

"Better?" she whispered, her eyes dancing. She still held his face in her hands.

"Better."

Lord Belanger cleared his throat again, more obviously this time.

"Please." Adelaide rolled her eyes and dropped her hands from his face as she turned toward her parents. She leaned back on her hands. "You two can't talk."

"Fine." Lord Belanger flushed. "I suppose that's fair."

A knock sounded at the door, and an older woman with a crown of gray braids walked in carrying a wool bag.

"Maggie!" Adelaide motioned the woman over with a warm smile. "This is Lord Hargreaves. He needs his ribs looked at."

The woman—Maggie, apparently—walked over to the bed, her gaze darting between Adelaide and Regulus with curiosity. She set the bag on the bed. "Take your shirt off."

He hesitated. He needed her care; but did it have to be here, in front of Adelaide and her parents? She would have to see someday, but he'd hoped it would be after they were married—when it wouldn't matter anymore. Well, he could hide the most embarrassing ones, at least. As he pulled off his shirt, he kept his back close to the wall.

Adelaide gasped, and heat rushed up his neck to his ears. He wished it was a gasp of appreciation, but he knew it wasn't. He was scarred. Several were from his time as a mercenary, like the one on his face. Many were from the last two years. The sorcery had healed him, but left scars. Some small and easy to miss. A couple were large, like the uneven white scar across most of his abdomen from the dragon's tail.

Maggie glanced up at his face, then turned her attention back to his ribs. "Hm."

He looked down. A stab of pain accompanied the movement. Blue and purple bruises marked yellowed skin over his injury. She pressed against the ribs with cold fingers. He gritted his teeth and flinched away.

"Hold still, dear." Maggie ran her fingers over his ribs.

Regulus stared at the gauzy green fabric suspended over Adelaide's four-poster bed, ignoring the ache and stabs.

"Definitely cracked," Maggie said. "And these..." She turned his arm to get a better look at the scabbed bite marks and red skin on his arm, then pulled him a little away from the wall to prod at the bite on his shoulder. He twitched against the prick of pain but tried to stay still.

"Anything you can do?" Adelaide put her hand on top of his.

"I'll salve the bites to fight infection, as I did with your arm. They should heal all right. The ribs will need salved, wrapped, and he'll need to keep movement to a minimum." Maggie pushed against his ribs again and he clenched his teeth until his jaw ached. "But they appear to be aligned and not threatening his lungs. He will heal, but it will take time."

The breaks had been worse before Adelaide started to heal them. Breathing had been difficult and agonizing, but he'd tried to hide the blood he'd coughed up. He hadn't coughed since she healed him. Adelaide looked downcast, so he gave her a reassuring smile. He couldn't say anything in front of Maggie, who he guessed didn't know about Adelaide's magic, but he hoped Adelaide saw the silent thank you in his smile. She had healed his arm, and his ribs weren't threatening to burst his lung. He counted that as a win. And Adelaide was alive and well, bigger win.

"Swing your legs over the side of the bed." Maggie fetched a stool from in front of Adelaide's vanity. She set it next to the bed and her forehead wrinkled when she saw Regulus hadn't turned. "This isn't an ideal angle, my lord."

Regulus gulped and did as instructed, his face already burning with humiliation. Maggie didn't seem to notice as she pulled a pot out of her bag, covered her fingers in sweet-smelling green salve, and began working the salve over his bruised ribs.

"Regulus…" Adelaide's fingers brushed his back, and he cringed. A chair creaked as someone shifted.

"There are many reasons someone is whipped," Lord Belanger said quietly. Maggie's fingers paused before resuming her ministrations. "Normally, I wouldn't pry, but you're pursuing my daughter. Discipline or torture?"

Regulus sighed and closed his eyes for a moment. "Mercenary discipline." He winced as Maggie bumped a tender spot on his side. "Happened once."

"What did you do that deserved a whip?"

Regulus chewed his lower lip. Would Belanger even believe the truth? But he'd promised Adelaide the truth. "Our captain was strict. My friend snuck out and missed his watch. I covered for him." *And earned extra lashes for my lie.* But Drez wasn't whipped, and that was all that mattered.

"You tried to hide your scars," Belanger said. "Why?"

He bowed his head as Maggie tended to the bite on his arm. "I am not ashamed of what I did. But…" He gulped. "My back looks like a slave's. That is unlikely to improve the opinion my intended's parents have of me." Maggie fumbled the jar, nearly dropping it as she scooped out more salve.

"Scars are nothing to be embarrassed about," Belanger murmured.

Lady Belanger cleared her throat. "Scars, especially unearned ones, are the least of my concerns."

"I don't want you ever to feel you need to hide from me," Adelaide said softly.

Their words soothed as much as Maggie's salve, but he still felt uncomfortable in the silence that followed. He looked over his shoulder at Belanger, grasping for a new subject. "We need to warn the king."

"I've already written His Excellency." Belanger rested his chin on his fist, watching Regulus thoughtfully. "I explained everything and recommended he postpone his annual birthday masque in a few weeks. I sent a falcon an hour ago."

The news brought no relief or consolation. Would the king even be able to stop the sorcerer—Kirven? The crying stone woman haunted his memories. *Death and destruction.* But they'd had to take the opal. Regulus suspected they had been seconds away from the sorcerer taking control of one of them. Now they had done the only thing they could—they had warned the king.

"Wait, his birthday masque?" Adelaide asked. Belanger nodded. "Prince Kirven attacked his parents on a Court Day, didn't he?"

"Yes…" Belanger's eyes widened. "When the castle was open and there were nobles present. He wanted a spectacle. And I was only worried about the security nightmare of a masque."

"Maybe he'll be patient enough to wait for the masque to attack," Regulus said. Maggie rubbed the cool salve over the bite on his shoulder. "That might give us more time to figure out how to stop him."

"But if the king cancels the masque, will he attack immediately?" Lady Belanger asked.

"We have warned the king." Belanger folded his hands. "And Kirven failed once before. Worry gets us nowhere."

Silence and the floral aroma of Maggie's salve filled the room. Dust particles floated in the sunlight angling through Adelaide's window between the dark, heavy curtains. Maggie put her salve away and pulled out a roll of narrow strips of white cloth. Regulus tapped his fingers against the bedspread.

"Lord Belanger—"

"Oh, Alfred. Please. Lord Belanger is a mouthful, especially among equals." Alfred raised a brow. "I hope you don't mind if I call you Regulus."

"Oh. Of course." He glanced at Adelaide, nervousness making him antsy.

"Hold still," Maggie chided as she tightly wrapped the bandages around his torso. He took a deep breath and stopped fidgeting.

"I feel the need to be more formal for this." He straightened his back, trying to look as confident as possible while sitting on a bed and having his wounds treated. "Lord Belanger, Lady Belanger. I would like to formally ask for your blessing to marry Adelaide."

Maggie froze, then wrapped more frantically. Lady Belanger frowned. Alfred crossed his arms and leaned back in the chair.

"I believe," Alfred said, eyes narrowed, "you mean to ask for my *permission*."

"Respectfully, sir, I do not." He met Adelaide's eyes. "Adelaide asked me to marry her, and if she'll still have me, I will." Adelaide smirked, her eyes glittering.

"She…asked you?" Lady Belanger sounded incredulous.

Adelaide giggled. "I think I more told him to marry me than asked."

Maggie tied off the bandaging and stuffed her things back into her bag. "That should do. My lords. My ladies." She curtsied and fled the room.

"No," Lady Belanger said, her accent thickening. "You're too young—"

"I'm twenty-one!" Adelaide protested.

"And how old is he?" Lady Belanger flung her hand toward Regulus.

Regulus pulled his shirt back on, grimacing at the ache in his side. "I'll be thirty in two months."

"Thirty!" Lady Belanger gripped the arms of her chair. "Why—"

"*Piahre,*" Alfred patted her arm. "They're closer in age than we are."

"That's different." Lady Belanger slumped back in her chair.

"How is it different?" Adelaide waved her hands. "Father had five children and was thirty-two when he met you. You were twenty!"

"Fine, but we hardly know him." Lady Belanger huffed. "We met Gaius before he asked to court Minerva. And then he courted her for several months before he asked for her hand. And you've been through a trying ordeal. This could be manufactured emotion—"

"My lady, with respect, I knew I loved Adelaide long before the events of the last few days." Regulus put his arm around Adelaide, trying to remain as friendly as possible without backing down.

"Gaius was afraid of Father turning him down," Adelaide said. "He wanted to ask sooner. Minerva told me as much. And I wanted to marry Regulus before any of this happened. Father...what do you think?"

Alfred paused before answering. "I think you risk being shunned by society if you marry a bastard and a mercenary."

"He—" Adelaide started, but her father held up his hand. Regulus' gut twisted with the sting of Alfred's bluntness.

"Your mother and I raised you not to live your life in narrow-mindedness. Let's review what I know about Regulus. I know his past. I know he caused you pain and put you in danger." Alfred stood and clasped his hands behind his back as he turned away from them. "Yet I know that he has repeatedly put himself at risk for your sake. He has shown a concern for your safety, and a protectiveness for his friends. I know that you love him, and I can see he loves you. I know he makes you happy and you trust him."

Alfred faced them with a sad smile. "And I trust you." He looked at Regulus. "But I have two questions for Regulus first. And I want your complete honesty."

Regulus inclined his head. Nerves made him twitchy, like he should be fighting or ready to fight. With a slow exhale, he focused on looking unconcerned and honest.

"Why did you become a mercenary?"

The direct question was like a punch to the gut. His arm slipped off Adelaide as a jumble of emotions overcame him. Through the glass of Adelaide's window, he watched a flock of small birds fly in a mass, like a black wisp of cloud.

"Why does that matter?" Adelaide asked. "He was a warrior. Like you."

At least that explained why she had never asked. Unlike most people, she heard mercenary and assumed warrior—not brigand.

"No, Ad." The gentle sadness in Alfred's voice hurt worse than if he had flat-out accused Regulus of being dishonorable. "I served my king. For duty and honor and to protect my family and friends. I need to know why he fought."

The birds dove into the sprawling branches of a massive oak. Perhaps the truth would help—at least they would know he wasn't just a treasure-hungry, blood-thirsty barbarian. Her father was right to ask. But the truth would highlight his other flaw.

"He's a good man," Adelaide said. "And so are his men. They're honorable—"

"I asked Regulus." Alfred tapped his fingers against his crossed arms. "And his silence is rather loud."

Regulus sighed. He focused on Adelaide, on the way his heart ached for her companionship. "You deserve the truth."

She shook her head. "It doesn't matter—"

"Yes. It does." He picked at some lint on the covers. "My guardian—a distant cousin—reviled me. I lived with him for twelve years, and he took every chance to punish me, to mock me, to remind me my birth was an unfortunate *mistake*. But I endured for the hope that after I was knighted, I could go home. Or at least somewhere I could be accepted." He worked his jaw, ashamed of what a naïve idiot he had been.

"A couple weeks before my knighthood ceremony, my father sent a note and a gift." He smiled ruefully. "It was a sword. Plain and unassuming, but expertly made. The note said he was proud and wished me the best, but he wouldn't attend my knighting."

Adelaide placed a hand on his thigh. He shrugged.

"I hadn't really expected him to come. But I had hoped." Regulus shifted, studying the twisting carved posts of Adelaide's bed. "About a week later, Dresden and I were out for a run. Three men attacked us. We weren't armed, but we fought them off and caught one." He paused.

He'd never told this story before. "Lady Arrano had sent them to kill me."

No one made a sound, but the shock in the room was palpable. Adelaide's hand slipped off his leg. Regulus avoided eye contact. He didn't want their pity.

"I finally realized the truth," he continued. "Even once knighted, that wouldn't be my world. Dresden was my manservant, and he was my only friend. I had no idea my father wrote me into his will in the event of my half-brother dying without an heir until I inherited Arrano two years ago. At eighteen, I had no family, no home, no future."

"I'm sorry," Adelaide whispered.

Regulus ignored his discomfort and continued. "I joined the first mercenary troop I found. Dresden joined me. Later, I led my own troop. I strove to be as honorable as possible." He summoned his courage and met Alfred's inscrutable gaze. "I regret that being a mercenary affects how people see me. But I don't regret what I did. I met good, loyal men who became my friends. I killed, but I also saved people. I am not ashamed of how I led my men."

For several tense moments, Alfred stared back. Adelaide gave his hand a gentle squeeze. Regulus was about to offer to answer any further questions they might have about his mercenary history when Alfred spoke.

"Thank you for your honesty." He was relieved to see kindness, not judgment, in Alfred's eyes. "Your birth does not concern me. Your actions do. But I have one more question, and I expect an immediate answer. From you, not Adelaide."

Regulus braced himself, trying to guess what he would ask. About his time as a mercenary? About serving the sorcerer? The worst thing he had ever done? He clenched his jaw as he flashed back to his hand squeezing Adelaide's throat as the sorcerer controlled him. Although that was only the worst thing he'd been *forced* to do. He had made many terrible choices as a mercenary. Alfred's gaze bored into him, like he was looking into his very soul. Regulus fought the urge to flinch under his scrutiny.

"Did you have relations with my daughter?"

Blood drained from Regulus' face. "No! I swear it—"

"Father!" Adelaide flushed dark red.

"I respect—"

"We didn't—"

"I wouldn't—"

Alfred held up his hand, silencing them both. Regulus held his breath, ready to protest. "I am satisfied. Wary, as fathers always are, but satisfied. I give you my permission *and* my blessing."

"Thank you, sir." Regulus let the tension out of his shoulders and allowed himself to breathe again.

"Alfred," Adelaide's father said, "please."

"Thank you, Alfred." Regulus inclined his head. Lady Belanger still sat back in her chair, her lips pressed together. "Lady Belanger? Adelaide loves you. I don't require you to approve of me." He was accustomed to living under the weight of everyone's disapproval. "But I do desire your blessing."

"Mother," Adelaide said softly. "Please."

Lady Belanger blinked, her eyes moist. The tendons in her neck stood out and her temples pulsed as she worked her jaw before speaking in Khast.

"Oh, Mother." Adelaide pushed off the bed. Regulus' hand fell off her shoulder as she moved to her mother and pulled her into an embrace. She said something in Khast into Lady Belanger's shoulder. Her mother's hands clenched her hair as she responded. Regulus watched, unsure what to do or where to look. He seriously needed to have Adelaide teach him some Khast.

When they separated, both women had tears on their faces. Regulus looked to Alfred, more than a little terrified. But Alfred was looking at his family, his own eyes watering. Lady Belanger said something else he didn't understand, then stood.

"Regulus."

He moved to that side of the bed and stood. She was an inch or two shorter than Adelaide and darker, but she looked up at him with similar dark brown eyes. A few strands of silver hair stood out against her black braid. She considered him, then hugged him a little too hard and immediately stepped back.

"You better not hurt my daughter."

"Never, my lady."

CHAPTER 8

ADELAIDE SMILED AS SHE DRIED HER TEARS. *"YOU'RE MY BABY girl."* The tenderness and fear in Mother's voice had nearly broken her. It didn't help Adelaide was still reeling from Regulus' admission his father's wife had tried to have him killed. Even in hiding, she had never known a life without loving parents.

But she hadn't expected Mother to be so hesitant. Sure, after those years together in that cottage, they could only have become close or hated each other. Adelaide loved Father, but until Regulus, she didn't think she could love someone as much as she loved Mother. And Mother had always been protective. She should have expected Mother to fight any suitor.

"I secretly hoped you would stay with me forever." Adelaide hadn't been able to keep from crying at that. But Mother understood, even if she didn't like it. *"I'm glad you've found someone you can love like I love your father. I just don't want to see you hurt."*

"There's something else," Regulus said as he sat back down on her bed, drawing her attention. "Something the sorcerer—or Kirven, I guess—said that I've been wondering about. Something that might help you get your magic back. If that's what you want."

"What?" Adelaide sat back on her heels. Hope swelled, followed by suspicion and doubt. "The sorcerer? I don't want anything to do with sorcery."

"It wouldn't be sorcery," Regulus said quickly. "At least, I don't think so. The sorcerer wasn't much for explaining things most of the time." He sat on the edge of her bed. "One of the ingredients he had me find was the root of a neumenet tree."

"Absolutely not," Mother said, folding her arms. "No."

Adelaide looked between them. "What's a neumenet tree?"

"According to the sorcerer, it's a tree that holds a lot of magic." Regulus looked inquisitively at Mother. "He said a long time ago people would try to conceive children under neumenet trees in the hope of their children being mages. And that it sometimes worked. What do you know about neumenet trees?"

Mother huffed and returned to the armchair. "When we realized Adelaide had magic, I read everything I found, trying to understand and determine how to help her hide."

"We had books on magic?" Adelaide gaped at her mother, hurt and anger cracking through her heart like searing lightning. "You hid them from me?"

"Yes." Mother pulled her braid over her shoulder and fiddled with it. "We hoped the less you knew, the easier it would be to keep your abilities concealed. To keep you safe." She bit her lip. "Maybe that was wrong, but I stand by our decision."

"And one of these books talked about neumenet trees?" Regulus asked.

"A few of them." Mother inspected the leather tie on the end of her braid. "Every living thing has some level of magic, tied inextricably to life itself. It is a reminder of Etiros, the creator and source of pure magic. Sentient beings with high levels of magic—like mages—can use that magic to affect the world around them. For unknown reasons, some non-sentient living things are like wells of magical energy. Neumenet trees are exceedingly rare and hold more magical power than any other known thing. There are legends about its power rubbing off on sentient beings that spend time in its shade, from birds to men. Some theorize neumenets actually *are* sentient."

Adelaide stared at Mother, stinging betrayal making her throat tense. "All these years…you knew about magic and didn't tell me?"

"Adelaide." Father looked at her, his eyes sad. "I lost a good friend and a few acquaintances when the Shadow struck. If there was even a chance not using your gift would keep you safe, I was willing to try it."

Father had mage friends before the Shadow? "You never told me that." She fidgeted with her hands in her lap.

"Some things are…painful to talk about. And difficult to hear." Father scratched behind his ear and bit his lip. "How do you tell your child you…" He shook his head. "You can't tell a child you found a dear friend strangled and hanging from his own balcony because he had the same gifting your child does." His voice shook. "I wanted you safe. I didn't want you terrified."

Silence filled the room as Adelaide stared at her hands. The very air seemed to press in, smothering her. It took her a moment to get her tongue working. "So this tree could help me?"

"It felt ancient and powerful," Regulus said. "Maybe if it can give an unborn child magic, it can restore yours."

"Perhaps," Mother said. "But you can't go running off on a hunch." She laid a hand on Adelaide's head. "Powerful sources of magic attract other powerful magical creatures, both good and evil. The tree might be dangerous. More importantly, it may be best if you are powerless, at least until the sorcerer is dead and can't take further interest in you. And I don't want you leaving this castle while that monster Carrick is out there."

"Best—powerless?" Adelaide sputtered. Mother couldn't begin to understand the emptiness she felt without her magic flowing through her veins. Or the fear.

A frantic rapping sounded on the door, and they all turned.

"Come in," Father called.

The house steward stepped in, clutching his cap in his hands, his eyes wide. His graying blond hair was a mess, as if he had been repeatedly putting the cap on and taking it back off. His bony shoulders scrunched up around his neck.

"My lord, we have a problem, if I may speak with you in private."

Father frowned. "Speak, Titus."

Titus twisted his cap. "Perhaps not in front of the ladies…"

"They will find out eventually," Father responded. "Out with it."

"My lord…we received back the falcon you sent to the king."

Adelaide stood and placed a hand on Regulus' shoulder. What could possibly have upset the steward so much about whatever message the king sent back? The steward shouldn't have even read a message from the king.

"That was fast," Father said, his brow wrinkling.

"It's dead, my lord."

Adelaide dropped onto the bed next to Regulus, her mind and pulse racing. Dead?

"A peasant brought it to us with an arrow through it, your message still in the container on its back." Titus tapped his foot. "He said a man named Carrick gave it to him and paid him to deliver the carcass to Belanger castle." He glanced at Adelaide, then stared at the floor. "The man also said Carrick instructed him to give Lady Adelaide his regards and to tell Lord Belanger to desist."

Adelaide's chest constricted, as if something was pushing on her sternum. She gripped Regulus' forearm and her hands and feet turned cold. Her face felt numb and her mind thrummed with a frantic buzzing. She was vaguely aware of her father dismissing the steward as she struggled to breathe. Her vision went out of focus.

Helpless. Powerless. Useless. She ran through the most likely scenario. The sorcerer would kill the king. Nolan would be a duke with an army of knights at his command. He would storm Belanger castle. Good men would die. Regulus would be killed. Maybe even her father. Nolan would take her. Sweat ran down the back of her neck.

"Adelaide." Regulus' voice cut through her internal scream. He rubbed her back. "Breathe, Adelaide." She took a deep breath. "We'll figure this out. All right?" His hand moved in circles over her taut muscles. His smooth, deep voice washed over her like a hot bath. "Chin up, *Tha Shiraa*."

Her breathing slowed. The tension in her shoulders eased as the weight lifted from her chest.

"We'll find a way through this together. Together, my brave tigress."

She nodded, her heart rate easing.

"Good." Regulus smiled. "Now, don't take this the wrong way, but your grip is like the jaws of a dragon."

"Hm?" She looked at her fingers digging into his sleeve. With a gasp, she released her death grip on his forearm. "I'm sorry!"

He shook his arm. "I think I was a few seconds from losing feeling in my hand." He winked and laughed nervously.

"That settles it," Mother said with finality. "You're not leaving this castle."

"I concur." Father's eyes flashed with a fury she had never seen. "I'll send another falcon tonight. Perhaps under cover of darkness it will make it. And I'll send messengers by horse and by foot. We'll have to spare a few knights to escort them. He can't stop them all. In the meantime, I'll have a guard posted outside your door. You're not to leave this room without at least two armed guards."

Adelaide's mouth hung open, but she couldn't formulate a response.

"Alfred, I understand where you're coming from, but I don't think that's going to work." Regulus continued to rub her back as he spoke. "I have experience with this. Carrick is nearly unstoppable, especially since he is eager to do his work. The sorcerer is likely stronger with the staff, and that may be reflected in Carrick's abilities as well. Your only hope is for your messengers to get past Carrick without him catching them. And we don't know if he is working alone or if he pulled some of his associates into his scheme with promises of fortune."

"What do you suggest I do?" Father said heavily.

"Send out *all* your falcons, to anyone and everyone you trust, all at once. Tell them to forward your message to the king. Hopefully one will get through, and no lives will be needlessly thrown away."

Father nodded but looked doubtful. "It's worth trying."

CHAPTER 9

MOTHER AND REGULUS PLAYED CHECKERS WHILE ADELAIDE laid on her stomach, hanging off the end of her bed. She tossed her dagger and caught it. Father had gone to write messages to all the dukes, several barons, and to a few lords. All she could do was wait. She hated it.

Mother had beaten Regulus for the third time, much to his clear disappointment, when the door burst open and Father flew in. "They're dead. Almost all of them."

"What?" Adelaide caught her dagger and sat up. Father's face was drawn and pale. He clutched an arrow in his hand.

"A servant went to the aviary to feed the birds." Father shook the arrow. "This was on the floor, with a small pouch and a note tied to it." He thrust out his other hand and opened it, revealing a shredded off-white wool pouch and a rolled-up piece of parchment. "The pouch was full of seed. The birds got into it." He clenched his fist around the pouch and note. "Poisoned. Most of them are dead, and a few are close. We're not sure if the others didn't eat any or if they haven't reacted yet."

Mother cursed in Khast, her eyes wide with horror. Adelaide gripped her dagger tighter. It seemed impossible. The aviary was located at the top of the south-eastern tower. Even though it had the largest window in the entire outer defense, someone would have to be a phenomenal shot to make that.

"We found a few identical arrows wedged in the moss on the sides of the window, and another inside," Father said, as if reading her thoughts. "They didn't have the pouch or note. He must have tried several times to ensure he would make the window."

"Who poisons an entire aviary?" Mother asked.

"The kind of person who orders a horse hobbled to send a message to its owner," Regulus muttered.

"I have to send messengers," Father said. He leaned back against the door. "And pray he doesn't kill them all."

"You can't send them to their deaths." Adelaide tossed her dagger onto the bed. "We have to figure out a way to send them safely!"

"Our king is in danger. Our home is under attack." Father's expression hardened. "This is war. Sacrifices must be made."

"But—"

"He's not wrong, Adelaide," Regulus said, his voice quiet.

She turned toward him, hurt and surprised. "They'll die."

"Many more people will die, including the king, if he's not warned," Father said. "It is my duty to try."

Adelaide shook her head. She *hated* Nolan. If only she had her magic. With her magic, she could keep Nolan from getting close enough to reach her. Keep him far enough away that his enhanced strength and speed and his immortality wouldn't matter. "Fine. But we need a back-up plan."

Father raised his brows. "I'm listening."

"Send the messengers." Adelaide looked at Regulus, then back at Father. "But let Regulus and I leave right after them for the neumenet tree." Mother and Father started speaking at once, so she shouted over them, "Listen!" They quieted, but neither looked pleased. "Nolan will be focused on the messengers. Send them out, and we can sneak out without him noticing us. If the neumenet tree can restore my magic, I'll be better able to defend myself. And if none of the messengers get through, then I'll go. If I have my magic back, I can get past him, I'm sure."

"That's a lot of if's," Father said with a shake of his head. "It's too dangerous."

"I'm not waiting here for him to take me!" She immediately wished she hadn't said it. But she couldn't keep her fear inside any longer, gnawing away at her heart.

No one said anything for a long moment. She stared at her blurred reflection in the dagger lying on her bed.

Father sighed. "I won't let that happen."

"Alfred." Regulus stood. "Adelaide's reasoning is sound."

"I don't care. She's not leaving this room if it means I have to chain her to her bed."

"Father!" She looked to Mother, but Mother lifted a shoulder, clearly siding with Father. "You wouldn't."

"The messengers will be sent tonight, in two groups, and will all take different routes." Father clutched the arrow and it snapped in half. "You two will be locked in your own rooms."

"Fath—"

"End of discussion." Father turned and opened the door.

"Wait!" Adelaide reached toward him, as if to stop him. He paused partway through the door. "What did the note say?"

"Nothing." Father walked out the door and she raced after him and grabbed his arm.

"Tell me."

"It's not your concern—"

She grabbed his hand and tried to pry his fist open.

"Don't make this harder, Adelaide." Father moved her aside, but she held onto his fist.

"I deserve to know." Her heart pushed against her throat. *He's only targeting you because of me.*

Father sighed and lowered his head. "It doesn't change any-thing if you know."

"I'd rather know than wonder." She tried to catch his eyes, but he wouldn't look at her.

Slowly, Father unclenched his fist. Adelaide took the crumpled, smashed scrap of parchment from his palm. It crinkled as she opened it. She walked closer to a small window in the hallway and held it up to the light. Nolan's handwriting looked just the same as in the love letters he had sent her what seemed a lifetime ago. Regulus walked up behind her as she read.

> *I'll tell you what I told Adelaide: You don't want to go to war with me. You can't stop the inevitable, Belanger. Stay out of my way. Final warning. Let's not make Adelaide fatherless if we don't have to, shall we?*

Regulus reached around her and pulled the note out of her hands. He read it, then ripped it in half and dropped it to the ground.

Father wrapped his arms around Adelaide and cradled the side of her head in his hand. "It's going to be all right." He kissed the top of her head, just like he did when she was little. She leaned into his chest, taking comfort in his warmth while he stroked her hair. "I've faced many enemies. I'm still here. Don't worry." He patted her shoulder and walked away.

But none were a man who couldn't be killed. Adelaide watched him walk down the hall, back tall, but with a heaviness to his steps that betrayed the weight he carried. She had always thought Father the strongest person she knew. Believed him to be unbreakable. A war hero with laughter and love in his heart. He had never looked so ragged. So unsure. For the first time, she looked at him and didn't feel like everything would be all right.

And it was her fault.

The room was made of layered shadows when Adelaide's eyes snapped open. She listened, trying to determine what had awoken her. She must not have been asleep long; in fact, she was unsure she'd even fallen asleep. Something metallic rasped at the door. Still lying down, she gripped the hilt of her dagger under her pillow and freed it from its sheath, watching the door through half-closed eyes. The door cracked open. Faint candlelight spilled into the room. With a creak, the door opened further. The candle on the floor illuminated a kneeling figure. She blinked against the bright light as the man picked up the candle and stood, her pulse quickening. Under the pillow, she gripped the dagger tighter and prepared to scream.

The man raised the candle, and the light glittered in his eyes and made his scar shine. Her muscles unclenched and she sat up.

"Regulus? What—"

"Shh." He walked in and closed the door behind him. A bulging bag hung from his uninjured shoulder. He'd found a sword somewhere, as one now hung at his left hip. "We're going to the neumenet tree."

"What?" She squinted at the candlelight.

"Unless you don't want to."

"No, I do—"

"Then get dressed. The second group of messengers are about to leave. If we're going to do this, we need to hurry. Plus, it's only a matter of time before someone finds your guards."

Adelaide tossed off the covers and hurried to her dresser. It almost surprised her how quickly she agreed. But it was her plan, after all. Even if the clandestine, against-Father's-orders-thing was unexpected. "What did you do? How did you get here?"

"I picked the locks. And I knocked your guards out. They'll be fine, although they might have a headache when they wake up."

Regulus winced. "And I don't envy them the experience of facing your parents."

Adelaide pulled an outfit she sometimes used for combat training out of her dresser and slipped behind her dressing screen. "You know how to pick a lock?"

"It's a useful thing for a mercenary to know."

Oh. She slipped out of her nightgown and struggled into the suede fitted trousers. Next, she slipped on a thin, sleeveless white undershirt and wriggled into a fitted sleeveless leather tunic she had based on a drawing in one of Mother's Khastallander books. With a hemline at mid-thigh in the front and just below her knees in the back, and slits up to her hips on the sides, it could hardly be called a dress. She tightened and tied off the laces over the bust. The back came up to her neck, but the front curved well below her collarbone.

From the dresser she grabbed tall riding boots, a black cloak, a belt, and a baldric with slots for throwing knives she had thought she would never use. Regulus' mouth fell open as she moved past him and sat on her bed to put on the boots.

"That's…you…" He cleared his throat, and she smiled to herself as she laced up her boots. "You look fierce, *Tha Shiraa.*"

Adelaide pulled her box full of weapons out from under her bed. She picked out five throwing knives and put them into the baldric before throwing it over her shoulder and across her chest. After feeding the belt through the sheathes of a couple daggers, she cinched it around her waist. She grinned as she stood and threw on her cloak.

"You're a bad influence, Regulus Hargreaves. This will be twice I've run off with you."

"It's your fault, really." The candlelight danced in his pupils. "You make me reckless." He grabbed her hand. "Ready?"

She stepped forward. "I'll lead. I know every hall in this castle. We'll be at the stables in no time."

"That's my tigress."

They snuck past the guards slumped against the wall next to her door and down the hall. Every moment they spent in the castle set her on edge, every little sound startling her, certain they had been caught. But they made it to the stables and found Zephyr and Sieger without a problem. They saddled them in a hurry, then stole through the shadows to the small servant's gate in the rear of the castle. Just large enough for a horse and rider, and easily blocked off, it presented little threat in case of attack. But it did provide an excellent way to slip out. The two guards standing in front of the gate straightened as they approached.

"Who goes—Lady Adelaide?" The guard on the right bowed. "I'm sorry, my lady, but you have to turn back."

"I command you to step aside." She put as much confidence and authority into her words as she could muster.

"Can't do that, my lady," the second guard said. "We're under orders from your father not to let anyone in or out without his express permission."

"Do you think I would be here without his permission?"

The guards exchanged a glance. "He'd be here if he wanted to give his permission," the first guard said.

Regulus stepped forward. "Look, gentlemen, you're doing a wonderful job. What are your names, so I can commend you to Lord Belanger myself?"

"Um, that's close enough—"

Regulus jumped forward and grabbed both men by the collar of their leather armor. He pushed them back into the stone wall, grabbed their helms, and knocked their heads together with a clang that was sure to draw all kinds of attention. One of the guards staggered in a daze to the side, then sagged against the wall. The other slumped to the ground. Regulus retrieved the key from the belt of the fallen man. He unlocked the door and pushed it open, then turned back, breathing hard.

"Better hurry before anyone else shows up." Regulus winced as he mounted Sieger. Adelaide bit her lip when he pressed a hand against his ribs and grunted.

She mounted Zephyr as a man shouted from further along the wall. Regulus kicked Sieger forward, and she urged Zephyr after him. They raced away from the castle, the wind from their speed pulling at her braid and cloak, the air cool and crisp on her face. She glanced back at the castle, at the cluster of torch-illuminated men near the door.

Be safe, Father and Mother.

CHAPTER 10

THEY DIDN'T DARE STOP WHILE ON FATHER'S LAND. TOO MUCH of a risk of either Father's men or Nolan finding them. Although, if Father's men found them, they'd just be taken back. Nolan was the bigger threat. If Father's men did find them, though, they'd be even more likely to come across Nolan on their return journey. So they rode. When they had put enough distance between themselves and Belanger castle, they stopped in a copse of ash trees surrounded by large bushes. They fell asleep in each other's arms.

Adelaide awakened to pinkish light filtering through the trees, casting long shadows. Regulus was already up, digging through the sack he had brought. She stretched her sore neck while massaging her left shoulder. Regulus reached into the bag and tossed her a red apple.

"How'd you get food?"

"I wandered into the kitchen before I went to bed. Said I liked to have food in my room in case I wake up in the night. The cook seemed confused and concerned I took so much, but he's the cook, I'm the guest and the lord, so he couldn't tell me no." He ducked his head and tied the bag to the back of Sieger's saddle. "Hopefully enough to get us to Holgren and back."

"Holgren? That's a—"

"Royal forest. I know."

She stood and brushed grass and leaves off herself. "What if we're caught?"

"I guess we'll figure that out if it happens?"

That didn't sound like a plan, but she didn't have any better ideas. So she mounted Zephyr and they continued on, toward a royal forest they didn't have permission to enter and a magic tree that may or may not be sentient.

They rode for hours in silence, but Adelaide didn't mind the comfortable quiet. The laughter and squeals of children carried through an overgrown hedge, and she wondered what hers and Regulus' children would look like. They would almost certainly be tall.

"I want to learn Khast," Regulus said abruptly.

She cocked her head. "You do?"

He looked over, his expression earnest. "I want you to teach me Khast. I don't know if I'll be any good, but…it's important to you, so I want to learn."

Adelaide could have laughed with joy, but she didn't want him to think she was making fun of him. "I'd love to teach you, *mareh piahre.*"

"Mar-ay pea-aw-ruh." Regulus said each syllable as if rolling it around his mouth, trying to get a feel for the sounds. "That's what your mother called your father. What's it mean?"

Adelaide gave him a teasing smile. "My love. My father likes to call my mother *piahre cha mareh gehvam.* Love of my life."

"Pea-aw-ruh chaw mar-ay gay-vam." Regulus sighed. "It sounds better when you say it."

Adelaide chuckled. "We'll work on it, *sumdir.*"

He wrinkled his nose. "Now you're just being cruel."

"Never, handsome."

Regulus blushed. "All right, how do you say beautiful?"

"Khast doesn't have a different word for beautiful and handsome."

"So…you're mar-ay soom-dear pea-aw-ruh? My beautiful love?"

His pronunciation sounded like someone trying to speak around a mouthful of marbles, but she grinned nonetheless. "Charmer."

Toward evening, they arrived at the edge of a forest. Wooden signs nailed to tree trunks proclaimed HOLGREN ROYAL FOREST. ENTRY WITHOUT ROYAL WARRANT STRICTLY PROHIBITED in faded white paint. They looked around, but didn't see anyone, so they continued inside.

Regulus paused. "Give me a minute to get my bearings. We don't want to waste time wandering about."

She reined in Zephyr. The fresh air smelled of moss and pine. A couple birds chirped somewhere nearby. Yellow edged in on the leaves of birch trees, announcing that summer was growing old.

A strange prickling ran across Adelaide's skin from head to toe. Almost like a breeze, but the air remained calm. Something deep inside her made her look to the right. The forest looked the same over there, but a voice—more of a sensation than actual words— seemed to tell her to go that way. As if Etiros himself were prodding her deeper into the forest. The familiar warmth of magical energy shuddered through her, brushing over the empty places in her soul and calling to her. She had urged Zephyr forward before she even realized it.

"Regulus," she called over her shoulder. "This way."

"What? Hey, where are you going?" Regulus directed Sieger closer. "Do…you feel something?"

"Yes." Her voice sounded detached. The pull increased. "I can feel it. Like a current sweeping me along."

The external pull of magical energy grew until it felt like it would carry her away. Her breaths came sharper and quicker until Adelaide and Regulus broke through the trees and she saw it. The pull stopped, and her jaw went slack. It was…unbelievable.

Clouds obscured the sun, but even so, the leaves on the gigantic tree shimmered like shards of silvery glass. Some of the light bent as it reflected, sending bright spots of color into the forest. Its black branches stretched out over a meadow and trees a half dozen paces away that bent away from its shade. The trunk looked big enough to fit a bedroom inside, and its black bark was glassy, as if the tree had been carved out of obsidian. She had to look up, shielding her eyes against the glaring light on the leaves, to see the top. Who knew trees grew so enormous?

They rode forward, but their horses got skittish, so they dismounted and walked. "Do you hear that?" She moved toward the tree as if in a dream.

"Hear what?"

"The tree." She couldn't describe the sound. Soft, nearly inaudible. Somewhere between a deep thrumming and a soft, wordless singing. The sound moved through her, calming and frightening her all at once. She reached toward the shiny bark, then paused, her palm hovering inches away from the glossy surface broken by angular edges that caught the light.

Warmth flowed between her hand and the trunk, and she felt the tree. Its life. Its tremendous age. Somehow, she knew, almost as if she had gotten a glimpse of it in her mind, that this tree had been tall when the rest of the forest hadn't yet begun to grow. It seemed to both call to her and warn her. She looked up at the glittering leaves above her. So high above the surrounding forest, they swayed in an unfelt breeze, flashing without a sound. A leaf separated from a branch and floated toward her, arcing back and forth like a falling feather. She caught it in her hand and its softness surprised her. No hard edges, despite looking like glass. She let it fall to the ground and looked back at the trunk.

A noise like a stifled groan behind her caught her attention and she spun around. "Reg—" She gaped at the empty space. Sieger and

Zephyr shuffled and whinnied near the edge of the trees. But Regulus had disappeared.

"Regulus!"

"Don't worry," a quiet, shrill voice said. "He's all right."

Adelaide turned toward the voice as she drew a dagger and a throwing knife. Her eyes widened, and she stepped backward. A fairy shorter than the length of Adelaide's hand flew less than a foot away from her face. A sleeveless dress of pale green embroidered with silver hugged the fairy's pale skin. Short reddish hair stuck out in all directions around her delicate face. Her wings beat the air so fast Adelaide couldn't make them out, other than to tell they shimmered with each movement.

"What?" Adelaide's voice squeaked, and she cleared her throat. "Who are...where is Regulus?" She pointed her dagger at the fairy, but the fairy tittered, her laughter like tiny wind chimes.

"This isn't about him," the fairy said. "It's about you."

Adelaide shook her head. "What do you want?"

"To help you, of course." The fairy smiled, showing pearly white teeth with sinister-looking points. Adelaide blanched.

"Where is Regulus?" She put as much force into her words as she could, even as she wondered how one fought a fairy.

"Oh, please. He's hardly the important one here, my dear." The fairy flitted side to side. "You're the mage. You're the interesting one."

Her breath caught. "How do you know what I am?"

"I can feel it, dear. Just like you can feel the neumenet tree. And I know what happened to you. I sense that, too." The fairy tilted her head and gave her a sympathetic look. "You were right to come here. The neumenet tree can help you. Reach out and take it."

Adelaide lowered her weapons. "Take what?"

"The tree's magic!" The fairy smiled again, and chills ran down Adelaide's spine. "You know how to do it, because it's been done to you."

Adelaide stepped backward. She flashed back to the feeling of her magic, her energy, her very life being drawn out of her. Even now the sensation of the tree's power only emphasized the abyss inside her where her magic had once been.

"No. Not like that."

"I'm afraid this is the only way."

"No. That's…that's sorcery. It's taking what isn't yours. It's *hurting*."

The fairy laughed again. "It's only a tree."

So were the trees around the sorcerer's tower. The ones so drained of life they turned white as bones. Trees sapped of energy until they blackened as if they had been burned. The sorcerer took their energy, their magic. And it killed them.

"I'm not a sorcerer. Sorcery takes. It steals and destroys and kills to further your own power." As she spoke, she became more certain. "That's why it's corrupted. It's been twisted from something that helps others to something that helps only yourself at another's expense. I won't get my magic back by becoming like him. Now where's Regulus?"

"Hm. Foolish girl." The fairy waved and pointed. Adelaide followed the line of her finger.

Regulus stood where she had last seen him, but his eyes were wide over his gagged mouth. Rope-like vines bound his wrists together, and more vines wrapped around his arms, tying them to his sides. Several fairies hovered around him, holding the ends of the vines that bound his torso. *Oh, Etiros, no!*

Adelaide's pulse quickened. She clutched her weapons tighter as her breathing became shallower. Not again. She couldn't watch him be hurt *again*. Her mouth went dry. "Regulus." Her voice cracked.

Regulus strained against the fairies, but somehow the tiny creatures held him without any struggle. He stilled and held her gaze, the message in his eyes clear. *Run.*

"There's your man." The fairy sounded bored. "Free him, if you want him back."

CHAPTER 11

ADELAIDE DREW HER DAGGER AGAIN AND STEPPED TOWARD Regulus. A blast of white light hit the dagger out of her hand.

"Free him," the fairy taunted.

With a growl, Adelaide drew a knife and threw it at a vine held by one of the fairies. The fairies on both sides of Regulus darted with surprising speed to the side, and Regulus stumbled sideways with them. Her knife sunk into his left shoulder and she cried out as he winced. Adelaide flinched and bit her tongue.

"Oh, dear." The fairy tittered, and the other fairies laughed with her. Their melodic laughter grated on Adelaide's taut nerves. "Better try something else."

She dug her feet into the ground and found every bit of magical energy left inside. It wasn't much, like a river reduced to mud. She pushed her energy out, sending blinding blue blasts at the fairies on either side of Regulus. The blasts hit the fairies, and they dropped backward, but held onto the vines and recovered quickly. Adelaide panted, sweat beading on her forehead as her vision swam. She didn't have another blast in her. She recalled the warning in the *Compendium*. Mages who drained themselves of their magic died. She looked at the first fairy.

"Please. Let him go."

"Free him."

"I can't!" She clutched her hands to the side of her pounding head. "Please!"

"Yes, you can," the fairy said in a sing-song voice. "Take power from the tree."

Adelaide shook her head. "I can't."

"You mean you won't." The fairy crossed her delicate arms. "I suppose we'll take him with us. He should make a good slave."

"No!" She held her hands out and stepped toward the fairy, her heart pounding.

The fairy flitted backward. "Lay your hand on the trunk. Pull its magic out into yourself. It has plenty to share, you won't kill it. You can't hold all the power it holds. Just take a little. Save your love."

She looked at Regulus, desperation making her heart pound. Blood ran down his arm from her knife. He struggled against his bindings, but to no effect. Even with her magic depleted, she could sense the magic holding the vines in place. She would need a great deal of magic to free him.

"I'm not a sorcerer," she whispered. Tears stung her eyes. "I won't hurt others to help myself."

"But you've already hurt your dear Regulus," the fairy reminded her. "And you could lose him forever."

No. No, no, no. She turned toward the tree and reached toward the trunk. *Etiros, forgive…* Her hand shook. This was wrong. Something deep inside whispered it shouldn't be like this. Stolen power would only leave her hungry to take more. Somehow, she knew. If she did this, she would become as power hungry as Kirven.

"I'm getting bored," the fairy said. "I think perhaps we should take our new slave and go."

"No!" Adelaide turned back to the fairy. "Please! I'm begging you!"

"Don't beg me, fight me!" The fairy thrust her tiny hands toward Adelaide.

White light slammed into her chest, pushing her backward. She had no strength to even raise a shield. The magic of the neumenet tree thrummed next to her, but she ignored it. *Etiros, I don't know what to do.*

Adelaide fell to her knees and hung her head as tears rolled down her cheeks. "Please. Don't take him." She wouldn't lose him now. Not after everything. "I won't steal power like a sorcerer. But I can't lose him." She looked at Regulus through her tears. He gave her a nod, and she knew he was agreeing with her decision not to steal magic, but it made the tears flow faster. She would watch him until he was gone. Unless…

"Take me, too," she choked out.

Regulus shook his head, eyes bulging. He tried to say something through the gag, but it was unintelligible. Adelaide looked at the fairy hovering above her.

"If you must take him, take me too. I won't leave him."

The fairy flashed a sharp-toothed smile. She flew down until she was right in front of Adelaide's face. "Give me your hand."

Regulus made more muffled grunting sounds as she held her hand out, palm up, toward the fairy. The fairy landed on her palm. She was so light; Adelaide hardly felt her. Her wings stopped beating, and Adelaide marveled at the two pairs of translucent, shimmery green wings. The fairy clapped her hands, the sound bizarrely quiet.

"Adelaide Diya Belanger, you've passed the test."

Adelaide gasped as power flowed from the neumenet tree into her. A rush of energy and life, a swelling in her very soul. If Kirven stealing her magic had felt like dying, this felt like the first breath of air after drowning. The colors around her flared with vibrancy. The smell of the grass, the pine trees in the distance, even the freshness of the dirt hit her with unexpected clarity as every nerve ending tingled with life.

The fairy fluttered back up, hovering a short distance away. Adelaide dropped onto her hands as her head spun, dizzy from the rush of magic coursing through her veins. Strong hands gripped her shoulders, and she looked up at Regulus' concerned expression. She grinned.

"My magic is back."

His features relaxed and he smiled. She pulled her knife from his shoulder and healed the hole it left behind. Then she healed his ribs. As soon as she stopped, he pulled her into an embrace.

She hugged him, then looked up at the fairy. The fairies who had been holding Regulus now hovered behind the first fairy. There were men and women wearing various earthy colors, all with the same delicate, beautiful features, but with skin tones from ebony to as white as the first fairy and everywhere in between.

"That was a cruel test," Adelaide said.

The fairy waved a hand. "But it was a good test. We are the guardians of the tree. It's up to us how we do that."

Regulus stood and helped her up. "But you didn't stop me from taking a root."

The fairy nodded. "There was strong, evil sorcery on you. A terrible corruption of protection magic. Stopping you would have been near impossible. Some things have to happen, and it is not up to us to determine why." The fairy smiled, but her fanged teeth still made Adelaide uncomfortable. "But I am glad to see you are free of your curse. It will make righting things easier."

"What do you mean?" Regulus asked before Adelaide could.

"You have made a wicked man very powerful." The fairy frowned. "The Staff of Nightfall has been broken and useless for hundreds of years. Because of you both, it is whole."

"I don't understand," Adelaide said. "What is the staff?"

"Hmm." The fairy rolled her eyes. "Doesn't anyone know anything anymore?" The fairy sighed, and Adelaide shuffled her feet, her shoulders bunching.

"You can store magical power in an inanimate object, such as a staff," the fairy explained. "When you use your magic, as you are aware, it eventually refills. Unless it's stolen, in which case, it usually takes an extra push to fully recover that magic. When a mage—or a sorcerer—puts magic into an object, that magic gets locked into the object. It can then help focus a mage's magic, making a little magic go a longer way. So while it takes an immense amount of power to create such an object, it later helps the user consume less energy to accomplish the same effect. Does that make sense?"

Adelaide nodded, although all the information made her light-headed.

"A powerful and twisted sorceress created the Staff of Nightfall. She imbued the Staff with corrupted sorcery tinged with her own cruelty, bloodlust, rage, and thirst for destruction. Because of this, the Staff works best when used for destruction, to bring pain and suffering and darkness. It took five mages to stop the sorceress and take the Staff. But such powerful magic is difficult to destroy. So they broke the Staff and each mage hid one piece. The pieces remained undisturbed until the sorcerer Kirven started looking for them. He never would have acquired them all without both of your help."

"I didn't have a choice." Regulus sounded resigned.

The fairy looked at him with pity. "I know. You tried, dear boy. But you learned the hard way not to make deals with sorcerers."

"My men—"

"Will die at the sorcerer's hand if he succeeds," the fairy said. "But you couldn't have known that at the time. Still. The fact remains, regardless of circumstances, that you both had a hand in creating a powerful threat to all creatures and people not only in Monparth, but in surrounding kingdoms as well."

Adelaide's gut twisted. Ironically, given the tiny creatures flying before her, she felt small. "Can't you stop him?"

"That is not our place."

"Why not?" Regulus snapped. "Are you cowards?"

The fairy turned red and clenched her tiny fists. "No. We will die if we leave the vicinity of the neumenet tree. It is the link to our realm. Why do you think the sorcerer sent you to gather the root? Because he couldn't be bothered? He knew what defended the tree."

"And didn't warn me," Regulus muttered.

"Adelaide." A male fairy with dark skin and wearing indigo hose and a periwinkle jerkin flew forward. His voice was also shrill, although deeper than the first fairy's. "We can teach you to use your magic. We can help you stop Kirven."

Adelaide looked to Regulus. His eyes reflected his uncertainty. The fairies had just bound and gagged him and threatened to make him their slave. Although then they helped her get her magic back and released him. But she was just one person. They said five mages had to destroy the last person to wield the Staff. How would she defeat him on her own? Was it even her responsibility? She hadn't wanted to give the sorcerer this power.

"You are one of only five mages in Monparth," the female fairy said, as if reading her mind. "The others are too weak or too young. You have strength and determination. And more magic than I have seen in a mage for decades."

"There has to be another way." Regulus put his arm around her. "Someone else who can help."

"It has to be you," the male fairy said.

Adelaide's shoulders fell. She wasn't prepared for this kind of responsibility. She had wanted her magic back so she would have a chance against Nolan and could warn the king. But then what? Did she really think the king's guards would be able to protect him? She considered how easily Nolan had incapacitated Regulus and Father. But then she remembered the sorcerer branding her with his mark. Remembered him pulling her magic out of her. She shivered. She didn't stand a chance against him.

"Don't agree to serve him, and he cannot claim you," the male said. Could fairies read thoughts?

"And the neumenet's protection is on you now," the female said. "If you had tried to steal the tree's magic, you would not have been able to. Unlike all other living things, in Etiros' mysterious wisdom, the neumenet tree's life cannot be stolen. Now your magic cannot be stolen, either. So, you see, you *are* the only one that can stop him. We will help you."

She rubbed her forehead. What else could she do? If no one else stopped Kirven… Nolan's note to Father invaded her thoughts. The king would die. Regulus would die. Her family might die. She would be lucky to die. Adelaide had told Minerva she wanted to use her magic to help people. If she refused to fight Kirven…she would have to face the possibility she had been lying to herself her entire life. That all she had truly wanted was power, not to help.

"All right." Adelaide hated how small her voice sounded. "Teach me."

The fairies smiled, their white fangs bright. "We will. But you have to come with us to our realm." The female looked at Regulus. "He must remain behind."

CHAPTER 12

"ABSOLUTELY NOT." REGULUS PULLED ADELAIDE CLOSER.

Minutes ago, he thought he had traded slavery to the sorcerer for slavery to fairies, of all things. He might not know much about magic, but everyone knew fairies were tricky. Manipulative. He had just seen that for himself. According to the stories, they also liked to trap people in their realm.

"We're leaving."

"That's not for you to decide," the female fairy said with a hiss. The other fairies whispered to each other. "You aren't ready, mage. Kirven has honed his skills for years. If you face him unprepared, you will die."

Adelaide curled into Regulus and placed a hand on his chest. "For how long?" she asked.

"As long as it takes," the male fairy said.

"Or until we run out of time," the female added.

Regulus fought the urge to draw his sword. It wouldn't help in this instance. "Why can't I come?"

"You're not a mage." The female stated this as if it were obvious. "If you came with us, you wouldn't be able to leave."

"You wouldn't let me leave?"

The male fairy rolled his eyes. "No, you wouldn't be *able* to. You need magic to leave the fairy realm."

"Why can't you teach me here?" Adelaide asked.

An excellent question, Regulus thought. *Tricksters.*

"We can't stay here long," the female said. "We weaken the longer we are in this realm."

"Can I talk to Regulus alone for a moment?"

The two fairies looked at each other, as if having a silent conversation. Regulus glanced toward the horses. If the fairies were telling the truth about weakening while in their world, maybe they had a chance at running away.

"Fine." The female waved her hand dismissively.

They stepped away from the fairies and Adelaide folded her arms over her stomach. Regulus tapped his leg.

"I don't like it."

"But they have a point." Adelaide bit her lower lip. He blinked. He needed to focus on the problem at hand and not how attractive that was. "What if it takes a mage to stop a sorcerer?" She kicked at the ground. "And I can't…" She looked away.

"Hey." He tilted his head and moved to catch her eyes. "Look at me." She met his gaze. "I don't trust them." He rubbed her arms. "But they are right about one thing. I can't make this choice for you."

"What would you do if you were me?" Adelaide glanced at the fairies, then met his eyes again.

He pursed his lips. "I'm done making questionable deals with people or beings with magical powers."

She took a steadying breath before turning back to the fairies. He followed her, hand twitching on the hilt of his sword. The fairies watched with crossed arms, wings beating faster than Regulus could see.

"Thank you," Adelaide said, "but…I don't want to leave this realm. I'll take anything you can tell me or teach me before you have to go back."

The fairies muttered to each other. The dark male in blue pulled on his hair. "Foolish. Why are the humans always so foolish!"

The lead female shook her head. Regulus had the odd thought that the movement should sound like a tiny bell. "Fine. You must practice. Practice until you can do three things at once without thinking. Practice until you don't have to picture what you're going to do first, you just remember how to do it on instinct. You have talent and much power, but little control. The more control and focus you have, the more precise you will be, and the less energy you will waste. Wasted magic will mean death when facing someone as powerful as Kirven."

"If you came with us, we would show you how to create your own staff," the male said. "Although it can take years to learn to craft one as fine-tuned as the Staff of Nightfall. But I suppose you can teach yourself. Start small. It's easier if you use something that was once living, especially if it had magical energy while it lived. Try to store magic in leaves from the neumenet tree. Build up gradually."

"We will teach you one thing before we go," the female added. "Protection binding. You've felt the corrupted, twisted version before."

"The sorcerer's mark," Adelaide said. Regulus tensed.

"Correct." The female flew closer. "Such a mark can only be bestowed if the bearer accepts it. It binds the giver to the receiver, and the receiver to the giver."

"It's difficult." The male swayed from side to side. "It's rather like putting magic into an object, but easier since people are natural receptacles of magic. You channel the magic into a person with a specific intent—to heal, protect, and unite. Think of it like healing and raising a shield all at once, but directing that energy into the person's very soul."

"It's draining," the female fairy added. "And takes time to recover due to the amount of magical energy sacrificed. So never attempt a binding unless you're sure you have time."

"You're certain you won't come with us?" The male tilted his head.

Adelaide reached back and Regulus took her hand. "I'm sure."

The fairies muttered and shook their heads.

"Then farewell." The female curtsied, her red hair falling into her face. "Stay here and practice as long as you can. The magic of the neumenet will help you. It has a way of guiding mages it favors, but it can only do so much. Return here and call for Jara if you change your mind. You're Monparth's best hope. Possibly its only hope." She looked at Regulus. "You both are."

Regulus swallowed back the knot forming in his throat. *No pressure.* Then the fairies vanished, leaving empty air. A glittering neumenet leaf drifted through the emptiness. He followed its slow descent as it arced back and forth until it landed on the grass.

"I can't do this," Adelaide whispered without looking at him.

He shifted. If he were honest, he was scared, too. The sorcerer had always intimidated him. But now…he sounded unbeatable. No, he wouldn't think like that. Not after he had fought for so long for his freedom. One thing Regulus had learned as a mercenary—every opponent was beatable. Some were just harder. He turned her toward him.

"Remember when I told you I took over the mercenary troop after the old captain retired?"

Adelaide knit her brows and looked up at him. "Yes?"

"He retired after his arm was crushed by a troll. He and two of the other mercenaries had gone to purchase supplies, got lost, and ran into a cave troll. One of the men didn't make it, and Captain Samuelson nearly lost his arm. He was an experienced, adept fighter. So was Jack—the man who was killed. Samuelson and Ivan almost didn't escape." *And later I lost Ivan to the sorcerer.* He pushed that thought aside.

She shook her head. "Why are you telling me this?"

"Because," Regulus took both of Adelaide's hands in his, "it was only a few days ago that *you* killed a troll. Do you remember? I do. I remember you looking fearsome and powerful, cutting the head off a mountain troll with a sword of light wreathed in flame. You can do anything, *Tha Shiraa*."

She lowered her eyes, her head drooping. "I couldn't even free you from some tiny fairies."

"First, fairies are notoriously one of the most powerful magical beings in the known world." He caught the hardness of what Dresden had termed his "captain voice" and tried to pull it back. "Second, you weren't at your full strength, so it doesn't count."

"But—"

"I'll help you. All right? I'll help you train. And then we'll stop Kirven together." He let go of her hand to lift her chin. "Who are you, Adelaide?"

"I'm…a mage?"

"You're the woman who ran at a group of armed men who were beating me. The woman who volunteered to go serve a sorcerer even though she was afraid." He smiled. She might not believe in herself, but he believed in her. "Where is the woman who killed a troll? Because that woman *knows* she's a mage. That woman is a tigress. So say it again."

"Regulus—"

"Say it like you mean it. I'm a mage."

She smirked. "No, you're not."

He rolled his eyes. "Say it, *piahre*." He felt a small amount of pride at how easily the Khast word rolled off his tongue, but this wasn't about him.

Adelaide huffed. "I'm a mage."

"Hm." He released her hand and stepped back. "I'm unconvinced."

"I'm a mage."

He forced his face to stay neutral. "Not feeling it."

"This is ridiculous." She planted her hands on her hips, her face reddening, but amusement sparked in her eyes.

At least the fear was gone, but he wasn't looking for mirth. He was looking for confidence. Her confidence had taken a hit since losing her magic and the fiasco with Carrick. More than anything, he wanted to see her as confident as she had been when she told Carrick off before the tournament. As confident as she had been when she told him she was going to marry him.

"Make me believe it."

"You know I'm a mage."

"Are you? You say you are, you tell me your magic's back, but—"

"It is! I'm a mage!" She held her hand out in front of her and her palm glowed blue. "I just healed you!"

He waved, pushing further. "You could do that yesterday. *Show* me what you are. Who are you, Adelaide?"

"I'm a mage! Reg—"

"Who. Are. You!" She stepped back, surprise at his harsh tone showing in her hurt expression. He wanted to apologize, but he didn't relent. Just like Dresden never relented when Regulus had been mired in despair. "Are you a mage or aren't you? Does your mother think you brave for nothing?" Her mouth fell open, but he pressed on. "Make me believe you're a mage! Because I'm doubtful right now. Who are you? Are you—"

"I AM A MAGE!" Blue light exploded from Adelaide in every direction, bending the grass. The light reached Regulus and knocked him backward. He scrambled to his feet. Adelaide's eyes glowed golden. She held her hands out to her sides, massive balls of flame hovering over her outstretched palms. "My name is Adelaide." She didn't shout, but her voice rang out across the meadow. "And I am a mage."

"There she is." He walked toward her. As intimidating as she looked, he had no reason to fear her. His wide smile pulled on his scar, but he couldn't stop grinning. "Yes, you are."

The fires over Adelaide's hands shrank then disappeared and her eyes returned to their normal rich brown. "You…" She scowled as he stopped in front of her. "You *scoundrel.*" She pushed against his chest, but without much force.

"Whatever works, right?" Regulus laughed. "I thought, it works on the mercenaries…"

"Don't you *ever* yell at me again." She crossed her arms.

He ducked his head. "Sorry. Never again."

Adelaide threw her arms around him and buried her face in his shoulder. "Thank you," she whispered. He wrapped his arms around her and squeezed, despite her throwing knives digging into his chest. She leaned back and met his gaze. "All right, Sir I'll-Help-You-Train. How exactly do you plan on doing that?"

"Oh." Regulus stepped back and rubbed the back of his neck. He gave her a sheepish smile. "I was planning on attacking you."

Chapter 13

Adelaide bit back a cry as Regulus sank the dagger into her left arm, halfway between her shoulder and elbow. He grabbed her opposite shoulder to steady her. Tears squeezed out of her eyes and her chest heaved with each labored breath. A crushed neumenet leaf glinted in the trampled grass at her feet.

"I'm sorry," Regulus murmured.

She nodded, unable to respond. Pinching pain surrounded the blade, while pulses of pain radiated up and down her arm in time with her heartbeat. He withdrew the dagger and she whimpered and sagged forward. Blood streamed down her arm. After being stabbed three…no, four times now, she thought she should be better able to handle it. But, by the fairy realm, it still *hurt*.

Regulus guided her right hand to the wound. "Come on. Heal it."

Adelaide's hand shook, but warmth spread across her palm, then over the wound. The area numbed so she couldn't feel the flesh knitting back together. The pain gone, she straightened and looked over. A vein stood out on Regulus' forehead, and his jaw clenched, emphasizing every angle of his temples and jawline. She finished healing herself and dropped her hand. Regulus exhaled but didn't relax.

"That's enough." He rubbed his eyes.

"I'm all right," she said to convince herself as much as him. "I can keep going."

"But I can't." He looked at her dagger smeared with her blood still in his hand. "I'm done. We'll practice another way. This isn't working. And…I won't hurt you again," he whispered.

"But it's all right. See?" She pointed to her arm. "You can't even tell."

"Yes, you can," he said, his voiced strained. "You have blood down to your hand. We need a new plan."

Adelaide was inclined to agree. She didn't enjoy getting stabbed. Not to mention the embarrassment of her repeated failures to stop him. She wasn't used to fighting with magic, but her throwing knives and daggers wouldn't prevail against Kirven. Regulus was quick, good at misdirection, and took advantage of the slightest opening. If he could stab her, what would Kirven be able to do with sorcery aided by the Staff?

"If I can't even defeat you, how am I supposed to defeat Kirven?"

Regulus mussed his hair. "Maybe you're not trying as hard because it's me? You could keep me from even getting close if you really wanted. You're subconsciously holding back."

He might have a point. She sighed. "Are *you* holding back?" His glance away told her everything. "Great. I can't even keep you from stabbing me when you're trying not to."

"Trying not to kill you." He turned red. "To be honest, I did try to stab you."

She sank onto the grass, her confidence dwindling again. "Do you try to stab Dresden when you train?"

Regulus sat down and cleaned off her dagger. "We train with swords. And we wear armor. There are bruises involved. I cut open his leg once. He had to be stitched up and limped for a week." He handed over her dagger. "The last couple years I mostly did defense. If they hit me, I'd be okay. But I had to be careful not to…kill someone by accident."

She turned her dagger over a few times before sheathing it. At least she hadn't backslid. After regaining her magic, she had worried all her progress over the last few months of practice would be lost. She could still conjure a flaming sword, raise a shield, throw a blast, and everything else she had painstakingly taught herself. If anything, she could do them faster—the neumenet tree's presence hummed through her, strengthening her grasp on her abilities. Despite all of that, Regulus kept winning.

"Maybe I should have taken up the fairies—"

"I'm glad you didn't." Regulus plucked blades of grass. "I would have gone crazy worrying if I'd ever see you again."

She smiled and elbowed him. "Aw. That's so sweet."

He threw a handful of grass at her. "Besides, your mother would probably have killed me if you vanished into the fairy realm. She's terrifying."

Adelaide laughed and brushed the grass off. "She's just protective."

His lips twitched toward a smile. "She threatened to slit my throat when you were unconscious."

"She did not!" At his serious expression, her chuckle died. "Sorry. She wouldn't…I don't think."

"I believe she would if it saved you." He handed her a neumenet leaf. The leaf shimmered, pinpricks of color dancing along its translucent surface. The soft and pliable leaves in contrast to their glasslike appearance still surprised her. "Here. Something you can practice that's not dangerous."

She pinched the stem of the leaf between her thumb and forefingers and rolled it back and forth. The leaf glittered as it twirled. "I have no idea what I'm doing."

"You're smart." Regulus laid back. "You can figure it out like everything else."

"Right." She stared at the leaf. Just…direct the magic into the leaf. Sure. Her palm glowed, and she imagined her power flowing into the leaf. Then she sensed it. The transfer of energy running down her hand and into the leaf. The leaf glowed blue. "Regulus."

He sat up and looked at the glowing leaf. "That was fast."

The magical energy stopped flowing, as if it had nowhere else to go. The leaf ceased glowing, and then so did her hand. *I guess an object can only hold so much power.* Adelaide spent the next hour practicing storing magic in leaves, then in neumenet twigs, and finally a couple of sticks of a pine tree at the edge of the meadow. That proved more difficult, and between fighting Regulus, healing herself, and all that magical transference, she was drained. She sensed the neumenet tree replenished her magic faster than it would otherwise come back, but she had used a lot.

"I think now's a good time for you to rest. Maybe try to sleep," Regulus said.

"I look that tired?"

He stroked her hair. "Don't worry. I'll keep watch."

"I'm not worried." She laid under the massive canopy of the neumenet tree and drifted to sleep within minutes.

Adelaide woke to a fire crackling in the darkness. Regulus sat next to her, staring into the flames. She stretched and sat up. "It's night?"

"Sun set half an hour ago. You hungry?" He held out a small cloth bag.

Inside, Adelaide found dried venison. Between bites of the tough, salty meat, she said, "I think we should only stay here one more day."

Regulus raised a brow. "The fairies said—"

"Yes, I know." She ate another bite. "But I want to find out if Father has heard anything about the progress of the messengers."

Regulus pursed his lips. The intensity of the unspoken question in his eyes made her uncomfortable.

"What?"

"I thought we were past secrets." He picked up a long stick from next to the fire and poked at the glowing embers. "Are you not being honest with yourself, or just not with me?"

Adelaide lowered the food to her lap. "I don't know what you're—"

"Why do you want to go back? Really?"

All right, there was another reason. But did she have to say it out loud? She tore off another piece of venison and tossed it in her mouth.

He sighed. "Information on the messengers will be important for plotting our next step. But it could wait. I don't want you ever to feel you need to hide from me." The softness with which he repeated her own words back to her pricked her conscience.

"I need to make sure my parents are safe." Saying it aloud somehow made the threat seem more real. "I'm afraid of what Nolan might do." She met his eyes. "Truthfully, I'm more afraid of him than Kirven. And I know that's stupid, but I can't help it. Kirven wants to rule. He'll kill the king and anyone who gets in his way. If it was only Kirven, maybe…" She trailed off, ashamed of herself.

"You'd be tempted to let him win." He didn't sound disappointed or disgusted. In fact, he sounded sympathetic. "I had the same thought. Would it be so bad? Maybe if we ignored him, he would ignore us. But he's vindictive. I doubt he'll feel satisfied with killing the king. I'm not sure anyone would be safe. And if he learns your magic is back… He'd see you as a threat. I don't think we can be free until he's dead."

"I know." She set the bag of jerky on the ground, her appetite gone, and pulled her cloak tighter around her arms. "And even if I could convince myself that wasn't all true..." She shuddered. "If Kirven gives Nolan the political and military power he wants, I'd never be safe. You and my family would never be safe. I'm more worried about that than the kingdom." She laughed weakly. "I suppose that's selfish."

"It's not selfish to want to protect the people you love." Regulus stood and offered her his hand. "Come on."

Without hesitation, Adelaide took his hand and he pulled her to her feet. "Where are we going?"

"Nowhere. But you need a distraction. So practice." He pointed at the fire. "Put up a barrier from the fire to the trunk of the tree."

They practiced for hours. Adelaide put up one barrier after another. Straight, curved, a complete dome over her and Regulus. Then Regulus made her keep a barrier up while she conjured and used lances, knives, and swords. The neumenet's power flowed alongside hers, as if guiding her, helping her learn. By the light of one of her spheres, Regulus set up a bunch of branches in the ground and had her knock them all down while he tried to break through a barrier. She sent the last branch flying into the forest and dropped the barrier. Regulus stumbled forward as she bent over, hands on her knees, breathing hard. Her stomach growled.

"All right. That should be enough for tonight."

She smiled at the pride in Regulus' voice.

CHAPTER 14

SUNLIGHT GLINTED OFF THE NEUMENET TREE'S LEAVES, CASTING a rainbow of color into the tendrils of mist drifting over the meadow. In the early morning light, Regulus imagined he could see how thin the veil between their world and the fairy realm was under the tree's canopy. Even if the ground under magical trees still proved hard and uncomfortable.

He had always hated sleeping on the ground. But with Adelaide pressed against his chest, the ground and his aching muscles didn't seem so bad. As their eyes met, the enchanting beauty of the meadow and neumenet tree faded away, leaving only her.

The sound of her gentle breathing. The dip in her waist where his arm fit so perfectly. Her gorgeous round face and soft brown skin, her dark brown eyes that held his gaze captive and tangled up his insides. The second the sorcerer was dead, Regulus was going to marry her and make sure he woke up to her every morning.

Adelaide ran her finger along his scar, tickling his skin and sending his mind careening in a dozen directions, several of which were less than innocent. But shame about the scars covering the rest of his body tainted his thoughts.

"What are you thinking about?" she murmured.

His face heated. "Um… How to help you train today."

Adelaide laughed, her eyes glinting mischievously. "No, you weren't."

"No," he admitted. "I was thinking about doing this." He leaned over, gripped her waist, and kissed her. "Every day." He kissed her cheek. "For the rest." A kiss against her neck that made her sigh. He smiled and moved his lips back to hers. "Of my life." She met his kiss and clutched the side of his neck. Her stomach rumbled, intruding on the moment and making him laugh against her mouth. "Hungry, *piahre?*"

"Using so much magic makes me starved." She gave him a quick peck and slipped out from under him.

He collapsed onto his stomach on the grass that was still warm with her body heat with a groan. A few moments later, Adelaide's shadow fell over him.

"Are you going to eat, or should I use your back as a table?"

Regulus sat up and rolled his eyes. She sat across from him and handed him some bread and roasted nuts. He raised a brow as she tore into the bread with as much gusto as one of his men after a hard training session. Her gaze moved from his eyes to his lips to his scarred cheek before returning to his eyes.

"I know you said you like my scar, and that I don't need to hide." He tossed some nuts in his mouth, trying to appear nonchalant. "But... I heard you gasp when you saw the rest. Are they..." His throat knotted. *Repulsive?*

Adelaide set her bread down. "They don't bother me." She moved toward him. Regulus wasn't ready for the shock that went through him when she slid her hand under his shirt and pushed it up. "They sadden me." She ran her left hand over the large scar from the dragon's tail. "This looks like it should have killed you."

He had to force his mouth to work, his mind was so consumed with her touch. "It would have, if the sorcerer's magic didn't pull me back."

"What happened?" She met his eyes, her brows knit. "Unless you don't want to—"

116

"Dragon."

"Oh, Etiros." Her hand left his stomach. "At the Glowers' party, when I asked you about the Black Knight and the rumors about a dragon… No wonder you were upset. I'm sorry."

He shrugged. "You didn't know."

She lowered her gaze, her right hand still holding up his shirt as her fingers trailed over various scars, warming his skin and making his breath hitch. "Are they all from serving him?"

"No. Mainly the worst ones."

Adelaide let his shirt fall and touched the long scar on his cheek. "And…this one?"

He worked his jaw and swallowed. "Not that one."

Her fingers slipped off his cheek. She settled back and picked up her bread. She wouldn't push him for the story, and he appreciated that. But he couldn't pressure her not to keep secrets and then do the same.

Regulus sighed. "First and most obvious scar, over a momentary, stupid decision. The first mercenary troop Drez and I joined isn't the one we stayed with. We'd only been with them two weeks when I got in a fight with the lieutenant and a few of his friends. They were drunk and bothering some poor barmaids."

He looked at the charred remains of the fire, remembering the feel of hands pinning down his arms and knees digging into his torso, the fist yanking on his hair to hold him in place. The agony as the knife traced over his skin.

"Drunk men still understand insults. And are still strong." He massaged the scar. Thinking about it made it hurt. "I'm just glad the fool with the knife was either sober enough or drunk enough not to cut all the way through. Drez cursed enough to make a sailor blush the entire time he stitched me up."

Adelaide placed a hand on his arm. "Stopping churls from bothering girls isn't stupid." He looked at her. She watched him with a warm smile. "It makes your scar more attractive."

He laughed through a frown. "I'm both bewildered and pleased I found a woman who finds my scar attractive."

"Well, you don't think I'm beautiful in spite of being half-Khastallander…" She trailed off, her smile vanishing as she stuffed the last of her bread in her mouth.

"Who would say something like that?"

She reddened and didn't look at him as she stood. "I'm ready to train now."

They spent the day training. Regulus challenged Adelaide to see how many things she could do at once, recalling the fairies' advice. Even when she grew tired, he pushed her. The sorcerer wouldn't stop when she was tired. And with Regulus' immortality gone, the best way he could help was by making her ready.

Adelaide dropped her shield and straightened. "I need a break—"

He hurled a large stone at her. She gasped and dove to the ground, but Regulus didn't pause and ran toward her. He knocked her back down just as she started to rise and grabbed her wrists, pinning her down. She smirked.

"If you want to kiss me, you can—"

"This isn't a game!" He released her wrists and stood, pacing back and forth. "Without a staff, the sorcerer bested fifteen of the best mercenaries I've ever met. According to the fairies, the Staff will make him stronger."

"You said…I can do anything."

Regulus stopped. Fear showed in Adelaide's eyes and a pang of sorrow shot through him. He knew what it felt like to question everything you thought you knew about yourself. He knelt next to her, trying to think of what Dresden would say.

"You *are* strong, Ad. But what separates a warrior from a champion isn't strength. It's perseverance. And it's training so their skills are the best they can be when they are tested."

An idea occurred to him. He could make his point and have fun.

"There's a coastal town in Hedengal where they tell stories of—well, I won't try to pronounce it, but it translates to 'the cliff-men.' Men who were battered like the cliffs by a stormy sea, but like those cliffs, they would not break. They killed the demon sea serpents that had been tormenting the town. They fought without rest from dawn until midnight, when the last serpent fell."

Adelaide huffed. "Legends make good stories—"

"Hey." Regulus turned and pulled up his shirt just enough to reveal a small knotted scar on his lower back. "Demon serpent bites burn. They spit saltwater in the wounds they inflict. My men and I fought too hard for you to roll your eyes at us." He released his shirt.

She stared. "Are you being serious?"

Regulus enjoyed her look of astonishment. "I should mention we also are forbidden from ever entering that town again after Caleb got caught kissing our benefactor's—the mayor's—daughter." He offered her his hand. "The point is, I'm pushing you because you'll need to be a cliff-woman to win."

"Okay." Adelaide took his hand and stood with a sigh. "You're right."

They left the tree at dawn the next day. As they reentered the forest, Adelaide paused to look back at the neumenet tree. "I can still feel its energy," she murmured.

Regulus shifted in his saddle. "Should we stay another day?"

She shook her head. "No. It isn't pulling me anymore. And I want to get back."

"Okay." He nudged Sieger forward. "But you should practice everything you can while we ride."

Sometimes Regulus would point out a branch to throw a magical spear at or ask her to see how long she could keep a shield up. He hoped the practice helped keep her mind off whatever Kirven and Nolan were doing.

The sun sank toward the horizon, turning the sky pink and the clouds burnished orange. A few hours away from Belanger castle, they heard voices ahead. Regulus had decided they should assume the worst and avoid everyone, so they moved into a copse of trees in a nearby field. The men kept talking, but no one came down the road.

"Let's keep to the field," he whispered. Adelaide nodded and followed him.

Three men stood next to a small fire on the side of the road. All wore swords and chainmail. Their horses were staked nearby.

"Sure, tell that to his face, coward." One of the men threw what looked like a bone into the fire, then wiped his mouth. "Yer more than happy to take his gold."

"His gold won't help if we're hanged!" another man said.

Regulus glanced at Adelaide and put a finger to his lips, then gestured to ride further from the small group.

"Then leave." The third man's deep voice carried loud and clear over the field.

"Yeah, if I have a death wish. Carrick's lost his mind." The second man cursed.

Regulus whipped his head around and locked eyes with Adelaide as her face drained of color. *No!* He shook his head, but she was already turning Zephyr back toward the road. Mentally cursing, he followed her.

"Carrick's got a plan," the first speaker said. His dark hair was pulled back in a short braid. "And he ain't lyin' about bein' immortal."

"Well, I don't see how that will save *my* neck if somebody finds out what he did." The man ran his hand through knotted blond hair. "His family connections won't save him or us this time."

Zephyr snorted, and the three men turned toward them, swords drawn.

"Hey." The man with the braid pointed. "That's her, right?"

CHAPTER 15

"WHERE IS NOLAN CARRICK?" HER HEART POUNDING, ADELAIDE drew two throwing knives and readied them as Regulus stopped next to her. "What did he do?"

The men circled them and raised their swords. "We don't want to hurt you," the deep-voiced man said. "But you have to come with us."

She threw a knife into his leg. He cursed and howled as he stumbled backward. "Where is Nolan Carrick?"

The blond bolted to one of the horses. She threw a knife at his neck, but he moved to mount the horse and it hit his back, bouncing off his chainmail. She cursed in Khast and drew another knife.

"Watch out!" Regulus' sword grated against its scabbard.

She looked back at the man with the braid just as he grabbed her cloak and pulled. She twisted and stabbed the knife into his forearm as she slid sideways in the saddle. The man cursed and leapt back, yanking her cloak against her neck so she tumbled out of the saddle and fell hard on her arm. Adelaide drew a dagger and staggered to her feet as Regulus ran up next to her. Her knife still stuck out of the man's forearm, but he had dropped his sword. Regulus held the tip of his sword to the man's throat.

"The lady asked you a question."

"He's at Belanger castle!" The man glanced at his friend, but he had sat down a few feet away and was trying to stop the bleeding from his leg. "He got some men together and took the castle by force."

"By force…" She swayed, suddenly dizzy. "Lord and Lady Belanger, are they alive?"

The man nodded rapidly. "Sir Carrick locked 'em up! But they're safe. I swear it! He said none of the Belangers could be hurt." She lowered her dagger, relief mixing with fear.

"Why were you posted here?" Regulus asked.

"To keep an eye out for you." The man swallowed hard, his eyes wide. "We was ordered to kill Hargreaves and take Belanger to Carrick. And if we couldn't, to let him know you're coming."

Oh no, the blond! Adelaide whipped around, but he was gone.

"How many men does Carrick have holding the castle?" Regulus looked eerily calm as he held his sword to the man's throat. Meanwhile, panic pushed against Adelaide's lungs and squeezed her throat. Incoherent thoughts of despair and anger chased each other through her mind.

"I don't know!"

"Think about it," Regulus coaxed. Adelaide wanted to shake the man. Or scream. Or cry. Maybe all at once.

"He brought twenty with him—"

"Nolan took Belanger castle with only twenty men?" Adelaide's eyes widened. "Was there a sorcerer with him?"

The man shook his head and glanced toward her knife still embedded in his forearm. Blood dripped from his elbow to the ground. "I don't know about a sorcerer! But you ever seen a man get run through with a sword and shake it off like a punch? You ever seen a man rip an arrow out of his throat and keep walking? Seeing that does things to men's spirits. He ripped a side door off its hinges, and we walked right in. We only lost a few men before the castle surrendered. Carrick locked up anybody who didn't join him."

"Join him?" Adelaide clenched her fist. "My father's men would never—"

"Carrick can't die and keeps saying he's gonna be the second most powerful man in Monparth soon. Greed and fear get men to do a lot." The man looked from her to Regulus. "I answered your questions. Please don't kill me!"

Adelaide and Regulus looked at each other. She hesitated before she stepped forward and pulled her knife out of his arm. "Go."

Regulus lowered his sword, and the man stumbled over to his companion. They ran to their horses, as best as the other ruffian could with a wounded leg.

"They'll go to Carrick," Regulus noted.

"That's probably where the other one went, anyway." She cleaned and sheathed her dagger and pressed the heel of her hand against her temple. "What if he's wrong? What if my parents are—"

"No." Regulus sheathed his sword. "He'd be an idiot to kill them."

She paced next to Zephyr. "We have to go rescue—"

"No."

"What?" She stilled and clenched her fists.

"You can't go near the castle. Absolutely not."

"Are you insane?" she shouted. "He has my parents—"

"Exactly." Regulus' eyes searched hers. "Think. Why? What will you do if he threatens them? If he puts a sword to your mother's throat? What would you do, Adelaide?"

She opened her mouth, closed it, opened it again, then snapped it closed. She wanted to say she would save them, she'd use her magic, she'd find a way. But what if she couldn't?

"We both know what you'd do," he said gently. "Because you've done it before."

Adelaide screamed and threw her knife into the ground with such force only the tip of the handle stuck out of the dirt. "Then what am I supposed to do? I can't leave them! What if he gets tired of waiting? I have to do something! I can't—"

A sob tore from her throat and she bent over, her chest seizing. She kept picturing Nolan standing over her parents' bloodied, lifeless bodies, that cavalier smile on his haughty face.

Regulus pulled her close and Adelaide sobbed into his shoulder. They had been outwitted. Outplayed. All Nolan had to do was threaten her parents, and she would surrender. Nolan knew it, too. When he threatened to tamper with Minerva's carriage, she had caved. He had pushed her at Arrano, and she had agreed to marry him to save Regulus and Gaius. He likely overheard her telling her parents she helped the sorcerer to help Regulus. She had a history of giving in to save others. Nolan had a history of being unbothered by hurting others. If she went to the castle, she would give herself to Nolan before she watched her parents suffer or die. But for all she knew, he would kill them if she didn't go, anyway.

Adelaide cried until her stomach hurt from gasping through her tears. Regulus held her close but didn't say a word. He let her cry and rubbed her back in big circles. Even when she could finally breathe normally again, she leaned against him. She had soaked his shoulder with tears, and more embarrassing, snot. Once her face was dry, she pulled away.

"What do we do?"

Regulus cupped his hand to the side of her neck and rubbed his thumb over her jaw. "They're going to be okay. But if Carrick is there, and the sorcerer is not, there is a good chance the messengers didn't get through to the king." She nodded, even though she couldn't think about that right now. Regulus sighed. "We're going to have to split up."

"What?" She grabbed his arm. "You can't leave me! And I'm definitely not leaving you! Not after—"

"Shhh." He smiled sadly. "You need to warn the king. You have a better chance of getting there, and once there, you can probably get in. You're Lord Belanger's daughter. I'm nobody. If we want any chance of preventing the sorcerer from seizing the throne, the king must be warned."

"But my—"

"I'll get my men, and we'll rescue your parents. We're mercenaries. This is what we do."

Adelaide shook her head. "Even with your men, how will you defeat Nolan? He has more men. And a castle! It's impossible."

He gave her a look of deep hurt. "Glad to hear you have so much faith in me. The men are going to be offended, too."

"I didn't mean…" She sighed.

"It's this or we both go to the king. Carrick has too much of an advantage over you. Your parents wouldn't want you to knowingly walk into a trap. Your father would want you to warn the king. So, I rescue your parents without you, or we leave your parents until after the king is warned."

She chewed on her lower lip. All right, fine. If she ended up captured trying to rescue her parents, they would be beyond livid. Father could be chained up in the dungeons, and he would still lecture her about tactical miscalculations.

But what if he *was* chained up? What if Nolan had put Mother in the dungeons? The thought of Mother, alone on a hard, dirty dungeon floor, shackles on her wrists, made Adelaide's blood run cold. What about her half-brother and his wife and their infant? Even though she didn't like Landon and Julia, they were still family. Nolan wouldn't put Julia and her baby in the dungeons, would he? Adelaide couldn't abandon them. But she couldn't hand herself over to him, either.

"It's the best way," Regulus whispered. He leaned his forehead against hers. "The king is warned. Carrick won't kill your parents when you're not around. I've done many stealth missions. I can rescue your family. I promise you, I'll get them to safety. Trust me."

She closed her eyes. His plan, though imperfect, made sense. This was the man who had fought demon sea serpents and dragons. He could sneak her parents out, right?

He shifted, holding the sides of her face in his strong, capable hands, and kissed her forehead. "We'll see each other again, *mareh piahre*. I promise."

"I'll hold you to that."

Regulus pulled her to him and kissed her urgently. Adelaide tangled her fingers in his black curls. If passionate kisses could ensure his survival, she'd make sure he lived to be a hundred. When they finally separated, she rested her forehead on his shoulder, her chest heaving and stomach doing flips.

"I need to go," he whispered. "The sooner I get to Arrano, the better."

She didn't want to let go, but she did. They gave each other one last embrace that said everything they couldn't articulate. He handed her his satchel with the last bits of food they had, and they mounted their horses.

"Swear to me you won't go near your parents' castle."

"I swear it." She swallowed back her sorrow.

"And promise you'll keep practicing your magic, even while riding."

"I promise."

Regulus turned toward Arrano. Adelaide watched him disappear into the twilight, then she adjusted course for the palace. She had a king to warn, and as much distance as possible to put between herself and Nolan.

CHAPTER 16

REGULUS RODE THROUGH THE NIGHT WITHOUT STOPPING, AND all the next day, too. Concern for Adelaide preoccupied his thoughts as the sun beat down on his back. He prayed she would truly head for the palace; that she would avoid any run-ins with Carrick or the sorcerer. While he believed separating had been their best chance at success, it would be days, perhaps weeks before he saw Adelaide again, and his anxiety for her safety added to his exhaustion.

He missed her. Her absence felt like when he reached for his sword but found he wasn't wearing it. It was a lost, unanchored sensation, and he wanted to remedy it as soon as possible. So, he shook away the drowsiness and rode on.

The sun had long set when he approached Arrano. The stars and a waning moon half-hidden behind clouds cast pale light on the outlines of his castle. Regulus rode toward the main gate, posture drooping. His dry eyes itched. A shadow on the ramparts above the gate moved.

"Halt! Who goes there?"

"Lord Hargreaves," Regulus called back wearily. He recognized the man's voice but couldn't connect it with a face. "Who's on watch? Maxwell?"

"Lord Hargreaves?" The guard sounded stunned. "Gerald, my lord. Maxwell's home with his family."

"Ah. Could you open the gate, Gerald?"

"The gate! Of course! Apologies, my lord!" Footsteps slapped hard and fast on the stone. A few moments later, a chain rattled and clacked, the portcullis lifted, and the great double doors of the gate groaned as they swung inward. Regulus nudged Sieger forward. The gate closed behind him and the portcullis settled back down with a clang. A torch bobbed toward him across the courtyard, held by a bleary-eyed stable boy, his shirt half-tucked in and twisted around his torso and his boots unlaced. Regulus dismounted and headed for the castle before the stable boy even reached Sieger. He called a thank you over his shoulder as his boots tapped against the cobblestones leading to the front door.

He didn't want to wake Harold, but he couldn't risk oversleeping. It took a couple knocks before Harold answered his door.

"My lord!" Harold blinked several times. "What—you're okay! But... I—"

Regulus half smiled. "Wake me at dawn, please. I can't sleep past then. And tell my knights to meet me in the hall for breakfast just after dawn. Oh, alert the cook, too."

"Yes, my lord." Harold's brow wrinkled. His eyes were full of questions Regulus was glad he wasn't asking, because he was too exhausted to answer.

Regulus rubbed his eyes. "Is my room locked?"

"Oh, yes, one mo—"

"Just give me the key." Regulus held out his hand. Harold's mouth twisted down, but he gave Regulus his copy of the key. "Good night, Harold." Regulus trudged up the stairs to his room.

Magnus knocked him onto his backside when he stepped into the room. "Okay, boy." He chuckled as Magnus whined and soaked his face with his large tongue. He tried to push the massive fluffy dog away, but Magnus seemed heavier and stronger than he remembered. "Down, Magnus."

Magnus whimpered, but moved off his chest. Regulus buried his fingers in the soft, fluffy brown fur on Magnus' neck as he walked past to his bed, giving him a quick scratch. He stripped down to his trousers and sunk into bed. Magnus curled up next to him. The dog wasn't Adelaide by any stretch, but his warmth brought some measure of comfort.

Morning and Harold's voice came too soon. Regulus washed his face and shaved but had no time for a full bath. He pulled on clothes and headed to the hall, Magnus close on his heels.

Dresden, Perceval, and Caleb already sat at the table. Dresden stood as Regulus entered the room, his angular features pinched with emotion. He had dark circles under his eyes and his thick black hair was a mess, but his beard looked as well-trimmed and kempt as ever. Regulus smiled and nodded. Drez nodded back, some of the tension leaving his face as he eased back onto his chair. But he sat forward with his back ramrod straight, as if too on edge to relax.

Perceval rubbed his hand over his morning scruff and narrowed his eyes at Regulus. His nose was bright red and peeling, likely from working the field around his cottage. Caleb's blond hair was even more tousled than usual, and the pitying look in his eyes as Regulus sat down made him wonder what they had been saying before he entered.

The door at the far end of the hall opened, and Estevan walked in. He smiled when he saw Regulus, creating deep dimples in his freckled tan face. They just needed—the main door swished open, and Jerrick strode in, panting like he had been running. He wore a bright orange shirt that contrasted well with his dark skin.

The men watched him intently with questioning eyes. Dresden's temple pulsed. But none spoke, respecting Regulus' right to tell them what he wanted, when he wanted. They had been called, and they knew it wasn't as friends. They sat tall and alert, focused on their captain.

Regulus opened his mouth to speak, but the door to the kitchens opened, and servants emerged carrying trays of food, plates, and goblets filled with water. He waited for them to place the trays of bread, butter, boiled quail eggs, and thick-sliced ham on the table. He loaded his plate, even though he didn't feel hungry between his worries over Adelaide and concerns for their upcoming mission. His men followed suit, albeit with more gusto, particularly Jerrick and Estevan, who were the youngest of the group.

Regulus cleared his throat as he spread butter over a piece of warm bread. "I'm certain you have questions. I will try to cover everything, but we are pressed for time." He ate a couple bites before continuing. "Much has happened since I left. Of first importance," he set down his bread and rolled up his sleeve, showing the underside of his forearm, "the sorcerer released me. My debt is fulfilled."

Dresden, still sitting forward like he was afraid to let his back touch his chair, froze with his fork halfway to his mouth. Perceval choked on his water. Estevan grinned. Jerrick muttered something in Bhitran that sounded like a prayer of thanks to Hallilek. Caleb slumped back in his seat.

"Then it's over?" Dresden lowered his hand to the table.

Regulus sighed. "Not really, no." He took a long drink. No one moved. "Unfortunately, the sorcerer *is* actually a prince. Prince Kirven. The king's brother. He is plotting to kill the king and seize the throne."

"So send the king a message." Dresden glowered. "Who is king doesn't concern us."

"Considering the sorcerer seems bent on death, destruction, and revenge…yes, it should concern us." Regulus tapped his finger against the side of his goblet. "But more directly, it concerns Adelaide and me."

"He took Lady Belanger," Perceval said, a stated guess more than a question.

"No. Adelaide is safe, or at least she was last I saw her. But if the sorcerer succeeds, neither of us will be safe."

"Everything he made you do, everything he did to you, and he can't leave you alone?" Dresden's raised voice echoed in the hall.

"The sorcerer? Perhaps. But, unfortunately…" Regulus' hand tightened around his goblet. He drew a steadying breath. "He has a new pet. A willing servant to whom he has promised wealth and political power for accepting the mark. If the sorcerer succeeds, Nolan Carrick succeeds with him. I'll be a dead man, and Adelaide…" He cracked open a quail egg with more force than necessary and began eating its soft-boiled contents.

The men stared in stunned silence. Finally, Caleb asked, "Carrick…has the mark?"

"Yes," Regulus said around a mouthful of bread and yolk.

"He's like you were?" Perceval waved the piece of bread in his hand. "Strong, fast…immortal?"

Regulus nodded as he took a large bite of ham. Dresden cursed. Repeatedly and at length, his face red. Regulus had expected a negative response, but Dresden looked as if he'd taken Carrick joining the sorcerer personally.

"Reg." Dresden's voice was low and strained, and he glared at the table like he was considering stabbing it. "Where's Adelaide?"

"On her way to warn the king. We're not sure if any messengers got through. If she does as we agreed, she's going to the palace."

"If?" Estevan swallowed a mouthful of food and tilted his head. "Why are you here, then?"

Regulus took a drink and set down the goblet harder than intended. He focused on the goblet. He needed to keep calm. To be a captain, not an emotionally compromised fool.

"Through a series of events, Adelaide and I were headed back to her father's castle when we learned that Carrick took the castle and is holding her parents hostage." He looked up, meeting each of their eyes. "That's why I called you here. We have a new assignment. We're rescuing Lord and Lady Belanger."

"From a castle?" Drez gestured to the men at the table. "With what army? You're not immortal anymore, need I remind you, and we'd be facing someone who is! Six men can't storm a castle. And then we'll have to face Carrick?" His hands fisted on either side of his plate. "Do you have a plan? Some secret that will give us an advantage? Do—"

"Enough!" Regulus slammed his fist on the table. Drez's objections had already occurred to him, and he knew his friend had a point. But he'd made a promise. "We leave in half an hour."

Dresden's eyes flashed. "That's not an ans—"

"Sir Dresden," Regulus snapped. "Am I your captain or not? Am I your liege or not?" He hated himself even as he said it, and he hated the hard look that slipped over his best friend's face, the uncomfortable way the rest of the men averted their eyes. But he didn't have time to waste arguing.

Dresden worked his jaw. "Regulus, attacking Carrick when he has the mark, especially in a castle, is—"

"We'll aim for stealth."

"And if we're caught?" Dresden demanded. "You—"

"Sir Jakobs! Do I answer to you? Or do you answer to me?"

Dresden's face darkened. He pushed away from the table and stood, his movements stiff. "I'll be ready in the courtyard in half an hour, *my lord.*" The tightness in his voice cut straight through Regulus, but he didn't soften his expression or flinch. They had an agreement. In private, Drez could say whatever he wanted, but he didn't question Regulus in front of the men. Dresden gave an abrupt, shallow bow, straightening with a momentary wince, and strode from the hall.

Jerrick leaned back in his chair with a disapproving frown. "He didn't deserve that. Especially not after what happened."

Regulus' stomach pinched at Jerrick's tone. "What happened?"

The men glanced at each other. None looked eager to share.

"What. Happened?"

Jerrick pulled at his shirt collar. "When Carrick came…we weren't here. Perceval and I didn't see them arrive. Estevan and Caleb were out hunting. When they couldn't find you, Carrick threatened to beat Dresden until you showed yourself. Sir Gaius convinced him not to."

Perceval scratched his stubble. "Sir Gaius and Lord Drummond left, but Carrick stayed to see if you would return." The men seemed fascinated with their food as Regulus' chest clenched.

"He beat him," Harold said from the stairwell. Regulus turned toward his squire. Harold's tear-filled eyes blazed. "You were gone! Carrick was angry, so he hit Dresden. He punched him, again and again. Then he had his knights tie Dresden to a tree, and he took a belt to him. Because he knew hurting Dresden would hurt you. Thankfully, that knight arrived saying he'd seen the Black Knight and Lady Adelaide, so Carrick only used the belt a few times, but he hit hard. The bruises haven't fully healed." Harold clenched and unclenched his fists. "I should have done something."

Regulus' stomach lurched and his hands shook. He swallowed hard. "No, Harold…" Guilt choked off his words. He'd abandoned Drez. But he hadn't thought…he couldn't have known… *I'm going to cut Carrick's head off.*

Harold slunk back up the stairs, shoulders drooping.

Regulus shoved his plate away, his appetite gone, but didn't get up. He wouldn't run away. The men ate in silence, glancing at him out of the corner of their eyes. One by one they left until only he and Perceval remained.

"He doesn't blame you, Captain."

Dresden should blame him. But blame wouldn't help them rescue the Belangers. "He might have a point about trying to infiltrate a castle being a bad idea. It will be difficult, and…" He rubbed his temple. "I don't want to know what Carrick will do to you all if he captures you."

"We'd follow you anywhere, Captain. Drez is just being cautious." Perceval stood. "I trust you, Captain. You always come through."

Reluctantly, Regulus looked up. "What if I'm not sure how to do this?"

"I'd be dead half a dozen times over if not for you. You know I wouldn't have settled down and served any random lord. Even Leonora couldn't get me to do that. But I'll fight anyone you ask me to. I'd die for you." Perceval tapped his hand on the back of his chair. "We all would, Captain."

"Thank you, Perceval. But I don't want anyone to die for me."

Perceval nodded with a smile. "That's why we'd do it."

Regulus slouched as Perceval left the hall. He tossed Magnus a piece of ham and returned to his room. It didn't take long to put on a gambeson and his lightest chainmail shirt over his shirt. He needed speed and flexibility more than he wanted the extra protection of plate armor. As soon as he'd strapped a sword to his side, he headed to the stables. Dresden was there, his scimitars crossed over his back, waiting for a stable boy to saddle his brown destrier. After Regulus spoke to another stable boy, Dresden came over to him.

"Can I speak with you?" Drez murmured.

"Actually, I was going to ask you the same." They stepped out of the stables. Dresden opened his mouth, but Regulus cut him off. "They told me what Carrick did." Dresden flushed crimson. "I'm sorry…" He struggled to find the right words.

"I told you I'd take a beating for you someday." Dresden smiled sadly and winked. "I'd say we're even, except a belt doesn't leave the scars a whip does."

"You never owed me."

"And you never owed me, but you don't listen."

Regulus ran his fingers through his hair and rubbed the pommel of his sword, his face burning. "Are you—"

"I'm fine now, Reg. Worse was not knowing if you were alive for the last week. Not knowing if you'd ever come back. Why didn't you send word?"

"We were… I… There was a lot…" He hung his head. "I should have thought to. I'm sorry."

Dresden sighed. "Now you show up, tell me the man who tried to have you killed and beat me is immortal and teamed up with the sorcerer while you're normal again, and you want to face him? I panicked." He crossed his arms. "But I apologize. I shouldn't have publicly challenged you."

Regulus sighed. "But I shouldn't—"

"No. I was wrong, and I deserved that."

Regulus shook his head. "You're my friend first, Drez."

"And you're my friend. My brother. Always." Dresden scratched his beard. "But you're my captain and my liege, too." He grimaced. "We can't be equals. No matter how much I wish otherwise."

Regulus winced. He wanted to argue Dresden's point about not being equals, but he couldn't. Not when raising Dresden to the knighthood had made his best friend his vassal. Not when he'd just exercised that authority in a way that highlighted their inequalities and probably made Dresden feel like a servant again.

"But between us, I'm concerned." Drez shifted his weight from side to side. "I don't say this to blame you, so don't hear that. Carrick hates you. Enough he took it out on me with his fists and a belt. He'd have used a whip if he had one." More guilt pricked at Regulus. "He thinks he's untouchable now he's in league with the sorcerer. If Carrick captures the men, what do you think he'll do to them? And you? He'll tear you apart."

Regulus fiddled with a strap on his gauntlet. "Which is why we won't act until we've scouted out the situation and agreed on a plan." He met Dresden's eyes. "I won't risk you all. The Belangers will have to wait until we have a plan that has a strong chance of success. But I have to try. I promised."

Drez smiled wryly. "A Hargreaves promise is a powerful thing."

Regulus sighed as the stable boys led out their horses. *I just hope I haven't made a promise I can't keep.*

CHAPTER 17

ADELAIDE CONSIDERED TURNING TOWARD BELANGER CASTLE several times, but each time she talked herself out of it. Thinking of Nolan leveraging her parents' lives against her made her shudder. She recalled his attack in the drawing room—his strength and speed, the lust and determination in his eyes—and fought a wave of nausea. Regulus would get them out.

After a couple hours, she stopped to sleep at the base of a birch grove. Every little sound put her on edge. The hard dirt felt more uncomfortable without Regulus' arms around her. She tossed in the prickly grass and woke from a troubled sleep at dawn, horrified at her decision.

What was I thinking? Without her there to stop him, Nolan would kill Regulus. Adelaide had been so worried about her parents, so relieved and ready to think *Regulus is a warrior, he knows what he's doing, he'll save them.*

But Nolan was immortal. She shouldn't have let Regulus try to take on Nolan. *I should go back and stop him.* And what? Leave her parents in Nolan's clutches? She couldn't do that, either. Regulus didn't need to take back the whole castle. Just get her family out. But how would he even find her family? And if Nolan caught him... *I have to stop him.*

Adelaide mounted Zephyr and headed toward Father's estate. *He seemed so confident,* part of her brain murmured. *He knows what he's doing.* But she remembered Nolan snapping Regulus' arm and hurried Zephyr on. With every mile she rode closer to home, doubt crept in. Father would want her to warn the king. She had promised Regulus she wouldn't go near Belanger castle.

She dismounted in a thicket of trees near the road and paced back and forth. *Save Regulus, risk the king and abandon my parents. Warn the king, risk Regulus.* She screamed and threw a knife at a nearby pine. It felt good, so she threw the rest.

Etiros, what do I do? She pried her knives from the tree, mounted, then dismounted again. Her eyelids drooped as she rested her forehead on Zephyr's saddle. *Regulus. My parents. The king.*

If she warned the king and Nolan killed Regulus, she would never forgive herself. If she returned to intercept Regulus, Nolan might catch her. Worse, if Father's messengers hadn't gotten through, the king would not be warned, and all would be lost.

What would Father and Mother do? Father would warn the king. Mother would save Father. She slumped against Zephyr's side. If she didn't warn the king, Kirven would make Nolan a duke and things would only be worse. The only way to stop Nolan was to stop Kirven. Her mistake in leaving Regulus couldn't be undone now.

Despite her writhing stomach, she turned Zephyr toward the palace, praying Etiros would protect Regulus and her parents.

As Adelaide tracked the sun and followed the roads toward the southwest coast of Monparth, she sent Father a mental thank-you for teaching her how to navigate and to Mother for teaching her geography. She kept her hood pulled low over her face, her hair braided and tucked out of sight, and her cloak drawn about her to hide her figure despite the warm sun. Whenever anyone approached, she left the road. That cost her time, but being accosted on the road would slow her progress more.

The supplies in Regulus' bag lasted the first day. She awoke much later than needed the second day, then had to scavenge fruit and raw vegetables from a nearby field. Every minute she wasted, she failed the king and Father.

On the third morning, she reached the royal township of Selcairn. Adelaide paused at the crest of a hill, looking over the largest town she had ever seen. Jumbles of buildings, mostly built of wood, sprawled out on both sides of a shining blue river. The narrow steeple of the township's chapel jutted above nearby slate roofs. A thin haze of smoke obscuring half the town indicated where the greatest concentration of shops must be. At least in such a bustling place, she might blend in. Maybe she could trade one of her knives for some food.

She continued down the hill, past peasants on foot, a small black carriage with a harried-looking driver and curtains pulled over the windows, and a group of brown-clad monks singing in a low drone. A young boy tossing a red wooden ball dropped his toy and chased it in front of Zephyr. Zephyr reared, and the boy screamed and scrambled backward as Adelaide struggled to rein in Zephyr. She dismounted and patted Zephyr's neck, calming him before tossing the boy his ball.

"Don't run in front of horses," Adelaide chided, her heart racing. "You could have been killed."

The boy ran off to a nearby woman, crying for his mama. Several people stared. A few pointed and whispered. Adelaide realized her hood had fallen off, and in the excitement, she had pushed her cloak back over her shoulders. She stood in the middle of the road, the knives on the baldric across her chest and the daggers at her hips on full display. She pulled her cloak around her and threw her hood up, but it was too late to stop the stares.

Someone wearing a hooded black cloak and riding a tan palfrey had stopped on Zephyr's other side when she turned to remount. She focused on her saddle, ignoring the spectator as she threw her leg over Zephyr's back.

"Where is a lovely lady like yourself going alone and bristling with blades?" a man's voice asked from under the hood. Something familiar about his voice made her pause, and she looked over.

The man looked up, his horse a little shorter than Zephyr and the man himself shorter than average. His hood shadowed the top of his face. A pale, round nose protruded over a long brown beard streaked with gray. Crimson accents stood out like blood against his layered black robes. One pale, knobby hand gripped the palfrey's reins. Her eyes locked onto the top of a gold staff, mostly hidden under his cloak. A dark opal with hints of blue and specks of red rested at the base of a hollow oval of gold spirals. Her gaze snapped back to his shadowed face as her hands went cold. A smile tugged at the corner of Kirven's mouth. Adelaide kicked Zephyr and the gelding shot forward.

"How rude!" Kirven shouted.

Something hit her side and launched her from the saddle. She groaned as she hit the ground. People on the road screamed and scattered. Adelaide lifted herself on her elbow and shook her head, trying to clear her double-vision as Zephyr bolted. Kirven's palfrey trotted up next to her.

"Where were you going, she-mage?" Kirven snickered. "Or, I suppose, just girl now."

Adelaide thrust her hands up and a blast of pale blue light sent Kirven flying off his horse. The palfrey galloped away as she scrambled to her feet and Kirven tumbled across the road. She threw off her cumbersome cloak and directed a blast of fire at him. He blocked it with a shield of lime green light before it hit him. The flames licked past him on either side of his shield as he lay on his back in the dry ditch on the roadside. She conjured a spear and threw it, then another blast of fire. *Keep him down!*

But Kirven stood, using the staff to help him up. He made his magical shield bigger and kept it steady against her barrage of hard light blasts, magical knives and spears, and fireballs. On the other side of his shield, the opal pulsed with a dark green glow. Kirven slammed the bottom of the staff into the ground. The road buckled and a ripple moved toward her across the ground that knocked her off her feet. The back of her head slammed against the packed dirt. Her pulse thudded in her ears and black dots danced in her vision.

"Interesting." Kirven's footsteps moved toward her. She blindly threw a barrage of light shards as she sat up, but his shield absorbed the shards with a soft hiss. The shield dropped in the same moment as he pointed the Staff at her, and a green blast of light exploded from the tip. Adelaide raised her own shield, but the force of the blast rattled her bones. She threw a fireball around her shield. Kirven raised a new shield in a blink.

Glowing green ropes snaked out from his free hand and curled toward her on both sides of her barrier. She expanded the shield, turning it into a dome completely covering her. The ropes stabbed at the barrier as she panted to catch her breath. Kirven let his shield fall and switched to firing a continuous stream of flames at her barrier. She knelt, chest heaving, while heat built within her little dome. Sweat soaked her neck and trickled down her forehead and into her eyes.

The barrier was getting more exhausting to maintain by the second. Worse, her dome was running out of air. Adelaide pushed to her feet, forcing the barrier into a wall. With a heave, she threw the barrier toward Kirven. He planted the staff in the ground and managed to stay on his feet. He scowled, his hood thrown back. She wanted a moment to gulp in the cooler air, but instead she heard Father's voice. *You have an advantage, you press it. A fight is never fair.*

She charged, conjuring a sword of light and flame. Kirven recoiled. He aimed the staff at her as she swung toward him with the sword. The blast from the staff, inches away from her chest, felt like a battering ram to the sternum. She sprawled on the ground, lungs burning, unable to breathe. Nothing but a pinprick of blue sky showed in the blinding whiteness. After a small eternity, she gasped in a giant breath and rolled onto her side, coughing and panting. Her throat was raw. The whiteness faded, but black hovered at the edges of her vision.

Something grabbed Adelaide's ankle, and she kicked it away. Green, glowing ropes raced over her arms and legs and around her neck. She tried to attack Kirven, but the ropes pulling at her wrists made it difficult. She saw the blast of magic just before it slammed into the side of her head. Her neck snapped to the side, and she knew no more.

Adelaide moved her heavy head and moaned. Her heartbeat pulsed behind her eyes. She fought to force her heavy eyelids open. Walls surrounded her, windowless but with long cracks between the boards that allowed narrow strips of sunlight into the shadowy room. The warm air smelled of mildew.

Ropes—real ones, not magic ones—wrapped around her, binding her arms over her torso and digging into her skin. Her arms were crossed in an X at her wrists, with her palms against her shoulders. She attempted to move her hands but could barely rotate them. More ropes tied her ankles together. Straw poked into her arms. Her knives and daggers were gone.

The small dark room was empty, save for a thick layer of dust, old straw scattered over the floor, and a three-legged stool in one corner. Perhaps it had been a shed in the distant past. Adelaide shimmied into a sitting position. A door to her right opened, spilling blinding sunlight around Kirven's outline.

"Good, you're awake." Kirven hurried inside, letting the door rattle closed. He set the staff in the corner, moved the stool closer, and sat down. "Now. Adelaide, isn't it?"

She glared. She needed to break free of these ropes, and soon. But she used her hands to perform magic, and with them tied in place, she was at a loss.

"I haven't been truly surprised in a long time, Adelaide." Kirven leaned forward, resting his elbows on his knees. He threw his hood back, and his eyes caught her off-guard. The whites were bloodshot around coal-black irises rimmed with a thin line of green. "I wasn't expecting to see you—much less with your magic back. Now, I usually kill people when I steal their magic, so the thought that it might return had occurred to me. However, I never would have guessed it would return so quickly, or so strong. Most interesting. Tell me, how did you speed the process?"

She clenched her jaw and glanced toward the Staff. Her head still ached, but at least the pounding behind her eyes had lessened.

"Look, mage." Kirven's tone turned sharp and impatient. "This can be quick and painless, or long and painful. How did you get your magic back so quickly?"

Adelaide glowered up at him, mouth set in a hard line.

He tugged on his beard. "I drained you of your magic. *All* of it, save the drop that kept you alive. If I had pushed a little further, I would have taken your life. But I promised I wouldn't kill you, and if I don't keep my word all the time, what good are my threats?" He grabbed her chin with cold fingers. "So believe me when I say, if you don't tell me exactly how you got your magic back in such a short span without the aid of sorcery, you will experience pain beyond what you can comprehend."

She stiffened. "You didn't kill me. My magic came back gradually. That's what happens when you let someone live." Kirven shook his head.

"I know you're lying. I could barely light a candle for three days after the amount of power it took to re-forge the Staff of Nightfall. That wasn't even a complete draining of my ability—thanks to the extra power from you. You're going to tell me how to speed that process up." His fingers dug into her jaw. "I do it by stealing energy from living things. It took an entire grove of trees and two hapless satyrs to get me back to full strength this time. But I know that's not what you did. Tell me."

"I can't help you."

The sorcerer's hand warmed. Pain moved through her jaw like a screw forced into her bones. Adelaide screamed as the pain spread. Down her spine, along her bound arms, through her legs. Every bone in her body felt like it would crack at any moment. She just wanted it to stop. Her own screaming rang in her ears and tears blinded her.

The pain vanished. Her chest pushed against her bound arms as she gasped for air. Her throat ached.

Kirven rubbed one ear with his forefinger. "Women's screams are so painful on the ears. Now. The truth."

She shook, staring at the moldy straw on the dirt floor as tears blurred her vision. She wouldn't help him. If she could just do some magic…

"Stubborn." He sighed and placed his hand on top of her head.

A shield! She squeezed her eyes shut and focused on creating a shield over her body. Her hands fisted. Kirven hissed and jerked his hand back. She opened her eyes to a pale blue shimmer over her skin, but maintaining it felt like trying to hold water in her hands.

"Clever girl." Kirven fetched the Staff and touched the end to her head.

Pressure built along her head until her grasp on the barrier shattered. Pain cracked through her skull and crushed her spine. She thrashed away with a scream as tears streamed down her face. He sat back down and lifted an eyebrow.

"Ready to talk?"

Adelaide trembled. Maybe it wouldn't help him. At the tree, the fairies had said Kirven didn't want to face them, that's why he sent Regulus for the root. And she'd had to pass a test—a test Kirven would fail. Besides, she didn't want any more pain.

"I visited the neumenet tree in Holgren Forest. There were fairies. They tried to trick me into stealing the tree's powers. I refused. Then the tree just…gave me back my magic."

"Was it coming back on its own before that?"

She licked her dry, salty lips. "Only a little. I tried to heal Regulus and passed out and then couldn't do anything."

"Mm. Disappointing." Kirven sighed dramatically. "Technically, I guess you were telling me the truth when you said you couldn't help me. So," he sounded displeased, "I suppose I owe you an apology for the torture. Still, you weren't being forthcoming, so that's on you."

On me! At last she stopped shaking. Her tears dried in dirty lines on her cheeks. If she hadn't already believed Kirven would make a terrible king, she was certain of it now.

"Speaking of His Saintliness, where is Hargreaves?"

No. She couldn't betray him.

"Let's not have a repeat of your reticence, shall we? I'd like to spare my ears."

Adelaide shuddered. She understood better now why Regulus had been ready to kidnap her, with that pain being the alternative. How had he even considered disobeying for so long?

"He went back to Arrano," she said, her voice tight.

"Did you two have a falling out?" When she didn't answer right away, Kirven grabbed her braid and yanked her head back so she was looking at him. "What happened to 'I love you?' And he seemed desperate to protect you. With his constant self-sacrificing, I wouldn't have expected him to let you wander about alone. What's he up to?"

If she didn't answer or lied, he would torture her again. But if she told the truth…what if he warned Nolan? Kirven sighed and wrapped his hand around her throat. Burning lines spread from his hand over her skin.

"All right!" The pain stopped, but he kept his hand on her neck. "We split up to cover more ground. He went to get his men."

"Why?" His wiry eyebrows knit together.

"To rescue my parents." Adelaide gulped.

"Typical. And I think I know where *you* were headed, but I'd like to confirm my suspicion."

"I was riding to warn the king."

"Foolish girl." Kirven pushed her back. She choked at the force of his hand against her windpipe. He stood and clasped his hands behind his back. "You and your father are nothing but trouble. Carrick told me your father figured out my secret. I recommended he kill Lord Belanger, but no." He wrinkled his nose. "He's obsessed with having you. It's clouding his judgment. I'm letting him try his way for now, because a willing servant works better in my long-term plans, and he believes he can control you."

His voice took on a hint of impatient annoyance. "I made a deal with him and put the binding on him because of his intelligence, ruthlessness, charisma, and ambition. A man with such a craving for power, with that much selfishness and so little regard for his fellow man, is an excellent ally in a war. Not to mention terribly easy to manipulate. He will be useful in restructuring Monparth's nobility to serve me—but that works best if he's happy with our arrangement. Also, I assumed he would kill Hargreaves. I'm disappointed he's not dead yet. Perhaps Carrick is less competent than I hoped."

"Then why didn't you kill Regulus?"

"Because," Kirven sounded like he was explaining something simple to a bratty and stupid child, "I gave my word. Haven't you been paying attention?" He ran his fingers through his beard. "Ah, well. I'll alert Carrick. I must be on my way again. There's a palace to scout and a masque to ruin. But first…" He placed his hand on her forehead.

"No, please!" She tried to scoot away, but the bindings prevented much movement. Her back pressed into the wall of the shed. She hunched down, making herself as small as possible. His hand burned hot against her forehead. Nothing else happened.

Kirven frowned. "What?" He pressed harder, forcing her head against the wall. The heat from his hand made her eyes water. He dropped his hand and stared for a moment before grabbing the Staff. He placed the end of the Staff against her head, then cursed and moved the Staff to her chest. Nothing.

"What aren't you telling me?" he screeched. "Why can't I take your magic?"

Oh. That's what he's— Searing heat spread from the end of the staff, spreading invisible flames over her skin.

"Tree!" she shrieked. The burning subsided. "The fairies said the neumenet tree's powers can't be stolen! It gave me my magic, so my magic can't be stolen. That's what they told me!"

Kirven's features slackened.

Adelaide cowered against the wall of the shed. "Please. That's what they told me. I don't know any more. I don't know any more."

He drew back the Staff. His shoulders rose and fell in sharp, tense movements as his expression became dark and dangerous. "Say you'll serve me."

CHAPTER 18

THE SUDDEN COMMAND TOOK ADELAIDE ABACK. "WHAT?"

Kirven bared his teeth. "I can't take your power as my own, but I can still ensure your magic serves me."

Serve…no. She remembered all too well how his mark burned. And he could torture her at any time. Take control of her body. He would force her to use her magic to harm.

She swallowed back her fear and straightened. *Etiros, give me strength.* "I'd sooner die." Her voice shook, but she stared him down.

Kirven crouched in front of her. "Say you will serve me, or I will torture you again."

"Because you never tortured Regulus while *he* served you? You'd torture me sooner or later." Adelaide raised her chin, even though her lower lip trembled. "I know what you're doing. You can't put the mark on me unless I agree. I won't."

Before she could so much as flinch, Kirven placed the end of the staff on her stomach. Pain spread like rope laced with sharp glass wrapping around her torso, then her arms, her legs, even her head. The invisible rope squeezed, and she felt like she should be bleeding everywhere. She fell to her side, writhing in mind-numbing agony. Her mouth was open, and she knew she was screaming, but she couldn't hear herself. She thrashed against the ropes, against the pain. Kirven pulled the staff back and she curled into a ball. Sobs wracked her body. Fresh tears raced down her face and neck, soaking into her tunic.

Kirven grabbed the rope around her torso and hauled her to a sitting position. She was crying so hard her eyes wouldn't focus on his face.

"Look at me!" He slapped her. She coughed, choking on her sobs. "Agree to serve me!"

Adelaide shook her head, even though she wanted to give in. A voice in her mind shouted to just say yes, it wasn't worth it, do anything to prevent more pain now, sort the rest out later. But she pushed that voice away. There would be pain later, even if she agreed. He would have to give up eventually. She had already helped this monster too much. Never again.

He grabbed her face and leaned in close. "If you don't agree to serve me, once I'm king, I'll torture your entire family. Your father. Your mother. Any siblings you have. Hargreaves. The pain you've just experienced? I'll make them feel it while you watch. Eventually, people can't take it anymore, and their minds break, like shattered glass."

A stifled cry shuddered through her. She pressed her eyes closed. *Etiros, please, no!* She couldn't serve him. But how could she refuse?

Kirven's fingernails dug into her face. "You will serve me, or you will watch your family suffer. And then you will suffer. Like this."

Ice seemed to spread from his hand, freezing and burning at the same time. Adelaide shrieked and broke free of his grip. Released from the pain, she curled against the wall.

"Serve me, or my first act as king will be to summon your entire family to their slow and excruciating deaths while you watch."

Adelaide cried silently. *Etiros, help me.* Kirven's words replayed in her mind. *"First act as king…while you watch."* To do that, he would have to leave her alive. If she lived, she would have a chance to escape and stop him. But she couldn't stop him if she agreed to serve him like Nolan had. She shivered. She would never choose the same path as Nolan.

Kirven wrenched her chin up. "Swear to serve me."

"No." It was a near-silent whisper, but enough for him to hear. Kirven snarled and backhanded her face. Her teeth cut into the corner of her mouth, and she tasted blood.

"Mages!" He threw together a string of nonsensical curse words in Monparthian, Khast, and languages she didn't know. He stopped short and looked at her, as if seeing her for the first time. "Mages…"

Kirven bent down and pulled a crimson handkerchief from his obsidian-accented belt. He dried her face, his expression calm. "I thought I had eradicated mages from Monparth, because no one knew of any." He dabbed at the blood on her lips. "You've been hiding all your life. I was surprised how much magic I pulled from you. All that power, and you hid. Why?"

"Because you killed everyone like me!"

"Not everyone." He smiled wickedly. "If I had killed *everyone* like you, I would have had to kill myself."

She recoiled, but already pressed against the wall, there was nowhere for her to go. "I'm nothing like you."

He dropped his hand and let the handkerchief fall. "I was you, once. A mage. Powerful, but clueless. Uneducated. Talented but without knowledge, just as you are. I couldn't help I was born a mage. But because of something out of my control, they took my birthright from me. Because of a centuries-old treaty, I wasn't allowed to be king.

"My *brother*," he bit out the word and spittle flew on her face, "would get everything that was rightfully *mine*. My throne. My crown. I could be his *advisor*. My brother and I studied together under the best tutors in government, military strategy, history, geography…but my parents refused to give me a tutor in magic. I was forbidden from even trying to use my power, punished when it accidentally escaped. My oh-so-loving father thought if I didn't know much about my power, I would be less of a threat." He laughed bitterly. "He was wrong. It just made me angry. When my mother caught me practicing, they forged a magic-suppressing cuff around my wrist."

New dismay contorted her face, but she shoved away the pinch of empathy. She wouldn't pity this monster.

He pursed his lips. "Your parents did the same, didn't they? Forbade you from accessing the energy burning through you, tried to force you to ignore the roar of power, to pretend you weren't what you are."

His words hit too close to her heart, and her gaze fell. Anger snapped her back to her senses, and she snarled at him. "Because of you! Because it wasn't safe!"

"Different circumstances, same lack of understanding." Kirven leaned back. "The difference between us is I didn't accept my cage. I left to find my own tutors. And you know what I discovered? Sorcery is far more interesting. More fun. More…useful." He reached toward her, and she shied away with a whimper from the torture that would doubtless accompany his touch. He grinned and leaned back. "See? Anyway, I learned quickly. Made some of my tutors nervous. I realized the best way to use a tutor was to have them teach you everything they knew, then kill them by draining their magic. Then they couldn't try to stop you, their knowledge died with them, and your power temporarily strengthened."

She grimaced as revulsion filled her.

"When I thought I was ready, I returned to claim my throne and punish those who denied me my birthright. But I miscalculated." He pulled the left side of his robe and tunic away from his neck and shoulder. Twisting white and pink scars covered every inch of exposed skin. "A gift from one of my father's mages." He shifted his collar back into place. "A burn covering most of the left side of my body. Don't worry," he said as she stared at his shoulder with horror, "after I learned how to track them all down, I killed every mage in the kingdom, including the ones who did this to me. So no one could stop me next time I tried to claim my throne. And yet," he cocked his head, "here you are."

"Then kill me." She'd meant it as a challenge. But her voice was so weak and desperate, it sounded like a plea.

"Don't you see? I'm offering to help you. To teach you. All this power, don't you want to learn how to use it properly? Don't you want to learn everything you are capable of?" Kirven's eyes narrowed. "You have a choice, Adelaide. On the one hand, you have a future as Carrick's wench. He's immortal, you can't fight that. A future filled with your family's pain and suffering. A future of using your talents only when your husband tells you to."

Her stomach churned, and she looked away.

"On the other hand, you have a future where *you* can show the world your power. You can control Carrick, not the other way around. You could avoid marriage to him. You can't have had an easy life, being half Khastallander. If you desire, you would have the power to punish anyone who has ever treated you as inferior for the way you were born. Agree to serve me, and I will make you the second-most powerful sorcerer in the world. I haven't waited so long to assemble the Staff of Nightfall to stop at Monparth. Together, we will conquer the known world. You could be ruler of Khastalland. I could even make you my queen. My empress."

She jerked her head up, her lungs seizing.

He laughed. "All right, never fear, I wouldn't force you. But perhaps one day you'd like to be queen. I'd even let you keep that self-righteous mercenary as your lover. All the freedom, all the power, all the status, all the wealth you desire. But even without the title of queen, you will be a sorceress of astounding power. You would never lose a battle again. Even Nolan Carrick would tremble at your feet."

"I don't want that." Adelaide shook her head, hard and fast, trying to dislodge the voice that whispered she did. "I'm not a sorceress. I won't corrupt my magic for personal gain."

"Then what's the point?" Kirven moved to the stool. "Don't be unreasonable. I am offering you power beyond belief. I am offering you freedom—from Nolan Carrick, from a society that judges you for your heritage and fears you for your magic. I'm offering you the chance to save your family and friends. Don't you want to protect them?" He crossed his arms. "Or I'm promising you the pain and suffering and death of everyone you care about. I'm promising you a life as Carrick's wife and plaything."

Adelaide trembled and fought growing nausea. It felt as if Kirven had peered into her soul and found all her deepest hurts, shames, fears, and desires. He took her experiences and emotions and twisted them to make his offer, his way of thinking, seem… tempting. *No. I'm not him. I won't become a monster.* She swallowed hard.

"Do you think you can bully me into joining you?"

"And bribe."

"I don't want anything you can give me."

It was half a lie, and she knew it. Part of her would love to relax, out of Nolan's reach. She could give in, and her family would be safe. Regulus would be safe. She could learn more about her magic. But the cost was too great. She remembered the haunted look in Regulus' eyes as he told her he had stolen and killed for Kirven. To knowingly agree to help the sorcerer murder the king and any other evil actions… Regulus would never look at her the same. Minerva would fear her. Mother and Father would be ashamed. And she would hate herself.

"I will *never* serve you."

Kirven's face hardened. He pressed the tip of the staff against her chest, pinning her to the wall. Her breaths came sharper, faster. "You will."

Adelaide's throat worked, but fear locked her words in her chest. Thousands of white-hot needles buried into her, ripping her apart. She screamed and curled forward. Her mind emptied of everything except the pain. The staff moved away, taking the pain with it. She fell onto her side and sobbed.

"Last chance." She barely heard Kirven over her weeping. "Will you serve me? Or will you watch as I torture your family?"

She squeezed her eyes shut and tried to control her crying. *I'll live. I'll get free. Regulus will come. The king will have guards. Kirven won't win. He can't. Etiros, he can't win.*

"Answer me!"

"No," she whispered.

"Fine." He cursed. "Suit yourself. I'll be back." He strode out of the shed, throwing open the door so it banged against the wall.

Her throat was raw from screaming. Her head hurt, especially across her forehead. She wanted to go to sleep and wake up in a world without sorcery and evil men who hurt others to get what they wanted. Adelaide closed her eyes, curled her knees toward her chest, and prayed for the unconsciousness of sleep.

She awoke to Kirven pulling her off the ground. Her head still ached, but not as much. Her throat was swollen and parched. Kirven pushed her into a sitting position. The sunlight coming through the open door and the cracks in the walls had dimmed and taken on an orange hue. Outside, the long shadows cast by the trees had deepened to black.

"You want to be difficult." Kirven moved slower and had bags under his eyes. "Fine. But I won't have you causing more trouble."

He twisted around and picked up something. Two thick half-circles of hammered iron connected by a hinge on one side. The open sides turned out a ninety-degree angle with a hole in each end. It was just large enough to encircle her neck. Her heart beat faster.

"What is that? What are you doing?" Adelaide tried to squirm away, but he closed the cold metal around her neck.

"You'll use your magic to serve me, or you won't use it at all."

She pulled against the collar. Kirven held it firmly as he slipped a small padlock into the holes where the two halves met. The lock clicked shut. He released the collar, and it settled against her skin.

Exhaustion overcame her panic as all her energy, magical or otherwise, drained away. Not like when Kirven had stolen her magic, but more like how she felt after using a lot of magic when training or fighting.

"What is this?"

"Magic suppressor." Kirven sat back and rubbed his head. "Tricky spell. Saps a person's energy. Takes a lot of power to create, which I'm not pleased about. But don't worry, I'll be at full strength to commit regicide. Fratricide, I suppose. You'll find using magic while wearing that exceedingly difficult. You could, but not for long, and you'd likely pass out from the effort." He sneered. "If you'd joined me, you would have learned how to do this yourself, instead of suffering the effects. But you're too hung up on ideas of being noble. A true match for the mercenary."

She wiggled her hands, contorting her wrists to grab the collar. She managed to lift it off her skin, but it didn't help the drained feeling. Resigned, she let it fall.

Kirven stood. "I've contacted Carrick. Someone should collect you before you starve." He paused at the door. "We'll see each other again. In the meantime, give some thought to who I should torture first—your father or your mother?" He shut the door behind him.

Adelaide laid back down. The collar weighed against the side of her neck. A single tear fell from the corner of her eye.

The plan had disintegrated. She had failed the king. She had been a fool to part ways with Regulus. If they had stayed together, maybe she wouldn't be in this mess. Perhaps if Regulus had been there, she might have won. Or escaped. And at least she wouldn't be alone. Or maybe Regulus would be dead. She shifted, trying to find a position that didn't hurt her shoulders, back, neck, or hips. That proved impossible.

With nothing else to do, her thoughts wandered. The only spot of light in her dark mind was that people had witnessed her and Kirven's magic on full display. Perhaps word would make it to the king, and he would be extra cautious. But that was small comfort against all her other concerns. Kirven was more powerful than she had feared. Would *any* amount of caution or security be enough to save the king?

And who would come for her? Would Nolan come himself, or would he send someone? What would he do when he had her? She pushed that thought away. Where was Regulus? Had he made it to Belanger castle yet? Did he stand a chance against Nolan?

"Please be safe, Regulus," Adelaide whispered. She cried herself to sleep.

Chapter 19

REGULUS PACED, HIS SWORD SWAYING AND CHAINMAIL RUSTLING with his swift stride. Caleb had been gone too long. He scowled at the sun half-hidden behind the trees lining the horizon. Much too long. If Caleb had been captured, the blame fell squarely on Regulus' shoulders. And if Caleb had been captured, that meant they had even less of a chance of success than he had feared. It would mean he had done the exact thing he had sworn to never knowingly do. He had led his men on a suicide mission. And he had left Adelaide to fend for herself to do it.

Thoughts of the last time he had led his men into a trap flashed in his mind. Images of friends' lifeless bodies, of ten graves. He shoved the memory aside. That wouldn't happen this time. He wouldn't let it. And the sorcerer wasn't here.

As he paced, his long shadow moved over the rest of his men. They sat on stumps or on the ground in front of their tiny make-shift camp of three low tents, their horses staked nearby. Estevan and Perceval played with dice while Dresden watched. Jerrick knelt with his eyes closed, his lips moving silently. Praying to Hallilek. He had a faith Regulus envied. Harold remained at Arrano—Regulus refused to put the youth in Carrick's path.

"He's fine, Captain. Cal's always fine, just tardy. Stop your pacing." Perceval threw down his dice and wrinkled his nose. Regulus did not stop pacing.

Estevan whooped. "Ha! That's two homemade mince pies for me!"

"You really shouldn't gamble your wife's cooking," Dresden said, his chin cupped in his hand. "Basically gambling away her labor. That's just wrong."

Perceval scowled. "You cheated, Wolgemuth."

"How?" Estevan rattled the dice in his hand.

"Check the dice," Jerrick said without opening his eyes. "His weighted one has a tiny nick on the corner."

Amid sounds of scuffling and grunting as Perceval tried to wrest the dice from Estevan, someone crested a nearby hill, his outline black against the setting sun. Regulus tensed and gripped the hilt of his sword. Behind him, his knights stood and watched the figure approach. The man waved, and fading sunlight highlighted his shaggy blond hair. Regulus dropped his hand from his sword. Caleb walked at a languid stroll, which did nothing for Regulus' mounting impatience.

"Well?" Regulus asked as soon as Caleb reached hearing distance. He tapped his foot, arms crossed. "What's the report?"

"Got some good news, some bad news, and some news I'm going to count as great but may be up for interpretation."

Regulus grunted, but Caleb just lowered onto a nearby moss-covered log. Dresden stood next to Regulus, and the rest of the men returned to their seats, the game of dice forgotten.

"Good news is, based on what the servants around the castle are saying, all the Belangers are alive." Caleb crossed his ankles and leaned back, propping his elbows on a protruding broken branch. "Bad news, the castle's well-garrisoned. I spotted ten men on the walls. Looked like more inside. But the stars have aligned, my friend."

Regulus cocked an eyebrow and waited for Caleb to continue. He should have sent someone less prone to dramatics, but Caleb had a way of making people comfortable and their tongues loose. Made him an excellent scout.

Caleb grinned. "Sir Immortal Brute has just left the castle all alone in a spectacular hurry, with no explanation other than he would be back in a day or two and instructions to keep the prisoners in good health."

"Carrick is gone?" Caleb nodded. "For at least a day?" Another nod. Regulus smiled and returned to pacing. This would make things easier. Maybe not easy, but easier. He stopped midstride. "He gave no indication of where he was going in such a hurry? Or why?"

"If he did, it wasn't in public. Hence the up for interpretation." A dreamy expression spread over Caleb's face. "I was chatting with a lovely milkmaid in the courtyard. A braid the color of honey, round, rosy cheeks, green eyes that positively demand a song—"

"Focus, Cal." Regulus rubbed his temple.

Caleb rolled his eyes. "Carrick jogged right past me on his way to get his horse. He was shouting about finding things just as he left them when he returns and threatening dismemberment if any harm came to the prisoners."

Perceval snorted. "It's a miracle you even heard that! Why the captain trusts you to stay on task, I'm sure I don't know, you philandering—"

"Oh, philandering, did you pick that up at university?" Caleb sat forward and pointed at Perceval. "I'll have you know I was on task. That milkmaid can get us into the castle." He gave an over-dramatic look of hurt. "To think I've called such an uncivilized oaf my friend."

"Not now, you two," Jerrick said.

Regulus gave Jerrick a grateful nod. "How can this milkmaid of yours get us in?"

"She's not my milkmaid." Caleb's eyes danced. "At least, not yet. But she's not happy with the current situation at the castle, and when Carrick left, was easily convinced to let us in. Two hours from now, just after dark, at eight and a half bells."

"Well done, Caleb." Regulus turned to Dresden and motioned with his head.

They walked a short distance away, followed by the sound of Perceval and Caleb's routine bickering and Estevan goading them both on.

"This could be good, but I don't like it," Regulus admitted. "Something strange is going on."

"Agreed." Dresden looked toward Belanger castle, its turrets just visible over the tops of the trees. "I can think of no good reason for Carrick to have left so abruptly."

"The sorcerer could have called him away." He chewed on his lower lip. "I don't like not knowing what they're up to."

Dresden rubbed his beard. "Or he could somehow know we're here. It could be a trap. Caleb's milkmaid could even be in on it."

"That occurred to me, too." Regulus rubbed the back of his neck. "But, even as blinded as he can be when it comes to women, Caleb would have noted if her behavior was suspicious." His chest tightened. "There is another possibility, though." His throat dried out.

"Carrick might have learned something about Adelaide's whereabouts."

"She wouldn't leave her parents behind. Splitting up seemed the best way to keep her away from Carrick." Regulus sighed. "But now I don't know where she is or if she's okay. I think I made a mistake. I should have dragged her to the palace if that's what it took."

Dresden gazed out at the sunset. Loud laughter rose from the camp behind them, the men unaware of the turmoil and fear in Regulus' heart. Drez turned to Regulus.

"There's no point in agonizing over what's done. We focus on the mission at hand. With Carrick gone and a way in, we can take back Belanger castle, not just get the Belangers out. So, let's plan."

Like it or not, Drez was right. He didn't have the luxury of spending energy and time worrying about Adelaide. She would have to take care of herself. He just prayed he had been right in believing she could.

Darkness fell and they crept toward the side door of the castle. The same one he and Adelaide had escaped through just a few days prior. Based on the fresh wood, the same one that Carrick had broken down. The mercenaries wore dark cloaks over their armor and moved with speed and stealth across the hill leading up to the castle walls. A dim crescent moon made it easier to blend into the night.

Regulus pressed against the wall next to the door. The fresh wood was reinforced with iron that gleamed dully in the faint moonlight. Dresden moved behind him, and the knights lined up against the wall. A gentle bell somewhere in the castle pealed once, signaled half-past eight. Regulus took a deep breath and knocked. Three rapid taps. Pause. Two slow taps. Pause. Three rapid taps.

A key scraped in the lock. Regulus drew his sword, nerves taunt and every muscle coursing with energy. The door opened without a sound—a blessing of new hinges. Regulus raised his sword. A small, pale hand held aloft a lantern. The flickering yellow light illuminated the wide-eyed face of a young woman with a gray shawl pulled over her head and shoulders. She stepped back and Regulus lowered his sword, scanning the darkness behind her. She beckoned them inside, and they followed.

Two guards sat slumped against either side of the door, sleeping. One snored and shifted position as they entered. Regulus grabbed the girl's shoulder and leaned in close to her ear. "Did you drug them?"

She shook her head, fear etched on her face. "The cook did."

"Carrick's men or Lord Belanger's?"

"Carrick's."

Regulus glanced down at the men. Still slumbering. But for how long? And they had aligned with Carrick. They chose violence the moment they entered this castle. He nodded at Estevan, then pointed to the men. Carrick had declared war by taking Belanger castle. He and his would reap what they sowed.

Silent as a shadow, Estevan slit both men's throats. The milk-maid pressed a hand to her mouth and the lantern shook in her out-stretched hand. Regulus took it, extinguished the flame, and set it down.

"Can you lead us to the dungeon?" Regulus murmured. She nodded, still staring at the corpses. Regulus turned her away with a flicker of shame. Adelaide deserved better than a killer. But taking a castle with only six men required the ruthless mercenary. The girl stood immobile in shock. "We need to move quickly…" He looked to Caleb questioningly.

"Susan," Caleb whispered.

"The dungeons, Susan."

Susan nodded again and drew a deep breath. She clutched her shawl against her chest and led them in the shadows along the base of the wall. Something moved ahead of them, and Regulus grabbed her arm to stop her. A guard carrying a torch approached. A soft whoosh passed Regulus' head and moonlight glinted on the edge of a blade before Estevan's throwing knife buried into the guard's throat. Regulus sprinted forward, caught the body before the sound of its fall could draw any attention, and lowered it to the ground.

Susan stifled a gasp. Her knuckles whitened as she gripped her shawl tighter. "I knew him."

"He's not locked up; he's a traitor," Perceval muttered. "Good riddance."

"It's Lord Belanger's choice what happens to the traitors," Regulus hissed. He looked at Estevan. "Let's try not to kill any of them again." Estevan and the others murmured disgruntled agreement.

They continued, moving from shadow to shadow across the courtyard. At a corner, Susan held up her hand for them to stop. She peeked around.

"One of Carrick's is guarding the door," she whispered.

Regulus moved her back and glanced around the corner. A large man leaned on the side of his shoulder against a door some twenty paces away. Regulus waved Caleb forward.

Caleb pulled his bow off his shoulder and nocked an arrow as he knelt at the corner. A soft thwang of the bowstring, and a short grunt followed by a muffled thud. Caleb stood and gave a quick nod. Regulus scanned the surrounding area before they ran to the door. Jerrick found the dead guard's keys and opened the door. Susan led them down a hall, then pointed to a descending spiral stone staircase.

"The dungeon is down there. From what I've heard, Carrick is only letting his own men be on guard in the dungeon." She glanced around, her wide eyes searching the shadows. "But Lady Belanger and Lady Julia are locked in their rooms."

"Don't worry, we'll get them next." Regulus smiled, trying to reassure her. "You've been very helpful and very brave. We can take it from here."

"Good luck." Susan fled.

"Permission to kill anyone not in a cell, Captain?" Perceval asked dryly.

Regulus adjusted his grip on his sword. "Granted."

They rolled their steps as they stole down the stone stairs. Quiet, indiscernible voices echoed up the stairwell. The stairs emptied into a guardroom. A few torches in iron ring sconces lit the room in orange light. Three men wearing chainmail and armed with swords sat playing a game with bone dice at a wooden table.

The guards jumped to their feet, but not fast enough. Estevan threw, and his knife buried into the throat of the guard on the right. His eyes widened and he fell backward. Caleb shot an arrow straight through the neck of the middle guard. The man fell onto the table. Jerrick ran forward, hefting his two-sided battle-axe. The last guard fumbled with his sword, his eyes darting to his deceased cohorts. Jerrick swung. The last guard's head rolled across the dusty stone floor.

Dresden was already crossing the room, double scimitars drawn, his gaze sweeping the hallway beyond the guard room. Perceval followed, broadsword in hand. Regulus stepped over the headless corpse and snatched the keyring off the hook on the far wall with a loud jangle. The sound of footsteps bounced off the stone walls as someone ran toward them down the hallway.

"Hey, what's—" The newcomer's sentence was cut short as Dresden sliced both scimitars in an X across the guard's neck. The body crumpled to the ground.

Regulus had grown accustomed to facing battle alone. But as his men worked seamlessly together, their movements coordinated, each one knowing the others had their back, he remembered why he loved leading them. *A wolf is strongest with its pack.* What a fool he had been to forget that. Facing enemies with his men—his brothers—was the only place he had ever felt comfortable. Until Adelaide. *Etiros, wherever she is, protect her.*

Regulus grabbed one of the torches from the wall and they continued, alert for more guards, but none appeared. They passed several empty cells before the dungeon opened further, spreading to the right and left. Someone moved in the cell to their left. A shorter man stood and walked to the door of the cells. The man leaned against the bars, taking in their appearance with confusion on his weathered face.

"Who are you? What do you want?"

"Lord Hargreaves." Regulus stepped closer. "Here to help Lord Belanger take back his castle."

"Lady Adelaide's Lord Hargreaves?"

"Yes." Regulus ignored Dresden's snicker and the laugh Jerrick hid behind a cough. A couple more men hidden in the shadows at the back of the cell came forward.

"Excellent. I'm Sir Ruddard. Lord Belanger's men are in the next few cells." Ruddard cocked his head to his right. "Lord Belanger and Sir Belanger are at the other end of the dungeons." He inclined his head in the opposite direction.

"Thank you. I'll be right back."

Dresden accompanied him down the hall while the others remained behind. No more guards met them. They found Alfred and his son sleeping in two cells at the end of the hallway. Regulus tried various keys in the cell door while Dresden held the torch.

"What do you want?" Alfred's hard voice echoed against the stone.

Regulus looked up and smiled. "To rescue you like I promised your daughter I would."

The color drained from Alfred's face as he scrambled to his feet. "Adelaide is here?"

"No." A key finally fit, and the lock opened with a satisfying click. Regulus swung the door open and Landon awoke in the next cell. "When we heard what happened, I went to Arrano to get my knights, and she headed for the palace to warn the king."

Alfred sagged against the bars. "Thank Etiros. But Carrick—"

"Left this evening and isn't expected back for a day or two." Regulus moved to the younger Belanger's cell and found the key quicker. Landon gave him an unreadable look as he strode out of the cell.

"My men—" Alfred started.

"We'll get them next," Regulus said. "The ones down here, anyway. Some of them—"

"Joined Carrick, I know." Alfred's expression darkened. "They will pay for their treachery in blood."

They freed Belanger's loyal knights, swelling their number by ten. Ten unarmed men.

Alfred's soldier instincts must have kicked in, because before Regulus could ask, he said, "The armory is in this building. I'll lead the way."

Dresden handed Alfred the torch. Several hallways and two spiral staircases later, Alfred, Landon, and the Belangers' knights rushed through arming themselves.

"Do you have a plan?" Alfred asked, buckling a sword belt around his waist.

"Depends on if you want any of the traitors alive after tonight." Regulus caught Estevan's smirk and the glint in Perceval's eyes, but ignored them.

Alfred's upper lip curled back. "If they weren't in a cell, they aren't my men."

"In that case, I'm sending my men in three groups to clear out the guards on the walls. We will head to the residence to find your wife and daughter-in-law. Your men are welcome to join, but my men will not take it well if they interfere in killing the traitors."

Sir Ruddard stepped closer, his jaw tight. "That won't be a problem."

"Good. Caleb, Perceval, take the east side." The two might bicker like rivals, but they worked together in battle like they shared one mind. "Jerrick, Estevan, west side. Dresden, see to the gates. All of you, take a few of Lord Belanger's men with you. The rest of you will accompany Lord Belanger and me to rescue the ladies." He made eye contact with Alfred and inclined his head in deference. "If that sounds good to you."

Alfred nodded. As they left the armory behind, Alfred murmured, "You have an interesting assortment of knights, Regulus. I dare say only two are Monparthian."

Regulus glanced sidelong at Alfred. "They were my mercenaries before they were my knights, if that's what you're getting at."

"You trust them?"

Regulus paused, reaching for the handle to leave the tower. "Do you trust me?"

"My trust was a bit broken when you disappeared with my daughter," Alfred's voice held an edge that cut right through him. "But I believe I do."

"Good. Then know you can trust my men. I trust them with my life." Regulus gripped the door handle and looked pointedly at Alfred. "I would trust them with Adelaide's life."

"Good enough for me."

Regulus opened the door and followed Alfred into the night. They hurried toward the central residential part of the castle, a multilevel building of soaring windows and gothic points. The other groups splintered off. Stealth was no longer required, but Regulus still noted with distaste how much louder Lord Belanger's men were than his own.

The front doors were locked. Alfred banged the pommel of his sword on the door. When no one answered, he banged again.

Regulus looked around the courtyard, catching sight of a man falling from one of the gate towers. "Is there another way—"

The door opened, revealing a bleary-eyed servant. "Lord Belanger?"

Alfred pushed past. "Where. Is. My. Wife!"

"In your rooms, my lord."

Regulus followed Alfred across the foyer as two men wearing only loose-fitting trousers ran in from an adjoining hallway, swords drawn. Regulus intercepted them while Alfred continued toward a door in the back corner of the foyer. The men hesitated when they saw Alfred, but Regulus did not. He drove his sword through the first man's stomach, turned as he withdrew his blade, and sliced across the second man's torso. Both men fell to the ground. Regulus followed Alfred up the flight of stairs behind the corner door. Landon headed in the opposite direction with a few of the knights. He did have his own wife to rescue, after all.

They ran up the stairs, Alfred taking the steps two at a time and Regulus close on his heels. The light of the torch in Alfred's hand sputtered, casting eerie shadows from suits of armor as Alfred sprinted down a hall. A man sat in a chair next to a closed door, head resting against the wall. He looked at them, then jumped up.

"You…Carrick said there was no way you could breach the walls!"

Before they reached him, the man unlocked the door and bolted inside. The door slammed in Alfred's face and the lock clicked. Alfred bellowed and jammed his shoulder against the door. It shook but didn't budge.

Regulus motioned for him to step aside. Alfred hesitated, but moved over, his face pinched. Regulus lifted his foot to kick at the door just as the door swung inward, and he nearly fell forward through the door. He stepped back in surprise. Lady Belanger stood in the doorway in a midnight-blue nightgown, eyes wild and shoulders heaving.

"Alfred!"

"Tamina," Alfred gasped out and dropped his sword. She ran into his arms and he lifted her off the ground, kissing her with such passion, Regulus turned away. He peered into the bedroom. The guard's body lay in a heap on the floor next to the massive four-post bed, just visible in the dim light from a gap in the curtains. The handle of a dagger protruded from his neck.

After a small eternity of tear-filled kisses, Lady Belanger turned toward Regulus. "Hargreaves." Her dark brown eyes flashed. "Where is Adelaide?"

"Hopefully safely on her way to the palace." Heat crawled up Regulus' neck as she stared him down.

"Alone!" She slapped him across the face. His mouth fell open as he touched his stinging cheek. Alfred grabbed Tamina's shoulders and pulled her back.

"Troll take you, you—"

"Mina!" Alfred held his wife back. "Regulus just saved us and ensured Adelaide didn't come—"

"I heard Carrick talking to that man," Tamina pointed in the direction of the body. "He said Kirven had sent word of where he could find Adelaide, and that Regulus might attempt a rescue." Her tone softened. "He didn't think you a threat against a garrisoned castle. And while part of me is pleased he was wrong," her hands formed fists, "Adelaide is out there *alone* with Carrick after her. His exact words were, 'I'm going to *collect* Adelaide.' Like paid-for goods. Why aren't you with her!"

Regulus stepped back, shaking his head. "No...she's on her way to warn the king. Her magic is back. Adelaide is strong and smart. She's okay. She has to be."

Tamina pointed at him. "First you run away with her when you were told to stay put. I suppose I should be thankful, because otherwise she would have been here when Carrick attacked. But then you leave her alone?"

"She wouldn't abandon you," Regulus said, his voice hoarse. "It seemed like the best way to keep her safe from Carrick."

"When did you last see her?" Alfred demanded.

"Three days ago? She's safe," Regulus said, trying to convince himself more than Adelaide's parents. He stared down at the blood giving his sword a red sheen. "I…" He swallowed. "I have to find her." He looked up, determination replacing his fear. "I have to go." He turned and pushed past the gawking knights blocking the hall.

"Where?" Alfred called. "You have no idea—"

"I'll head for the palace." Regulus clutched the grip of his sword until his fingers hurt. "I'll follow the route Adelaide most likely would have taken. Or I'll track Carrick. One way or another, I will find her." He lowered his voice, guilt carving a hole in his chest. "I have to."

CHAPTER 20

BETWEEN THE MEMORY OF THE TORTURE, THE COLLAR LEACHING her magic, and the gnawing in her stomach, Adelaide felt light-headed and dizzy, even lying on the ground. A night and most of a day had passed since the sorcerer had left her in the shed. She'd slept poorly. It was impossible to get comfortable, and fear of Kirven and his torture haunted her dreams. She grew weaker with each passing hour. Worse, she reeked, although she could now ignore the scent of urine. So far, she had managed to avoid defecating on herself. But she had begun to worry whether her magic would return when she got the collar off. How she would remove it, she didn't know, but she would find a way.

At this point, she was even too exhausted to be angry. She had spent part of the morning trying to escape the ropes, or even to stand up and hop her way to the door with the idea of breaking it down. When that proved futile, she had sat with her back against the wall, her rage building, lashing out at everything that had gotten her to this point. At the center of which, in the moment, had seemed to be Regulus. Adelaide finally understood why Mother had been so angry with him.

Regulus had gotten her involved with the sorcerer. Regulus had made an enemy of Nolan Carrick. Regulus was the reason Nolan had found Kirven and was now unstoppable. Regulus had the idea to split up, hadn't been there to help her when Kirven attacked. But as the pain in her empty stomach increased and the day dragged on, her anger cooled.

Regulus hadn't wanted to serve Kirven. He hadn't wanted to take her to Kirven, either. And Adelaide had made an enemy of Nolan, too. She had agreed to splitting up. Maybe the person who deserved the blame for her predicament was herself.

In the end, she decided to blame Kirven. He was behind all this pain. Everything—her years of hiding her magic, Regulus' pain, her capture, Nolan's immortality—came back to him. That spark of righteous anger kept her from utter despair. Sooner or later, someone would come, that's what Kirven said. They'd have to untie her, and she would make her escape. She would find Regulus. And somehow, someway, they would see that Kirven didn't hurt anyone else.

Adelaide was lying on her back, watching a bat trying to find its way out of the rafters, and wondering what it would be like to fly and if insects tasted any good, when the door to the shed opened. She squirmed to a sitting position and squinted at the influx of evening sunlight and the figure outlined in the doorway.

No. Not him.

"Gracious, Adelaide!" Nolan dashed forward and knelt next to her, brow wrinkled.

"Don't touch me!" Her voice croaked. *Why did he have to come himself?* Adelaide wriggled away, her heart racing. He grabbed her shoulders, looking her up and down. She hated the involuntary whimper that caught in her throat. But unlike Kirven's, Nolan's touch didn't hurt.

"Did he hurt you?"

"As if you care." Her stomach twisted and emitted a strange groaning sound.

"I care. He left you like this?" Nolan sounded surprisingly upset. "Have you eaten?"

"Yes, he left me like this. And how could I have eaten?" She wiggled her fingers by her shoulders.

"Hold on." Nolan darted out of the shed and returned a moment later with a bag in hand. He pulled Regulus' dagger from the back of his belt and cut the ropes off her torso. Adelaide groaned as her arms fell to her sides. She would have clawed his eyes out if her cramped muscles had allowed her to move her arms.

He took a wineskin from the bag and offered it to her. "Water?"

She tried to reach for it and moaned. Her muscles prickled everywhere they weren't numb. Her arms didn't want to obey.

"Here." Nolan poured water over her chapped lips. She felt ridiculous, but thirst got the better of her pride and she gulped down the water. He placed the wineskin on the ground and picked up her right arm.

"What are you doing?" She jerked her arm, her eyes widening, but he didn't let go.

"Relax, love." He started rubbing her arm from the shoulder down.

She tensed, but eased as feeling returned to her arm. Fine, let him help. It would only restore her strength faster.

"Better?"

Adelaide didn't want to admit it, but it was. She nodded, and he moved to her other arm.

"Kirven told me your magic is back. I'm happy for you." He stopped massaging her arm and brushed his fingers over the collar. "You wouldn't have to wear this if you joined us."

She shifted away. "You're not happy for me. You think having a wife with magic will make you more powerful."

Nolan returned to massaging. "What can I say? I'm attracted to power." He finished rubbing her arm and kissed her shoulder. She jerked away with a shudder. Nolan sighed and pulled a few pieces of jerky out of his bag. She devoured them, not caring they were dry and tough.

"I like your attire." He handed the water over, and she begrudgingly accepted. His gaze wandered over her. "Very enticing."

She threw the open wineskin at him. Water splashed his face, and she smiled with satisfaction at his irritated frown. She lifted her chin, trying to look as dignified as possible. "I need to relieve myself."

His nose wrinkled. "Pretty sure you already have."

She blushed and he snickered, making her face heat more. "Laugh when you've been left bound in a shed," she muttered.

"All right, all right." He picked up a long piece of rope from the ones he had cut off her torso and tied it to the loop in the side of the collar, next to the lock. "I'm not going to let you just run off," he said in response to her withering look. He cut the ropes off her ankles.

It took Adelaide a couple tries to stand on her aching legs and numb feet, but she managed it with a little assistance from Nolan. He picked up his bag and wineskin and waited outside the door while she relieved herself.

"Done yet?" he called. She scowled as she exited the shed.

A few maple trees were spaced between little groves of ash and birch. A soot-blackened wooden frame of what might have once been a cottage stood several feet away. She sucked in a deep breath of the fresh air, appreciating anew the warmth of the sun and the coolness of the evening air on her skin.

Nolan gave her a once-over. "Come on. You need to clean up." He strode off, the rope attached to the collar leading her after him. "There's a stream down here."

"Fine," she said through gritted teeth. However, she was thankful for the opportunity to rinse off her clothes.

Nolan stood on the bank next to her boots while she sat in the shallow stream and attempted to wash off some of the smell. He leered. "This might be easier if you took your clothes off."

Heat covered her head from scalp to collarbones. She turned away and scrubbed more furiously at her fitted trousers. He just laughed.

"I'm going to kill you." The words spilled out before she thought better of it.

He stopped laughing. "First, that's a rude thing to say to your knightly rescuer and future husband. Second, you must have missed the part where I can't die."

She glared over her shoulder. "I'll try cutting your head off. I'd like to see Kirven heal that."

His lips pursed. "We really need to work on your attitude. Plotting to kill your betrothed is frowned upon."

"We are *not* betrothed."

"Yes, we are. You agreed, remember? Besides, if we're not, why am I sticking my neck out for you?"

She stood with her back to him and squeezed excess water out of the skirt of her suede tunic and tried to press water out of her trousers. "What are you talking about?"

"Prince Kirven would have killed you if not for me. You're welcome." He paused, as if waiting for a thank you, but he was not about to get one. "But His Highness isn't interested in threats to his power. I told him I can control you, but if you misbehave, he won't hesitate to kill you. And that's not what I want."

Adelaide turned, water dripping from her trousers. "Don't pretend this is you being self-sacrificial."

"I can protect you easier if you marry me."

"I don't need or want your protection!"

"Really?" He lifted his brows. "If that's true, why were you bound on the floor of an abandoned shed?" He pulled on the rope.

The collar pressed against the back of her neck and she stumbled out of the stream toward him. "If you didn't need my protection, you wouldn't have a magic-suppressing collar around your neck." He drew her in until she was standing in front of him. She stared down at the grass poking up between her toes.

"Look at me, Adelaide," he pleaded. She clenched her jaw, annoyed at his constant playacting. "Please." With a huff, she looked at him. "Stop fighting Kirven and marry me, and I can and will give you anything and everything you can possibly desire. You won't have to wear this collar. You can use your magic. You want tutors in magic? I'll send to every kingdom to find the best ones. You want silks? I'll order dresses in every color in any style you choose. You want exotic fruit? I'll send to the edges of the known world for them. You want to travel? I'll take you anywhere. You want to meet your mother's family? I'll find them for you. What do you want, Adelaide? I'll make sure you have it." He looked at her, his eyes gentle, begging. His love-sick puppy act sickened her. "Just love me."

She crossed her arms. "I want this collar off."

"Once we're married. After you've sworn your loyalty to me in front of witnesses."

"Now."

Nolan sighed. "I try to be your knight in shining armor, and you act like I'm the dragon. You'll see. I can be cruel, I know, but only when necessary. I won't be denied or disrespected. But I can be kind." His blue eyes shone with affection that caught her off-guard. "I can be the man you deserve, Adelaide. The man you need." He rubbed the back of his fingers down her arm in a soft caress.

She shivered, and not just from the cold of her wet clothes.

"I will give you all the riches of the world. I will fill you with ecstasy and live for your pleasure, if you let me."

He ran his thumb over her cheekbone. Adelaide swallowed back the bile pushing against her throat and turned her head away. She stepped back, but the collar dug into her neck, keeping her close to him.

"Stop fighting me." Nolan's voice dropped to a seductive murmur. "We could be unstoppable. We could do anything. Let me in, Adelaide." For a moment, the tenderness of his tone took her aback. Gentle longing filled his eyes. His ability to lie, to play a part, astounded her. No wonder he had seduced so many. Only because she denied him did she have the displeasure of seeing his true nature.

"Untie the rope at least. Please." She tried to look harmless and innocent as he regarded her, lips pursed.

He shook his head. "You're not ready yet."

"I'm not going to marry you!" Adelaide grabbed the rope and turned to run. Nolan's grip was too strong, even with her sudden movement. She released the rope and stood erect with her back to him.

"I am your destiny, one way or another." His voice hardened as he grabbed her elbow, his fingers digging in around the joint, and wrenched her back around. She bit her tongue to keep from crying out. "You can sit in splendor at my right hand, or you can kneel at my feet. The choice is yours. But either way, you will be mine."

Nolan lifted her chin, placed his other hand on her back, and pressed his lips to hers. Her skin itched with disgust as she stood momentarily frozen. He kissed her softly, then more forcefully when she tried to pull away. She pushed against his chest, but he locked his arms around her. His hand on the back of her head held her in place. She squirmed and thrashed, her arms pinned between their bodies, trying to break away. Her lips hurt from trying to deny the press of his mouth. His lips left hers and she gasped in a deep breath. He brushed a kiss against her jaw.

"Be mine, Adelaide." He kissed the side of her neck above the collar.

"Stop," she rasped. She shook as she pushed against him. She couldn't breathe.

Nolan lifted his head. His eyes glinted with hunger. "Why don't you want me? How can I be driven mad with the thought of you, and you won't spare a glance my way?" He kissed her shoulder, ignoring her struggling. "You fill my dreams; your smile steals away my concentration. I see you when I close my eyes, and it's not fair."

His mouth hovered above hers. With his hand still holding the back of her head like a vise, Adelaide couldn't turn away. Her heart pounded against her chest and she pressed her eyes and mouth closed.

"You've gotten under my skin," he murmured. "Some half-Khastallander girl with skin the color of dark amber, the product of an alliance between a lord rich with the spoils of war and a merchant's daughter. You aren't topping any list of most wanted maidens."

How flattering. She pushed her head back against his hand to no avail.

"You were just the answer to my marriage predicament, but I can't stop thinking about you. I desire you with every fiber of my being, with every bone in my body." He gave her a quick peck on her closed lips, then pulled back. She risked opening her eyes.

Nolan watched her, his eyebrows pinched. "Does no part of you desire me?"

Adelaide clenched her jaw. "No."

She sent a burst of magical energy out of her palms and into his chest. It was tiny for how much effort it took, but he stumbled back, his arms slipping and allowing a small space between them. She sent another shockwave and he let go as he staggered backward. Dark spots danced in her eyes, and she shook her head, trying to clear away the dizziness. She swayed and leaned forward, supporting herself on her knees.

Nolan straightened, face flushed and eyes dark. "I'm tired of you!" He pulled on the rope and she fell to her knees on the grass. "I'm tired of you fighting me! I'm tired of you choosing that scarred bastard mercenary over me! I'm tired of losing to that stuck-up mongrel nobody who doesn't deserve his title or castle and certainly doesn't deserve you. I'm tired of wanting you and being denied. I'm tired of you acting like I'm some cruel monster."

"Then stop behaving like one!" She sounded braver than she felt. Those small uses of her power had drained her, and she didn't have much energy left to so much as stand, let alone fight. That scared her, because she didn't know what Nolan would do next. *Etiros, protect me.*

"You think me cruel?" He strode toward her. Adelaide tried to crawl backward, but he drew in the rope, stopping her. "So be it. If that's what you want, I can show you cruelty." He backhanded her face, making her cheek sting and throb. "I can be your monster."

"Nolan, please..." In spite of herself, a sob tore from her throat and tears squeezed out of her eyes.

He knelt in front of her, his expression softening. "It doesn't have to be like this." He wiped a tear off her cheek with his thumb. "Stop fighting me." He grabbed her waist and pulled her closer.

The truth sank into Adelaide's chest like a rock. She couldn't fight him. Not right now. Not for long, anyway. She wanted to be strong, but she was exhausted. The collar drained her, leaving her weak. Weak, tired, and scared. She hadn't recovered from Kirven's torture yet. Nolan's strength dwarfed hers, and even if she wounded him, he would heal. This wasn't a fight she could win.

She wanted Mother. She wanted to be a little girl again, watching with fascination as Mother sewed a new dress for her in a Khastallander style and told her Khastallander fables. Back before she knew the extent of the world's cruelty. When she climbed too high in the trees and cried and Mother crossed her arms and said if her brave little tigress, her *shiraa*, could get up, she could get down.

Nolan's hand gripped her thigh as he forced her onto his lap. As numbness settled into her chest, she didn't feel like a tigress. She didn't feel brave. Mother had raised her to defend herself, and she couldn't. *Give me courage*, she prayed. *Give me strength. Protect me.* Her mind raced, searching for a way to stop him. Suddenly, she remembered Regulus' dagger, stuck in the back of Nolan's belt. She needed to stall him. To distract him long enough to get ahold of the dagger. His hands roamed as he leaned toward her.

"Nolan." Her voice came out in a croak. She cleared her throat. "Nolan, I…I'll marry you." He froze. "I just need—more time." She gulped against the lump in her throat. "I'll marry you."

He narrowed his eyes. "I've heard that before."

"Please." She blinked back a few stray tears and edged her hand toward his waist. "You're right. I'm not ready. But I won't… I won't fight you. On, on our," she exhaled slowly to steady her voice, even as the words killed a part of her soul, "on our wedding night. If you wait." She met his eyes. "Please." *Please don't let him notice*, she prayed as her hand hovered near the back of his belt.

His eyes narrowed. "What about after our wedding night?"

"I'll…" She licked her dry lips. She would have to lean toward him to reach the dagger. "I'll be a dutiful…affectionate wife." Cold clawed at her insides.

A slow, self-assured smile pulled at the corner of Nolan's lips. "Swear it."

"I promise." Adelaide leaned forward as she reached around behind him. Her fingers brushed the hilt of the dagger. With a quick pull, she freed it from his belt and slashed toward the rope, her heart pounding. Nolan caught her wrist, stopping her before the blade met the rope. She looked from the dagger to his eyes, her moment of bravery spent. He watched her with eerie calm, his mouth drawn into a hard line. His hand clutched her wrist so hard she feared her bones would snap.

"I'm sorry," she whispered, his silence more unnerving than shouting. "I...I panicked. I'm sorry."

He pulled her hand away and she dropped the dagger, hoping he wouldn't break her wrist again. "Why, Adelaide? Why don't you want me? Why do you continue to fight me?"

She shook her head, too tense to say anything. Nolan pushed her back onto the ground with force that hurt her shoulders. He grabbed the dagger and stood, still holding the rope. The sun had nearly set; dusk gathered around them. The first stars stared down from the darkening sky; cold, distant, and uncaring.

Nolan turned the dagger over in his hand. "I'm of two minds, Adelaide. Part of me wants to keep trying to be your knight, to show you I can be compassionate. To give you time to accept the inevitable." He crouched and put the edge of the dagger to her throat, right above the collar. "The other part of me is done trying to win you over."

You were trying? She tried to move her neck away from the blade, but his hand followed her. She lost her balance and fell back, propped up on her elbows. He crawled over her, the knife still pressed to her throat. The metal rested there, one faulty move away from opening a wound that, in her weakened state, she wouldn't be able to heal. Her stomach twisted, threatening to push up the jerky.

"Nolan, please..."

"Do you have any idea how frustrating you are?" He released the rope to trace the top edge of her tunic. His fingers stopped at the ties of the bodice.

Adelaide curled her fists, her nails digging into her palms. Her breaths came in rapid, shallow gasps. *Stop, please, make him stop.* "I'm sor—"

"You're maddening. I've had ladies throw themselves at me. I've had women beg me *not* to stop." He tilted his head. "But the problem isn't me, or even you. You want me, you just don't realize it yet." He leaned back, returned the dagger to his belt, and picked the rope back up.

Every muscle in her body was taut as a drawn bow as she watched him, hope a weak spark in her shuddering chest.

"When Hargreaves is dead, when he's no longer confusing you, you'll finally see me. When I'm the only thing between you and Kirven's wrath, you'll realize how generous I've been. You'll come crawling. You'll beg me to take you. And when you do…" Nolan leered and leaned closer, his voice teasing. He ran his fingertips down her spine, and she shivered. "You'll wish you had given in sooner."

Not likely. Adelaide bit back the retort, careful not to stir his anger again. She fought to keep her expression blank and not betray her disgust and terror. He seemed to have decided to stop, at least for the moment, and she wouldn't risk antagonizing him into changing his mind.

CHAPTER 21

"CARRICK!" REGULUS' SHOUT BOOMED THROUGH THE TWILIGHT air. A flock of birds in a tree beyond Carrick and Adelaide took flight, their wings rustling as they soared into the pink-tinged sky. Adelaide was lying on the ground, propped up on her elbows. Carrick leaned over her, holding a rope tied to a collar around her neck. Indignation boiled Regulus' blood. He kicked Sieger forward and raced down the hill toward them. Dresden and Alfred followed close behind.

Nolan sighed as he stood, pulling Adelaide up with him by the arm. "What are *you* doing here? How did you even get here?"

"Turns out you're not the only one good at hunting," Regulus snarled as he jumped off Sieger's back and drew his sword. In actuality, one of the servants had overheard the sorcerer telling Nolan where to find Adelaide. Drez and Alfred had insisted on coming, too, and they had pushed their horses hard to catch up. Sweat frothed on Sieger's neck.

Nolan wrapped his arms around Adelaide and held her against his chest. A human shield. Regulus ground his teeth.

"Lord Belanger?" Nolan frowned. "How…unexpected. I really didn't think you could actually pull off a rescue, mercenary."

"Unhand my daughter!"

Adelaide looked at them, eyes wide—with hope or fear, Regulus wasn't sure. He stalked closer. Why wasn't she doing something? Had she lost her magic again? His gaze flicked to the iron collar around her neck. Did that have something to do with it?

"Ah, and the Carasian servant." Carrick grinned. "Did you give your master my message?"

Regulus glanced at Dresden. Dresden had turned dark red.

"I wish I'd had the time for a more comprehensive belting," Carrick said. "Did he tell you those stripes were for you?"

"Enough!" Regulus' voice shook.

"Three against one," Carrick said. "And I'm not wearing armor and they are. Don't you think that's unfair, love?" He kissed Adelaide's shoulder, just below the collar, maintaining eye contact with Regulus. Adelaide flinched as his mouth pressed against her skin, and Regulus focused in on a bruise on her cheek. *He hurt her.*

"Let. Her. Go." Regulus took an offensive stance, ready to sprint forward at the hint of an opening.

Carrick raised a brow. "All right." He dropped his arms, then hit Adelaide hard on the side of her head. Alfred screamed as Adelaide crumpled into Carrick's arms. Regulus' heart fell like a stone. Carrick lowered her onto the ground. "Don't worry, she's just unconscious. I wouldn't kill my bride." He stepped over her still form. "What are you waiting for?"

Regulus lunged forward and swung at Carrick's neck. Carrick dove under the blade with unsettling speed and pummeled into Regulus' torso, wrapping his arms around Regulus as they toppled. Regulus grunted, the air knocked out of him. His sword slipped from his grip as he landed hard on his back with Carrick on top of him.

"I'm going to finally kill you, mercenary." Carrick punched Regulus in the face, and Regulus groaned as his cheekbone cracked. He wrapped his legs around Carrick, gripped his shirt, and twisted, rolling Carrick onto his back. He punched Carrick's mouth, and blood seeped from Carrick's lips.

Carrick growled and caught his fist. Regulus punched with his left hand, catching Carrick in the temple. Carrick shouted and wrenched Regulus' arm, then threw him to the side. Regulus jumped up, his right shoulder aching, as Carrick scrambled to his feet and picked up Regulus' sword. He barely escaped Carrick's manic thrust. Carrick sliced and Regulus jumped back. The tip of the sword scraped across his chest, the sword clinking against the chainmail.

Two curved blades protruded out of Carrick's chest. Carrick stared at Regulus, mouth hanging open in a silent scream. *Good job, Drez.* As Carrick fell to his knees, Dresden withdrew his scimitars. He swung at Carrick's neck, but Carrick met one scimitar with Regulus' sword and grabbed Dresden's other hand. Dresden strained against Carrick. Regulus grabbed Carrick's shirt and tossed him to the ground. Carrick groaned, but rolled onto his back as Regulus reached for his sword, moving too fast. His fingers dug into the grass. *Too slow. I'm too slow!*

Carrick kicked his ankle, and Regulus collapsed to one knee as Carrick rolled away and sprung to his feet. A little pain couldn't stop him right now. He needed to *get up!* Drez blocked Carrick's desperate swing. But then Carrick released his grip on the sword with his right hand, reached forward, closed his hand around Dresden's neck, and shoved. Regulus scrambled to his feet as Dresden fell onto his back, coughing and wheezing. *Not my best friend, cur.*

Regulus aimed a punch at the back of Carrick's head. Just before his fist made contact, Carrick leaned forward and turned. His boot rammed into Regulus' gut, knocking him backward. Regulus gasped, his abdomen throbbing and lungs struggling to pull in air. Dark spots flickered in his vision. Carrick sneered and thrust the sword at Regulus' heart. The blade pressed into the chainmail, but Carrick kept pushing until he fell onto his back. His chest ached.

Carrick stomped on his sternum, and something cracked. Regulus sucked in air against the suffocating pain as his vision blurred.

"Let's see what my new strength can do." Carrick stood over him, straddling his middle.

I have to move. But his body wouldn't listen. Carrick raised the sword and brought it straight down with the speed of a viper. Against the superhuman impact, and with no give as Regulus lay braced against the ground, the chainmail broke.

The sword ripped into his gut with hellish pain, its momentum stopped only when it hit the chainmail on his back. Regulus gasped; strangled, staccato groans of agony as tremors ran up and down his body. He'd nearly died enough times to know—he wouldn't survive this. But all he could think about was Adelaide. *Get her away, Alfred.*

"No!" Drez screamed. "Regulus!"

Carrick released the sword and turned in time for Dresden to bury both scimitars in Carrick's stomach. Carrick bellowed in pain as Dresden withdrew his blades. Regulus' hands shook, but he grabbed the blade and tried to push it out. The sharp edges cut through his leather gloves, stinging as it split open his palms. Shallow, pain-inducing breaths wheezed in his throat. Through his blurring vision, he saw Carrick throw Drez aside like a rag doll. *No...* He tried to call Dresden's name, but couldn't speak. Darkness encroached along the edges of his sight.

"I told you I would kill you, mercenary," Carrick panted.

He grabbed the hilt and twisted. Regulus' scream came out strangled. The blade scraped out of his stomach as Carrick withdrew it. Tears ran down his temples into his hair. Carrick dropped the sword and stumbled away, pressing his hand against his blood-soaked middle as he headed toward Alfred and Adelaide. *No!* Panic forced Regulus' dying body into action.

"Carrick!" He coughed up blood, but he fought through the pain and managed to get to his knees. He'd endured worse. "I'm not dead yet."

Carrick glanced over his shoulder, then laughed. "You're good as."

Regulus tried to stand and fell back to his knees. He was dying, and this time, there was no stinging sorcery dragging him back from the brink. He had failed to protect Adelaide. *My fault...* He fell forward. He raised his head and tried to warn Alfred, but his tongue wouldn't work.

Pain overwhelmed his senses. The world went in and out of focus. *I'm sorry, Adelaide. I'm sorry. I love you, and I'm sorry.* His eyelids felt heavy. He had the odd thought of being terribly thirsty. He looked at Alfred, trying to see past him to Adelaide. To see her one last time.

Alfred moved aside. Adelaide sat up, and Regulus wondered if he was dreaming, or maybe already dead. Or halfway between the realm of the living and the afterlife. Adelaide's eyes glowed golden as she leapt to her feet. Wings of fire spread out behind her back and a sword of light and flame appeared in her hands. His avenging angel. The world faded into darkness. He let his face fall onto the grass.

Goodbye, Adelaide.

CHAPTER 22

NOLAN'S FACE TURNED GHOSTLY WHITE. WITH THE COLLAR gone, Adelaide felt lighter, but also furious. All fear vanished. She raised her flaming sword to swing for his neck. Before she got the chance, Nolan fled. She sliced the sword through empty air. An arc of flame flew off the glowing magic blade and singed Nolan's back as he ran. She started after him, but movement in her periphery caught her attention.

Dresden ran through the dark, weaponless. Not after Nolan, but somewhere else. She traced his trajectory to a mound in the grass.

No, not a mound.

Regulus.

The scream she emitted hardly sounded human. The magic sword vanished. She raced toward his still body. Dresden beat her to him and rolled Regulus onto his back as she slid to a stop. Even in the dim light, she could see the blood that covered his abdomen and had pooled on the grass. His eyes were closed, his features deathly pale and still. His chest wasn't moving.

"No, no, no," Dresden muttered. "Regulus? Can you hear me?" He touched Regulus' neck, searching for a pulse. "Please, Reg."

Tears burned her eyes and soaked her cheeks as she knelt next to Regulus. She reached out tentatively. "Regulus…"

Dresden made a strangled noise in his throat. "Don't you abandon me now, Regulus. Please." He adjusted his fingers on

Regulus' neck, pressing as if that would induce a pulse. "Reg?" His hand slipped away as he sobbed.

"No!" Adelaide grabbed Regulus' blood-soaked chainmail, choking on her sobs. Her chest burned with the effort of breathing and her stomach muscles tensed and knotted to the point of pain. Mucus ran out of her nose and mingled with her tears. "Regulus, you hang on!" She placed her hands over the wound on his stomach. Soft blue light illuminated the ragged tear in his chainmail and blood-soaked gambeson.

"He's gone, Adelaide." Dresden's voice was deadened and hopeless.

"No." She shook her head. She could feel it. The tiniest bit of life. A spark of energy deep in his chest. "He's hanging on. Just barely." But she detected the wound, too. She sensed the hole through his body and the damage done to his organs. "Please, Etiros. Please."

Her palms glowed brighter as she focused all her magic on Regulus. From deep inside working out, she pulled him back together.

"Come back to me, Regulus," Adelaide whispered. "Don't leave me." *Don't leave me. I'm sorry I blamed you, even for a moment. I'm sorry I didn't stay with you. I'm sorry I didn't stop Nolan. I'm sorry your pain is because of me again. But don't leave me.*

Her tears dripped onto her hands and mixed with Regulus' blood. She sensed the wound closing, healing, the blood reabsorbing, but the flicker of life in his chest sputtered on the edge of going out.

"Come on," she muttered. "Etiros, please. COME ON." The light glared brighter. "I love you. I love you. I love you." The wound closed, but still he didn't move. She moved her hands, searching. His sternum was cracked. She healed his chest, then his battered cheek and pulled off his gloves to heal his cut hands. Still he showed no signs of improving. "Regulus?"

Dresden felt Regulus' neck again. "Reg…?" He shook his head. "He…he's lost too much blood." Tears traced lines down the blood marring the side of Dresden's face.

"No…he can't…I can't… Regulus." Her voice cracked. Adelaide laid across his chest, holding on to his shoulders. "I can't…stop. Can't stop them. Not—not without you," she whispered between sobs and gasps for air. "I love you." She broke down weeping onto his shoulder, numb to everything. Numb to Regulus' limp body beneath her, to the tears on her face.

"Can't…breathe…" Regulus' voice was so quiet she almost didn't hear it over her crying. She gasped and straightened. His eyes were open, and she sobbed again as they met hers.

"Regulus?" Dresden choked out.

"I'm…tired." Regulus blinked sluggishly. She placed her hand on his chest. The spark of life shuddered, losing the fight to hold on.

"No, no, don't you go to sleep!" She grabbed the sides of his face. Her lower lip trembled. A tear fell from her chin onto his cheek.

"I love you, too." Regulus sounded thin and reedy. Completely unlike himself. "I'm…sorry."

"No, you have nothing to be sorry for." She stroked his hair, her hands shaking. "I'm sorry! I—"

"Shhh." He closed his eyes. "You didn't…do…anything… wruh…"

"Regulus!" Adelaide pulled his head toward her, and he opened his eyes. An idea occurred to her. She didn't know if she could do it, and she'd already used so much magic, but she had to try. She had to. "You want to marry me, right?"

"Yush…"

"You want to bind yourself to me forever?"

"Ad…I would—have…"

"I am yours." Her voice trembled. "Say you're mine. Forever."

"Yes. I…your…sh." His eyes fluttered shut.

"No, you don't." Adelaide wiped away her tears and set her jaw. She pushed up the sleeve on his right arm and placed her hand over his scars.

Warmth spread across her palm as energy pulsed from her chest down her arm. *Protect him. Heal him. Tie his life to mine.* She put every ounce of healing power, all the energy she would use to create a protective barrier larger than any she had conjured before, into him. Her power drained away, emptying out of her and filling him. Even if she poured herself out and her magic was gone forever, she didn't care, so long as it worked. Even if it killed her. It *had* to work. *Etiros, let this work. Please!* Regulus' arm glowed blue under her hand.

The flicker of life in Regulus' chest flared back to full strength. She felt a bond between them, like a cord connecting her heart to his. Felt him like he wasn't just next to her, but he was in her heart, in her very soul, and she in his. Her hand slipped off his arm and weariness made her sway, her vision clouding over. A black mark stood out on his skin, over the white of his scars.

The overlapping knot design had no beginning and no end, just one never-ending line, crossing over itself to form two interlocking hearts connected by a diamond. White spots drifted through her sight as she stared at the mark. She closed her eyes. She just… needed…a moment…

CHAPTER 23

REGULUS SAT UP WITH A GASP, NEARLY HITTING HIS HEAD against Dresden's in the dark. Every muscle vibrated with energy. He felt like he had just jumped into a freezing lake while half-asleep, and the jolt to his system had erased any feelings of tiredness. He grabbed at where the sword had pierced his abdomen. His chainmail was sticky with blood, but it was like the wound had never been there.

"Regulus." Dresden sobbed and hugged Regulus to his chest, his body shaking as he squeezed so hard Regulus couldn't breathe. When Dresden pulled back, his face was streaked with tears.

"Are you hurt?" Dresden shook his head, and Regulus looked around. "Where is—" *Adelaide.*

Alfred held her across his lap, leaning over her ashen face. Regulus' heart nearly stopped until her chest rose with a small breath. He moved toward them.

"Adelaide?"

Alfred didn't look up as he stroked her head. "She did something to heal you, and then she just…fell over. I think she fainted, but she's barely breathing."

"What?" Regulus touched her braid where it fell across her shoulder.

Alfred sniffed, and Regulus realized he had been crying. "She healed your wounds, but you were still dying. And then she put her hand on your arm. I don't…" He drew in a ragged breath and kissed her forehead.

"You were nearly gone," Dresden said. "I thought you—" His voice cracked, and he broke off.

"She wouldn't let you go," Alfred murmured.

Dresden snuffled. "She said… Your arm… Oh, no. No. I know what she did." Regulus looked back, surprised by the horror in his friend's voice. "Look at your arm, Reg."

Regulus frowned down at his arms. His right sleeve was pushed up to his elbow under the chainmail.

"The underside." Drez sounded resigned, almost bitter.

He turned his right arm over and lifted it. The chainmail slid back to his elbow. A new black mark stood out against his skin; an intricate knot of interlocking shapes formed from an unbroken line. He squinted in the dim moonlight. Two triangles, their points extending toward the sides of his arm, formed a diamond between two…hearts?

He ran his fingertips over the mark. A comforting warmth spread up his arm at the touch and the strangest humming sensation nestled deep in his chest, almost in his soul. The humming drew his gaze toward Adelaide. He took her hand. Something inside him tugged toward her. An ethereal connection he couldn't explain, but that made him feel at ease and energized at once.

"She marked you," Drez said angrily, "just like the sorcerer."

"No." Regulus smiled and caressed the side of her face. "Not at all like the sorcerer."

"She made you agree you wanted to be bound to her forever. She used magic to put a mark on your arm, and somehow that kept you alive when you should have been dead. Doesn't that sound familiar?" Frustration laced Drez's voice.

"This isn't sorcery." Regulus turned toward Drez. "This isn't about control. It doesn't hurt. It feels completely different. Less one-sided. It even looks different. This isn't slavery." He looked back at Adelaide's face. Even in sleep, exhaustion pulled at her features. "This is love."

"I hope you're right." Drez sighed. "At least you're alive. I…"

"I'm okay." Regulus clapped Dresden's shoulder. "Thank Etiros you are. If I'd woken up and you…" He swallowed hard.

Dresden crumpled and rubbed at his beard. "I thought I lost you. You looked like—" He stopped himself with a shake of his head, but Regulus could imagine what he was going to say. Like any of the friends they had lost as mercenaries. "I won't forgive you if you die," Dresden muttered. "I won't forgive *me* if you die."

"Drez—"

"I couldn't save you." Dresden's head sank further. "I kept staring at you, trying to think of what I should have done differently so you wouldn't be lying there. My friend. My *brother.* Always there to protect me, and every time it matters, I can't protect you!" He looked up, his eyes brimming with tears.

Regulus stared at Dresden, at a loss for words. Part of him wanted to point out he wasn't always there. He hadn't been there when Carrick beat Dresden. And it wasn't Dresden's fault Carrick was immortal and unstoppable.

"I can't see you like that again." Dresden forced a smile. "You're not allowed to die. Ever."

"Okay." Regulus smiled weakly. "Only if you never die."

Dresden laughed, the sound tight and pained. "Deal."

CHAPTER 24

AS THE SUN ROSE THE NEXT MORNING, CLEARING AWAY THE FOG rising off the nearby stream, it became clear Adelaide would not awake anytime soon. Regulus washed the blood off his clothing as best he could and put his chainmail and his gambeson in his saddlebag. His long-sleeved gray shirt now was bloodstained and had a hole over his stomach, but they had no thread or needles with which to mend it. They found a shed nearby where Adelaide had clearly been held, and the fury in Alfred's eyes rivaled Regulus' own. They let Adelaide sleep through the day, exchanging concerned glances and wondering if they should move her. And wondering when they should continue to the palace.

Alfred wanted to warn the king, but he also wouldn't leave his daughter. Regulus had determined never to part ways with Adelaide again. Dresden didn't stand a chance of convincing anyone to even let him in the palace. Besides, they were exhausted from riding through the night and all day to find her. So they waited and prayed as the day turned to night and another day dawned and Adelaide still did not wake.

At least Regulus had convinced Dresden that Adelaide wasn't a sorceress and hadn't enslaved him. The marks looking nothing alike helped. Dresden teased him about how it looked like hearts. But he still looked at Adelaide with a mixture of distrust and fear. Not that Regulus could entirely blame him—Drez and Alfred had confirmed that he hadn't been hallucinating. In her fury, Adelaide had sprouted a pair of fiery wings.

Unfortunately, though, Carrick had escaped. Regulus blamed himself. If Adelaide hadn't left her pursuit of Carrick to save his life, perhaps she would have succeeded in killing the villain. If anything could break the bond to the sorcerer, it would probably be a weapon of pure magic. Maybe cutting him in half would do the trick.

Regulus sat next to Adelaide, watching an eagle circling high above the trees. Alfred had left to stretch his legs. Dresden had gone in search of fresh food as midday approached. Adelaide stirred, the grass rustling against her tunic. He laughed with relief and wetness rimmed his eyes as she stretched out on the grass with adorable soft grunting noises. She squinted against the bright sunlight.

His grin pulled at his scar. "Morning, *sumdir.*"

She smiled groggily and propped herself up on her elbow. "You're alive." She eyed his torn, stained shirt. "A mess, but alive."

"All thanks to you." Regulus cupped his hand to the side of Adelaide's face and caressed her cheek with his thumb. Her smile vanished and fear flooded his mind. She flinched, pulling away from his hand. He drew his hand back, his stomach dropping. "What's wrong?"

She shook her head and forced an unconvincing smile that made his heart twist. "Nothing, everything's fine. I'm sorry."

"What aren't you telling me?" he asked quietly. Uncertainty lingered in her eyes.

"Nothing." She rolled her shoulders and looked around. "What time is it?"

"Approaching noon. It's been two days since we found you, though."

"Two days! I slept that long?"

He shrugged. "When the fairies told you about how to do a binding, they did say you would need a lot of time to recover. How are you feeling?"

"Still—" She yawned. "Still tired. But better. I can feel my magic returning. Strengthening. And I'm not drained anymore, it's a relief to…" She faltered, her eyes going out of focus as her fingers drifted to her neck.

"The collar," Regulus said, confirming his suspicion. "The one your father broke off. It somehow suppressed your magic, didn't it?"

Adelaide's gaze fell. "Kirven… I met him on the road. He defeated me. Bound me. When he failed to steal my magic or convince me to serve him, he put that collar on me." She shivered. "It sucked away my power, my energy. Just…a constant drain."

"Hey, it's okay." He moved closer and put his arm around her, pulling her in as he kissed her cheek. Instead of relaxing, she stiffened and inhaled sharply. Hurt pierced his heart. "Adelaide?"

"I…I'm sorry." She quivered in his arms.

Inexplicable sorrow and fear coursed through him. It was when a sensation of a name, more than an actual thought, accompanied the surge of anxiety that he understood. *Nolan.* Somehow, he was sensing Adelaide's emotions.

His jaw tightened. Anger and regret fought for dominance in his soul. "What did Carrick do?"

"Nothing." She pulled away and stood, her back to him. But not before he saw the tears that glistened in the corner of her eyes. "Nothing happened."

"Then why are you afraid?" He kept his voice gentle, even as he wanted to shout and fume. "I can sense your fear. Your sadness."

Adelaide glanced over her shoulder at him. "What?"

He stood and walked around in front of her. "The bond you created…it's different from the sorcerer's. When I touch you, I can…feel you. Your emotions. Your soul."

"You feel it, too?" she whispered. "This...connection. Like we're..."

"Part of each other," Regulus finished. She nodded. He inclined his head so their eyes were at the same level. "So why can't you be honest with me?"

She turned and took a couple steps away. "Where's my father? And Dresden?"

"They'll be back shortly."

"You got my family out." She didn't look at him. "My mother? And Landon and Julia and their son?"

"They're safe and unharmed." He hoped that was all she was worried about. "We took back Belanger castle. They've taken precautions; Carrick won't get in again."

She glanced back and said, "Thank you," before she turned away again.

Dread that Adelaide blamed him for her capture grew in the pit of Regulus' stomach. But he hadn't detected anger, only fear. And he didn't like not knowing why she was afraid. He couldn't help if he didn't know the problem. "What's wrong? Talk to me, *shiraa*."

"Don't..." She hugged herself and ducked her head.

Regulus furrowed his brow. Something had happened. And he didn't want it to be what he thought it was. "Don't what?"

"Call me that," she whispered.

He took a step back, stunned. "What? Why?"

"I'm..." She shook her head. "I need... I'll be back." She walked toward the stream, but he strode after her and caught her elbow. Adelaide whimpered and pulled away, drawing into herself. For the moment their skin touched, Regulus felt her spike of panic. She looked at him, eyes wide and face red. "I...I didn't... I'm sorry. I don't know..." She reached toward him, then dropped her hand.

He eyed the yellow-green bruise on her right cheek. "He hurt you." When she lowered her gaze to the ground, her chin resting against her chest, that was all the answer he needed. He exhaled through his nose. "You're safe now."

"Am I?" Adelaide didn't look up. "I couldn't fight them. I was…weak."

His heart broke. "Adelaide." He reached for her again, then stopped, remembering her reaction. "You aren't weak."

"I *am* weak." She sank onto the grass.

He couldn't stop himself. He sat next to her and pulled her into his arms. She turned and leaned against his shoulder.

"It's okay," he said. "You don't have to tell me."

"I lost, and… I was helpless. And then the collar…" She hugged his waist like she was holding on for her life. Her chest heaved. "When Nolan… I was afraid and weak. I'm not—brave." She hiccupped and tucked her face into his shoulder.

Regulus rubbed her back, rage a fire in his veins. *That…* A slew of vile names for Carrick raced through his mind.

Adelaide turned her head to speak again. "He didn't even… I'm all right, really." Her hands clutched the back of his shirt. "He just scared me."

"He's a monster," Regulus said through gritted teeth.

Adelaide shuddered. "I antagonized him. He…" She buried her face in his shirt, her voice muffled as she continued. "I prayed he would stop. Maybe that's why he did. But I…I didn't help matters. I was stupid. Reckless. Defiant. And now…when…when… I'm sorry."

Every word she spoke ripped him apart, piece by piece. Her tears finally broke through, seeping into his shirt. She didn't need to finish the thought. He sensed her regret, her fear, and he knew. Knew that when he had touched her, she had flashed back to Carrick touching her.

"Oh, Adelaide." Regulus swallowed against the swelling in his throat. "No. It's not your fault. You didn't do anything wrong. He shouldn't have laid a finger on you. His behavior is his. Do you hear me?" His chest shook with each jagged breath.

"It's not your fault," he continued. "Don't blame yourself and don't you dare feel guilty. You did nothing wrong. Nothing you did excuses his actions. And you're not weak for being scared or upset." He stroked her back as her breathing deepened, becoming more regular.

"And I'm not angry with you," he added, sensing her dread. "I don't blame you for shying away. *I'm* sorry. I wouldn't have…" His anger threatened to break into tears. "You have every right to not want to be touched."

Adelaide didn't respond, but her storm of emotions calmed.

"You did nothing wrong," he whispered. "But I did. I never should have left you. I should have been there. I should have protected you." His throat tightened so much he felt strangled. "I failed you. I'm sorry. I'm so, so sorry."

After a moment, Adelaide mumbled into his shoulder, "It's all right."

"No, it's not." He took a deep breath, steadying himself against the growing ache behind his forehead. "I—"

"No." She shifted, turning so her cheek laid on his shoulder. "It's not your fault, either."

"But—"

"I did blame you." Adelaide's admission cut deeper than the sword that nearly killed him. "Briefly. I was alone, and scared, and…angry. But I realized it wasn't your fault." She drew in a long, shaky breath. "You said it yourself. Kirven's actions, Carrick's behavior," her voice hitched, "it's theirs. Don't take blame that isn't yours."

Her words released a chain Regulus hadn't even realized he'd placed around his heart. He'd been blaming himself for the sorcerer's actions for two years. How could he tell her she wasn't responsible for other's evil while blaming himself? She never blamed him. His men never blamed him. But he still blamed himself.

"Regulus." Adelaide's voice was soft, timid. "If it's not my fault, it's not yours, either. You have to stop blaming yourself."

He exhaled slowly and rested his cheek on top of her head. "I know," he murmured. "Still, I should have been there. I promise I will be in the future. No more splitting up."

"Yes." She linked her fingers behind his neck and snuggled closer. "No more splitting up."

Her fear and hurt abated. He wanted to kiss her forehead but didn't dare. Not yet. He would gladly give her all the time she needed. He wouldn't so much as hold her hand if that's what it took for her to overcome any lingering fear. So help him, he would not remind her of Carrick. Adelaide relaxed, and Regulus thanked Etiros that she trusted him enough to let him hold her.

CHAPTER 25

WHEN ALFRED RETURNED FROM HIS WALK, HE DIDN'T SAY ANY-thing about finding Adelaide on Regulus' lap. Maybe he was too relieved she was awake. Or maybe he didn't care. They hadn't spoken much while Adelaide was asleep, but Regulus sensed an increased respect from Alfred that he suspected had much to do with nearly dying and Adelaide pulling him back.

Alfred hugged and kissed his daughter, although Adelaide shied away even from her father's touch. He told her how relieved he was she was alive and how much he loved her. But he didn't ask any questions or pressure her to talk about what had happened.

Dresden returned carrying two rabbits and several fish while Alfred was telling Adelaide how impressed he was with her magical abilities. Regulus went to help Dresden with the fire and preparing the kills. Adelaide left to relieve herself, and Alfred came and sat next to Regulus. He pulled a knife from his belt and took one of the fish.

"Did she say anything about what happened?" Alfred asked.

"Why are you asking me and not her?"

Alfred paused, his knife halfway down the trout's belly. He scowled at the limp fish like it had threatened him. "I didn't want to ask her questions she might not be willing or able to answer. But I thought maybe she would have told you, if she was going to talk to anyone." He opened and closed his mouth a few times, like he wanted to say more. As he gutted the trout he said quietly, "Have you ever been captured?"

"Other than by the sorcerer? No."

"Right." Alfred glanced at him. "You mentioned he'd use the mark to punish you. Adelaide may not have the mark, but somehow, he tortured her."

"What?" Dread made Regulus dizzy. "What makes you—"

"I *have* been captured."

Regulus looked up in surprise. So did Dresden from the rabbit he was skinning.

"Most people don't know." Alfred looked around before continuing. "I was acting as King Olfan's double." He turned and pulled up the edge of his shirt with his pinky, the knife still in his hand. White scars crisscrossed his back and a large, knotted scar marred his side. He let the shirt fall back down. "I know what happens when you anger vengeful, powerful men."

He returned to the fish, but Regulus stared. Alfred looked calm as ever, but now Regulus realized his strength wasn't from never being weak. He had earned his strength through survival.

"Some things are difficult to speak aloud," Alfred said, his voice strained. "She was smiling, but I recognized the pain and fear in her eyes. The nervous energy. The hesitation to be touched. The way she's standing, making herself smaller. Something more happened to her than whatever caused that bruise on her cheek. Whether she healed it, or whatever Kirven did left no marks..." He shook his head. "I want to know she's all right, but I can tell she's not."

Regulus caught Dresden's eyes as Dresden tied the first rabbit over the fire. Dresden looked as shocked as he felt. Alfred was intent on cleaning the trout. But his jaw tightened, and wrinkles deepened around his eyes and across his forehead.

Regulus focused on scaling his own fish. He should have known. He thought only Carrick had hurt her. That the sorcerer could torture someone who didn't bear his mark hadn't occurred to him. And who would torture a woman? After everything else the sorcerer had done, he shouldn't be surprised. But he was still furious. He squeezed the fish and a scale sliced into his palm. He winced and held his hand up to inspect the cut, but the pain vanished as it closed in front of his eyes. As if by magic.

"When they realized you were just a lord…" Dresden started, pulling Regulus' focus back to Alfred's story. "Why didn't…" He shook his head and started on the second rabbit.

"Why didn't they kill me?" Alfred asked without looking up. "They still hoped for a ransom. I escaped by pure luck and some sheer stupidity on my captors' part. But I would have been caught again if it hadn't been for Tamina."

What? Alfred set aside the cleaned fish and grabbed another. His worried features had softened, a hint of a smile pulling at the corner of his mouth. But Regulus saw Adelaide returning, so he dropped his questions and returned to preparing the fish.

Adelaide sat on the opposite side of the fire. Whether because she didn't want to watch them gut the fish and rabbits or because she wanted space, Regulus wasn't sure. She'd healed the bruise on her cheek, and he wondered if her magic had hidden anything else. Or if, like when the sorcerer tortured him, she had nothing to show for her suffering.

"Adelaide?" Dresden looked up from the rabbit. "Thank you. For saving Regulus." Adelaide nodded, and he tied the second rabbit over the fire, looking uncomfortable. "So. Fiery wings, huh?"

"Fiery wings?" Adelaide frowned and shook her head. "Did I miss something?"

"Wait, you're saying that wasn't on purpose?" Drez whistled. "I don't know if that's better or worse. Either way, it was terrifying."

"Who, me?" Adelaide looked to Regulus, her face drawn and anxious. "What did I do?"

"Ad, you…" Alfred added his fish to the stone. "When you got up…"

"You went all avenging angel," Drez said, settling back on the grass. "With these huge wings of fire at your back and a flaming sword and everything."

"I suppose that's why Nolan ran away as fast as he did." She drew her knees up to her chest and stared at the fire.

Alfred's right, Regulus thought with a stab of shame. Her shoulders hunched forward, her chin tucked behind her knees. Making herself small. A hollow look had settled behind her eyes.

"I barely saw it," Regulus said. He willed her to look at him. "But you looked incredible." She finally lifted her gaze to meet his. "You were incredible."

She bit her lower lip. "I didn't even realize… That seems like a waste of energy."

"Anything that scares your enemy isn't a waste," Alfred said. "It's a tactical advantage."

"So is having a soldier who can't die," Drez said. The suspicion in his voice was impossible to miss. Regulus gave Dresden a look of warning, but Drez was focused on Adelaide. "I can't be more thankful my best friend is alive. But what did you do to him, exactly?"

CHAPTER 26

ADELAIDE WRAPPED HER ARMS AROUND HER LEGS, GLANCING back and forth between Dresden and Regulus. She didn't like the accusation in Dresden's tone. Regulus' eyes widened, then his features hardened.

"We talked about this, Drez."

"You say it's not sorcery, I want to hear from her how she did it and what she did." Dresden didn't take his searching gaze off her for a moment.

The cooking rabbits sizzled, filling the air with savory aroma and making her stomach tighten. She was too tired and too hungry to argue.

"She saved you, and I'm grateful," Dresden said. "But how? She was captured by the sorcerer, who could be controlling her—"

"She doesn't have the mark, Drez!" Regulus sounded on edge.

"We don't know how easy it is for a mage to become a sorcerer," Dresden countered, challenge in his tone. "I won't watch you be a slave all over again! I want proof—"

"I'm not a sorcerer." Adelaide rested her forehead on her knees. "If I were, I wouldn't have..." The memory of Kirven's torture returned, and phantom pain slid over her body.

"Wouldn't have what?" Dresden asked.

"Enough." Father used his commanding officer voice, and Dresden's mouth slammed shut. Father was no poet, but he had his own way with words. "She saved Regulus' life. Why isn't that enough for you?"

"Because the sorcerer saved his life a lot, too." The agitation left Dresden's voice, replaced by resignation. "For two years he tried to earn his freedom or break free in another way. Do you have any idea what it's like for your friend to—" He shot a glance at Regulus. "The point is, I don't want to see him suffer again."

"I would never hurt Regulus." She met Dresden's eyes, hoping he would see the truth in hers. "Surely you know that."

After a moment, Dresden relaxed. "I know you love him. But what if you don't even know what you did? Will you remove it if it harms him? *Can* you remove it?"

"I told you, it's different, Drez." Regulus sighed. "Less one-sided. More like we're both connected to each other. And there's another difference." He held up his hand, showing his palm for some reason. "I cut this hand on a fish scale a little bit ago. It healed almost instantly—and there wasn't a chance of it being fatal. And the healing process didn't hurt."

"Hm." Dresden waved a hand. "But that's tiny. Maybe that's why it didn't hurt."

Regulus picked up the knife he'd used to clean the fish and wiped it off on his pant leg, then stuck it in the fire to finish cleaning it. "Fine. Let's check."

"Regulus!" Adelaide gasped and stood. "Don't you dare!"

"It's a protection enchantment, right?" He looked at her, completely calm.

She did *not* feel calm. "I mean…yes, but I don't know how…or what…"

"Well, if it doesn't work, you can always heal me anyway." Regulus grinned. "Besides, it can be payback for misguided training at the neumenet tree." With that, he plunged the knife into his upper arm.

214

"Regulus, this is—" At the exact moment the knife cut into Regulus' arm, just as he winced, Adelaide grabbed her own upper arm and winced. It wasn't like when he had stabbed her at the neumenet tree. More like an echo or memory of that pain. Still sharp, but not as painful as the real thing. He pulled the knife back out. As his arm healed, the pain in her own arm subsided and a tiny amount of her power left her.

Regulus looked down at his arm and wiped away the bit of blood smeared over his skin and the edges of the hole in his sleeve. "Good as new."

"I…felt that," she whispered.

All three men looked at her.

"What do you mean, you felt it?" Father's brow furrowed.

"Not like actually being stabbed, but a softened version. An echo of the pain."

Regulus looked horrified. "Are you sure?"

Adelaide hesitated. Maybe she *was* just remembering the pain of being stabbed in nearly the same place. She needed to know. "I'm going to turn around, and then you do it again, somewhere else. I don't want to ask you to hurt yourself again, but—"

"Okay," Regulus said, his expression grim.

She turned around. A moment later, something slashed across the back of her right calf. Deep, too, but more of a quick stinging sensation than an actual cut. She grimaced and grabbed at her calf, but it was unharmed. The pain subsided, and she turned back around. Regulus had turned white as the clouds drifting above them. Dresden's mouth hung open. Father's expression was stoic and unreadable.

Regulus looked at her, the blood on the back of his right calf, then back. "That's…no." He shook his head. "No." He stood and charged past Dresden toward her, rolling up his sleeve. "Take it off."

"What?" She drew back. "No!"

"I'm not letting what hurts me hurt you, too." He shoved his arm toward her. "You have to remove it."

"But…" She stared at the mark on his arm, her mind racing. "It's a small amount of pain. And I don't bleed. It's all right—"

"No, it's not!"

"I agree with Regulus," Father said. She shot him a hurt look.

"You said this thing is more two-sided," Dresden said. "So what happens if she gets hurt?" She hadn't thought of that.

Regulus turned toward Dresden. "I don't really care—"

Adelaide snatched the knife out of Regulus' hand and jabbed it into her thigh before Regulus could stop her. She sucked in a breath through clenched teeth. Compared to the pain Kirven had put her through, this was minor. She pulled the knife back out. The wound continued to bleed down her thigh, showing no signs of healing. She tossed the knife toward the fire and held her glowing palm over the throbbing cut until it closed.

"I…didn't feel anything." Regulus sounded ashamed.

"So not completely two-sided then," Dresden said. "But it seems like the benefit is all yours right now, Reg. Which I'll admit doesn't seem like sorcery's methods."

Adelaide glared over Regulus' shoulder. "I told you. I'm not a sorceress."

"So you can't hurt him, or force him to do something—"

"No!" She crossed her arms. "At least…I don't think so."

"It doesn't matter," Regulus said. "I want it off."

"And I don't want you to die!" Tears pricked her eyes. Why couldn't she just be angry without feeling like she was going to cry? She was too tired for this. "Nolan can't die. It's only fair you have the same advantage."

Dresden stood and walked over next to them. "What if you tell him to do something? If he disobeyed the sorcerer, that mark caused him pain."

"I know that," Adelaide snapped. Still, Dresden's worrying was getting to her. "Regulus, Dresden is annoying me. Punch him in the face."

Regulus blinked. "What?"

"Punch him!" She didn't want Regulus and Dresden to fight. She hated it. But she needed to prove to herself Dresden's concerns were unfounded.

"Adelaide…" Regulus rubbed the back of his neck. "I've never laid a hand on Dresden." He winced. "Not by choice, anyway."

Her gut twisted as she remembered that Kirven had made him attack Dresden twice. "Does the mark hurt?"

"What—oh. You were testing…" Regulus half chuckled as relief eased his expression. "No pain. Nothing."

Dresden pursed his lips. "Good. But I still don't like that it works similarly."

"Sorcery is corrupted magic," Father said. "That's hardly surprising." He still sat next to the fire. "But I don't like that you're feeling his pain, either, Adelaide."

"See?" Regulus held his arm up. "Please."

"If it didn't hurt me, would you still want it off?"

Regulus shifted and averted his eyes.

"I thought you agreed it wasn't sorcery?" Her self-assurance faded.

"No! It's not that." Regulus sighed. "No, I wouldn't. I wouldn't care either way, if it stayed or not, so long as I have you. But it *does* hurt you, so I want you to remove it."

"I thought I lost you." Adelaide released a shaky breath, trying to stay in control of her emotions. "I can't—I won't go through that again." She pushed his arm away, his concern hitting her mind as she touched him. "Please."

Regulus looked down at her hands on his arm, then back at her eyes. "Okay." He pulled the sleeve back down.

"And you," she pointed a finger at Dresden. It shook, undermining her anger. "Don't you ever accuse me of sorcery again."

Dresden glanced away, but otherwise looked unapologetic. "Only if you don't do anything sorcerous."

"If I wanted to be a sorcerer, I already would be!" She bit her tongue. She didn't want to talk about this. Not in front of Father. Not to Dresden. She turned toward the fire and sat down. "The fish are burning."

Regulus sat next to her. Dresden and Father turned their attention to the fish while Adelaide stared at the flames. Her own screams echoed in her memory. *Stop thinking about it, stop.* But she imagined Kirven's mocking black eyes in the ash. A weight pressed against her back. Adelaide leapt aside with a short, strangled scream. Everyone froze.

Regulus stared, his mouth hanging open, his hand still suspended midair where he had tried to rest it on her back. To comfort her.

"Sorry," she mumbled. "You startled me."

They ate in silence, but she didn't miss Father's poorly disguised concerned glances or the questioning, pitying looks Dresden sent her way. Regulus sat close, a deep line between his eyebrows. She didn't need their pity. It just made her feel weak all over again.

Full for the first time in what seemed an eternity, Adelaide laid back in the grass and suppressed a yawn. "We need a plan. To stop Kirven."

"You need to rest," Father said. "We can worry about that later."

"We have to warn the king. Kirven mentioned the masque, but the sooner the king is warned, the better." She sat up, even as her mind begged for sleep. "We should leave immediately."

Regulus and Father looked at each other.

"I'm fine." She swallowed a yawn.

"We can leave tomorrow morning," Father said. "That still gives us enough time."

"But—"

"Please, Adelaide," Father pleaded. "Rest. For me."

"So what if I'm a little tired? If it was one of you, you wouldn't wait."

"You're exhausted." Father pointed to himself and Regulus. "And we are, too. We've hardly slept. We could all use the rest." He gave her another look of deep concern. She got the feeling that, somehow, he knew she'd been hurt far worse than a bruised cheek.

"All right." With a huff, she laid back down. It didn't take long for the warm sunlight to lull her to sleep.

When Adelaide opened her eyes, dark pressed around her. Kirven stood over her, his face illuminated by a sickly green glow from the opal in the Staff of Nightfall. She screamed and went to blast him back, but her hands were bound behind her back. *No. No, no…*

She stood and ran, but every leaden step only covered a few inches. Something pulled against her neck and she fell backward. The collar. Oh, Etiros, he put the collar back on. Panic pressed against her lungs. She looked around, frantic, as Kirven moved closer, holding the rope tied to the collar in one hand and the Staff of Nightfall in the other.

"Where's Regulus and my father?" Her voice sounded raspy and weak.

Kirven shook his head. "You cause so much trouble, you and your mercenary. You couldn't just go with Carrick, could you? Couldn't be a good little girl." He pointed the staff to her right. Father was tied to a tree, his mouth gagged and his head hanging forward like he was unconscious.

"Father!" He didn't move. *No...* She tried to stand, but Kirven pushed her down with the end of the staff.

"I promised I would torture your family if you didn't join me." Kirven knelt before her.

Nolan stood behind him, leaning on the pommel of a sword and watching impassively. Blood ran down the blade, soaking into the ground. Some instinct told her it was Regulus' blood. Her heart seemed to stop beating. Kirven squinted, then looked over his shoulder, following her line of sight.

"Oh. He's just waiting his turn." He placed the end of the staff on her chest. Ice spread from the edge of the staff, freezing and burning all at once. She screamed.

"Adelaide!" Kirven shouted. "Adelaide!"

Something gripped her shoulders and shook her. She continued to scream, writhing on the ground.

"Adelaide!" Kirven's voice morphed into Regulus'. "Adelaide, wake up. WAKE UP!"

Adelaide bolted upright and fought free of the hands holding her shoulders and her hand. "Let go!" Her chest heaved as she gasped for air and struggled to bring the faces hovering over her into focus. "Don't hurt me!"

Regulus released her shoulders and sat back on his heels, his expression terrified and pained. Kneeling on her other side, Father released her hand. He looked like he had aged ten years, his face was so drawn. Dresden stopped mid-pace behind Regulus. Faint sunlight still lit the pale blue sky, and the few clouds had an orange tint. No sign of Kirven or Nolan.

"You're safe." Regulus' neck corded. "Just a dream. You're safe. No one's going to hurt you."

"Reg?" Her voice broke on a sob.

"Ad." Regulus pulled her into an embrace.

Adelaide wrapped her arms around him and cried. It didn't matter it was embarrassing. The tears had decided to fall and would not be stemmed. She sobbed into Regulus' chest for several minutes, and her stomach and chest ached when her tears were finally spent.

"I'm sorry," she murmured as she pulled away.

"There's nothing to apologize for," Regulus said.

"For you," Dresden said. Adelaide looked up in confusion. Dresden sighed. "There's nothing you need to apologize for. But…I do." He crossed and uncrossed his arms. "I…shouldn't have doubted you. You've clearly been through a lot. I'm sorry."

She nodded, unable to say anything. Dresden strode away. She pressed a hand to her pounding skull.

"I wouldn't agree to bear the mark again." Waking up screaming like a child felt foolish. Even though she didn't want them to know, she owed them the truth. "Kirven—"

A violent shudder made it difficult to speak as she recalled the pain he had inflicted on her. That he had threatened to inflict on her family. She curled in on herself. Words failed her. How could she tell Father the truth? That she hadn't known a person could experience that much pain and live?

"You don't have to explain." Father knelt beside her and stroked her head. "They'll fade." His voice was barely a whisper. "The memories. The dreams. And the pain. They won't last forever."

He already knew. A sob tightened her throat as she met Father's gaze. "When?" She focused on the love in his eyes and let his calm wash over her.

Father shook his head, still stroking her hair. "I don't know. But they will. I've…been where you are. This feeling of—being broken. It's a lie. You will heal." He kissed the top of her head. "You're so, so strong, my dear. Don't doubt that, all right?"

Adelaide nodded, even though she didn't feel strong. She felt worthless; useless and used. *Broken* seemed right. *It's a lie.* But right now, she didn't know how to heal. How to wait for the memories and the dreams and the pain to fade.

"I think I'll sleep easier when he's dead. When they both are."

Father's lips drew into a hard line. "You don't have to be the one to face them—"

"Yes, I do." She looked down, fiddling with the edge of her tunic. "You don't know what he can do. It's going to take more than some knights to stop him."

Father obviously wanted to argue, but there was nothing he could say. He stood with a sigh. "Your mother will blame me for your insistence on being the hero, but that stubbornness is all her." He patted her head, then walked away.

Regulus rubbed her back. "I wish I could blot out what Kirven did to you," he whispered, his voice hoarse. "I..." His strong arms wrapped around her. Protecting her. Shielding her.

Adelaide leaned against him. "I'm all right."

By the way Regulus tightened his grip on her, like he could hold her tightly enough to press all her broken pieces back together, she knew he didn't believe her.

CHAPTER 27

REGULUS DIDN'T LET HIMSELF SLEEP UNTIL ADELAIDE WAS sound asleep in his arms, which took a while. He didn't care to know the specifics of her nightmare. That she had mumbled for him and her father and then screamed like she was being burned alive was more than enough for his aching heart and guilty conscience.

When she asked him not to leave her side, he swore he wouldn't. He didn't care that Dresden looked amused when he curved his body against Adelaide's back. Or that Alfred tightened his mouth so much his lips turned white when he wrapped his arms around her, and she curled her hands around his forearm. He only cared that Adelaide felt safe, that she slept comfortably, even when his own arms fell asleep.

He was thankful to be the first person awake in the early dawn. During the night, they had shifted. Regulus was on his back, and Adelaide lay on her stomach across his chest, her head resting on his shoulder and her left leg hooked around his left leg. The fingers of her left hand had intertwined with his right. Her heart beat a gentle rhythm against his ribs. A hot stone seemed to burn in his stomach and his skin tingled. He hardly dared to breathe, afraid he'd disturb her slumber.

Birds sang nearby, their chirps competing with the gentle flow of the stream. The air was crisp and cold, more like the beginning of harvest than the end of summer. He stroked Adelaide's unraveling braid, undoing the strands as the sky turned from a dusty pink to a washed-out blue. Green leaves swayed in a breeze that didn't reach the ground, revealing the occasional tinge of yellow and orange.

He smiled, relishing this moment of peace. Adelaide's warmth, the gentle beauty of a new day. This was what he wanted, every day for the rest of his life. Well, maybe inside, on a bed with pillows. A pinch had developed in his neck.

Drez tossed onto his side on the other side of the ash-filled fire pit. More important than Regulus' discomfort, it seemed wise to get up before Alfred. He eased his hand out of Adelaide's, but she stirred as he tried to move out from under her.

"Five more minutes," she mumbled as she wrapped her hands behind his neck.

Regulus chuckled. "You make a compelling argument," he whispered in her ear, "but—"

"Too cold." She turned her head, hiding her face in his shoulder, and mumbled something he couldn't make out.

"Okay, but only to protect you from the cold."

"Good," she said, her voice still heavy with sleep.

A sparrow flitted through the air above him, catching insects. No part of him wanted to get up. He wanted to stay like that forever. Sorcerers and immortal creeps be damned. He put his hands on her waist, thinking he would just pick her up and move her over. Instead his hands developed a mind of their own and moved over her waist, tracing up her back and tangling in her hair. She filled his mind, all other thoughts sinking into blurry shadows.

Adelaide shifted, and he sensed her sleepiness fall away. Her love and desire shot through him, mixing with and heightening his own. Regulus closed his eyes and breathed in, trying to calm his racing heartbeat. She turned her head and her breath slid over his neck. His right hand wandered up and over the back of her neck, her skin warm and soft under his fingertips as he brushed his fingers through her hair. He gripped her waist with his other hand. A flare of anxiety and fear edged into his mind as she tensed. Guilt and sorrow squeezed at his chest and he released her waist and opened his eyes.

A dark shape hovered above him as something hard dug into his side opposite Adelaide. He grunted and Adelaide gasped. Regulus squinted against the light as Alfred bent down and pulled his arms off her back. His face burned like he'd been sitting inches from a roaring fire. Alfred's eyes flashed, his face and neck flushed. Adelaide scrambled off Regulus, her cheeks darkening. Alfred drew his arm back, his hand curled into a white-knuckled fist. But instead of punching him, Alfred reached down, gripped the front of Regulus' shirt, and pulled him up so his mouth was next to Regulus' ear.

"You go too far," Alfred whispered, voice tense. "I won't have you taking advantage of her weakened state. Even without what she's been through, show some restraint." He pulled back so they were eye-to-eye. Regulus' tongue stuck to the roof of his mouth, his fists pressed into the dirt. It took all his courage not to bow his head in submission at the withering look Alfred gave him.

"I'd give you a proper beating instead of just a boot to your side," Alfred said, "but I can't hurt you without hurting her." He shoved hard against Regulus' sternum, pushing him backward.

Adelaide stood with her arms wrapped over her stomach. "Father—"

"No." Alfred pointed at Adelaide. He opened his mouth, shut it again, then dropped his hand. "You're not married to him yet," he said as he strode past.

Regulus rubbed his sternum, wondering if Adelaide had felt that, too. She met his eyes apologetically but didn't look like she felt the throb in his own chest. The dull ache dissipated quickly, however. Points to Adelaide's magic for ensuring he didn't have a bruised side or sternum.

Alfred glared every time their paths crossed while they ate some apples and fish for breakfast and prepared to leave. Dresden had awoken just as Alfred landed a swift kick in Regulus' side, and every time their eyes met, he looked on the brink of laughter.

The sun had breached the horizon when they were ready to depart, their scarce supplies packed up and the horses saddled and bridled. With Zephyr gone, Adelaide headed toward Sieger with Regulus close behind. As she reached for the saddle, Alfred cleared his throat.

"No." Alfred's tone left no room for argument, but that didn't stop Adelaide.

"No, what?"

"You can ride with me, or Regulus can ride with Dresden."

Dresden wrinkled his nose and lifted an eyebrow.

"Fath—"

"Or someone can remain behind." Alfred's glare made Regulus' blood run cold. Adelaide looked to Regulus.

Regulus glowered. "Respectfully—"

"Respect?" He recoiled at the intensity of Alfred's voice. "Respectfully, Lord Hargreaves, you push the limits of propriety with my daughter, and I've had quite enough." Alfred held out his hand. "Ad, let's go."

After a tense moment, Adelaide spun around and mounted Sieger. "Regulus?"

"Uh…" He looked from her to Alfred's red face.

Alfred stalked over and snatched Sieger's reins. "We're not leaving. Not until I am certain you're away from his wandering hands."

Adelaide fidgeted. "Father."

"I apologize for any impropriety," Regulus said, "but I promise—"

"Promises are easily broken when opportunity abounds." Alfred narrowed his eyes. "Your choices are to ride separately, or Regulus can have his hands tied behind his back."

"Father!"

"Final." Father and daughter stared at each other for several moments. Regulus was torn between saying he could ride with Dresden and agreeing to have his hands bound when Adelaide lowered her head, her shoulders slumping.

"Yes, Father." She looked miserable as she went to dismount.

"Wait." Regulus put his hand on her knee, then drew it back as the corner of Alfred's mouth turned down in displeasure. He took a step away from Sieger's side, his face burning. "Sieger is the biggest horse we have. You two can ride him, my lord." He hadn't meant to sound so disappointed, but truthfully, he was.

Alfred nodded, and Regulus mounted Alfred's gray stallion, ignoring the disbelieving judgement in Dresden's eyes. They had enough concerns without making his betrothed's father hate him. As much as he resented Alfred's harsh turn, he understood. Alfred had barely forgiven him for sneaking Adelaide out of Belanger castle. Not to mention that Alfred had to wonder, if Regulus was willing to get that...comfortable with Adelaide with her father a few feet away, how comfortable might they have gotten when they were alone?

It didn't matter the answer was they had been focused on things like not dying or getting kidnapped by fairies and when Adelaide practiced magic she slept like a hibernating bear. Alfred was her father, and if years of managing mercenaries had taught him any-thing, it was that fathers tended to be fiercely, even irrationally, pro-tective of their daughters. Assurances of self-control and respect rarely soothed an outraged father.

They rode in silence. The tension was palpable, making the morning stretch on. Guilt weighed on Regulus' shoulders. He had embarrassed Adelaide and seriously offended her father. Far worse, he had scared her. The sensation of her anxiety had lasted only a moment, but it was enough to sink claws into his heart.

They stopped to eat around noon. Adelaide tied Sieger near a half-dried up brook while Alfred approached him, his face stern.

"Can I trust you for two minutes?"

Regulus ground his teeth. "Yes, my lord."

Alfred wandered off to relieve himself, and Regulus approached Adelaide, although he resisted the urge to touch her.

"I'm sorry," he said quietly.

"Don't be." Her smile both lifted the weight on his shoulders and made the pang in his heart worse. She placed one hand on his chest and touched the ends of his hair with the other.

"I got carried away. And…" He hung his head. "I scared you. I felt it."

Her hand pulled back from his hair, her smile fading. "I'm sorry. I didn't—"

"Hey, you don't have anything to be sorry about. And don't step on my apology." He forced a smile. "I don't ever want to scare you."

Adelaide shook her head. "No, it's not… I'm not afraid of you, Reg. I'm not sure I ever could be. Not after everything." She leaned her cheek on the top of his shoulder while her hand drifted to the side of his neck. "I didn't mean to react like that. It's not your fault."

As her skin touched his, her conflicting emotions skidded over his consciousness. Sorrow. Doubt. Nervousness. Anger. Guilt. Fear. But not of him. His hand fisted at his side. Of Carrick. Regulus closed his eyes and attempted to steady his nerves. Instead, his mind jolted. Shadowy, disjointed glimpses of scenes through Adelaide's eyes flickered behind his closed eyelids.

Carrick leering as he pulled Adelaide toward him out of the stream. Carrick holding her immobile against his chest as he forced a long, rough kiss on her. Adelaide pushing him away, her magic bright against the darkness of the memory. Carrick grabbing Adelaide's waist and thigh and pulling her to him. Regulus experienced her fear, her panic, her hopelessness as Carrick held a dagger to her throat, then changed his mind. Carrick leaned over her, his eyes lustful and expression gloating. Adelaide's remembered terror seeped into Regulus. Carrick's words slipped into his mind, muffled and distorted. *"When Hargreaves is dead... Come crawling... Wish you had given in sooner."*

Regulus stumbled backward, his eyes flying open. His pulse throbbed in his head. The ground tilted. He was aware of Adelaide shouting his name and Dresden running over as he teetered and fell onto all fours, shaking. He pressed his eyes closed against the double image of grass floating in his vision.

"What the hell did you do?" Dresden shouted. "Tell me what you did!"

"I—I didn't! I don't understand—"

"What is going on?" Alfred demanded.

"*She* did something to him!"

"No, I—"

Regulus held up a trembling hand, silencing them as he took several deep breaths. When he finally opened his eyes, the world stayed level. He rocked back onto his heels and wiped his hand across his forehead. He opened his mouth, to tell Adelaide he was okay, to tell Alfred everything was fine, to tell Dresden not to yell at his betrothed. But all that came out was a broken, "Adelaide."

"Regulus?" She wrung her hands.

"I saw," he said hoarsely. "I saw what Carrick did."

Adelaide paled and took a step back. Her jaw quivered as she shook her head. "No...that's not... Oh, Etiros. No."

"I'm so, so sorry, Adelaide. I'm sorry. I'm sorry."

"Stop—stop saying that." Her eyes glistened with unshed tears.

"I…" Regulus slammed his fist into the ground. "I don't know what to do! I don't know what else to say!" He punched the ground again and released a deep-throated scream. "I should never have left you. I failed you, and I'm sorry." A tear raced down the side of his nose while he stared at the grass stuck to his knuckles.

What would she want? For him to listen? To hold her? To leave her alone? He couldn't forget what he saw, what he felt of her emotions. He wanted to help, and he didn't know how.

"Tell me how to make it right." His voice cracked. "Tell me what to do!"

Adelaide knelt in front of him. Her fingers lifted his chin. He wasn't prepared to feel her emotions, but they hit him anyway. Humiliation she had no reason to bear. Grief that struck at his heart like a hammer. Rage that had turned ice cold. And love he didn't deserve.

"Nolan Carrick owes me an apology." The strength in her voice belied the tremor of her lips. "You're not the guilty party."

She placed her hands on his shoulders, then moved them up to the back of his neck, her thumbs rubbing back and forth behind his ears. "You really…" Her lips parted. "You don't think I'm weak. You don't blame me for being afraid."

Regulus pushed her hair out of her face. "I would never. And you're so much stronger than you realize. So much stronger than I am." *I don't know how you're holding together.*

Adelaide laughed through her tears. "Please. Where do you think I'm getting my strength?" She embraced him, her body pressing against his. As he hugged her back and tucked his face into her shoulder, he promised himself that so far as was in his power, he would never leave her alone again.

After a while, she pulled away. "I need to, um…you know. I'll be right back." His hand slipped down her arm as she stood and walked away.

Alfred watched her go, his expression pained. "Did Carrick…" Alfred's neck bulged as he swallowed.

"He kissed her and put his hands on her." Regulus stood, feeling weary, ill, and murderous. "He threatened her. And he…got too close. But no."

"I suppose I should be thankful for that," Alfred said, his voice hollow. "But I'm too angry and heartbroken to care. He violated her mind, if not her body." He met Regulus' eyes. "Carrick has to die."

CHAPTER 28

ADELAIDE WASHED HER FACE IN THE BROOK. THE COOL WATER somehow eased some of the emotional strain. She didn't understand how this bond she had created worked. Why and how had Regulus seen her memories? When she first realized what had happened, she had thought she might either faint or vomit.

Regulus not only knowing but watching what Carrick had done…her failure to stop him… It added to her humiliation. She had feared he would see her as broken and used and worthless as she felt. Yet when she touched him, she sensed no judgment or disappointment. Just understanding, sorrow, and love. And fury.

She splashed water onto the back of her neck and massaged her tight muscles. She had also sensed his pride as he told her she was strong. If only she could agree. Simultaneously wanting Regulus' touch and dreading it didn't feel strong. Neither did the way the involuntary memories of Nolan's assault or Kirven's torture sent her pulse racing. But Regulus and Father looked at her and called her strong.

The gnawing in her stomach drove her back to the others. Dresden intercepted her and held out a handful of fresh-picked black berries.

"We just found them. Over there." He gestured to the left, not meeting her eyes. "They're sweet and refreshing." He pushed his hand out further.

"Oh…thank you." Dresden didn't look at her as she scooped berries out of his hand. Her fingers broke the thin skin on some of them. Purplish-red juices stained her fingertips and the flesh of his palm.

"Listen, I…" Dresden sighed as he closed his fingers around the remaining berries. "I'm sorry for yelling." He scratched his beard. "Reg is…he's my brother. Not by blood, but he's my brother all the same. He's protected me since we were children, and I will always protect him. I nearly lost him, and…" His throat corded.

"You were afraid."

"I can't thank you enough for saving him. But his soul was dying under the sorcerer. I can't watch that again. I can't." Dresden took a deep breath and met her eyes. "I wasn't afraid, I was terrified. If he'd died fighting for you, or if you'd enslaved him, even by accident, it would be my fault. But I shouldn't have doubted you, and I'm sorry."

Adelaide stared. "I forgive you, but…how would it be your fault?"

"Ah, he wouldn't have told you that." A sly smile spread over Dresden's face. He looked over as Regulus approached. "Reg, you didn't tell her my part in enabling your romance, and frankly, I'm offended."

She expected Regulus to scoff and brush Dresden's comment off. Instead, he turned bright red. "Drez—"

"Regulus almost didn't go to the Drummonds' party." Dresden tossed a couple berries into his mouth with a toothy smile. "I talked him into going." He elbowed Regulus. "Forced him to talk to you, too. The frowny-faced coward. Talked him out of giving up on pursuing you several times. Plus, there's our little secret." He winked, much to Adelaide's bewilderment.

"Secret?" Regulus demanded.

"Aw, don't tell me you've forgotten about the pastries." Dresden arched a brow.

Pastries? The nalotavi. Regulus' sweet and slightly ridiculous note. Dresden's postscript confiding that Regulus thought he had thrown that note away in favor of a more restrained message, but Dresden had thought she'd like that one better.

Adelaide smiled, then giggled. Regulus looked affronted, which for some reason made her laugh more. All her stress welled up and bubbled out of her in gut-squeezing, shoulder-shaking laughter.

"You were right, you know," she wheezed, her hand pressed against her stomach. "It was sweet; and I liked it."

"See?" Dresden slapped Regulus' shoulder. "I always have your back."

She wiped a tear from the corner of her eye while Dresden sauntered away. Her laughter died out, but her smile remained. Especially as Regulus watched her with a deep crease between his eyebrows and an expression like a lost puppy.

"Dresden exchanged the letters you wrote when you sent me the nalotavi." She slipped her hand into his. "He wrote at the bottom he thought the original was more honest."

"Oh, great." Regulus' embarrassment crept into her mind through their connection. "Just…excellent."

Adelaide giggled and leaned against his shoulder. "I liked it. In fact, I hope you don't stop writing me sentimental letters when we're married. Or giving me nalotavi."

"Marry me and I'll ask Sarah to bake you nalotavi every day if you want."

"You do know how to charm a girl." She kissed him as his abashed delight traveled through their bond.

Dresden hadn't lied—the berries were ripe and juicy. They walked hand-in-hand over to the horses. Father handed her some leftover cold fish. He looked calmer than when she left, but she still caught the flicker of pained worry in his eyes. They ate quickly and prepared to continue their journey.

Adelaide planted a kiss on Regulus' cheek while Father's back was turned before mounting Sieger. Regulus moved toward Father's horse, but Father stepped up to the stallion's side and mounted before Regulus could. Regulus stood stock-still. He gave her a helpless, confused look.

Father looked down at Regulus. "Don't stand there. We don't have all day, and I doubt you'll keep up long on foot." He turned his horse toward the road.

Relief and joy washed over Adelaide. Regulus turned toward her, looking unsure. With a grin, she motioned him over with her head. He cast one more look at Father riding in the direction of the road, then jogged to Sieger's side.

Once he settled into place behind her, he plucked the reins out of her hands. His torso bumped against her back as he whispered in her ear, "Can—would you mind...if I kiss your forehead?"

She didn't know if she wanted to laugh or cry, the gentleness in his voice almost too much to bear. Unable to force a response past her tied tongue, she nodded. His lips pressed against her temple. With the contact of their skin, Regulus' love and desire to protect her sank into Adelaide like an ache. He leaned back and prodded Sieger to follow Father.

The rest of the day passed more comfortably, with Regulus' arms around her while they rode. After they stopped for the night, it didn't take her long to fall asleep, tucked against Regulus' side.

The next morning passed in the same manner, but in the early afternoon they crested a hill and Adelaide's mouth fell open like her jaw had unhinged. The rolling green hills continued before them, but beyond, stretching into what seemed like an eternity, was an expanse of glittering deep blue. A cool, salty breeze tugged at her hair.

"Is…is that…?"

"The Ismuire Sea," Father said.

She leaned back against Regulus, staring. The expanse of the water beckoned her. When Adelaide was little, she had told Mother she wanted to visit Khastalland. Mother had asked if she wanted to go by land or sea. She had said she didn't care, she just wanted to see all the places in Mother's stories.

But as Adelaide looked across the lush hills at the water glittering like diamonds and sapphires, she wanted the sea. She wanted to touch the sea, to step in it and see what it felt like. To sail out into it until the land disappeared from view. She wanted to know the sea and find out if it would accept her.

They rode to a path that followed the coast. As they neared the water's edge, the sound of the sea built. She had always assumed the sea would sound like a river, but somehow bigger. It was nothing like a river.

The water pushed and pulled at the shore, the rushing swoosh of the waves building until they fizzled out before receding and smashing against a new, incoming wave. Stones along the shore clacked against each other as waves moved over them, making the water whisper. The rhythmic rustle and crash of the waves held a melodic beauty that would make a musician envious, with an unpredictable wildness that was both exciting and alarming. White-crested waves broke along the shore, bubbling and swirling between massive boulders as the sea breathed.

Regulus placed his hand on top of hers. She sensed his curiosity, then his amusement as he said, "It is incredible, and beautiful. I can't believe you've never been to the sea." He removed his hand. "Dangerous, too."

Sir Ruddard had told Adelaide and Minerva about the one time he traveled on the sea. It was a favorite story of his, because he got to dramatize how close he was to death in an abrupt, terrible storm.

He always insisted he saw mermaids that day. Or maybe sirens, he would say. The howling wind sounded too much like singing for his comfort.

The sea passed in and out of sight as the trail wound through pines and birch trees and across gentle valleys and hills. They entered a grassy valley with a stream running through it that emptied into the sea. Between two protruding rock cliff-faces topped with pines, a sand and pebble beach surrounded the stream's outlet.

"I think we need a quick break," Regulus said, turning Sieger toward the sea. She looked at him over her shoulder. His eyes danced. "I don't need the bond to know what you want. Your entire body is straining toward the sea."

"We're nearly to the city," Father protested, but Regulus followed the stream, urging Sieger to a canter.

Adelaide couldn't suppress her giggle. Regulus halted Sieger at the edge of the beach and hopped down. He reached toward her waist, then paused, his concern reflected in his eyes. *Oh, Etiros, I love him.* She grabbed his hands and guided them to her waist. He smiled, his scar pulling one side of his upper lip higher in that lopsided way she loved, and lifted her off Sieger's back and set her on the ground.

She pulled off her boots and pushed her trousers up to her knees. The water was colder than it looked, but not unpleasant. Careful not to slip on the loose pebbles, Adelaide waded into the sea. The waves, smaller here in this protected little beach, pushed and pulled on her legs, messing with her balance. She continued until the water was sloshing onto her thighs, soaking her trousers. A receding wave pulled a pebble out from under her foot and her arms pin-wheeled as she leaned to the side.

Regulus caught her arm, steadying her. She grinned up at him. His loose black hair swayed in the sea breeze as he laughed, rich and deep. The sunlight reflected off the rippling water, flickering over his face and making his light gray eyes sparkle. He was so attractive it made her heart physically hurt.

His eyes met hers, his hands still holding her arm to keep her steady. She didn't need the bond to tell her what he was feeling. She felt it too. The sound of the waves filled her mind, soothing her nerves. She turned toward him. Before Adelaide could even raise her lips to his, Regulus' arms wrapped around her and he lifted her into the air. She leaned over him, cradled his face in her hands, and kissed him like she had been waiting her whole life for his salty kiss.

CHAPTER 29

SOMETHING SLAMMED INTO REGULUS' RIBS, JOLTING HIM awake. He reached for his sword as the shapes in the shabby inn room clarified in the dark. The beds where Alfred and Drez were sound asleep, the hole-ridden curtain over the discolored glass window, and the table and two chairs beneath it. Satisfied it was just Adelaide's elbow that had awoken him, he set the sword back down on the rough wooden floorboards.

The old inn wasn't pretty, and the flat, straw-stuffed mattresses stank of body odor. The thin wool blankets itched. But it was indoors and boasted one of the cleanest taverns Regulus had seen. Rain had started shortly before they arrived at the royal town of Crelburgh at dusk, and they had arrived exhausted. Anything was better than sleeping in the rain.

Adelaide shifted beside him. "Won't." He squinted at her in the feeble light. She curled into a ball, her eyes squeezed shut. "No." She tossed over on her back and kicked his knee.

"Ad?"

"Please," she whimpered, her eyes still closed.

Oh. A deep heaviness settled into his chest. He gently shook her shoulder. "Wake up. Come on, wake up."

"Leave him alone," Adelaide mumbled. Her terror tickled his mind as he touched the bare skin of her arms.

Regulus sighed and closed his eyes, trying not to panic. Instead, his panic increased when her nightmare leapt into his mind. Figures stood outlined in eerie green light as he looked out of Adelaide's eyes.

A rope bound Adelaide's hands together, the palms against each other, and disappeared into the darkness. The sorcerer stood before her, both hands gripping the Staff of Nightfall. Carrick stood next to him, one hand on Alfred's shoulder, the other on Tamina's shoulder. Alfred and Tamina knelt with their wrists chained.

"I made you a promise, mage." The sorcerer extended the staff toward Alfred.

"No! It's not their fault! You can't do this!" Adelaide lunged toward her parents, but something caught on her neck and yanked her backward. "You're not king yet." Desperation rang in her voice as she stared at the tip of the staff hovering over her father's chest. "You said after you were king!"

"I *am* king."

Adelaide's eyes flicked up to the sorcerer. To the crown on his head that hadn't been there a moment before. "No. No!"

Regulus forced his eyes open and the nightmare vanished. "Adelaide! You have to wake up." He shook her, but she didn't open her eyes. "Wake. Up!"

Her eyes opened wide, the whites stark in the darkness. She grabbed his arms and her fingers dug through his sleeves as she looked around.

"Hey, it's okay. You're safe. Your father and mother are safe. The sorcerer and Carrick aren't here."

Her face relaxed and she leaned into him. He stroked her back, her chest heaving.

"Wha goin' on?" Alfred mumbled.

"Nightmare," Regulus said. "You can go back to sleep."

Alfred mumbled something, and a few moments later, his breathing deepened again.

"Wait." Adelaide pulled back to look into his face. "My parents?" She bit her lip. "Did you…see my dream?"

"I closed my eyes while touching you. I didn't mean to," he added, hoping she wasn't offended. "It just happened." She didn't respond. "Do you want to talk?"

She shook her head.

"Okay." He wrapped his arms around her. He could feel her heart still racing. "If you change your mind, I'm here." He held her while her breathing and heartrate slowed and wished he could do something more.

"Kirven…" Adelaide's voice was barely a whisper. "He promised to torture my family in front of me until they went mad from the pain. And you. But not until after he's king, so I thought we could stop him. But… I don't know if we can."

His fingers brushed against her bare arm. The fear and hopelessness he sensed seemed so unlike the woman who just a couple weeks ago looked at him and said she would help free him. Who said if the sorcerer went back on his word, they would find another way together. She had been through so much, and it made his heart feel squeezed and hung out to dry.

"I'm not giving up." Regulus rubbed her back. "You have endured so much. Don't give up now."

She nestled closer to his chest. "It's just…hard."

"I know." *Etiros knows just how much.*

Adelaide reached under his right sleeve and her fingers rubbed the scars from his attempts to remove the sorcerer's mark. "How did you stay strong and keep hope for two years?"

"I didn't." He sighed. "Dresden wouldn't let me give up. He…"

Honesty. He needed to be honest. He had seen all Adelaide's fears, all her pain. He couldn't hide his from her. Maybe it would help, somehow, to know she wasn't alone.

"Shortly after I took the oath, I refused to rob a cathedral. The sorcerer…if he'd maintained control a few seconds longer, I would have murdered Dresden. Harold barely escaped, too." Regulus gulped against the lump lodged in his throat. "I went to the cathedral after that. Killed an innocent monk. While I was gone, Dresden somehow convinced Harold to stay. Later, Dresden found me after I tried to cut out the mark, and when that failed repeatedly, tried…" His mouth felt dry. "I tried…"

His throat closed as the locked-away memory came crashing back, along with the recollection of his pain. His wretched hopelessness, fear, and self-loathing.

"Please, Drez."

"I won't. Don't ask me to."

"I've tried everything else! I—I need you to behead me. Please. Please."

Dresden had taken Regulus' bloody sword and tossed it aside. Bits and pieces of what Dresden had said echoed in his mind. *"This isn't how you win. I'll help, Regulus, I promise. This is temporary. You're more than your failures, mistakes, your worst moments, or the sorcerer's actions. You can't leave me. I'm not abandoning you. You're my friend, my brother. The world is a better place because of Regulus Hargreaves, and I won't see the world become worse by losing you."*

Adelaide sucked in a breath and pulled away, but before her skin left his, he sensed it wasn't out of shock or disgust. She simply couldn't bear feeling his emotions.

"Reg…" She clapped her hand over her mouth and looked toward Dresden. "I didn't mean to…" Her voice was jagged and raw, and a hint of moonlight caught in the silent tears on her cheeks.

Oh. No. "You…saw?" He wiped away his own tears.

She threw her arms around him. "I'm sorry."

Regulus now understood how horrified Adelaide had been when he accidentally spied on Carrick's attack. The realization she had not only seen him at his lowest and most vulnerable, but lived his memory of it, crushed him. But Adelaide didn't turn away. He leaned into her embrace, but avoided touching his skin to hers, careful not to flood her with his emotions again.

"I lost hope," he said past his tight vocal cords. "I saw no way forward, and the guilt…"

She rubbed his back and arms and moved closer against his chest. Comforting and accepting him as his emotions choked him. Her unflinching love soothed his battered heart.

"But Drez didn't abandon me or judge me," he continued quietly. "He never stopped believing in me. He was always nudging me forward, insisting I keep living my life like it was normal, because it would be someday. He came up with a mantra to ground me when my thoughts got too dark. And he got me Magnus. To 'give me a reason to leave my room.'" *Which did help, actually.*

Regulus shifted. Part of him felt exposed and ridiculous. Part of him was relieved to tell her, to talk about it.

"I'm glad you have him," Adelaide whispered.

"Me too." He licked his lips. They still tasted salty from the afternoon of sea breezes. "No one is strong all the time, Ad. Even tigers run from fire and hunters." He kissed her hair. "That's why we all need each other. I thought I was being strong by separating myself and putting up walls. I thought I was protecting my friends. But Dresden was right. Being a lone wolf made me weaker, not stronger, and only hurt the people I care about."

Adelaide squeezed him tighter.

"I don't expect you to be fearless." Regulus stroked her hair. "But I hope you'll stand with me and try to do what's right. Together."

After a moment, she responded. "Thank you. For being honest." She felt for his hand in the dark and gripped it, and her determination, heartache, and love poured into him. "I think I can manage together."

CHAPTER 30

IN THE MORNING THEY ORDERED A TUB OF HOT WATER brought to their room. Alfred gave Adelaide coin to purchase new clothes for herself and Regulus while the men washed up. Even though Regulus had argued against Dresden and Alfred coming to rescue Adelaide, he was thankful they had insisted. Thankful to have Dresden, and thankful Alfred had had the foresight to pack a good amount of coin.

He wished he had the rest of his men with him, too, but it was better this way. Safer to travel in a smaller group. Better that he hadn't endangered their lives any further. And comforting to know Caleb and Perceval had stayed to help protect Belanger castle while Jerrick and Estevan had returned home to keep an eye on Arrano.

Regulus was scrubbing his back when someone knocked at the door. Dresden, his hair still dripping, finished fastening his trousers and threw the door open. Adelaide's eyes widened and her face turned dark red as she looked from Drez's bare chest to Regulus sitting in the wooden tub to the ceiling. Regulus tensed, his skin on fire even as a traitorous grin pulled at his lips. She shoved a pile of clothes against Dresden's chest and spun away.

Alfred slammed the door closed, one boot half laced. "Do you have a brain, man?"

Drez laughed. "I'm not sure which surprised her more, Reg. My excellent olive-skinned physique and masculine chest hair, or the fact you're naked."

Alfred whacked the back of Drez's head and stomped back to his bed to finish putting on his boots. Drez held the bundle of clothes with one hand and rubbed the back of his head with the other. He mouthed "ow" to Regulus as he dropped the clothes onto a bed.

"This should look fetching on you, Reg." Dresden held up a deep green dress.

"That's clearly Adelaide's, you egotistical bearded nit-wit."

Drez laid the dress out on the other bed before he finished dressing. Once Regulus had shaved and dressed in the new clothes—a pair of black trousers that were a touch tight, a blue tunic, and a black belt—the men left the room. The inn's staff changed out the water for fresh heated water, and Adelaide went in to get cleaned up. Alfred stood watch outside the door while Regulus and Dresden got food and drink from the tavern on the ground floor of the three-story wooden building.

The vegetables were mush and flavorless, but the bread was fresh and the mead decent. They got more than a few stares and curious glances. Regulus' scar and Dresden's Carasian complexion and nose often drew attention, so it wasn't new.

Regulus and Drez split up, talking to other tavern guests and fishing for information about if anyone had seen or heard anything about the sorcerer or Carrick. People either didn't care to talk or didn't know anything. Regulus intimidated the barmaid, judging by the way she kept looking at him then away, and she seemed suspicious of poor Drez.

Accordingly, they hadn't discovered anything when Alfred came down the creaky stairs with Adelaide. She looked lighter, as if some of her turmoil and pain had washed off with the dirt and grime. Her dark green dress brushed the floor. Fitted sleeves covered her arms, but the wide neck left the tops of her shoulders bare. A silver cord tied around her hips hung down the front of the dress, swinging as she walked. She had pulled her hair into a thick braid that cascaded over her shoulder.

Drez nudged Regulus' arm with his elbow. "Stop gawking."

Adelaide swept across the floor and kissed Regulus' cheek. "You can gawk if you like, *piahre*." She stepped back to look him up and down with an appreciative smirk. "So long as you don't mind me gawking in return." It was difficult to restrain himself from kissing her in front of a tavern full of strangers.

The entire time Alfred and Adelaide ate, Regulus was acutely aware of the stares Adelaide received. Ladies didn't frequent inns or taverns, so the patrons' curiosity wasn't surprising, but it put Regulus on edge. Especially the roving looks some of the more disreputable-looking men gave her.

The moment Adelaide and Alfred finished eating, Regulus rushed them out the door. They rode to the towering palace walls, where Alfred gave the guards his name and showed them his ring with his rearing unicorn crest. One of the guards led them inside the walls.

Compared to the palace gardens, the garden in Arrano's court-yard was a peasant's bean field. Trees Regulus had never seen within Monparth's borders stretched toward the sky. Flowers in every color and shape with strong fragrances bloomed amid all the greenery that grew along winding paths of white stone. They passed three marble fountains, one with a woman pouring water from a jar over her nude body, another of three leaping dolphins, and one of a crane with its long neck extended into the air and water shooting out of its beak.

He glimpsed a chapel between the trees that looked more like a miniature cathedral with its high arches. White plaster covered the walls of the palace so that they shone in the light, even with the partial cloud cover.

The guard spoke to a servant who led them inside the palace. Rose marble bannisters curved next to granite steps covered with a long red carpet. The servant didn't lead them up the steps, instead turning into a narrow hall to the right that ran through several rooms. Tall stained-glass windows of nature scenes, knights, ladies, and magical creatures illuminated each room. They walked through the first few rooms too quickly for Regulus to register anything other than each room appearing to have a specific color scheme and lots of opulence. Another red carpet ran down the length of the hall, through all the open doors.

The servant left them in a room with several plush armchairs upholstered in turquoise with bronze legs. A rug embroidered with a floral pattern covered the floor and a tapestry of a stag hunt covered most of the long wall opposite the windows, except for a plain door. A rose marble fireplace nestled in the wall to their right, a mantle held over it by two bronze statues of kneeling women in gauzy dresses. A huge painting of a noblewoman with rosy cheeks and a small dog at her feet hung on the wall opposite the fireplace.

Alfred sat in one of the chairs and Adelaide followed his lead, but Regulus felt awkward in all the finery and just stood near the empty fireplace with his hands clasped behind his back. Dresden was apparently fascinated by the tapestry and stood squinting at it.

After several minutes that dragged on, the door next to the tapestry opened. A thin, tall man in a deep blue doublet with silver embroidery on his belt, cuffs, and boots entered. He bowed as Alfred stood.

"Lord Belanger. I am His Excellency's steward, Sir Michael." Sir Michael clasped his hands in front of him. "I am told you are asking for an audience with His Excellency?"

"That is correct, Sir Michael." Alfred bowed, but not as deeply. "I am afraid I come bearing grave news. It is a matter of life and death that I speak to His Excellency immediately."

"Life and death?" Sir Michael raised an eyebrow. "Perhaps if I had more information—"

"The king's life is in danger," Alfred said, his tone sharp. "If you tell him I said so, I am certain he will want to speak with me. I *must* speak to him directly."

Sir Michael looked uncertain. "His Excellency is quite busy. But I will pass on your message and see what the king would like to do." He left, the door clicking shut behind him.

Adelaide sat on her hands and swung her legs. "Well. I don't think we'd have gotten an audience with the king on our own, Regulus."

"Seems that way." Regulus pursed his lips. "Do you think he will listen?"

Alfred sat back down. "Yes."

They waited for an hour. When Sir Michael returned, he threw the door open. Sweat glistened on his forehead as he motioned them through the doorway. "His Excellency will see you immediately."

Regulus and Dresden looked at each other. Maybe he shouldn't be surprised. Alfred had nearly given his life for the king's father, after all.

Sir Michael rushed them down hallways with paintings of royals and showed them into a small room with no furniture save for an empty small wooden throne with red cushions. After collecting their weapons, the steward left them, closing the door behind him. Against the throne leaned a sword with a gold hilt formed in the shape of a dragon's head in a scabbard of gold, ivory, and onyx.

Behind the throne, a floor-to-ceiling clear glass window illuminated the room. The fireplace to their right had a gold mantle supported by statues of gold dogs. A door opposite the fireplace opened and the man from the portrait Alfred had shown them walked in.

The king, like his brother, was short. No silver had yet touched his short brown beard. A simple gold crown sat on his head, holding his long brown hair in place. He wore a crimson cloak with gold edging over a black doublet embroidered in gold and black hose. Every finger bore a ring. Gold embroidered his belt and gold buckles shone on his boots.

Alfred dropped to one knee and bowed, and Dresden and Regulus did the same behind him while Adelaide curtsied low.

The door closed behind King Gawain as he walked to the throne. "Rise, Lord Belanger and companions." Regulus waited for Alfred to stand first. The king sat down. "We are glad to see you, old friend."

Alfred inclined his head. "I wish it were under better circumstances, Your Excellency."

"Yes. Our steward told us you fear for our life." The king rested his chin on his fist. "Explain."

"Your brother is alive, Your Excellency. He has obtained a powerful magical weapon and plans to kill you at your birthday masque."

King Gawain paled and leaned back in the throne. When he spoke, his voice was quiet and tense. "How do you know this?"

"My daughter and her betrothed have met him." Alfred gestured back toward them. "And he told my daughter as much."

The king shifted his piercing gaze to Regulus, then Adelaide. "Kirven told you his identity and plans?"

Adelaide offered another small curtsy. "Yes, Your Excellency."

"And how did you come into contact with a sorcerer?" The suspicion in the king's voice made Regulus wince. He stepped forward and bowed.

"Your Excellency, she met him because of me."

The king raised an eyebrow. "And you are?"

"Lord Regulus Hargreaves of Arrano, Your Excellency. And for two years, I served the sor—Prince Kirven."

King Gawain's expression turned cold. "He was stripped of his title."

Regulus bowed his head. "He still fancies himself a prince. He did not tell me his name, but he called himself the Prince of Shadow and Ash."

The king's eyes widened, but he quickly recovered. "You served him? Why?"

"To save my men's lives, Your Excellency."

"And how did Lady Belanger meet him?"

Regulus winced. He knew this would come up, but it didn't make it any easier. He glanced to Adelaide. "He needed a mage. He demanded I bring Adelaide to him to help recover a relic." His collar suddenly felt itchy. "The last piece he needed to re-forge a powerful weapon, the Staff of Nightfall."

"You are certain?" The king leaned forward, gripping the arms of his throne. "He has the Staff of Nightfall?"

"You've heard of it?" Alfred asked.

"Rumors. I thought it was a myth." Regulus noted Gawain's abandoning of the royal we. The king dragged a trembling hand across his brow and his eyes shot over to Adelaide. "Wait. A mage? You're a mage?"

"Yes, Your Excellency."

"Prove it."

Adelaide held her fist out in front of her, her palm glowing a faint cerulean while she conjured a sword of blue-white light. The light sword vanished as she dropped her hand.

"Your name is Adelaide?" The king asked. She nodded. "Approach us, Adelaide." Adelaide approached, her footsteps hesitant. "Kneel."

She knelt, and the king stood and drew the dragon sword. Adelaide's hands shook at her sides. Regulus reached for his own sword, but his scabbard hung empty and useless at his side. He stepped forward. Alfred stopped him with an arm against his chest. He looked at Alfred, panic clawing at his heart. Alfred shook his head, but his features were drawn and afraid.

"Lady Adelaide Belanger, as your king, we request that you join our personal guard," King Gawain said solemnly. "We ask that you live and die to protect us. Do you agree?"

Wait, what! Regulus' mouth fell open.

Adelaide looked up at the king. "I…"

"Your king requests it," the king repeated with a stern expression. "Will you heed our call?" With a sinking feeling, Regulus understood. It was not a request.

"Yes, Your Excellency." Adelaide's voice quivered.

The king nodded. "Very good. Please repeat these words. I, Adelaide Belanger."

"I, Adelaide Belanger."

Regulus wanted to intervene. To pull Adelaide to her feet and tell the king he couldn't force her into his service. But to do so would be treason. His hands fisted. The king continued, Adelaide repeating each line.

"Swear to uphold the laws of Monparth, and to serve my king and the royal family. My will and aim are now and forevermore to serve and protect the king."

Adelaide swallowed, stumbling over the words.

An ache settled behind Regulus' forehead. He was going to lose her. What if the king wouldn't permit them to marry? What if he couldn't even see her?

"I swear before the king, before Etiros, and before those gathered here," the king continued, Adelaide repeating. "That I will give my life and death to protect the king of Monparth."

Her shoulders dipped as she repeated the oath.

"Until my death or the king's word release me."

"Until…" Adelaide took a shaky breath and Regulus' heart snapped in half. "Until my death or the king's word release me."

King Gawain raised the sword. Only now did Regulus notice the gold script running down the length of the blade, but he couldn't make out the words. The king touched the sword to Adelaide's shoulder. "We hold you to your vow, Lady Adelaide Belanger, member of the royal guard and shield to the king." He sheathed the sword and let it fall against the side of the throne. "Arise, Lady Belanger."

Adelaide stood and moved back. She glanced toward Regulus and Alfred, her eyes big as a frightened deer's. This wasn't how this was supposed to go.

The king looked to Alfred as he sat back down. "Thank you, Alfred." Then he looked at Regulus. "Lord Hargreaves. You spent two years in Kirven's service. Any information you can give is desired."

Regulus had to clear his throat before speaking. Anger at the king's selfishness flared hot on his skin. King Gawain hadn't given Adelaide any more of a choice in serving him than Kirven had given Regulus. "He was secretive and told me only what was necessary to fulfill his commands."

"Why for two years?" The king strummed his fingers against the arm of his chair. "You said you served him to save your men. Did he capture them?"

"No…well, yes. He threatened their lives but released them when I agreed to serve him."

"And you continued to serve him because…"

Because, like you, he puts people in agreements they can't get out of. "He put a mark on my arm that bound me to him. It caused me great pain if I did not obey. And he could use it to control me. To force me to hurt my men. After he received the last piece of the staff, he released me for payment of the life-debt he claimed I owed him."

"A mark?" The king leaned forward, curiosity in his expression. "Where? Show us."

Regulus shook his head. "It disappeared when he released me, Your Excellency."

"Hm. So no proof, then. Your story seems questionable. We wonder if we can trust you, Lord Hargreaves."

Alfred answered first. "I assure you, Your Excellency, he is honest and loyal."

"I have the scars to prove my *story*, Your Excellency." Regulus hesitated. According to the laws of Monparth, he owed the king his allegiance and thus his complete cooperation and honesty. Even if he didn't believe he owed this self-absorbed monarch anything. "And…I have another mark. One put there by Adelaide's magic. It is different, but—"

"Show us."

Reluctantly, he stepped forward and rolled up his sleeve. The king inspected the mark.

"Interesting. What is its purpose?"

"Protection and healing," Adelaide said. "He was dying from a fatal stomach wound inflicted on him by Kirven's lackey, Nolan Carrick. It was the only way to save him."

"Carrick? The baron's son?" The king frowned when Adelaide and Regulus nodded. "Troubling news indeed. Is the baron aware?"

"We do not believe so, Your Excellency," Alfred said. "But I cannot say without a doubt." The king stroked his beard.

The seconds dragged on while the king stared into the distance. Regulus rolled his sleeve down and stepped back, thinking about how underdressed and out of place he was amidst all the gold and splendor of the private audience chamber. It made him once again feel like a fake. A mercenary pretending to be a lord.

As if he suddenly remembered they were still in the room, the king looked back at Regulus. "Protection and healing? What does that mean?"

Regulus didn't want to answer, but when the king asked a question, you answered, and you told the truth. "If I'm hurt, I heal. When I had the sor—Kirven's mark, I couldn't die. I don't know if that's the case with Adelaide's, but it seems likely. I also have noted some increased strength."

The king tilted his head. "Indeed. Lord Hargreaves." By the glint in the king's eye, Regulus knew what he would say before he said it. Resentment surged. "As your king, we request that you join our personal guard. We ask that you live and die to protect us. Do you agree?"

Regulus stiffened, his jaw clenching. So this would be his lot. He would exchange servitude from one brother to the other. One thing comforted him as he knelt before the king. At least he would be with Adelaide. He met the king's eyes as he knelt, not caring if the king saw his fury. "I agree, Your Excellency."

CHAPTER 31

THEY SPENT THE NEXT HOUR AND A HALF IN THE KING'S audience room answering his questions and telling him everything they knew about Kirven, Nolan, and their plans. Which wasn't much. Adelaide's feet and lower back ached from standing. Regulus had looked even more unhappy about being drafted into the royal guard than she felt. At least the king hadn't taken his title. King Gawain had explained Regulus would be Lord of Arrano in name, but so long as he was in the guard, his position as a guard trumped any other responsibility or title. But he had been demoted from the nobility in practice, if not on parchment. It was completely unfair.

The king had asked Dresden what his story was, and his curt response of, "I'm a mercenary. I'm just an armed escort, Your Majesty," did not impress the king. Adelaide suspected that was purposeful. A way of avoiding the fate that had befallen her and Regulus.

When King Gawain was satisfied that they could give no further information, he left them with instructions to wait for a servant to escort them out.

Father's perfect posture crumpled the moment the door closed. He rubbed his temples. "I'm sorry. I didn't think—you're a *woman*. I thought he might ask for your help, or accept if you offered, but I never… I would have had you both wait in town if I had known. I'm sorry." His brows pinched as his eyes filled with worry and sorrow.

"Self-righteous, egotistical, arrogant…" Regulus threw out a few less savory words.

"Someone could hear you," Adelaide hissed.

"Let them." Regulus crossed his arms. "I'll do what I swore. But I never swore to be happy about it or act grateful to be made a slave all over again."

"You'll be paid," Father said, his voice weary. "That's technically not slavery."

"Who cares about technicalities," Dresden muttered.

"It's also not my choice." Regulus turned and looked at Adelaide, a wretched sadness undercutting the rage in his eyes. "Can I even marry you now? Is that allowed?"

She couldn't believe that hadn't occurred to her. She had been too surprised by the king's non-request, too frightened and confused by the sudden change in her life trajectory to think through all the consequences. Then getting through the questions about Nolan and Kirven had reopened her emotional scars, especially when she had to admit to Kirven torturing her. At least she hadn't been forced to talk about Nolan's intentions. Regulus and Father had avoided the issue, and she had been more than happy to do the same.

"Royal guards are permitted to marry, although they rarely do." Father shook his head. "Marriage can present difficulties when you're required to live in the palace with the other guards. But…surely the king doesn't expect Adelaide to live in the barracks." She didn't like the uncertainty on his face.

"Out of the question," Regulus said. "You seem to know a decent amount about this. The vows mentioned the king could release us. How often does that happen?"

The pained look Father gave her nearly made her sick. Adelaide leaned against the golden fireplace mantel, fighting a bout of dizziness. Regulus rushed to her side and slipped his arm around her waist.

"There are typically two reasons a royal guard is released from service." Father spoke slowly. "Old age or injury that renders the guard unable to perform his duties."

Dresden cursed, and Father cast him a disapproving scowl.

"This isn't fair," Regulus protested. She didn't need to touch his skin to detect his fury. "He's using us! Just like—"

"Enough," Father interrupted with finality. "What's done is done. Perhaps once Kirven is defeated, the king will release you. There have been instances of kings releasing guards from their service with a generous pension for service beyond the normal purview of the royal guard."

A small spark of hope ignited in Adelaide's soul. "Really? When? Recently?"

"King Gawain has never done so, but his father did, once."

"Oh." Regulus sounded like something had clicked in his mind. Like he finally understood something she still couldn't even see.

"Oh, what?"

Father sighed. "Adelaide... You know I don't like talking about the war." She stared at him, uncomprehending. "I knew what the king wanted as soon as he asked you to kneel and drew that sword. Because King Olfan did the same thing to me."

"You...were a royal guard?" He was a warrior, everyone said. A general.

"For a time, yes. I paid for my release with my blood." His eyes filled with sorrow, pity, and pain. Her heart twisted. "It was only afterward that I led his armies."

She leaned against Regulus. Why was Father being so vague? "I don't—"

The door they had entered through opened. A young woman entered wearing a simple black dress, her hair drawn back in a bun, accompanied by a boy holding Regulus, Father's, and Dresden's swords.

A middle-aged man with red-blond hair and a powerful build followed just behind them. A red sash hung across his chest over a cobalt coat with brass buttons. The man turned toward her and Regulus.

"Lady Belanger and Lord Hargreaves of Arrano?"

They answered in the affirmative. Regulus removed his arm from her waist so he could bow, and she could curtsy.

"I am Captain Russell of His Excellency's Royal Guard." Captain Russell inclined his head toward them. "Welcome to the guard. Come with me."

The woman curtsied toward Father and Dresden. "If you will please follow me, my lords, I will escort you out of the palace."

Panic gripped Adelaide's chest. Wait, this…was goodbye? Regulus took his sword from the page while Adelaide walked to Father.

"I…" The sudden fear she would never see him again cracked down her sternum. "I—"

"Disobedience and tardiness are not tolerated in the Royal Guard regardless of your gender, Belanger," Russell barked.

She gulped back her fear. "I love you, Father." She hugged him tightly. His returned embrace nearly squeezed the air out of her lungs. She held on longer than she should have, but she couldn't bring herself to let go. Neither, apparently, could Father.

"I love you, too," Father whispered. "My brave daughter, my *shiraa*." He kissed the top of her head. "It's going to be all right." She clutched the back of his shirt.

Russell cleared his throat. "I'm not accustomed to being kept waiting, Belanger. This is your last warning."

She let Father go and blinked back her tears. She would not cry in front of Captain Russell. Russell strode out of the room. She followed, slipping her hand into Regulus' as they followed him down the hall. She cast one last glance over her shoulder at Father and Dresden following the servant woman in the opposite direction.

"His Excellency told me you both are assigned to his personal guard, but he didn't specify why." Russell looked back at them, his expression halfway between curious and disgusted. "I don't know what use a woman can be in his guard." He eyed their joined hands. "I guess that's why you two are to have your own room separate from the barracks. Ridiculous."

He looked back in front, keeping up his rushed pace. Adelaide cast Regulus a relieved glance. At least they wouldn't be separated. The scarred side of his mouth pulled up in a slight smile and he squeezed her hand.

"I will show you to your room and explain how the guard works," Russell continued without looking back. "Lieutenant Beale will orient you later. You will be notified of your schedule once I've worked that out. Apparently," he said with annoyance, "the king wants one of you on his personal detail as often as possible, but he had a meeting to attend and couldn't explain."

Russell opened a door to a plain spiral stone staircase and led them down, instructing them to close the door behind them. Archer's loops in the wall provided the only light and let in the outside air. They were in the back of the palace, based on the glimpses Adelaide caught out the narrow slits as they passed them.

At the bottom landing, Russell paused. His gaze trailed over her from head to toe and back. "What's the truth? Seems there should be an easier way to disguise a royal affair. And that doesn't explain," he pointed at their joined hands, "this."

Adelaide gasped. "That's not—"

"She's not his mistress!" Regulus' grip on her hand tightened.

"What, not yet?" Russell raised his eyebrows. "You don't have to keep up the act with me. I know every secret the king has, including the ones the queen doesn't."

Regulus' indignation melded with Adelaide's horror and embarrassment through their bond. "The king needs my protection." She hated how high-pitched her voice sounded.

Russell snorted. "I'm sure you have many useful skills." He eyed her in a way that made her want to hide behind Regulus, but she stood her ground and scowled.

"In fact, I do." She threw a small ball of fire at the stone wall less than a foot away from Russell. He jumped.

"You…you're a…"

"Mage." The fear in his eyes pleased her more than it should have.

"And you're…?" He looked at Regulus.

"Her betrothed. And maybe immortal."

"Right…" Russell nodded slowly. "Right." He opened the door to a cobblestoned courtyard bordered by wooden buildings.

Servants rushed back and forth. Some carried baskets, boxes, and sacks. A few led livestock. Russell led them behind the palace, then entered another door. The hallway here was undecorated, the stone floor barren. They walked past several doors, passing male and female servants from small children to older women with silver hair tucked under headscarves, then turned down another corridor. Finally, Russell opened a door and motioned them inside.

The small room had a worn green rug, a simple wooden dresser, a small square wooden table with two worn chairs, and a bed covered with a faded green comforter and two flat pillows. Nothing hung on the bare stone walls, none of which had windows. The only light came in through the open door. A glass oil lamp sat on the table next to a couple pieces of flint.

A servant's room. Disappointment pinched her gut, but Regulus squeezed her hand. At least it wasn't a dirt floor and wasn't the barracks. Russell stood near the table, hands clasped behind his back.

"You have taken a solemn oath to serve and protect the king, whether that be by your life or your death." He looked quizzically at Regulus as he said *death*. "I have no idea if this will work differently, so for now I'll give you the usual orders. You will report for meals in the barracks mess hall when assigned. You will be assigned a time to report to the barracks courtyard for training. You will not speak to any members of the royal family unless addressed first, and you will keep your answers short and refer to the king as Your Excellency, the queen as Your Majesty, the crown prince as Your Highness, and the princesses as Your Grace.

"You will address the members of the court as my lord and my lady. You will report to me or the officer on duty before and after each shift with your fellow guards. You will follow all orders given by myself, Captain Matthews, and Lieutenants Beale, Breck, and Antar promptly and without question. You may not leave the palace grounds without the consent of the officer on duty. You will address your captains and lieutenants as sir.

"Disobedience will be punished according to the severity of the offence and if it is a repeat offence, ranging from withheld meals to time in the stocks to lashings to execution and other punishments at the discretion of the assigning officer. Is that clear?"

"Yes, sir," they said in unison.

"Someone should come measure you for a uniform at some point today, Hargreaves. I don't know what we're doing about clothes for you, Belanger." He shook his head, then continued. "Lieutenant Beale has been notified to find you here and should arrive presently. Any questions you have may be directed to Lieutenant Beale, as I will be off duty for the remainder of the day." Russell turned on his heel and headed out. He paused in the doorway.

"One other thing," Russell said over his shoulder. "I don't know why the king didn't tell me about the…um, magic. Maybe His Excellency wants it kept secret. Until we're told otherwise, keep your cards to yourselves." He departed, leaving the door open.

Adelaide sank onto the bed, relieved to be off her feet. The frame creaked under the thin mattress as Regulus sat next to her. "Well. At least we're together."

Regulus gently held the side of her head and pulled her toward him. "My life has taken some unexpected turns since meeting you." He kissed her temple. "But you're worth it."

Her face warmed. His sincerity pulsed through their connection, comforting her and loosening the knots in her back. He rubbed her shoulder and kissed her forehead, then her cheek. She turned toward him, meeting his lips with hers. Her arms circled around his waist.

Someone cleared their throat. They leapt apart and stood. A man dressed in the same uniform as Russell but with a black sash instead of red stood in the doorway, arms crossed and mouth turned down. His brown hair was cut close to his head. He had a stubbly beard, thick eyebrows, and light brown skin that might have just been a dark tan.

"I'm Lieutenant Beale. You must be Hargreaves and Belanger." They confirmed as Beale continued to scowl. "Follow me."

CHAPTER 32

LIEUTENANT BEALE LED THEM ACROSS THE COBBLESTONE courtyard to a stone wall, through a set of open double doors into a dirt-floored courtyard that extended to the palace wall. A two-story wooden building stood in the far-right corner with rows of small windows without glass and with open shutters. A one-story building occupied the far-left corner. Shirtless men were everywhere she looked. Some sparred with each other while others hefted and tossed stones. A few fired arrows into dummies stuffed with straw. Some stretched or ran in place. A few at a time, the men noticed their arrival. Whispers went around the courtyard as Beale lead them toward the smaller building. Men stopped what they were doing to stare at them. At her.

Adelaide hated it. She wanted to hide. Regulus put his arm around her shoulders, drawing her into his side. A couple men let out a low whistle. Someone said, "What's a lady doing here?"

Another man said, "Her handler's awfully protective. Must be expensive." Heat rushed up the back of her neck.

"So, what, officers get a pass on the no women in the barracks rule?" another man muttered.

Beale halted and turned around. "Since your attention is off your training anyway." His raised voice carried over the courtyard. "Meet the two newest members of the king's personal guard. Regulus Hargreaves and Adelaide Belanger."

"Sir, you're saying the woman's…one of us?" A man with bulging muscles wiped sweat off his glistening forehead.

"No," Beale said tersely, "His Excellency says she is."

The men glanced at each other, whispering. Adelaide gripped her skirt and fought the urge to flee the courtyard. She wanted to press into Regulus' back to hide from their stares. Instead, she lifted her chin and looked around the courtyard, daring them to challenge her.

"She need a sparring partner?" A lanky man who looked a little younger than Adelaide leered. "I'll volunteer."

"You aren't even that good, Tom," called out another man. Adelaide couldn't find him in all the staring faces. "We all know I'm the best at hand-to-hand combat. I could give her some pointers. Demonstrate some moves." This was greeted by snickers and exclamations of agreement and offers to teach her. Adelaide clenched her teeth so hard she feared they might crack.

"Enough." Beale started back toward the low building. "Back to your exercises, men."

A chorus of "yes, sir's" answered him, but the men only half-heartedly returned to their training, their eyes still following her. Beale opened the door and walked inside. Long rows of tables bordered by wooden benches ran the length of the mess hall. Some twenty men sat at the tables, chatting and eating.

"This is the mess," Beale said. Eyes turned toward them, widening when they saw Adelaide. "You'll eat your meals here." He pointed toward a counter with a window into the kitchen at the far end of the hall. "You'll give your name and get your food there during your time slot."

Regulus shuffled his feet. "Perhaps it would be better if Adelaide—"

"You arguing with me, Hargreaves?" Beale rounded on Regulus, stepping up so they were face-to-face. Or close. Beale's head ended at Regulus' eyes.

"No, sir, I just think barracks discipline might suffer—"

"Well, if your lady didn't want to eat with the guards, she shouldn't have joined."

"She didn't have a choice!" Regulus glared down at Beale.

"What was that?" Beale squinted. "Didn't Captain Russell tell you the rules?"

Regulus looked lost for a moment, then said, "She didn't have a choice, sir."

"Well, she doesn't have a choice about eating in the mess, either, unless and until the king or Captain Russell or Captain Matthews say otherwise."

Adelaide felt Regulus about to protest again, so she squeezed his hand hard. She could handle it. It wasn't like she couldn't protect herself. She wouldn't be collared. Not this time.

Regulus grunted. "Yes, sir."

"Good." Beale led them to the other building, which she guessed must be the barracks. The men watched her all the way.

"They'll get used to it," Adelaide whispered to Regulus, hoping she was right. "It's just novel now." Regulus worked his jaw in response, the veins in his neck bulging.

Inside the barracks, Beale took them into a room with a large desk, a wall covered in parchment with schedules written on them, and a round table with four chairs. Two men sat at the table playing cards, both wearing the same outfit as Beale, including the black sash. The one on the right had a small scar running through his left eyebrow. His brown hair fell in a thin braid down his back. The other man had thick, wavy black hair and the same dark olive complexion as Dresden but was taller and much huskier.

"This is the officer's command center," Beale explained. "Assignments and schedules are posted here. You will report to this room to debrief before and after every shift protecting the king. Do you understand?"

"Yes, sir."

"This is Lieutenant Breck," Beale continued. The man with the scar nodded. "And Lieutenant Antar." The olive-skinned man waved. "These are the new recruits, Hargreaves," Beale jutted his thumb at Regulus, "and Belanger." He jutted his thumb at her.

"So, it's true." Breck stood and looked them both over. "Don't get why the king wants some foreign girl to protect him."

"Hey, I'm foreign," Antar said.

"Well, at least you're a man and a soldier."

"I'm Monparthian," Adelaide said with rising indignation. "My father is Lord Alfred Belanger."

"Don't much care who your father is," Breck said, his eyes narrowing. "But I *do* care about you following protocol, woman or no. Did you get the full rundown of the rules or what?"

Dammit. "I apologize, sir." She bowed her head, hoping that would show enough deference to stay his wrath. "And we did, sir."

"Ah, you know new recruits, Breck." Antar propped his boots on the back of one of the other chairs and crossed his ankles. "Always takes a little while to adjust. Slip-ups happen." Antar smiled. "I'm sure you'll work on it, right, sweetheart?"

She managed not to let her irritation show as she replied, "Yes, sir."

"You call all your soldiers sweetheart, sir?" Regulus asked. *Oh. Great.*

Antar's expression darkened. "I could if I wanted to, sweetheart."

Adelaide sensed Regulus' anger rising, and she grabbed his arm with both hands. He looked at her, eyes flashing. She gave a small shake of her head. He took a deep breath and relaxed.

"Guess the girl's got more brains than you," Breck said. "That attitude you're showing has no place here. It'll get you in trouble. But by the look of that scar, you're acquainted with trouble. Where'd you get it?"

"As a mercenary," Regulus said flatly.

"You were a mercenary?" Breck looked surprised, and Antar looked impressed.

"For nine years. A captain for five of those." Regulus glared back at Breck, a hint of pride in his voice.

"Ah, so that's the cause of the disrespect in your tone." Breck's mouth curled down. "You think you're better than me."

"I mean no disrespect, sir." Regulus sounded unconvincing as he stared down Breck.

Adelaide looked to Beale. "Sir, is there anywhere else we need to know how to find?"

"Don't change the subject to protect him, girl," Breck said.

"Breck," Antar said with an easy wave of his hand. "Let them be."

"Sure." Breck tilted his chin up. "Soon as scar-face apologizes to his superior for his disrespectful tone."

Regulus tensed. *Please*, she thought, remembering Russell's list of punishments. *Just get it over with.* She heard Regulus grind his teeth.

"I apologize, sir." He sounded almost sincere. Almost.

"I still feel disrespected." Breck crossed his arms. "Kiss my boot to make it up to me, guardsman." Adelaide stared at the lieutenant in disbelief. Regulus didn't move. "If I have to tell you again, you won't get dinner." Still, Regulus didn't move. He probably figured going hungry for a while was worth skipping the humiliation of kissing Breck's dust-coated boot. To be honest, she didn't blame him. "No dinner, then. Kiss my boot, or I'm taking your supper, too."

Regulus stood immobile. This was insane. She looked at Beale and Antar, but Beale just watched and Antar looked mildly amused. She gave Regulus' arm a gentle tug. This was getting out of hand. He didn't even look at her.

Breck shook his head and tapped his foot. "One more chance, but this time you're looking at a night in the stocks."

Adelaide's mouth fell open. That wasn't a legitimate order. That punishment did not fit the crime. But she didn't dare say so, not with the gloating expression on Breck's face and the disinterest Beale had in the whole situation. She slid her hand from Regulus' sleeve to his hand, hoping he would receive her desire to give in. Her fear of being without him that night.

Regulus started at her touch. Some of the fire left his eyes, but his expression remained tense. "Yes, sir."

Regulus got down on his knees and kissed the tip of Breck's boot. As he straightened, Breck kicked him in the chest. Regulus fell back against the wall next to the door. Adelaide yelped, both at the unexpected attack and the ache in her own chest that indicated just how hard Breck had kicked him. She leaned over Regulus, praying he wouldn't lose his temper and make things worse. His chest heaved, but he didn't say anything.

Breck nodded, a self-satisfied smile on his face. "Still no dinner or supper for you."

"I'm sorry," she whispered as she helped Regulus up.

His face was red, but he whispered back, "Don't be."

A hand grabbed her upper arm. Adelaide shied away and scrunched her shoulders toward her ears. *Pull it together. It's just your arm.* All the same, fear made her rigid. Regulus' thumb rubbed her hand. His love and even somehow his anger gave her more confidence and she relaxed.

"I don't get it," Breck said as he squeezed her arm. "More muscle than I expected, but not enough to be much use. And seems skittish." He released her and sneered. "A week's wages says the king requests her on night shifts."

Beale laughed. "Do I look like a fool to you? I'm not betting against that." Adelaide's face burned. "Ah, look. You've upset her." He laughed again.

"That's enough," Antar said, his voice quiet but firm. "I apologize for my fellows. You're free to go back to your room."

"Thank you, sir." She pulled Regulus out of the barracks, Breck's complaining about Antar's sour attitude fading behind them. They kept a rapid pace until they were back in their room with the door closed. She hovered a sphere of light in the center of the room.

"The king's an idiot," Regulus spat. "He didn't pause for a moment to consider what a bad idea putting a woman in the guard was."

"Being angry won't change it." She pulled him down next to her on the bed and gripped his shirt. "I understand, but please, don't do something like that again."

"I've done enough groveling and being pushed around in the past two years to last me a lifetime."

She couldn't argue with that, but her own irritation with his stubbornness continued to grow. "I know. But—"

"They don't scare me." Regulus' eyes narrowed. "I—"

"It's not only about you!" She shoved his chest and released his shirt. "Did you consider how your actions affected me? Now if I want to eat, I have to face the mess hall alone. I almost had to spend the night alone. Did you think about that? Did you think of me? Well, did you?"

"I…" His face fell. "No. I didn't."

"No. You didn't." She huffed and stood. "Together, Reg. That's what you said. Together!"

"I'm sorry—"

"You're not a lone wolf, Reg, you—"

"Ad." He grabbed her hand. "I know. I'm truly sorry." The genuine regret on his face and the sorrow roaring through their bond made her anger deflate. "It won't happen again. I swear."

"Thank you."

Someone knocked and Adelaide groaned. "Two minutes. Can't we have two minutes to process?"

The person knocked again, so she stepped toward the door before she remembered Russell's orders to keep her magic secret. She crossed to the table, lit the lamp with her magic, and vanished the glowing sphere before answering. An older man with a mustache stood at the door, holding a large cloth bag. He stepped back as he saw her.

"I…may have the wrong room." He glanced past her to Regulus, then looked back at her. "I'm Phillip, the tailor? I'm here to fit Hargreaves for a royal guard uniform and was told to tell Belanger to report to the mess hall anytime within the next hour for dinner?"

Adelaide sighed. "I'm Belanger." She stepped aside to allow the tailor to enter and nodded toward Regulus. "He's Hargreaves."

"I…don't understand." Phillip's brow wrinkled. "You're a royal guard?"

"That's correct." She looked at Regulus, then back at Phillip. "How long will getting his uniform fitted take?"

Phillip set down a bag and started pulling clothing out of it. "We should be done within half an hour."

She turned around while Regulus changed into the uniform Phillip had brought, then sat on one of the chairs and watched while Phillip measured and pinched and pinned and smoothed and re-pinned. When he finished, he had Regulus maneuver out of the pin-filled uniform.

"I should get this back to you by this evening," Phillip said with a nod, then left.

Concern etched Regulus' face as he pulled his boots back on. "Are you going to eat?"

Adelaide wanted to say if he wasn't eating, she wouldn't, either. However, she *was* hungry. And, more importantly… "For all I know, I could get in trouble if I don't." She kicked at the floor. "Do you think…they'll let you in, at least? Even if you can't eat, you could just sit there, right?"

"Well, we can try."

Fewer men were training in the courtyard, but they still stared and whispered. She kept her chin up and avoided their stares, her fingers intertwined with Regulus'. They entered the mess hall. Regulus pointed at an empty table.

"I'll wait there."

The boy behind the counter looked no older than fourteen. He looked at her in surprise as she stepped forward after the man in front of her moved down the counter.

"Belanger," she said. The boy gaped for a moment, then checked a list tacked to the wall just inside the window.

"Uh…guess you are on here." He handed her a long wooden plate and a rough iron fork. "Help yourself."

"Thank you." She loaded some potatoes, beef roast, and peas onto the plate. She felt the eyes of every man in the mess hall on her as she walked back to Regulus and sat. "That was the most awkward walk of my life," she whispered, trying to lighten the mood. Regulus cracked a halfhearted smile.

Footsteps alerted her to the approaching men before four guards sat down, one next to her, the others with clear disappointment opposite her. Their plates clattered as they set them down. Regulus straightened, but Adelaide focused on eating her dinner.

"So," the man across from her said. He was wiry and looked to be about thirty, with lots of freckles. "How'd you become a guard? Thought they didn't take women."

"King's request," she said between bites. Perhaps if she answered some of their questions, their curiosity would abate.

The man whistled. "Why? That's rare. I don't get what you can do that we can't." He grinned. "Well, other than the obvious."

"I'm sworn to protect the king, same as you." Adelaide worked to keep her voice even. "Nothing more and nothing less."

"Maybe you're a spy, or something?" This from a man in his mid-twenties, with a blond ponytail and pencil-thin lips. "You'll blend in with the nobles, so they don't know you're a guard. Is that it?"

She shrugged.

"Told you." Ponytail reached behind Freckles to slap the third man's shoulder. "Pay up."

"Hey now." The third man had a deep baritone voice that somehow made him less ridiculous than his balding head made him appear. "A shrug doesn't count." He leaned his elbow on the table. "You know some foreign language, is what I think. You'll be a stealth interpreter. When people think the king can't know what they're saying."

She was so surprised, she said, "You think the king made me a guard so I could listen to people gossip in other languages?"

"Ha," Ponytail said. "That's pretty clearly a no. At the very least, you're wrong, so I should still win."

"That's not how it works, Rob."

"You just don't want to keep your end of the bet." Ponytail—Rob, apparently, made a grabbing motion with his hand.

"No one's right or wrong yet," Baritone said before shoveling an oversized bite of potato into his mouth.

The man to her left scooted closer until his thigh touched hers. She gripped her fork in her fist. "You want a fork in your eye? Back.

Off." He made a sour face but shifted back over so they had a small space. Regulus snorted.

"Hargreaves!" Adelaide nearly spilled peas everywhere as Breck's shout echoed through the mess hall. Breck cursed as he tramped toward them, his boots clacking. "—do you think you're doing in mess?"

"Not eating, sir." Regulus kept his tone even and respectful, but irritation stormed in his eyes.

"Get out."

"Sir?" Regulus' brows drew together. "I haven't eaten, sir—"

"You want to miss breakfast, too?" Breck grabbed the back of Regulus' shirt and pulled him off the bench. "Get out!"

Regulus blew air out his nose, gave a clipped, "yes, sir," and left.

Adelaide sat frozen, watching Regulus stomp out. The side of the fork cut into her fingers, she squeezed it so tight. She could have eaten more, but she picked up her plate and stood. Breck's hand gripped her shoulder and pushed her back down as he sat next to her.

CHAPTER 33

ADELAIDE'S THICK TONGUE STUCK TO THE ROOF OF HER MOUTH. She couldn't think of anything other than Breck's hand on her shoulder.

"You didn't finish your food."

"I'm not hungry anymore, sir."

"Don't take more than you can eat, then." Breck still gripped her shoulder. "I don't like to see food wasted. Finish eating. That's an order."

"Yes, sir." She took another bite. Her heartrate rose, but she breathed easier when Breck removed his hand.

"Here's the thing, Belanger." Breck rested his elbow on the table and turned toward her. "I don't know what's going on. I don't know why you're here, or what the king's playing at. I don't know if this is some crazy test, or if you made someone powerful very angry, or if it's an elaborate and pretty transparent way to cover up that you're in the king's bed. But you're not an exception because you're a woman. You have to follow orders, same as everyone else."

She stared at her plate. "Yes, sir. I know, sir."

"And tell your lover or handler or whatever Hargreaves is I don't care if you two were chosen by the king for whatever mysterious reason. That doesn't make you better than us."

"No, sir."

Breck grabbed her hand holding the fork and stabbed the tines into a piece of roast. "I said to eat." He moved her hand toward her mouth. Her face burned as she bit the roast off the fork. "Good." He released her hand.

Adelaide shoveled down food, but her appetite was gone. She finally finished and picked up the plate. Before she could stand, Breck slung his arm over her shoulders, keeping her on the bench. A tremor ran down her spine.

"Got somewhere important to be?"

She chose her words carefully. "I should return my plate, sir."

"Lewitt can take care of that. Can't you, Lewitt?"

"Yes, sir." Freckles reached across the table and took her plate, stacking it on top of his own before carrying them to the tub in the corner.

"Tell me about yourself, Belanger." Breck smiled, and it made her stomach churn. She was going to lose her dinner. "Tell me a secret."

"I don't like being touched, sir." She sat still as a statue, staring at the empty space where Lewitt had been sitting.

"Hargreaves' attitude isn't rubbing off on you, is it? I'm leaning more and more toward you two angered someone. Who was it? Was it the king himself? What'd you do? Ah, you *didn't* get in his bed, is that it?"

"Sir, I want to protect the king." Her fingers curled against the tabletop. "I want to be a good royal guard, sir. To do that, I need rest. May I please go, sir?"

"Rest? How boring. Or are you just wanting to bed Hargreaves?"

Adelaide felt her face and ears go red. In that moment, she truly understood Regulus' earlier actions. She twisted free and jumped off the bench.

"I didn't say you could go!" She stopped midstride and slowly turned around. Breck had stood, a cruel smirk twisting his mouth. "Come back here."

She took a deep breath and stepped toward him.

"Closer."

Another step. She could see the rings of brown in his murky green eyes.

"Closer." Breck grinned, taunting her.

"May I please go, sir?" She stepped closer, her boots nearly touching his. He grabbed her hips and pulled her to him, and she bit back a cry. A couple of the men watching snickered. She leaned back, her heart thumping in her ears. *Don't cry.* "Sir, this is hardly appropriate."

"You being here isn't appropriate." His hands moved up her sides.

No. No, not again. Consequences and punishments be hanged; she was through. She wasn't weak this time, and she wasn't powerless. Adelaide grabbed Breck's wrists and pulled his hands off her. The surprise on Breck's face almost made her smile.

He yanked his hands away. As she turned and headed toward the door, he grabbed her braid and pulled. She winced but didn't turn around. Anger burned in the pit of her stomach.

"Sir, respectfully, if you don't let me leave right now, I will embarrass you in front of all these men."

Breck laughed. "I think it's going to be the other way around, girl." He grabbed her shoulder and turned her toward him. "Making threats against an officer. Tsk, tsk." He leaned forward, his gaze drifting to her mouth as his fingers dug into the back of her shoulder. "Kiss me to show how sorry you are."

Never. She slammed her palms against his chest, releasing a blast of magical energy. Breck flew backward two table lengths then skidded across the packed dirt floor before his shoulders knocked into the wall under the counter. Adelaide didn't wait for him to recover, she rushed out the door. Regulus was leaning against the wall just outside.

"Hurry." She grabbed his hand as she sped past.

"What happened?" Regulus strode next to her. "Is everything—"

"BELANGER! Stop right there!"

She closed her eyes, her shoulders slumping as she stopped.

Regulus glanced at Breck. "What. Happened."

"Both of you, on your knees!" The guards in the courtyard stared.

Adelaide cursed in Khast and lowered onto her knees in the dirt. Regulus did the same beside her, but his anger built alongside her own

"I don't know what just happened." Breck stopped in front of them, his face red and lips pulled back in a snarl. "But the punishment for attacking a ranking officer is twenty lashes."

"What?" Regulus gripped her hand so hard it hurt.

"Someone bring me the whip!" Breck shouted. "Before I decide to flog each and every one of you dawdlers!" He sneered. "Policy is bare-backed."

"I'll take her punishment, sir." Regulus' rage and panic mingled with her fear.

"Not the way it works." Breck cocked his head. "But you can get some lashes, too, if it will make you feel better."

"Sir, please." Regulus bowed his head. "Give me as many lashes as you want. She…she can watch. But—"

"But nothing!" Breck glowered down his nose at her. "She attacked me; she'll be stripped and lashed."

Adelaide's chest heaved. She was not about to be stripped in the middle of a courtyard full of men. She didn't deserve any lashes, and Regulus definitely didn't. Not to mention she would feel both whippings. "You wanted to know a secret, sir?"

Her fury overpowered her dread, leaving a reckless storm in her chest. Maybe Mother and Regulus were right. Maybe she was a *shiraa.* She didn't even care if she was breaking Captain Russell's order to keep her magic secret.

"You wanted to know why the king wanted me in the royal guard?" She smiled. *Let the tigress play.* "Be careful what you wish for, sir."

She let go of Regulus' hand and stood, taking a few steps away. Breck watched in confusion and outrage. She had no idea if this would work, but if she had done it before subconsciously, she could choose to do it—right? The familiar magical warmth spread across her palms against her dress. *Come on. Fire and flames.* Adelaide pictured what she wanted, and heat flared at her back.

"Oh…" Breck cursed and stepped back. Shouts and whispers echoed across the courtyard. She glanced to the side and smiled when she saw red and orange flames fanning out in the shape of a massive wing.

"Any other questions, Lieutenant?" She summoned a sword of magic light in her right hand, just for the fun of it.

"What are you?" Breck took another step backward.

"I'm a mage." Satisfied that Breck looked sufficiently terrified, Adelaide let the wings and sword vanish. Silence filled the court-yard. Regulus stood, and they headed toward the gate, every royal guard within the wall watching them, unmoving. But the men's stares didn't make her feel small anymore.

"You think you get a pass because you're a mage?" Breck said, snapping out of his stupor. "You still swore an oath! You still have to obey me!"

She cast him a cold glare. "Take it up with His Excellency."

"I'm still your commanding officer!"

At that moment, Lieutenant Antar strolled in from the entrance to the courtyard. "What's going on here?"

"Belanger disobeyed a direct order, assaulted me, and is trying to avoid punishment." Breck sounded manic.

"Sir," Adelaide tried and failed to keep her anger out of her voice, "Lieutenant Breck assaulted *me* and I defended myself. He ordered me to kiss him, and I did not comply. I will not be accepting a punishment I do not deserve."

Regulus made a disgusted sound in his throat and started to turn around, but she grabbed his hand and stopped him. She had already defended herself. He didn't need to further stoke Breck's rage and get them in more trouble.

"Huh." Antar looked at her, clearly impressed, then looked at Breck. "What do you mean, she assaulted you? You're at least twice as strong as she is."

"She's a filthy mage!"

Antar raised his brows. "A…what? No, no, wait. That makes so much more sense." He shook his head and chuckled. "Did you actually order her to kiss you?"

Breck opened and closed his mouth. "She was being insubordinate and insulting."

"Breck, you're a disgrace." Antar nodded at her and continued across the courtyard. "Have a good day, Belanger. Hargreaves."

"But—" Breck started.

"Don't make me report you to Captain Russell," Antar said. "You've already got two strikes this month for abuse of power."

As they walked to their room, Regulus leaned over and murmured, "That was risky."

"It was riskier not to."

"I'm proud of you."

"Well, maybe hold off on the praise until we determine if I've just made our lives a living hell." Her stomach still felt uneasy.

"I'm sorry," Regulus said quietly. "That should never have happened. I should have been there, like I promised."

"It's not your fault." They turned into their little room. "And it wasn't…" Her voice dropped. "I've been through worse."

"Doesn't make it okay." Regulus closed the door, plunging the room into darkness.

She created an orb, the soft blueish light filling the room, and sat on the bed.

"Are you sure you're all right?"

"I had the opportunity and means to fight back." Adelaide laid on the bed and rested her hands on her midsection. "Somehow, that helps."

He shifted and his brows pinched. "If I ever make you feel uncomfortable, if you need me to back off... You know you can tell me, right?"

Sorrow accompanied a swell of love. "Thank you," she whispered. She shifted over and patted the bed. He hesitated, then laid next to her and wrapped his arm around her. Adelaide nestled against him, thanking Etiros for Regulus.

"I always want you to feel safe with me."

"In your arms is the only place I feel safe right now," she murmured.

A guard arrived shortly with orders to give them an exhaustive tour of the palace. Regulus got his uniform that evening, and a servant delivered several dresses for Adelaide. Adelaide skipped dinner, opting to stay with Regulus. A servant delivered a parchment with their schedule for the next day. They would have breakfast together, but the rest of the day one would be on duty when the other wasn't. The following days were similar, and often they had late night and early morning shifts. The king wanted one of them on guard whenever possible, which made it difficult to see much of each other.

Adelaide asked for a set of throwing knives and dagger and wore them on her belt, which seemed to help some more with the other guards' opinion of her. They still stared, but they gave her space. The king didn't care if the guards knew she was a mage, but wanted it kept a secret from the nobles, so she practiced magic behind the mess hall.

Breck glared whenever he saw her, took every opportunity to make suggestive comments when the other officers weren't present, and relished every order he gave, even if it was, "Tie your boot laces, Belanger." But he didn't try to touch her again.

Guard duty was boring. She hung back, standing in the shadows, observing anyone the king interacted with. Listening to him talk and talk about harvests and food supplies, trade routes, taxes, approving marriage arrangements, and laws and bylaws. She practiced forming her magic into various shapes behind her back or while guarding the king's chambers at night to pass the time.

Despite having a son and two daughters, the king and queen rarely interacted. Adelaide discovered Russell had been telling the truth when she watched a lady-in-waiting her own age enter the king's chambers one night. It made her sick.

The king held a meeting with the officers of the royal guard, a few of his top knights, and Regulus and Adelaide on the third day, four days before the masque. Breck turned pink when he saw them in the council chamber. The king elected not to cancel the masque. He hoped to catch Kirven and wouldn't be dissuaded. Captain Russell suggested a double, but the king said his brother would know, and wouldn't reveal himself to a double.

After the meeting, Adelaide secured permission to go into town and buy masque-appropriate clothes for herself and Regulus. She had managed to convince the king that if she and Regulus blended in with the crowd, they stood a better chance of finding Kirven and Nolan before they could attack. She found a dress she would only need to alter slightly and bought matching material to make

Regulus' outfit. More importantly, the trip gave her an opportunity to visit Father.

They sat in the inn's tavern, quiet during the mid-afternoon slump, sipping on ale. The place smelled of spilt food and drink mixed with soapy water as a maid scrubbed the dented wood floorboards. Occasional clatters rose from the kitchen, and whenever a worker passed through the door to the back, the scent of preparing stew drifted through. Adelaide wrapped both hands around her tankard and gazed at the candle flickering on the table between them. They'd tucked themselves into a shadowy corner where Adelaide drew less attention.

"You don't have to go," she said. "Weapons aren't allowed; what could you—"

"The king has granted me permission to bear my sword. Sir Jakobs, too." Father leaned back in his chair. "Jakobs has an unfortunate lack of respect for his king and takes his cavalier attitude a bit far sometimes, but I rather like the fellow. Yesterday, he—"

"This isn't about Dresden." She stared at the lingering foam along the wall of her tankard. She still hadn't told Father about Kirven's threats. But she couldn't risk him falling into Kirven's hands. "Even if you have a sword, Nolan is still immortal, Kirven is—"

"Adelaide." He reached across the table and pulled one hand away from her tankard and held it. "Do you have so little faith in me?"

She looked up and softened at the gentleness and determination in his green eyes. "I'm just…afraid."

"Fear is a healthy emotion, in its place. Fear helps prevent recklessness. Warriors don't face battle unafraid. They face battle because they are fighting for something they value more than they fear the battle." Father squeezed her hand. "What are you fighting for?"

"You. Mother. Regulus, Minerva, everyone. My own freedom. But mostly to protect the people I love." *To protect you from Kirven's wrath.*

"Love." He nodded. "Love will always conquer fear, my tigress."

She drew in a ragged breath. "I don't feel like much of a tigress lately."

Father rubbed his thumb over the back of her hand. "When your mother and I told you about The Shadow, you hid under a blanket and cried. But when we told you about the cottage and learning to hide your magic, you were so upset about leaving your siblings you said you weren't scared of shadows, even mean ones. You still had tears in your eyes, but you lifted your chin and crossed your little arms and said you didn't need to hide."

"I was four, I barely understood."

Father just smiled. "You've always had the heart of a tigress. That heart is still in there. That determination. That boldness."

Adelaide worked her throat. "But if I fail—"

"If you fail, the outcome will be the same as if you don't try. But you have a real chance to succeed." Father's head bowed as sadness overtook his expression. "Adelaide… I won't apologize for trying to protect you. I did what I thought I had to, but I was wrong. I wish I could have helped you be more prepared. But I've never doubted you. I am in awe of the things you can do."

He met her eyes. "I'm proud of you. Proud of you for doing what you know to be right, even when it's dangerous. Proud of the kind, strong, selfless young woman you are. Proud of the dedication you're showing in learning to use your power. Whether you defeat Kirven or not, I'm proud you're my daughter. And I believe in you."

"Thank you." Her choked words came out in a whisper. She wiped at her eyes. "I should go. I need to get back before my next shift."

He released her hand and they both stood. Father pulled her close. "I love you."

She leaned her head on his shoulder and embraced him. "I love you."

Father kissed the top of her head. "It's going to be all right."

He couldn't know that. And yet, for some reason, when Father said it, it felt true. He patted her back. "I'll see you at the masque."

Between guard duty and practice, Adelaide and Regulus struggled to find time together as the masque approached. In her spare moments, Adelaide worked on their masque attire. Regulus often fell asleep watching her sew. When she crawled into bed, he'd pull her close in his sleep. She'd often wake to find him already gone, and every time, she hated it.

The day of the masque, Adelaide's nerves buzzed and exhaustion dragged her down. Sleep had evaded her the night prior, and when she had slept, she had nightmares. Dresden weeping over Regulus' mangled corpse. Minerva, heavily pregnant, trying to run from Kirven. Mother screaming, but Adelaide couldn't find her. A giant Nolan towering over her, laughing as he locked a collar around her neck and dragged her away. But Regulus had been there, holding her together every time she woke up.

Regulus couldn't sit still, so they walked through the gardens, holding each other and not saying a word. They didn't need to. What their bond didn't convey, they shared with a look. They would face Kirven and Nolan together. If they won, they would win together, and if they fell, they would fall together. But that night, Adelaide knew, either Kirven would die, or Monparth would fall.

CHAPTER 34

REGULUS LEANED AGAINST THE WALL OUTSIDE THEIR BED-room door, waiting for Adelaide to finish changing. He pulled at the edge of the dark turquoise doublet Adelaide had made. The material was velvety and rich, and not really his style. He would have been satisfied with the black long-sleeved shirt he wore under the doublet, but Adelaide insisted he needed to look the part. At least she wasn't forcing him to wear hose, just narrow-legged black trousers, and he wasn't wearing his uniform. He hated that uniform that declared his choices had been stolen.

He rubbed the pommel of his sword. It would make him stand out a little, as the guests would be required to surrender any weapons. But, bewilderingly to Regulus, it wasn't unheard of for lords to wear fake swords to these events, bladeless hilts attached to empty scabbards, just to keep up appearances. His weapon wouldn't completely undermine their plan to move unnoticed through the guests, looking for the sorcerer and Carrick.

The bedroom door squeaked open and Regulus pushed off the wall. Adelaide swept out in a matching turquoise dress of the same velvety material as his doublet, her hands behind her back. The wide, low vee of the neckline bared her shoulders. The sleeves split open at the middle of her upper arms and hung to her thighs, lined with satiny gray material. A narrow gray cloth belt embroidered with twisting silver circled her hips, the long ends hanging down in the front. A thin silver chain hung from her neck with a small, teardrop-shaped crystal. Her dark hair fell in loose curls over her shoulders and down her back.

Regulus opened his mouth, but his tongue stuck in place. She smiled. "Tigress got your tongue?"

"You…" His voice cracked and he blushed. He cleared his throat. "You are breathtakingly beautiful. I don't know that you'll really be blending in as the prettiest girl there."

She laughed and pulled two narrow black masks decorated with turquoise swirls from behind her back and gave him the larger one. "You look striking, too, *sumdir*. Ready?"

"Almost." He placed his hand on her back and pulled her close, brushing his fingers across her cheek. He sensed her flutter of giddy nerves and anticipation. "I love you, Adelaide Belanger. Whatever happens today, I love you until the sun fails to rise."

He kissed her, desperately and tenderly. Her hand gripped the side of his neck, her fingers cool against his skin. Between the delight rippling through him and the sensation of her desire, he barely managed to stay standing.

"And I love you, Regulus Hargreaves." Her eyes shone up at him. "No matter the outcome. Until the sea swallows the land, I love you."

He kissed her nose between her eyes, then tied on his mask. It only surrounded his eyes, and for a moment he regretted it didn't hide his scar. But Adelaide liked his scar. He smiled. "Let's go to a ball."

They walked arm-in-arm across the servant's courtyard to the side livestock gate, Adelaide carrying her skirt up to keep it clean. As part of their objective of blending in, they would enter with the other guests, starting their surveillance in the reception line. If they could catch Kirven and Nolan before they even made it into the palace, even better. As they approached the wall, Breck stepped out of the shadowy recess of the closed gate.

"About time you two were leaving. Thought you were going to be late." His gaze traveled slowly over Adelaide.

Regulus tensed and pressed his hand against his thigh to keep it from curling into a fist. "We'd best be on our way then, sir."

"The point is for you to blend in." Breck circled them. "I'm just checking that you look up to the task." He walked back around and nodded. "I suppose you look like guests, but Belanger's going to be useless with all the men that will be trying to plaster themselves to her and talk her out of that dress."

"Sir, we need to join the guests," Adelaide said, her tone dark.

"All right, all right." Breck opened one side of the double doors and held it open for them to pass through. He picked the door on Adelaide's side, so she would have to walk past him. Regulus wanted to move her to his other side, but Breck would find a way to make that into some grave offense. As they passed, Breck said, "Remember, your only concern is to protect the king. Not to see how many nobles you can lure into dark corners."

"Substitute servant girls for nobles and you've given yourself some great advice, sir," Adelaide said. Regulus nearly tripped over the cobblestones. "See you in the ballroom, sir."

Breck called her a couple words that made Regulus' hair stand on end, but Breck turned back inside and slammed the gate closed behind him. Regulus grunted. "So I get scolded for making him angry, but you get to do it?"

She didn't answer right away. "I'm going to face Kirven and Nolan today. Breck and his pettiness seem pretty insignificant right now."

"Oh." He moved his arm around her waist. "How are you feeling?"

"I'm scared, Reg. I'm terrified I'll fail again." She looked up. "But I'm determined. I'm ready to face them. For you, for myself, for Father and Mother. For Minerva and Gaius and their unborn baby. For Dresden and Perceval and Estevan and…" She frowned.

"Caleb and Jerrick and Harold," Regulus said.

She nodded. "Even for Landon and Julia. Even for the rest of my half-siblings. Just because I don't like them doesn't mean I want them and their families to live in a world where Kirven is king and might hurt them because of me. But I'm afraid I'll fail them all."

Regulus spoke quietly. "You're not solely responsible for protecting all of Monparth."

"I think I am. I think we are. And we don't even have a plan. Just…" She sighed. "Find each other if we see them. Get the staff, kill Kirven and Nolan. That's not a plan. That's a goal."

"Well, think of it this way: without a plan, we don't have to worry about if things don't go according to plan."

She scowled. "That's the worst attempt at positivity I've ever heard."

He smiled. "Sorry. Why do you think I keep Caleb around?"

"And I thought you just liked his music," she said with a laugh.

They rounded the front of the palace walls and found the reception line already stretched to the front gate. Men and women of all ages in ornate outfits and masks of every color stood gossiping and laughing. Regulus scanned the crowd as they joined the line. The masks further complicated their task. Everyone had tried to talk the king into at least changing the party so it wasn't a masque, but the king said that would signal that something was wrong, and he didn't want to worry his people or alert Kirven. Regulus believed the king was an idiot, but he was also the king, so idiocy ruled the day.

A group of three men in their early twenties stood in front of them, chortling and holding small open flasks. Apparently, they'd decided to start the party early. They wore ridiculous hose and doublets in flashy and obnoxious colors. One looked over his shoulder, sunlight glinting on the silver inlay on his violet mask.

"Hey." The man nudged one of his fellows. "Look at what just fell from the heavens."

Regulus rolled his eyes as the other two men turned toward them. His arm was still around Adelaide's waist, but either the young noble didn't notice or didn't care.

"I actually crawled out of hell," Regulus said. "But thanks for the compliment." Adelaide giggled.

The noble squinted at him, then laughed too. "This your husband?"

"Betrothed," Adelaide replied.

One of the other men wiggled his eyebrows. A vivid green mask covered the right half of his face. "What I'm hearing is I still have a chance." He held out his flask. "I'm Will. Care for a drink?"

"No thank you, Will," Adelaide said with an amused snort.

"I'm Thomas," the first speaker said. He pointed at the third noble, who wore a crimson mask. "That's Sean. And the angel's name is...?"

"Adelaide," she said, before Regulus could say *none of your business*. "But I'm quite human."

"Where are you from, Lady Adelaide?" Sean asked. "Carasom? Khastalland?"

Regulus felt her stiffen as she said, "Nueres Duchy."

"Oh." Sean pointed at Will. "Will has relatives in Nueres. But where were you from before that? Khastalland, right?"

Regulus winced. He'd seen Dresden lose his cool over similar lines of questioning in the past. Jerrick and Estevan hadn't been born or raised in Monparth, so it didn't bother them unless someone implied they didn't count as Monparthians, despite their status as knights of Monparth.

"My mother's womb," Adelaide said flatly. "Who was in Nueres." She shuffled her feet. "But she was from Khastalland."

"Ah, see?" Sean snapped his fingers. "I knew it."

Regulus looked around, scanning the growing line behind them. No one looked like Nolan or the sorcerer. He turned back to the intoxicated young men. "Do you know anyone else coming to the masque?"

"Sure," Will said. "Lots of nobles. None that could wear that dress so well, though." He winked at Adelaide. Regulus could have punched him, but he restrained himself.

"Have you heard if any of the Carricks are coming?" Adelaide asked.

"Duke and Duchess Carrick come every year," Thomas said. "Not sure if any of their sons are coming."

"Henry said he saw the youngest, what's his name?" Sean said. "Nathaniel?"

"Nolan," Will said.

"Yeah, that's it. Said he saw him carrying some boxes for some older man over in the merchant's district a couple days ago. Said he planned on coming. Why?"

Regulus and Adelaide glanced at each other. She placed her hand on his chest. "Regulus used to be good friends with the Carricks. He was hoping to reconnect and introduce us."

"I wouldn't do that." Will laughed. "Or if you do, keep a close eye on your lovely lady. Nolan Carrick has a reputation for charming the ladies."

"Does he?" Adelaide murmured.

"Well," Regulus said, "at least I don't have to worry about the three of you."

Thomas and Will laughed, but Sean turned red as his mask. "At least we've still got our looks." Sean traced his finger down across his cheek to his chin, mirroring Regulus' scar. Regulus' mouth turned down and the tops of his ears burned.

"Don't worry, Sean," Adelaide said. She turned toward Regulus and ran her fingertips over his scar, making his skin tingle. "Maybe one day you'll grow out of those boyish features and look like a man, too." Regulus couldn't help himself. He leaned over and kissed her.

"Well, then." Will pulled at his collar. The young men turned around and returned to their flasks, commenting on the ladies they could spot ahead of them in line.

The line moved forward at a slow but steady pace and continued to grow behind them. They scanned the crowd, looking for any sign of Kirven or Nolan, but couldn't get a good enough look at anyone. Captain Russell and Lieutenant Beale stood just outside the doorway, checking for weapons and scanning the passing faces for anyone who matched the descriptions Regulus and Adelaide had given them.

"See anything?" Russell whispered as he pretended to check Regulus' sword.

Regulus shook his head. "Too many people. Too many masks."

"Masquerade." Russell cursed. "I hope you have better luck than we're having once you're inside. They're passing us too quickly."

They continued inside, up the red-carpeted staircase and into the cavernous ballroom. Massive crystal chandeliers with dozens of candles hung from the vaulted ceiling. Candelabras with intricate metalwork covered in gold leaf stood on pillars between the towering stained-glass windows. Tables covered with food arranged into the shapes of animals, flowers, and magical creatures lined the sides of the long room. A group of musicians played softly in the far corner.

The royal dais stood empty, but the hall was filling with guests and a low buzz of constant conversation mixed with the sounds of the harp, lutes, and flutes. Royal guards stood on either side of every entrance and exit, and in front of every window. Servants carrying trays of silver goblets filled with deep red wine wove through the guests. Regulus realized he had frozen, gawking at the overwhelming opulence.

"We should probably split up to cover more ground," Adelaide whispered before kissing his cheek. She slipped out of his arm and breezed away, looking unconcerned and like she wasn't bearing the weight of the world on her shoulders. He watched her move among the guests, her above-average height helping him track her.

With a sigh, he turned away. He wasn't much for talking at parties, but he was a good listener. He meandered through the hall, listening for Carrick or the sorcerer's voice or for anyone to say anything about Nolan Carrick or anything suspicious.

CHAPTER 35

ADELAIDE WANDERED THE BALLROOM AS DISCRETELY AS possible, but she couldn't avoid people's eyes, their whispers, or sometimes their conversation. She faked politeness and, as the hall filled and the music changed from peaceful background music to dances, gently turned down a couple offers to dance.

The afternoon sped on. The angle of the sunlight through the stained-glass windows changed and dimmed as evening approached. She saw Regulus several times, but no sign of Kirven or Nolan. Part of her felt relieved, as if nothing would actually happen. But deep down, she knew that was ridiculous. They would be here. Sooner or later.

She nursed a goblet of wine and scanned the crowd. Breck stepped up next to her, far too close for her comfort. "Getting intoxicated on duty, are we?"

Adelaide snorted. "Blending in as per your orders, sir."

"Right." He put a hand on the small of her back. She couldn't repress her shudder, and her involuntary reaction made Breck snicker. He leaned in to whisper, his breath tickling her ear. "Don't get carried away. If you get drunk while on duty, that'll be that lashing I owe you." He walked away.

She pressed her eyes closed, then left the goblet on a nearby table and continued to meander. Couples twirled around the dance floor, making her wish this was just a party, and she was in Regulus' arms. She looked across the dancers, searching for Regulus. Just seeing him would help calm her jittery nerves.

Someone stepped up behind her and a gentle hand brushed her hair behind her shoulder. A slow smile pulled at her mouth.

"You look ravishing, love," Nolan whispered close by her ear.

An invisible rope coiled around her chest. In spite of how much she had thought about being strong when she saw him, she trembled. Something sharp pressed against her ribs as he kissed the side of her neck. Her stomach lurched. Her breath stuttered and the muscles in her neck and back went taut.

"How'd you get a weapon in here?" Adelaide whispered, trying to control the pounding of her heart.

"Oh, it's just a tiny blade I had up my sleeve." Nolan ran his knuckles over her jaw in a caress that made her skin crawl. "But it's enough to do some decent damage. Nothing you can't heal, based on the fact Hargreaves is alive. I'm disappointed, but I suppose I'll simply kill him a second time."

"I'm surprised you had the mettle to show up after you ran away last time." The tip of the knife pressed deeper into her side, threatening to break through her dress.

"I had been run through with a sword four times," he snapped. "I knew it was pointless to waste my time fighting you in that state. It was a tactical decision."

"Right. I'm going to turn around now." She turned slowly, but he didn't stab her. Nolan wore a black doublet with gold stitching, and a matching mask. Facing him made Adelaide flash back to the last time she saw him, and it made her dizzy. *Focus. It's different this time.* She kept her voice low. "As a member of the royal guard, I'm placing you under arrest for treason."

"Really?" Nolan laughed. "So, the rumors around town a woman joined the royal guard are true. I suspected it was you." He adjusted the knife's point against her side. "But if you arrest me, you'll be too busy with me to find Kirven."

"Where is he?" She looked around. "Is he here?"

Nolan clicked his tongue. "What would be the fun in telling you that?" He took her hand. "May I have this dance?"

"Are you going to stab me if I say no?"

"It's just a dance." He smiled. "Don't say no and we won't have to find out."

"Fine." She lifted her chin, determined not to let him see her fear. "But put the knife away or I'll step on your feet."

He chuckled. "Maybe I want to keep it out to make sure you don't try anything stupid."

"Maybe I'm trying to keep a low profile until I find Kirven and think dancing is as good a way to do that as any." She met his eyes, even as her stomach twisted in on itself.

"Deal." Nolan's hand left her side and he slipped the short, thin knife up his sleeve then showed her his empty hands. "Satisfied?"

"I will be when you're either dead or in prison."

Nolan took her arm. "With that mouth, you're awfully lucky you're so attractive." A crooked, leering smile replaced his frown as he pulled her against him on the dance floor. "But at least your mouth is excellent for kissing." He pressed his lips to hers. Adelaide gasped and pulled back, but he yanked her forward again.

"Ah-ah," he murmured against her mouth. "Don't cause a scene, love. You wanted to blend in." Her legs shook and she squeezed her eyes shut, the blood draining from her face as he kissed her. He pulled back and moved her hands into position for the dance.

She stumbled over the first several steps, her mind numb. She could still feel him, taste him. Her knees shook. She tripped and mumbled an apology. *We should have had a better plan.* As they brushed past other couples, she searched for Kirven to keep her mind off

Nolan. Why did Kirven have to be so short? She caught glimpses of Regulus on the other side of the room, his head rising above most of the other guests. She focused on him.

"I feel like you're ignoring me, which makes you a poor dance partner." Nolan pulled her closer. "Give in, Adelaide. I know you want to."

Panic squeezed at her throat. *I'm not helpless. I'm not trapped.* But it didn't feel true, and her heart hammered against her ribs like it wanted to escape its cage. She stared over his shoulder; every ounce of her shaking concentration focused on moving her feet in time to the music.

Captain Matthews and Lieutenant Breck stood conversing near one of the servant entrances, near two other royal guards. She wondered how to lead their dance toward them without being obvious. Surely the five of them could restrain Nolan. She purposefully mis-stepped so Nolan's foot landed on top of hers. She gasped and dropped her hand from his shoulder, exaggerating her limp.

Nolan steadied her. "Are you all right?"

"I think I just…need to sit down for a moment." She put some weight on the foot and stumbled, wincing and sucking in a breath to sell it. Not that it didn't hurt—her big toe throbbed—but it wasn't *that* bad. She put a hand on his shoulder. "Help me off the floor?"

"Least I can do." He beamed as she leaned on him and took the opportunity to loop his arm around her waist. She tried not to let her aversion show while she hobbled toward a bench near Matthews and Breck. She kept her head turned toward the bench but looked toward the officers. Breck caught her gaze and rolled his eyes, looking disgusted. Adelaide glanced toward Nolan, then back at them. Breck just shook his head.

Nolan helped her onto the bench. "Here, let me look at it." He knelt and pulled her boot out from under her dress.

Adelaide risked looking over her shoulder at the officers and pointed at Nolan. She dropped her hand and looked back just as Nolan looked up from her boot.

"Feels swollen. But, you know," he said, massaging her foot through her boot, "it wouldn't have happened if you'd done the proper steps."

"I know."

"I am sorry, though." His hand moved to her ankle, wandering up her calf as he smirked, his eyes filled with desire. Her throat constricted. "Let me make it up to you."

"Belanger," Breck said, approaching with Matthews. Nolan looked at them, his brow creasing. "If you're trying to point out that you're doing the exact opposite of what I said—"

"It's Nolan Carrick." Adelaide's palms glowed blue. *Time to try something new.* Nolan stood, but the ropes she formed out of her magic curled around him, tying his arms to his sides. Matthews and Breck drew their swords. The people standing near them gasped and moved away.

"I'm disappointed, love." Nolan strained against the glowing ropes. Keeping them in place felt like trying to maintain a barrier against Kirven's attacks. "But you're too late."

Trumpets bugled, signaling the royal family's arrival. Adelaide looked toward the dais, her heart sinking as the crowd turned toward the end of the hall. The king walked to the large gilded throne in the center of the dais, trailed by the royal family. Guards stood in a line in front of the dais. The king raised his hand in a welcoming gesture.

The windows imploded. Women screamed and men shouted as colored glass crashed across the room. Most of the candles went out. Nolan kicked Adelaide in the face, and she catapulted backward over the bench. Her mask cracked in half and fell. Pain exploded over her face and blood poured out of her nose. She lost control of the ropes binding Nolan as her vision blacked out; her pulse hammered in her face.

Her head weighed her down and her eyes watered. Adelaide's hand shook as she held it to her shattered nose, unable to see anything as she healed herself. The ringing in her ears added to the cacophony of the hall. The pain subsided, her nose making sickening snapping sounds as it returned to its normal shape. Her vision cleared.

By the time she straightened, which couldn't have been much more than a minute, Nolan was gone. Breck lay on the floor, his eyes glazed over and his head at an impossible angle. Matthews slumped against a glass-covered food table, blood trickling out of his mouth and pouring out of his stomach. Breck's sword was missing. Worse was the chaos in the ballroom.

Kirven floated over the crowd, a swirl of green light around his feet. His flowing black and blood-red robes glittered with gold embroidery. He held his arms out to his sides with the Staff of Nightfall in his right hand. Green lightning crackled from the top of the staff, reaching into the panicking crowd. Screaming echoed in the rafters as men and women, young and old, nobles and servants, were struck by the grasping tendrils of lightning and fell to the glass-strewn floor, their lifeless bodies smoking. She could never shield them all, and despair tugged at her soul. Nobles ran past, but cries of anguish dragged Adelaide's attention toward the exit. Kirven had blocked it. The lightning stopped, leaving behind the smell of burned bodies.

"Hello, brother." Kirven's voice resounded over the hall and the crowd quieted, too shocked to say anything. A shudder raised goosebumps on Adelaide's arms. This wouldn't be like last time. She was more prepared.

Guards huddled around the royal family. Barriers of shim-mering green light and blocked the doors behind the dais. Father and Dresden stood among the guards shielding the king from Kirven, their swords drawn. Her gut pinched. *No.*

"I have no brother." The king's voice carried through the hall.

"Now that's just cruel," Kirven said. "But then, I *am* here to claim my throne and kill you and your family, so fair." The opal in the staff emitted an emerald glow.

Adelaide shoved her hands forward. The blue light barrier rose in time to block the fireball Kirven threw at the cluster of guards. She expanded the barrier until it reached from floor to ceiling and wall to wall. Kirven cursed. People screamed and shouted about sorcery and magic as they pushed to get through Kirven's barrier.

"The windows!" someone shouted. Guests and servants scrambled out the now-empty windows.

Kirven barraged Adelaide's barrier with bursts of green light, flames, and more lightning. The guards attempted to break down Kirven's barriers over both rear doors. Satisfied she could keep the barrier up, Adelaide conjured a spear and threw it at Kirven's back. At the last moment he turned and knocked the spear away. He looked around, face twisted in anger, searching the surging mass of bodies escaping through the windows.

"Belanger!" He hurled a massive fireball into the crowd, and she barely managed to shield the fleeing innocents. "Where are you?"

Adelaide opened her mouth, but before she could answer, she gripped her side and doubled over in pain. It felt like someone had stabbed through the side of her abdomen, just above her right hip. *Regulus.* The link hurt more than usual. Maybe because maintaining the gigantic barrier and healing Regulus at the same time strained her power. Maybe because it was a worse wound. She panted, grimacing as she forced herself to straighten.

A barrage of green shards flew at her and she erected a barrier over herself and the guests escaping near her. Her magic drained as the barriers and Regulus' wound pulled her power in three directions. Her grip on the larger barrier was slipping. Kirven turned back toward the dais.

"You're wearing my crown, brother." Kirven pointed the staff at the dais. A steady stream of green light pummeled into Adelaide's barrier. She dropped the barrier over herself and fought past the retreating crowd, intent on keeping the barrier up. The king had to live. Father had to live.

"Kirven!" She broke through the last guests, glass crunching under her boots. "I'm ready to try again."

CHAPTER 36

THE GAPING SWORD WOUND IN REGULUS' SIDE PULLED TOGETHER and his breathing steadied. The light from Kirven's assault and Adelaide's barrier at his back cast the glass-strewn hall in an eerie teal glow. Regulus glared back at Carrick and squared his shoulders as he raised his sword, dripping with Carrick's blood. Carrick tilted his head, his face furrowed with pain from the deep slash healing across his torso.

"Are you…" Carrick eyed him. "Healing?"

"Looks like you're not the only immortal on the battlefield today." Regulus inched his right foot forward, pushing away broken glass to get more secure footing.

"She can do that too, huh?" Carrick looked impressed, but also outraged. He moved into a defensive position. "You have a mark, too?"

"Not like yours. Mine doesn't make me a slave." Regulus thrust his sword toward Carrick's chest, but Carrick parried the attack.

"Kirven!" Adelaide's voice rang out. Regulus and Carrick looked toward her. "I'm ready to try again."

Regulus swung for Carrick's neck, taking advantage of his split focus. Carrick blocked and countered with a thrust of his own. Their swords clanged together as they circled, glass sliding beneath their boots while they avoided the charred bodies of masque guests.

Out of the corner of his eye, Regulus caught glimpses of Adelaide and Kirven battling with flashes of blue and green light and red flame. He couldn't worry about her right now. He had his own fight.

Adelaide raised her shield just in time to stop another blast of crackling green lightning. Her hair clung to her sweat-soaked forehead and neck. She yelled and sent two streams of flame toward Kirven, but he just held out the staff and extinguished the flames. How did he make it look so effortless? She conjured several spears of blue light and hurled them toward Kirven, followed by a blast of light and another stream of fire.

Kirven raised a shield that easily absorbed every attack. Meanwhile, her breathing grew more labored by the moment. Movement on the dais caught her eye. She threw a haphazard barrage of knives to keep Kirven focused on her. One of Kirven's barriers, the one blocking the exit to the left of the dais, had vanished. The guards hurried the royal family out the door, followed by Father, Dresden, and the guards, including Captain Russell. *Thank Etiros.* Now she just needed to keep her barrier up long enough for them to escape.

"You're tiring, girl." Kirven pointed the staff at her. Half a dozen fingers of lightning cracked toward her, and she surrounded herself with a barrier. The assault continued for seconds that felt like hours. The lightning stopped, and she dropped the shield. Adelaide conjured ropes of blue light and snapped them toward the Staff of Nightfall. If she could pull it out of his hands…

Kirven laughed and sent a stream of fire at the ropes. He clicked his tongue. "Theft is a serious crime, Adelaide."

With a grunt, she let the ropes vanish. She raised her hands, conjuring a shield above Kirven's head, then slammed her hands down. The shield crashed into Kirven's head. He cursed as he fell, but shoved the tip of the staff toward her before she could attack again. She raised a shield, but the blast from the staff knocked her backward. She tripped over the hand of a charred body and fell onto her back.

"Guess you actually have some skill, mongrel." Carrick dodged Regulus' thrust and countered, but Regulus blocked the blow. Carrick aimed a cut at Regulus' leg, which Regulus parried. "Too bad it won't be enough."

"I'm going to cut your head off," Regulus said through gritted teeth as Carrick blocked his attack.

Carrick flashed a cocky grin. "Funny, Adelaide said something similar—just before I kissed her. She has such soft, sensuous lips."

Rage rushed over Regulus like fire on his skin. He lunged, but his heel slid on glass and he slipped to one knee. Carrick sliced toward his neck. Regulus blocked, the impact shuddering down his arms. He pushed Carrick's blade away and jumped to his feet.

Adelaide cried out. Instinctively, Regulus looked toward her. She had fallen onto her back, and she raised a bleeding hand with bits of glass glittering in the cuts. Carrick's sword sliced across Regulus' abdomen. Regulus moaned. Adelaide yelped and clutched her stomach. Blood seeped out of Regulus' gut, and he stumbled backward as his vision swam.

Instead of seizing his advantage, Carrick ran for the dais. Regulus turned in confusion. Adelaide's barrier was gone, but so were the royal family and their guards. Carrick ran through the door to the left of the dais. Regulus grunted and pressed a hand to his stomach as the numbing warmth of Adelaide's magic healed his wound. How long ago had the king left? Only human, mortal guards stood between Carrick and the king. He had to—

"You stupid, annoying, nuisance of a mage!" The sorcerer shouted.

Regulus glanced over his shoulder. The sorcerer stood on the ground, the top of the Staff of Nightfall aglow. He lifted the staff and a blast of jade light exploded toward Adelaide. She raised her hands, a sapphire shield covering her. But her elbows bent, her hands lowering under the constant barrage of the sorcerer's attack. Regulus ran toward the sorcerer, his only concern helping Adelaide. The blue light of Adelaide's shield faded. Regulus launched into the sorcerer, knocking him to the ground.

The sorcerer thrashed, but Regulus crawled over him and reached for the Staff of Nightfall. His fingers brushed the staff. He just needed to pull it out of the sorcerer's grip… A snap of greenish lightning cracked off the tip of the staff and slammed into his chest.

Regulus felt like he was being ripped apart with white-hot claws and pushed back together by searing hands at the same time as the lightning traveled through his body. He went rigid, unable to even scream to process his pain. But he could hear Adelaide screaming, and that was almost worse. His sight gave out, going completely white. Then cool numbness pushed back the searing pain, starting from his feet and moving up toward his chest, as Adelaide's healing magic fought the sorcerer's destructive magic in his body, gaining ground inch by excruciating inch.

The sorcerer shouted, the crackling sound of the lightning intensified, and a strangled scream escaped Regulus as a fresh wave of torment pushed through him. *Just let me die.* But the comforting healing sensation shoved back, chasing the jagged rending of the lightning out of his convulsing body. *No, no dying today.* He latched onto the soothing sensation of Adelaide's magic, focused on their bond and his love for her. The pain faded as the searing sorcery fled from Adelaide's magic. A resounding crack split the air as the lightning released Regulus, and he collapsed onto bits of sharp glass.

The sorcerer screamed curses between cries of pain. Regulus blinked and his vision cleared. The sorcerer knelt in the dimly lit hall, cradling his right hand. Giant red blisters covered his palm. The Staff of Nightfall lay on the ground between Regulus and the sorcerer, its light extinguished and smoke rising off the entire length of the staff.

"What is this?" the sorcerer shrieked. "What is this? What did you do?" He looked at Regulus, his eyes wide and bloodshot. "This isn't possible. The spell rebounded onto the staff. That's not possible!" His palm glowed green and the skin repaired itself.

Regulus shook his head as feeling returned to his limbs. Adelaide lay sprawled across the floor, her eyes closed but her chest rising and falling. He wanted to go to her, but he had an opening to kill the sorcerer. Spotting his sword, he moved toward it. He grabbed the hilt just as green ropes wrapped around his wrists. The sword slipped from his hand.

"Why aren't you dead?" The sorcerer stood. A third glowing rope curled around Regulus' neck, cutting off his air. He gasped and tried to reach toward his neck, but the ropes holding onto his wrists wouldn't let him. The sorcerer clenched his fist and a glowing moss-green sword shimmered into existence in his hand as he walked to Regulus.

"It's high time you died." The sorcerer ran the sword through Regulus' chest. The pain nearly made Regulus pass out. His scream stuck in his strangled throat, coming out in a thin moan. The sorcerer withdrew the sword. Sword and ropes vanished, and Regulus fell face-forward onto the ground. His chest was on fire. He couldn't breathe. Blood pooled beneath him. From where he lay on the ground, he saw Adelaide bolt upright, her hand clutched over her sternum.

"Regulus!"

Slowly, the fire blazing in his chest cooled and the pain numbed. Adelaide ran toward him. At the last moment, she changed direction and snatched the staff off the ground. She slid across broken glass until she stood in front of him, the staff clasped in both hands.

"He's not yours anymore." The challenge in her voice forced a smile to Regulus' face.

The sorcerer laughed. Regulus pushed himself to his knees, and the sorcerer's laugh died on his lips. "What… Oh." He slapped his forehead. "You put a bond on him. Idiot."

"Your Highness!" Carrick ran into the hall, panting. "The king has escaped. I can't find him."

Relief filled Regulus as the sorcerer cursed.

"I'll take that back." A coil of green rope shot from the sorcerer's hand and ripped the staff away from Adelaide, pulling her forward.

Adelaide conjured a flaming sword. Kirven held his hand forward, but Adelaide blocked the blast of flames with a shield of magical light. Regulus turned his attention to Carrick—right as Carrick slammed the pommel of his sword between Regulus' eyes.

Adelaide panted, sweat trickling down her back as she braced herself against Kirven's fiery assault. She maintained the shield with her left hand, the flaming sword still held in her right. Pain exploded between her eyes, but she couldn't look back at Regulus as she focused on withstanding Kirven's attack. Kirven raised the staff, then slammed the end into the ground. A small tremor raced toward her, enough to knock her off balance. Kirven cursed and fumbled the staff. Her foot slid across glass and she fell onto one knee.

"Should we go, my lord?" Nolan said.

Kirven waved his hand and a blast of green she didn't have time to block knocked her sideways. "Yes, but not empty-handed."

He sent a dozen ropes toward her, leaning heavily on the Staff of Nightfall and looking pale. She raised a barricade around herself and tried not to worry how much strength she had left. A rope broke through her barrier and grabbed her wrist.

"Hargreaves is unconscious?" Kirven asked. Carrick answered in the affirmative and Adelaide looked toward Regulus. He lay in a heap on the floor. Her heart twisted, her concentration breaking. Another rope got through and circled around her waist.

"Good." Kirven wiped his forehead with his sleeve. "Take him and go."

"What?" Carrick sounded as stunned as Adelaide.

"Are you stupid, boy?" Kirven shouted. "Take him and get out of here now!"

In her surprise, she lost all control of the barrier. The ropes wound around her arms, her legs, her waist, her throat. She strained against them, watching helplessly as Carrick ran past her, Regulus thrown over his shoulder.

"No," she choked out past the rope tightening around her neck. She let a blast of magical energy radiate off her entire body. The ropes disintegrated. She gasped in air.

"You've gotten better," Kirven panted as he walked toward the entrance to the hall. "I'm too tired to continue fighting you right now."

She stumbled to her feet and threw an arc of fire, but a green barrier stopped it. Kirven raised his left hand. Emerald light swirled around his legs, lifted him off his feet, then sped him toward the entrance. Adelaide darted around the barrier Kirven had left up. It disappeared as she passed it while Kirven floated out of the hall doors. She hitched up her dress and chased him.

A green shimmering barrier blocked the door behind him. She ran into it and was pushed back. "No!" She threw a fireball at it, but it held. "No, no, no!" She conjured a sword and attacked the barrier, but still it held. "Regulus!" She pounded the barrier with the sword, then stepped back and threw a stream of fire at the door. It flickered but didn't break.

"No!" Wait. The windows. *Idiot!* She turned and ran to the nearest window and climbed up onto the sill, ignoring the shards of glass cutting into her palms. She fell three feet to the ground outside and twisted her ankle. "I don't have time for this!" She tried to run without healing her ankle, but it slowed her progress and every step was excruciating. She cursed in Khast and stopped to heal her foot.

She didn't see a trace of Kirven, Nolan, or Regulus in the front garden, so she hurried on. One of the royal guards knelt over a bleeding guard on the ground next to the open font gate.

"Where are they?" she screeched. "The sorcerer and Nolan Carrick and Regulus Hargreaves! Did you see them?"

The guard looked up, eyes wide, and pointed a shaking hand out the gate. She ran past into desolate streets. Kirven and Nolan were gone. And so was Regulus.

She fell to her knees on the cobblestones and screamed. A blast of flames flared around her, turning the stones black. Another shrill scream ripped up her throat, leaving it raw, and echoed against the palace walls.

CHAPTER 37

EVERY PART OF ADELAIDE FELT NUMB AS SHE DRAGGED HER feet back inside the palace. She stood in the middle of the empty, silent great hall as night fell, dark and lifeless as the emptiness that had settled in her chest.

The king had escaped. Kirven had said something was wrong with the Staff of Nightfall. She had stood her ground, and Kirven had run away. These things should have comforted her. They didn't.

She had failed. Kirven and Nolan had escaped. The bodies of those she had failed to protect littered the floor of the hall. Kirven had taken Regulus, and she didn't understand why. Her bond would heal a lot if they hurt him, at least. But it wouldn't spare him from pain—or her from experiencing an echo of whatever pain he felt. It wouldn't prevent Nolan from cutting Regulus' head off his shoulders. Her stomach turned and she swayed. Footsteps sounded on the dais and someone entered holding a lit torch. She looked up, her mind blank.

Dresden stood on the dais, staring into the shadows. Blood stained his torn sleeves and covered his shirt and the bandage wrapped around his middle. He pressed his left hand against his side.

"Anyone here?" He held the torch high. "Regulus? Adelaide?"

She couldn't even find the energy to respond. As he walked further into the hall, the edge of the torchlight reached her.

"Adelaide?" Glass crunched under his boots in the stillness. "Adelaide?" He stopped before her, looking around in confusion. "Where's Regulus?"

She shook her head. Dresden paled. "D-dead?"

She shook her head again.

"I don't under… Captured?" She nodded. Dresden stumbled back as if slapped. "No… Reg…" He cursed and kicked at the glass.

"I tried…" Her throat constricted. She stared at the glass glittering in torchlight on the floor between them.

Dresden took several deep breaths. "I'm sorry, Adelaide. I need to tell you something." His voice was too low, too gentle. Her stomach knotted. "There's not an easy way to say this. It's…your father."

She jerked her head up, her throat closing. The drawn look on Dresden's face sucked away her breath.

"Adelaide…" Dresden sighed. "He's—"

"No." She shook her head. He couldn't be about to say what she feared. Tears burned in the corners of her eyes. "Where is he?"

Dresden's expression was pained. "He died a noble—"

"No!" She shoved Dresden's chest. *Died. Died.* "No, you're lying. You're wrong!" Her shrill voice wavered as her shoulders shook. "He's not… No." She pushed him again and felt a twinge of remorse as he groaned and clutched at his bloodied side.

He dropped the torch onto the floor and grabbed her shoulders. "Adelaide—"

"He can't be dead." Her head hurt like it had been hammered. She pictured Father's face, his eyes crinkling as he laughed. A sob shook her entire body. "He's not dead!"

Not Father, who was always there. Father, who had kissed her head and told her not to be afraid when he told her about the Shadow. Father, who always made her believe that somehow, everything would be all right.

"Adelaide—"

"No, you're wrong." She was supposed to save him. To save them all. "Where is he?" She broke free of Dresden's grip, sobbing as tears made his face difficult to see. "Where's my father?"

"I'm sorry. Your father is gone."

She rubbed her eyes and his face came back into focus. In the shadowy light of the torch on the floor, she saw the truth in his eyes. *No.*

"Take me to him. I—I can—" She gulped back her sobs, trying to talk past the ache in her throat. "I can save him. I can heal him. You have to take me to him!" She'd heal him, and he'd laugh and say she was as stubborn as Mother.

Dresden shook his head. "I'm sorry, Adelaide. It's not like Regulus. He's gone. I don't think even you can resurrect the dead."

"No, please…" What was left of her heart broke with a pain that was physical. Father's green eyes filled her mind. The sound of his voice as he teased Mother. The love and protectiveness in his face every time he called her *my daughter.* She had failed him.

Light flickered in the doorway behind the dais. "Clear," someone said. "Lay them out on the dais."

Adelaide stared at the doorway as guards carried bodies into the hall. Her chest constricted. Dresden tried to turn her away. "Adelaide, don't—"

She released a blast of light against his chest, knocking him to the ground, and ran to the dais, ignoring Dresden's cry of pain. She recognized the faces of the guards on the ground but didn't know their names. Another guard carried in a body not wearing a royal guard's uniform. She froze while the man placed the body on the dais next to the others. She stumbled forward as Dresden came up behind her, holding his torch in one hand and clutching his side with the other.

"Adelaide…"

She stared down at Father's ashen, lifeless face. His glassy eyes stared at the ceiling. The blood covering his chest glistened in the light of Dresden's torch.

Adelaide sank to her knees. "Father? I—I'm…here." She brushed her fingers over his cheek. His skin was too cold. His unseeing eyes didn't move. Her jaw quivered. "No, you can't, you have—you have…to stay."

She moved her trembling hands over his body. Her palms glowed as she searched for a spark of life. Nothing. She could sense the wound that went through his still, unmoving heart. She tried to heal it, to pull his heart back together and force it to beat again. "Tell me it—it's going to be all right. Pl…please, Father."

His heart didn't beat. His lips didn't move. Adelaide lifted his stiffening torso and cradled him in her lap as she rained tears on his unblinking face.

"I'm sorry, Father. I—I—I… I tried—" A sob swallowed her words. Her soul shattered like the stained glass covering the hall floor. She clenched his shirt and buried her face in his shoulder, choking on the sharp and bitter scent of his blood.

Dresden pulled her to her feet and Father's body fell back to the floor with a sickening thud. She screamed. Dresden dragged her away. Her legs shook and she collapsed, nearly pulling Dresden down on top of her. Her wails echoed in the vaulted ceiling. She howled her pain into the air until her throat was so raw, she couldn't make a sound, and then she pounded her fists against the floor.

Bits of broken glass cut her hands and her blood dripped onto the floor, but she didn't care. She couldn't feel the pain. There was too much pain in her heart for her body to feel anything. Dresden knelt and pulled her against his chest, preventing her flailing. She wept silently into his shoulder until she fell asleep, too exhausted to keep her eyes open.

When Adelaide awoke, she was lying in the dark on top of the bed in her and Regulus' little room. Her head throbbed. Everything came back at once. Regulus had been taken. Kirven and Nolan had escaped with the staff. And Father was... Father was...

Dead. The word bounced around inside her skull, making it pound more. She turned onto her side and curled into a ball. Her throat felt like it had been tied in knots and then untangled. She made a sound like an injured dog. Movement somewhere in the room made her freeze.

"Adelaide?" Dresden's sleepy voice. "Are you awake?"

After a moment, she said "yes," but no sound came out of her mouth. She cleared her throat. "Yes." Her voice sounded scratchy and thick.

"Do you need anything?" Dresden murmured. "I have water..."

She licked her dry lips. They tasted of tears. "Water would be good."

She managed to conjure a small orb of light. The light hurt her eyes and made her headache worse, which seemed impossible. Dresden sat in one of the chairs by the table, squinting. Dark bags circled under his heavy eyelids. He picked a large canteen up off the table and handed it to her. Swallowing was almost painful, but the water soothed the tightness in her throat.

Adelaide stared at the canteen in her hands as the question she both wanted and dreaded to ask burned in her chest. She took another drink. The water helped her headache, if only a little. Blood from her broken nose had dried on her chest and the bodice of her dress. Cuts and scrapes covered her hands, especially the fleshy sides of her palms. Parts of her skirt and sleeves were singed. And none of it mattered.

It took a moment to find her voice. "What happened?" The words came out in a croak. She took another drink and cleared her throat again. "How did my father…." Her eyes filled with tears. "How'd he die?" She finally met Dresden's eyes. "Were you there?"

Dresden hesitated. "We followed the royals. A guard or two was left every so often to slow down anyone who might try to pursue. We got to a locked brass door. The king unlocked it, and the guard captain and a few other guards accompanied the royals inside. It leads to some underground maze with several exits for the royal family to escape if need be."

He took a deep breath. "Three guards, your father, and I remained to guard the door. Good thing, too, because Carrick ripped the door off its hinges—after he caught me in the side," his hand drifted to the new, clean bandage on his left side, "cut off the hand of one of the guards, and severely wounded the other two. Your father stood his ground the longest. He bought the king time to escape."

She swallowed back a whimper.

He shook his head, admiration sparking in his eyes. "I would never have expected someone of his age to move so fast. He didn't think. He just fought." Dresden sighed heavily and his gaze left hers. "But Carrick was too fast and too strong. Alfred didn't stand a chance. He was stabbed through the heart. He died quickly."

Against her will, an image of a sword thrusting into Father's chest filled her mind. She tightened her jaw against traitorous sobs. She pressed her eyes closed as her stomach roiled.

"I was supposed to keep him safe," she whispered.

"He wouldn't want you to blame yourself," Dresden said quietly. "I spent several days with him, and I know how much he loved you."

His words meant to comfort just made her loss more acute.

"Your father never thought you needed to protect him. He just wanted to protect you. He would gladly have given his life for you, and he would never blame you."

She trembled as tears dripped off her chin. She wanted to tell Dresden to stop, stop talking, stop trying to make her feel better. Where once had been a father's love, now was an aching, empty loneliness. She didn't want him to try to ease her pain. But she couldn't make herself speak.

"He made his choice to stand his ground and defend the king." Dresden's eyes met hers, but instead of pity she didn't want, she saw unexpected understanding and determination. "He knew the risk. He didn't have to bring a sword or follow after the king. He didn't even have to come to the masque."

"If you think he didn't have to come," Adelaide whispered, "you don't...didn't know him very well at all."

"That's my point." Dresden leaned forward in the chair. He winced and clutched his side with a sharp intake of breath.

"What am I doing?" She wiped at her eyes and moved over to Dresden. "You're hurt. And I'm...I'm..." *Useless.* She held her hand over his side. The cut was long, but didn't touch any of his vital organs, and whoever had stitched him up had done a good job.

"Adelaide—"

"Almost done." She wasn't sure she wanted to hear what he had to say. Every word was just another strike, the hit of a hammer against an anvil, forging Father's death into an inescapable reality.

She finished healing his side. "You'll have to pull the stitches out." She headed back toward the bed, but Dresden caught her hand.

"Thank you. But you need to listen. Because if you can't forgive yourself, you're going to break. I've seen it before."

She pulled her hand away and sat on the bed.

"Your father knew what he was doing; he was aware of the danger, and he did it anyway because that's who he was. He was a good man. A brave man. He deserves your pride, not your self-blame."

"I don't want to be proud." She rubbed away a tear with a shaking hand. "I want him back." *I want my Father back. I want him to embrace me and tell me everything is going to be all right.* Her teeth chattered as she tried to stop crying.

Dresden didn't respond, and she was thankful. She didn't want platitudes or expressions of pity or pointless apologies. If she had resented Nolan before, that rage had frozen over into stone-hard hatred that threatened to drag her down and drown her in the storm-tossed waters of her hopelessness and sorrow. But some part of her whispered it wasn't really Nolan she hated; it was herself. Maybe Dresden was right. If she couldn't forgive herself and accept Father's sacrifice, she was going to crack. She clenched the worn blanket in her fists. Father was dead, and Regulus was gone, and Mother was—*Mother.*

"How am I supposed to tell my mother…?" Adelaide buried her face in her hands. How could she even cry this much? How could her heart hurt this much and not just kill her?

She didn't know how long she cried. Ten minutes, twenty, thirty, five. Time had ceased to have meaning. When she stopped, she took several deep breaths. "I think I'm going to go for a walk."

"Um…" Dresden cleared his throat. "A…Lieutenant Bell? Ball? A lieutenant said you're to report to him as soon as possible. Technically, he said the minute you wake up. He wanted to wake you, but I wouldn't let him."

She should have known. Duty first. "Can…can you come with me?"

"Of course."

They walked through the dark night to the barracks, an orb floating above them to light the way. She guessed it to be around three in the morning. A guard on duty at the entrance to the courtyard said Beale was in his chamber, but had left orders that if she came, to show her straight in. The guard led them to the end of the first floor of the barracks and knocked on a door. No one stirred inside, so he knocked again, harder and longer. A muffled voice shouted for them to enter. The guard bowed and departed, and Adelaide pushed the door open.

Beale sat on his bed, rubbing his eyes. His uniform coat was on but open over a white undershirt. His boots laid on the floor, but thankfully he was still wearing his trousers.

"Ah, good. Belanger." He rubbed the back of his head. "I need a report of what happened in the hall after the king left."

"Where is the king?" Weariness made her voice small.

"Safe. The royal family have been escorted to various places to hide. The king wants you to join him at once. But first I need to know what happened and what we're looking at going forward." He glanced toward Dresden. "I got a report from Sir Jakobs about what he knows about the attack. But I was knocked unconscious by Kirven's initial blast. I'm working blind here."

She relayed everything that happened. Her fight with Kirven. How Kirven tried to kill Regulus and she passed out, but something had happened to the Staff of Nightfall. How it seemed to not be working properly and be causing Kirven pain. Kirven and Nolan taking Regulus. She hung her head.

"I'm sorry, sir. I failed."

"You gave the king a chance to escape," Beale said. "The king is alive because of you. You did your duty. And you tried. And survived, which is more than I can say for...far too many of our men." He dragged his hand down the side of his face. "Captain Russell accompanied the king. Lieutenant Antar is gravely wounded and may lose his leg, possibly his life. Captain Matthews and Lieutenant Breck are dead. Five guards sustained minor injuries, five are critically wounded, ten are dead, and seven are missing, suspected desertion. Best guess, they panicked when attacked by a sorcerer, ran with the guests, and are too afraid to come back."

Adelaide nodded. The punishment for abandoning your post was at minimum thirty lashes and two days in the stocks without food or clothes.

"That leaves us with only twenty-five guards." Beale clasped his hands together. "And the threat is still out there. So I need you to pull yourself together, Belanger. We don't stand a chance without your help."

"Where are the wounded?" She sounded more tired than she had hoped. "I can help them."

Beale perked up at that. "Most are in the infirmary, at the beginning of the hall." He stood. "Lieutenant Antar is next door."

He led them into Antar's room. Antar lay on his bed, his damp hair plastered to his head. He muttered incoherently under his breath. Blood soaked through a thick bandage wrapped around the top of his right leg. Beale moved to unwrap the leg, but Adelaide stopped him.

"I don't need to see it."

And truthfully, she didn't want to. She held her hand over the bandage. Her magic flowed out and into Antar, and she got a sense of his wound. The wide cut went deep, partway through the bone. A sensation she hadn't encountered before surprised her until she realized what it was. An infection was already spreading through his body.

"I don't know if I can heal this," she admitted. "Why didn't they amputate already?"

"He insisted they wait until morning. I think he was hoping to die first."

She focused on mending the bone, the torn muscles and severed veins and nerves. Antar stopped muttering and his breathing deepened. The infection was harder—she had never dealt with that before. She tried to kill it, as if burning the infection out. When she had done everything in her power, she turned to Beale.

"He's technically healed, but I don't know if he will live. He's lost a lot of blood."

"I understand. Thank you for trying." Beale led the way to the infirmary, and she spent the next hour healing the guards. By the end, she felt more like a ghost than a person.

"I need to sleep," she mumbled. "I have to…to…have to regill. Refain." She shook her head. "Regain my energy. Wait for my magic to rurn…return."

"Yes. Yes, of course." Beale looked like he thought she might topple over at any moment. "We need you at your best, Belanger. Get some sleep."

She fell asleep within moments of collapsing on the bed. She only barely registered that Dresden had followed her and settled back into a chair. Somehow, his presence made the ache in her soul a little more bearable. But Regulus' absence next to her felt like a hole in her heart as she slipped into a deep sleep.

Light was stealing into the room in the cracks around the door when Adelaide bolted awake with a scream trapped in her lungs. She arched her back and flailed her arms and legs but couldn't break free of the bone-crushing pain pummeling her body. She rolled off the bed and hit the ground hard. Dresden jumped off the chair and grabbed her shoulders as she pulled in a wheezing, strangled breath.

"Breathe!" He dodged her wildly swinging hands. "What's wrong?"

She found her voice, and a single word leapt from her throat in a shriek. "Regulus!"

CHAPTER 38

SOMETHING ROUGH POKED INTO REGULUS' BACK AS HE groaned awake. He shifted. Metal clanked, aggravating his throbbing head. What was going on? Something weighed down his arms. He pried his eyes open. Pale, early morning sunlight illuminated the trees and meadow around him. The almost inaudible crash of waves sounded in the distance. The blackened bark of an oak tree pushed into his back. He recognized the dull, lifeless black of the tree and the shriveled, charcoal leaves curled on the edges of the branches. He'd ridden past the same thing on his way to the sorcerer's tower too many times.

Carrick and the sorcerer sat on stumps on either side of a small fire several paces away, turned away from him and eating something that smelled savory and made his stomach growl. Regulus went to move his arms and found he couldn't. He looked down.

A thick chain wrapped around his chest and the tree several times. Another chain connected to shackles around his wrists, then wrapped around his forearms before also wrapping around behind the tree. The right sleeve of his shirt had been cut off. He strained against the chains, but only succeeded in bruising his chest and making his wrists hurt. He glared at Carrick and the sorcerer, but they continued eating and paid no attention to his grunting and the clinking of the chains.

"Hey!" He tried to use his legs to push himself up, but the chains were too tight. "What am I doing here?"

They finally looked at him. Carrick's mouth curled into an irritated snarl as he chewed, but the sorcerer just wiped his fingers on his robe, picked up the Staff of Nightfall, and stood. Carrick glared up at the sorcerer, then tossed down the last bit of meat in his hand and followed the sorcerer toward Regulus.

"You are here," the sorcerer said, thinly veiled fury in his voice, "because of this." He held the top end of the Staff of Nightfall in front of Regulus' face.

At first, Regulus didn't understand. But as he looked closer, he saw the source of the sorcerer's rage. Two deep, jagged cracks ran through the opal mounted in the top piece. Spots of murky white marred the shiny black surface. The purple, blue, and red flecks looked dull instead of glittery. The sorcerer tossed the staff aside.

"I don't know how to fix it," the sorcerer spat. "Every time I use it since I tried to kill you with it, it doesn't work properly and burns my hand. But perhaps, if I can better understand this," he bent and placed his fingers between the chains on Regulus' right arm, on top of Adelaide's mark, "I can understand exactly what happened and fix it."

"Well, if you're hoping I can explain," Regulus said with a glare, "I can't. I was unconscious when Adelaide put that there, and I know nothing about magic."

"Oh, I don't need you to explain." The sorcerer straightened. "I know what that is, even if I've never seen one before. Honestly, I thought the lover's bond to be purely hypothetical. First time I've been wrong in quite a while."

The way Carrick clenched his fists and tightened his jaw at *lover's bond* lit a satisfied spark in Regulus' chest. Let the cad try to argue he could win Adelaide's heart now.

"There are three known bonds," the sorcerer said. "The servant's bond, sometimes called the slave's bond, which I perfected and with which you're well acquainted." Carrick frowned at that, and Regulus nearly laughed. "The protection bond, which is the most common but still not widely used because few people are so selfless as to let another essentially borrow some of their magic. Finally, the lover's bond. Obviously the rarest, since I didn't believe it existed outside of legend."

The sorcerer stroked his beard. "But the lover's bond is also the strongest, the hardest to break, and most closely unites the bearer and the giver." He sat cross-legged next to Regulus. "So you don't need to explain what it is or how she put it there, or even how it works because I'm aware your stupid brain doesn't understand it. But I do want you to explain what you have experienced since receiving it. What are its effects? What changes have you noticed?"

"Let me say this plainly and simply." Regulus rested his head against the tree. "As Adelaide said: I'm not yours anymore. I don't answer to you."

The sorcerer shook his head. "You always make things so difficult." He placed his palm against Regulus' chest. The pain was immediate, and worse than anything Regulus had experienced when he had the sorcerer's mark. Somewhere in the back of his mind he wondered if it was because of the direct proximity of the sorcerer, but he was too consumed with the pain to think clearly. He screamed, struggling against the chains but unable to do more than kick his legs. His boot hit the sorcerer's side, and the sorcerer's hand left his chest. Regulus gasped for air as the world tilted and shifted before his vision cleared.

The sorcerer rubbed his side and cursed. "All right. Let's try this again. Tell me about the effects of the bond."

Regulus glared. He wanted to tell the sorcerer to go to hell. But he also didn't want to experience that pain again. More importantly, when what hurt him hurt Adelaide, he couldn't go asking for punishment. But would that information help the sorcerer fix the staff? A malfunctioning weapon would help Adelaide defeat him.

"This shouldn't require that much thought, Hargreaves." The sorcerer stood. "If you won't tell me, I suppose we'll just have to do some research. Carrick." He motioned toward Regulus. "Have fun."

Carrick grinned and pulled a dagger from the back of his belt. "My pleasure."

"No, wait." Regulus struggled to sit up straighter as Carrick crouched next to him.

"Afraid of a little blood, mongrel?" Carrick laughed. "Where should I start? Maybe I'll reopen that scar of yours." The blade glinted as it moved past Regulus' eyes.

He squelched his rising panic. It would be better to pretend to play along, give obvious information, than let them hurt Adelaide. And he didn't want to be tortured, either. "I heal."

"Tell me something I don't know," the sorcerer spat.

"Little things heal, too. Nicks, bruises."

The sorcerer squinted. "And that's it? You're holding out on me, Hargreaves. Do it, Carrick." Carrick grinned and moved the point of the knife to the top of Regulus' scar.

"No!" The chains clinked as Regulus fruitlessly tried to raise his hand to stop Carrick. "That's it, it works like yours, but without the pain! Please! I heal, there's no pain, she can't control me, that's it." The point of the knife touched his skin. "Don't! That's it, I swear. Please!"

The sorcerer held up his hand, and Carrick scowled as he lowered the knife. "Hm." The sorcerer tilted his head, his gaze drilling into Regulus. "You're not afraid of pain. You know you'll heal, so it's not a fear of a wound. What are you so afraid of?"

Dammit. He met the sorcerer's gaze and tried to keep his expression closed, to betray nothing. The sorcerer's eyes narrowed as he thought. "You only have ever begged me to spare others, never yourself. Others… Wait. The mage cried out like she was in pain, but I hadn't hit her." He looked to Carrick. "But you hit *him*." He looked back to Regulus. "What aren't you telling me, mercenary?"

Regulus set his jaw and glared right back.

"Cut his face open."

"Finally." Carrick brought the knife back up. From the way the corner of the sorcerer's mouth twitched upward, Regulus suspected he already knew the truth.

"All right!" Regulus lowered his gaze. "Adelaide feels my pain."

Carrick froze, the point of the knife hovering just above the top of the scar. "What are you talking about?"

"When I'm hurt, she feels an echo of my pain. Not as intense as actually receiving the wound herself, but she still feels it." Regulus looked up at the dead branches above him. "When we realized, I tried to get her to remove the mark. But she wouldn't." He looked back at Carrick. "Please. Anything you do to me, you do to her."

Carrick tilted his head. "So it doesn't actually wound her?"

"There's no mark or blood, no."

"But she feels your pain? Your injuries?"

"Yes!" He knocked his head back against the tree. "Do you not understand, or do you not believe me!"

"No, I believe you. And I understand." Carrick's eyes glinted. "I understand that when I do this," the tip of the dagger cut into Regulus' face as he pulled the blade down the length of the scar while Regulus screamed, "she'll know exactly what is happening to you."

Regulus clenched his teeth, his chest heaving and eyes watering. Carrick stood and moved back to give the sorcerer an unobstructed view of Regulus' mutilation. He had cut deeper than the original scar, slicing all the way through the cheek so that the skin curled away from the side of his face. Regulus moaned, the pain like fiery needles over the side of his face. Then the pain faded away. He breathed deeper. The skin curled back and pulled together. Regulus unclenched his jaw and opened his eyes.

The sorcerer stood stroking his beard, expression impassive. Carrick's brows lifted toward his hairline. Regulus spat blood toward Carrick's feet. Carrick stepped back, his top lip pulling up.

"Interesting." The sorcerer tugged on his beard. "All very interesting."

Regulus sighed. Sooner or later, the torture would break him, and he would have put Adelaide through all that pain, just to give in. He couldn't let them hurt her. "Please. I'll tell you anything I can. Just…stop hurting her."

Carrick looked to the sorcerer, who nodded. With clear disappointment, Carrick crossed his arms.

"You said you were unconscious when she bound you," the sorcerer said. "That shouldn't be possible. You should have to agree to a binding."

"I did, apparently. I don't really remember." Regulus glowered at Carrick. "Carrick had run me through with a sword, and I had mostly bled out. Adelaide healed the wound, but I was still fading. She asked me if I wanted to be bound to her for life, and I didn't really understand what she was asking, so of course I agreed. Then I blacked out. I came to a couple minutes later, Adelaide had passed out, and I had this mark."

"How long was she out for?"

"About a day and a half, two days."

The sorcerer clasped his hands. "Any other side effects?"

When Regulus hesitated, Carrick twirled the knife in his hand.

"When we touch—actual skin contact—we can feel each other's emotions." Regulus shifted against the tree trunk, but there was no getting comfortable. "Any skin contact, I can sense her emotions. And a couple times, I've seen what she's thinking about when I close my eyes while touching her."

"Examples," the sorcerer grunted.

Regulus fixed Carrick with a withering stare. "She was scared and upset, and I was trying to comfort her. I closed my eyes, and I saw her memories, as if looking through her eyes. You know what I saw, Carrick? I saw *you*. I know what you did."

Carrick reddened and glanced away, then recovered his neutral expression. At least he had some sense of shame.

"And you." Regulus turned his attention to the sorcerer. "She has nightmares. About what you did to her, what you threatened to do to her family. I tried to wake her one night and closed my eyes, barely more than a blink, and my mind was pulled into her nightmare."

"No wonder my spell backfired," the sorcerer muttered. "This bond is stronger and deeper than I would have dreamed possible. But then, magic born out of self-sacrifice is always strong, because the price paid for it is so high."

"Sacrifice?" Regulus' brow wrinkled. "Why, because I nearly died?"

"That's part of it, yes. You sacrificed yourself for her, but the amount of energy she put into you to create *that* mark—she was ready to give up her power entirely to save you. She could have killed herself with the effort."

What? Regulus' mouth fell into a silent *oh*. A surge of love and gratitude fought with guilt. *No wonder she slept for so long.*

The sorcerer crossed his arms and shook his head, his features sagging and weary. "When I used the staff on you, the sorcery in it tried to overpower the magic in you to kill you and failed. All that destructive magical energy had to go somewhere, so it did—back onto my staff." He snarled the words. "I had hoped it said something about her power, that she might have the strength to repair the staff. But this," he pointed at Regulus' arm, his disgust apparent, "this isn't because of the power of her magic, just her love. It's a cyclical strengthening based on your sickening affection for each other. Your love strengthens the bond, the bond strengthens your love, and so forth, making the protection magic in you stronger than the destructive magic was in the staff. It's useless to me, unless I want to use you as a shield."

"Oh, yes," Regulus said with a scowl, "how *dare* something exist you can't twist to use for your own selfish needs."

The sorcerer lifted an eyebrow, then waved his hand. "Carrick, he's all yours."

"What?" Panic crawled up Regulus' spine. "I answered your questions! I won't beg for myself, but for Adelaide? Please. Don't." He desperately looked at Carrick. "I'm begging you. Don't hurt her."

"Actually," the sorcerer said, "what I want more than anything right now is to hurt your precious mage for making a mess of all my plans. I'd do it myself, but I'm tired, and need to rest and think so I can figure out where to find my stupid brother."

Regulus clenched his fists in a useless gesture of defiance. "But—"

"Carrick, don't cut any appendages off, especially not his head." The sorcerer sounded bored. "Other than that, go ahead and let all that rage and resentment that's been making you insufferable out on him." The sorcerer started back toward the fire, then paused. "And for the love of sorcery, gag him so I don't have to listen to his screams and protestations."

"I answered your questions!" The chains dug into Regulus' chest as he strained against them. "No, you can't—I answered your questions!"

Carrick pulled off his blood-stained doublet and cut a long, thick strip, paying no attention to Regulus.

He switched tactics. "Carrick, you have to realize this won't help you win her. She won't forgive you."

Carrick shoved the fabric into Regulus' mouth and tied it behind his head. "I'm not trying to win her heart anymore, mercenary. She doesn't want me, and she likely never will. She won't forgive me, anyway." Uncertainty flickered over his expression. "Not after I killed her father."

Regulus stopped straining against the chains. Her father… His eyes bulged. Alfred Belanger was…dead? Carrick killed him? *Oh, Adelaide.*

"He got in my way." Carrick shrugged, but from the tone of his voice and the pinch of his brows, he was troubled. "I'd kill you, too, but apparently I'm not allowed." He shifted over to Regulus' right arm. "I had hoped once you were dead, she would be free to want me. But I see now…" He dug the dagger into Regulus' forearm and began cutting around the mark. Regulus screamed into the gag. "She's given her heart too completely to you for it to ever be mine. She could have had my love. Now she will know my vengeance."

Carrick pried the chunk of flesh bearing Adelaide's mark, the mark of a lover's bond, out of his arm. Regulus sagged against the tree, black spots clouding his vision. Bile rose in his mouth but had nowhere to go against the gag, so he swallowed it back down. He closed his eyes and bit down hard on the gag.

Numbing warmth spread over his forearm until the pain faded away. Still, tears soaked into the gag pulling at the sides of his mouth. He let his head fall forward and leaned in exhaustion against the chains. Carrick rubbed at his arm, and Regulus opened his eyes as Carrick pulled his hand away. On his arm, beneath the smeared red, Adelaide's mark stood out as clear as ever.

"Hm. Unsurprising, but disappointing." Carrick flicked a spray of blood off the dagger. "I want to be clear, though." He used the dagger to lift Regulus' chin, forcing him to look at Carrick's face. "I've admitted I can't force her love. But I will still have her. I've never been one to walk away. My parents said my reckless, bullheaded determination was cute when I was a child, but is…what was it? Boorish now. But then, I was always their least favorite son." He turned the dagger so the edge sliced into the underside of Regulus' chin. "I don't like losing. Adelaide will be my wife, even if I have to keep her collared and chained."

Regulus pushed his tongue against the gag, trying to force it out of the way so he could tell Carrick off. His face burned from his neck to his scalp. He pulled at the chains, willing them to break even as the shackles cut into his wrists and the effort pulled at his shoulders. He kept his eyes locked on Carrick's and hoped Carrick could see his rage.

"I never liked you, mercenary. A peasant masquerading as a lord." Carrick lowered the dagger. "But trust me, at this point, I hate you as much as you hate me." He stabbed the dagger into Regulus' thigh. Regulus grimaced, then groaned as Carrick dragged the dagger down several inches. "Maybe His Highness will let me keep you. If Adelaide misbehaves, I can just hurt you." He twisted the dagger. Regulus shook as he bit back a scream. "Knowing that her bad behavior will spill your blood and cause you both pain might help keep her docile." He pulled the dagger out of Regulus' leg with a sickening squelch. "Should help with holding her to her promise."

Promise? Regulus raised his eyes from his leg to Carrick.

Carrick laughed. "Oh, she didn't tell you? Before you came barreling in and nearly got yourself killed, she promised me that once she and I are married—and we will be—she will be, and I quote, 'a dutiful, affectionate wife.'" He sneered.

Regulus felt like he had been punched in the gut. Was that the only reason Carrick had stopped that day? He pulled at the chains, his muscles bulging. He pictured his hands closing around Carrick's neck. The chain made a squeaking groan as it pulled against the tree.

336

But it wouldn't break. There was no point, so he stopped struggling and sagged against the chains, his head hanging as guilt crushed him.

"That's right." Carrick examined the blood-soaked tip of the dagger. "Be a good mongrel dog and accept your leash."

Chapter 39

Adelaide gripped Dresden's arm, steadying herself as she nearly fell over in the middle of the entrance to the guards' courtyard from the pain in her leg. There had been a short window without pain—meaning Regulus wasn't in pain. She had changed her dress during that window, then headed to the barracks to ask Beale if he had heard anything about where the sorcerer might have gone. But getting there was proving difficult. Every wound inflicted on Regulus not only caused her pain but drained some of her energy to heal him. The pain in her leg faded. She let go of Dresden's arm and straightened.

"Why are they doing this?" Her voice trembled.

Dresden shook his head, his eyes pinched. "Maybe to see how much he can take. Or to keep you weak. Maybe just for the fun of it."

Her stomach clenched. She could see Nolan hurting Regulus just to hurt him. But surely Regulus would have told him that it hurt her, too. She remembered Nolan kicking her face and shattering her nose. And then he killed her father. Clearly, he didn't care about not hurting her. At least there was a twisted upside to that. Maybe it meant he didn't want her anymore. But, no. She recalled the glint in his eyes as his hand slid up her leg. He simply no longer cared if she wanted him.

They had only gotten a few yards into the courtyard when she grabbed her throat. *Can't...breathe...* Stabbed. They had stabbed Regulus in the throat. Dresden wrapped his arm under hers, supporting her. A tear slid down her cheek as she dropped her hands from her throat.

"The pain is that bad?"

"It does hurt. But not as much as it's hurting him. And that's worse than the actual pain." She pulled away and ran across the courtyard. "I have to find him!" She clenched her teeth and tried to ignore the stab of pain in her left hand.

She threw open the door to the barracks. Beale and Antar sat in the briefing room. They looked up as she entered, stopping mid-conversation.

"Has any information come in about where the sorcerer might be?"

Beale shook his head. "No, but that's not—"

"*Someone* had to have seen something!" She stomped her foot. "Someone must know—" She gasped and clutched her stomach as something prodded, pinched, and twisted. She grimaced against the pain, against the knowledge of what was happening.

"Are you okay?" Beale stood and reached toward her.

She held up her hand and he stopped. "I'm fine," she said through gritted teeth. "It's Regulus. We have this bond. I can feel—" She leaned against the doorframe as pain sliced down her bicep. "His pain. They're torturing him."

Beale and Antar exchanged a look. "I don't understand," Antar said. "Why don't they just kill him?"

"They can't." She had forgotten they had never explained Regulus' abilities to the officers, only to the king. "The bond. It constantly heals him so he can't be killed."

"He…what?" Beale shook his head. "That's impossible."

"How're you feeling, Lieutenant Antar?" She looked pointedly at his leg.

Antar flushed. "Tired, but otherwise fine. Thank you. I should have said that already."

"You're welcome, but that's not my point. My point is, why should it be impossible?" She pushed off the doorframe. "Now, I *have* to find Kirven and Regulus. This torture is a constant drain on my power. The longer they hurt him, the less energy I'll have to fight Kirven." *And the more pain Regulus will experience. And me.* Something stabbed between her ribs. She groaned and grabbed the spot.

"She feels only a fraction of his pain," Dresden said behind her, his voice tight. "If she's in this much pain, Regulus is…" He gulped. "He needs help."

Beale shook his head. "I'm sorry, Belanger. My orders are to send you to the king, not out looking for the sorcerer."

"Fine." She straightened. "I'll find them without your help." She turned and nearly ran into Dresden standing in the doorway.

"Belanger." The tone of Beale's voice stopped her. "If you leave now, it won't just be abandoning your post. It'll be counted as desertion. You'll be hanged."

She hesitated. An invisible blade sliced across her jaw. *This can't continue! Kirven, Nolan, whoever is doing this, they have to get tired of it, right?* She whimpered as pain dug deep into the front of her shoulder, just above her armpit, and twisted back and forth. Dresden grabbed her shoulders as her eyes watered and she moaned. The knife or whatever it was dragged out of Regulus and she felt her power healing him as the pain abated. She squared her shoulders. Without looking back at Beale, she said, "So be it," and pushed past Dresden out of the room.

They were only a few feet from the barracks when Beale's voice rang over the courtyard. "Adelaide Belanger, you are under arrest for desertion, a crime of treason against the king. Men, seize her."

She stopped mid-stride. The dozen or so men around the courtyard looked over. No one moved. Adelaide grabbed Dresden's hand and sprinted toward the gate. Beale shouted at the men, and they drew their weapons and started after them.

"Stay back!" Adelaide threw an arc of fire behind her as she ran. The guards slowed but didn't stop. They were almost to the gate when two men stepped in front of them, their faces white. With a wave of her hand, she blasted them out of their path. Their pursuers were all behind them now. She blindly threw a blast of energy behind her and heard a couple men grunt. They ran through the gate and she skidded to a stop and whirled around. She raised her hand, and a shimmering blue barrier filled the open gate. The closest guard tapped the barrier with his sword. A burst of energy pushed him back.

"Let's go." She strode away from the barricaded gate, her jaw set.

Dresden hurried after her. "Do you have a plan?"

"Get out of the palace. Find Regulus." She turned toward the livestock gate, the closest exit, and dodged a servant boy leading an obstinate goat. "Kill Kirven and Nolan."

"Remind me never to let you and Regulus plan anything alone," Dresden said. "He's a great fighter, a firm but understanding captain, and an inspiring leader, but his plans usually need some help to be actual *plans*."

"I'll figure it out." She strode toward the gate and ignored the shouting voice in her head agreeing with Dresden, telling her she was making the same mistake they had made before the masquerade. The guard on duty glanced between them.

"Um, no one told me—"

She cut him off, conjuring a ball of flames above her right hand. "Unlock the door."

The guard paled. "I…I can't without orders—"

"Then give me the keys and I'll do it." The flames flared larger and hotter.

"I really wouldn't try her if I were you," Dresden said, a flicker of amusement in his voice. "The love of her life has been taken and she's on the war path."

The guard backed toward the gate. "I'll be thrown in the stocks."

Adelaide groaned. She dropped the flames and shoved her hands forward. The blast pushed the guard back and up against the gate with a crash. He slumped to the ground, unconscious. She pulled the keys off his belt and opened the lock holding the crossbeam in place. She pushed the gate open and tossed the keys on the guard's chest before striding out of the palace. Once they were well away from the palace walls, she stopped. She needed a direction. Walking with no destination would waste precious time. And every minute she wasted was another minute that Regulus—

Wait. She stared at Dresden.

"They stopped."

"What?" Dresden looked around the narrow, shadowy alleyway between two tall wooden buildings. His hand gripped his sword as he watched the townspeople walk by the opening of the alley, busy with their lives and their shopping as if their king wasn't on the run. "Who—wait. The pain? It stopped?"

"Yes. What does that mean?" She should have been relieved, but irrational fear clawed at her mind. They couldn't have found a way to kill him—could they? No. No, she wouldn't lose Father and Regulus. She couldn't.

"It means he's okay for the moment," he said, his voice calm. "Now, we need a plan. We can't just wander around, hoping to stumble across them before the guards find us." He stroked his beard. "If they're torturing him, they're unlikely to be in town. Even with a gag, that would make a lot of noise and draw too much attention. If the sorcerer was worn out from your fight, they wouldn't have gone terribly far. He must have needed to regain his energy, just like you did, which is probably why they didn't start on Regulus until this morning."

He spoke so matter-of-fact. It reminded her of the way she once heard Father and some of his friends discussing how to find and corner a hobgoblin that had been causing havoc in the gardens. Methodical, dispassionate. But this was *Regulus* being tortured he was talking about.

"They'd likely want to stay close enough to town that they could sneak in and listen for gossip on where the king is," Dresden continued. "But they wouldn't want to be too close to the palace in case of search parties while they're recovering and getting whatever it is they want from Regulus."

She leaned against one of the buildings. The rough wood snagged on her dress, but she didn't care. "How are you so calm?"

"I'm not calm!" Dresden slammed his palm into the wall. "I'm trying to be *controlled.* Controlled keeps you from making stupid decisions and wasting time or getting killed. Regulus might not be great at coming up with plans, but he never meets the enemy on their ground without stopping to think. You know how many mercenary troops had as high a success and survival rate as ours? Not many. Because he never made a move without sending out scouts. He never broke camp until he had consulted with his lieutenants. He tried to avoid going in somewhere when he didn't have a way out." He sighed. "Until the sorcerer. He gave up and got reckless after that. It's part of why he would never let us go with him. But that's irrelevant."

Adelaide looked up at the sliver of blue sky peeking through the narrow space between the wide top floors of the buildings. Some kids ran past the alleyway, laughing as adults shouted at them. She massaged her forehead. "All right. Do you have an idea?"

"Just…give me a minute to think!"

She closed her eyes and leaned her head back against the building. *Where are you, Regulus? Where would they take you?* His face filled her mind. His intense gray eyes. His lopsided smile from the pull of his scar. The gentleness in his strong hands as he held her. She needed his strength right now. The way she felt protected when curled against his side. *I need you, Regulus. Where are you? Please, Etiros. I need to find him.* Something tugged at her gut. A gentle current, almost like the pull of the neumenet tree, but different. Her eyes flew open.

"Dresden." She stepped into the alley, heading toward the back of the buildings. The pull grew, and she knew in her heart. "I can find him."

Adelaide raced through the twisting streets of the town. A couple times she had to back up and retrace her steps when the pull shifted, and she realized she had missed a turn. Dresden tried to tell her to slow down, that they should form a plan, but the thrum of energy leading her toward Regulus overpowered his protests. *I'm coming, Regulus. I'm coming.*

They left the town behind. Farmers watched in confusion and irritation as they cut across fields and leapt over low stone walls. But for whatever reason—perhaps their clothes marked them as nobles, or the farmers thought with sorcerers on the loose it was better to ignore strangers—no one tried to stop them. The air cooled and smelled of salty sea air. The pull of their bond strengthened, but she forced her feet to slow.

"We're getting close," she said.

Dresden grabbed her arm, forcing her to stop. "How close do you think we are?"

She tugged on her hair. "It's difficult to explain, and it's inexact. I know he's that way," she pointed toward the trees on the other side of an apple orchard just ahead of them. "I don't know how much past the orchard. Could be a couple feet. Could be ten paces."

Dresden pinched the bridge of his nose. "Okay. We need to go slowly. I want to rush in, too, but our best bet is to surprise them, and to do that, they can't hear or see us coming." He pointed to the hedge circling the orchard. "We should keep to the outside of the hedge, stay low, instead of cutting across the orchard. If we can, we need to get Regulus *before* confronting the sorcerer and Carrick. That will make our chances better and prevent the possibility of them hurting Regulus and making you both useless."

His bluntness made her wince, but she nodded. "Once Regulus is free, we need to prioritize Kirven. So long as he's alive, we can't kill Nolan. And the best way of stopping Kirven is to get his staff."

"Good thinking." Dresden sighed. "That will have to do. There are too many variables with all this magic involved. No point in making a plan that might fall apart."

They crept along the outside edge of the hedge at a maddeningly slow pace. They were so close to Regulus it made her skin tingle. But that also meant they were close to Kirven and Nolan. And that made her stomach churn, which reminded her she hadn't eaten breakfast. The gnawing in her stomach added to her nervous energy as they darted across the empty space between the hedge and the trees, as quickly and quietly as possible. She led the way toward Regulus through the trees. She wanted to hurry but forced herself to move slowly, watching the ground to avoid any dead leaves that looked crunchy or sticks that might snap and give their approach away.

"—honestly, I should be torturing *you* for letting Gawain escape!" Kirven spat. Adelaide dropped into a crouch and moved away from his voice and closer to where she sensed Regulus.

"Then get it over with," Nolan said. Adelaide's breath caught as grief and anger slammed into her at the sound of his voice. "You're the one who said you could easily take care of Adelaide if she was there. Besides, if you had taken your shot faster, she wouldn't have had time to raise that barrier." Nolan groaned. *You deserve that and more*, Adelaide thought as she edged toward an opening in the trees.

"And if we had just killed her, she definitely wouldn't have been able to."

Nolan grunted. "Not the agreement."

"If she gets in my way again, I'm killing her," Kirven said, his words heated.

Adelaide and Dresden crouched behind a couple of trees. Regulus sat chained to an oak tree that looked like it had been through a fire. His head rested against the black tree trunk. A blue gag pulled against his mouth and his eyes were closed. Dried blood stained his right arm and the chains binding it and covered his legs, his neck, his torso, even his face. She leaned against the tree, light-headedness making her vision black out until her head cleared. Oddly, the Staff of Nightfall lay in the grass at Regulus' feet. Kirven sat several paces away, his back toward them. But Nolan stood across from Kirven. If they left the cover of the trees, he would see them.

"Didn't you already try that at the palace?" Nolan clenched and unclenched his fist, his face red. "You couldn't even manage it then. And we should have taken *her*. What was the point of taking Hargreaves? You made a mistake—" Nolan screamed and doubled over. Adelaide ran out of the trees, Dresden close on her heels. She slid across the grass to the side of the oak furthest from Kirven and Nolan. The air reeked of Regulus' blood.

Chains. How to break chains? Fire? No. Cut through them with a magic blade? It might work. She looked at the chains around Regulus' chest, then at the shackles around his wrists. Which should she try to remove first? Both needed to come off, but the moment they did, they would make noise. Nolan had stopped screaming. She risked leaning out around the tree. Nolan stomped away from

Kirven, his back to them. Good. The Staff of Nightfall lay on the grass, so close. Staff first, or Regulus first? Regulus first.

She moved closer to Regulus and touched his shoulder. His eyes snapped open, full of silent pleas for mercy that made her heart bleed. He relaxed when his eyes met hers, the terror in his expression replaced with joy. She smiled and held a finger to her lips, then untied the gag. He moved his jaw as she dropped the rag to the ground. She leaned close and murmured in his ear, "I thought we agreed no more splitting up."

"I'm glad to see you," he whispered, "but you shouldn't have come."

"You would have come for me." She pressed her hand to the side of his face, against the blood caked over his jawline. "Together, remember?"

He glanced toward Kirven and Carrick. "Alright, but we need to hurry."

"Hey." Dresden crouched next to her. His face tinged with green as he looked at Regulus, but he shook his head and looked in control again. Regulus looked exceedingly displeased to see Dresden. "Isn't that the staff? Should we take it?"

"What are you doing here?" Regulus hissed. "This is magic and immortals. They could kill you."

Oh. She hadn't even stopped to think of that when Dresden followed her. She had been too focused on Regulus. Too focused on herself.

Dresden grinned, but it was full of sorrow and pain. "Somebody had to watch your girl's back with you off getting captured."

An idea occurred to Adelaide. She had no idea how to break the staff, or if she even possessed the power to do so. But they could at least ensure Kirven didn't have a chance to use it against them—and keep Dresden safe. "Dresden, you should take the staff and run." She glanced toward Kirven and Nolan. They still weren't looking. She kept her voice low. "Take it far from here."

"It's a good idea." Despite his hushed tone, Regulus' words held urgency.

Dresden shook his head. "And leave you two?"

She placed a hand on Dresden's arm. "I can't lose anyone else."

"I won't abandon my brother," Dresden whispered fiercely.

"Look at me." Weariness laced Regulus' voice. "I won't let this happen to you. I can't let Carrick hurt you again."

Again. Adelaide recalled Nolan's taunt. *"Did he tell you those stripes were for you?"* Her hands fisted.

"Please, Drez. I need to know you're safe."

"And I need you safe," Dresden shot back. "We protect each other, remember?"

Adelaide sighed. "Regulus can't die. I can defend myself from Kirven's magic, and Nolan won't kill me. You have to go."

"I can help," Dresden pleaded. "Reg, you know I can—"

"Drez…" Regulus rested his head against the tree. "Don't make me order you."

Dresden's expression turned stony. "Please don't do this."

Adelaide looked helplessly between them and glanced toward Kirven and Nolan. They were still turned away from the tree, but it was only a matter of time.

"Sir Jakobs." Regulus looked apologetic as he locked eyes with Dresden. "As your liege, I command you to take the staff and flee immediately, and don't come back." He hung his head. "As your brother, I'm begging you. Please go."

Dresden worked his jaw. "Fine. I'll find you when you return to the palace." With one more glance at Kirven and Nolan, Dresden grabbed the staff and ran.

Good. She watched Dresden disappear among the trees, taking the Staff of Nightfall where Kirven couldn't reach, then turned back to Regulus. "Can you grab the chains on your arms, so they won't fall when I unlock them?"

In response, Regulus gripped the chains. *How…maybe like closing a wound, but opposite?* She held her hand over the shackle on his left wrist and closed her eyes, but couldn't sense the lock. She detected Regulus and the blood pumping in his veins. *No.* She knit her brows together, concentrating. This wouldn't work. She needed… *Key.*

Such an obvious answer. She conjured a rough key shape and inserted it into the lock. At last, she sensed the inside of the lock, and she morphed the key until it fit, then turned it. The shackle made a click that sounded terribly loud to her ears. She glanced toward Kirven and Nolan, but they still weren't looking. She moved to his other side, closer to Kirven. *Okay, focus. Form the key, shape it…* The lock clicked and she smiled.

"I hoped you'd show up, mage."

CHAPTER 40

THE SOUND OF KIRVEN'S CALM VOICE SLITHERED DOWN Adelaide's spine. She whirled around and stood, shielding Regulus. Kirven moved toward her, a self-assured smile on his face. Carrick followed, his sword drawn. The clink of metal indicated Regulus had released the chain on his arms.

"I'm glad you're here, Adelaide." Kirven nodded. "We can have a nice talk."

"I'm not here to talk." She conjured a sword and hoped she looked intimidating. Nolan eyed them both but didn't attack. Probably waiting on an order from his master. "Where's your staff, Kirven?"

Kirven frowned, then looked down. His head jerked back up. "What did you do with it?"

"It's long gone. A friend took it; I don't know where. He might have thrown it into the sea for all I know."

Kirven's eyes flashed. He clenched his fists, his shoulders scrunching toward his ears. He relaxed and his expression returned to bored neutrality. "You're protecting him with your life when that's not necessary. Standing over him, placing yourself in harm's way, when he can't die because you already protected him with your bond."

When he said it like that, it did sound stupid. She *could* die. "I won't let you hurt him anymore." She looked at Nolan. At the blood staining the ends of his sleeves and splattered on his shirt, trousers, and boots. Regulus' blood. Guards' blood. Father's blood. Anger and sorrow kicked at the inside of her chest, a caged and wounded animal that wanted out.

"Why?" Her voice broke. She hadn't meant to say that. It just came out.

Nolan's cocky, unconcerned façade cracked. For a moment, she saw regret in his eyes. Then it was gone. "I'm sorry. He shouldn't have gotten in my way."

His careless words hit her like fists. Her emotions built, threatening to crush her. Adelaide willed back her tears. *No. Not now. You can't fall apart right now.* She saw the green light out of the corner of her eye too late. She'd been too focused on Nolan and her hurt to stay on guard. The blast knocked her sideways, throwing her several feet from Regulus and the tree. She grunted as she hit the ground. *Stupid!*

Nolan held his sword to Regulus' neck. Regulus glared up at Nolan but didn't try to move. Cautiously, Adelaide walked closer, her hands at her sides as Kirven watched her with an impassive expression.

"Ready to talk?" Kirven stroked his beard. "Or should I have Carrick find out if your precious Hargreaves can regrow limbs?" Nolan stepped on Regulus' right hand and held the sword at his wrist.

"No!" Adelaide held up her hands submissively. "I'll talk."

"You owe me, mage." Kirven crossed his arms. "Your lover's bond caused my spell to rebound and cracked the opal in the Staff of Nightfall. I could, with some effort, replace the opal. But I fear the damage runs deeper than that. Your friend may have taken the staff, but it was already useless to me. You owe me a replacement weapon."

"I can double-check under my bed, but I don't think I have another staff imbued with sorcery lying around."

Kirven rolled his eyes. "I had something else in mind." The look in his eyes, the sly half-smile, and she knew. A lump grew in her chest. "You."

She swallowed. "I've already given you my answer."

"Carrick, remind her what's at stake—but nothing that might not heal yet."

"No, wait—" She reached toward Nolan and Regulus, but Nolan jabbed the sword into Regulus' side. Regulus groaned and Adelaide stumbled forward, grabbing at her own side and biting her tongue against the pain. Nolan pulled the sword further down into Regulus' hip. Adelaide moaned and fell to her knees as Regulus screamed.

"Stop!" She struggled to stand. Nolan withdrew the sword. Regulus' blood dripped off the blade and she turned her face away.

"You took my greatest weapon from me," Kirven said. "One I worked for nearly twenty years to find and reassemble. You owe me a new weapon."

Energy drained out of her to heal Regulus. A new thought occurred to her. The warning in the *Compendium*: *"drained of magic until they perished."* Might she reach a point she couldn't heal Regulus, even with the bond? Would Regulus die if they kept this up? Would *she* die? She needed to find a way to stop them, and soon.

Adelaide shoved her hands toward Nolan. A blast sent him flying. She ran toward Regulus, but Kirven put up a green-tinted barrier between them. *Fine.* She conjured a sword and turned toward the tree. With all the strength she could gather, she brought the sword down on the chains. *Please, work.* The glowing sword of magical energy carved deep through the chains and the blackened trunk. With a clatter, the chains fell to the ground. Regulus leapt to his feet and lunged at Kirven as Adelaide ran around the barrier.

Nolan intercepted Regulus before he could reach Kirven. His blade protruded from Regulus' back, glistening crimson in the sun.

Pain tore through her body. Regulus bent forward, and Nolan's stone-hard face appeared over his shoulder. It was too much. The pain, the sight of Regulus impaled on Nolan's sword. The fact it felt like watching a repeat of Nolan killing Father.

Adelaide fell to her hands and knees and dry heaved, her stomach clenching. Nolan tossed Regulus down next to her. The retching stopped, but her entire body trembled, and tears wet her face. Her energy drained further as Regulus healed. Her fists closed around grass. Dirt rolled under her fingernails. This had to stop. She couldn't take much more. She raised her head.

Kirven cocked an eyebrow. "Have you figured it out yet?" She nodded.

Regulus grunted as he sat up next to her. "Figured what out?" He rested a hand on her back. His touch comforted her despite her hopelessness.

"Tell him." Kirven jutted his chin toward Regulus.

"Tell me what?" Regulus gently pulled her up until she sat back on her heels.

The realization of Kirven's plan made her heart twist with guilt. She met Regulus' eyes. His anger melted, replaced with concern. She took a shaky breath and tried to force her hands to stop trembling. "I'm running out of energy…out of magic. To—to heal you."

Regulus' face went slack. "What does that mean?"

"You really are dense," Kirven cut in. "Magic, like energy, gets used. You run, you have to rest. You use magic for any reason, you have to rest. Hargreaves, you get hurt, your bond heals you by stealing magical energy from Belanger. With no time to rest, she'll run out. And when she does," he smiled maliciously, "one of three things will happen. One, the bond will break, and Hargreaves will die. Two, the bond will leach off Belanger's own life until she dies. Or three," he shrugged, "you'll both die."

Her headache returned, and she closed her eyes against the throbbing behind her forehead. Regulus grabbed her hand. She felt his confusion, his fear. Then his sadness. His guilt. There had to be a way to win. If she could just get them to leave Regulus alone long enough to defeat Kirven, then maybe they would stand a chance.

"There is another option, though," Kirven said.

Adelaide opened her eyes. She wouldn't do it. She'd die before she served him again. And she knew Regulus would, too.

"You don't have to run out of energy." Kirven held his hand toward the closest tree, a birch sapling a few feet away. Green tendrils of light stretched from his hand to the tree. The leaves curled in on themselves and blackened. Black veins crawled up the tree trunk and spread until it was totally black. Still Kirven didn't lower his hand. The tree shuddered, and its leaves all fell off at once with a soft whoosh. The bark disintegrated, leaving behind wood as white and dry as old bones. Kirven lowered his hand. He took a deep breath that swelled his chest. "Ah…" He smiled. "That's a bit better."

She stared at the tree. She could sense Regulus' disgust. That… was wrong. Kirven didn't just use the tree, like cutting down a tree for a building. He…consumed it. His sorcery reached into the tree and sucked its life, its energy, right out. Just like the fairies had tried to trick her into doing at the neumenet tree. Just like he had done to the forest surrounding his tower. Just like he had done to *her*.

"Try it," Kirven coaxed. "You'll like it."

"No."

"Tens of thousands of people in Monparth," Kirven muttered, "and I had to find a mage with a conscience." He held out his hand and glowing green ropes snaked over the ground. She conjured a domed barrier over herself and Regulus.

"Adelaide." Regulus' voice was heavy. "Is that true?"

She plucked blades of grass. "I don't know. But I know I'm tired. And it gets more exhausting every time you're hurt."

"Oh, Ad." She felt his wish through their connection as he guided her hand to the blood-covered mark on his arm. "You have to remove it."

"This is my choice." Adelaide pulled her hand off Regulus' arm and cradled his face in her hands. "Forever. That's what I asked you. Did you want to be bound to me forever, and you said yes. I'm yours, and you're mine. Is that still true?"

His heartbreak rushed through her. "Of course it is."

She pressed her lips to his. "Then stop asking me to do what I cannot."

"You can't stay in there forever, you know," Kirven said as he and Nolan circled the dome in opposite directions, hunters on the prowl. "You might as well give up now."

Regulus brushed his fingers through her hair. "I'm ready to fight when you are."

"Fighting isn't worth it," Kirven said. "You'll lose."

"What you fail to realize," Regulus said, his gaze never leaving hers, "is that we will die before we serve you." She smiled sadly. *Together. Love conquers fear.*

Kirven made a sound like a growl. "What you fail to realize is I won't stop at killing you. You think your family and friends will be safe when you're dead? You think just because I can't make you watch I won't still enjoy torturing them for all the trouble you've caused me?"

Adelaide released Regulus' face as her hands went cold. Fear tore up her insides. She dropped the barrier.

CHAPTER 41

REGULUS STARED AT ADELAIDE. SHE COULDN'T BE GIVING UP. She wouldn't… But then, he had seen her nightmares. "What are you doing?"

Adelaide slowly stood and faced the sorcerer. "I make you a counter-offer."

The sorcerer stroked his beard. "Speak quickly."

"You think your sorcery makes you so strong. Then fight me— fair and square. No hurting Regulus to hurt me. No help from Nolan." Regulus stood and grabbed her hand. She pulled it away, but not before he sensed her determination. "Chain Nolan and Regulus up and have a fair fight."

The sorcerer laughed, but it was sharp and angry. "Why would I do that?"

"You defeated me before, but you were cheating, using the staff. You've already cheated today." She held her hands out to her sides. "I'm tired and weakened. So what are you afraid of? Do you think my magic is stronger than your sorcery?"

"Of course not! And it's not cheating to use every tool at your disposal. Why would I waste energy when I can just continue to torture your mercenary lover until you break?"

Regulus flinched. *Please, no!* But a warning bell went off in his mind. She wouldn't. He had to be wrong, she—

"Because if you win and I survive, I'll serve you," Adelaide said quietly.

"Adelaide!" Regulus turned her toward him. "Absolutely not." He would rather Carrick cut him to pieces than Adelaide enslave herself. Ideally, though, the bond would break and let him die first. He understood why she wouldn't remove it, but he wished she would. He was tired of the pain.

Sorrow made Adelaide's eyes look dull and lifeless. "My father is…dead." She swallowed. His heart clenched at the brokenness in her voice. "I can't let any more of my family die because of me." She turned back to the sorcerer, leaving a hollow ache in Regulus' chest.

"But if you win," Adelaide said, "whether I live or die, you have to promise no harm—no pain, no capture, no killing—will come to my family or Regulus' men." Carrick snorted.

The sorcerer raised a brow. "And if you win?"

"I'll kill you."

Adelaide and the sorcerer glared ice daggers at each other. Regulus eyed the distance between himself and the sorcerer and tried to judge how far behind him Carrick stood without looking. He could still remember the feel of Carrick's blade through his heart. The excruciating feeling of dying without the release of death. Until Adelaide's magic had eased the pain. Until he had stolen her magic, weakening her.

It wasn't fair. If Regulus could just reach the sorcerer, maybe he could break the monster's neck. But if either the sorcerer or Carrick attacked him first, all he would accomplish was weakening Adelaide further. Despair pressed against his lungs. No. He wouldn't give up; not on Adelaide.

The sorcerer fiddled with his belt. "You know what you're agreeing to, if you lose and don't die?"

"I'll accept the mark." Adelaide's shoulders slumped.

No. Regulus wanted to say they should take their chances fighting together, fight until death if need be. But if they lost, her family would suffer. Dresden and the rest of his men would suffer. *Etiros, help us!*

"You realize I'll marry you off to Carrick," the sorcerer continued. "You're too annoying and wearisome to have around all the time. Besides, in a moment of shortsightedness, I technically did promise he could have you."

Regulus bristled. "You can't force her to marry him!"

"What about the mercenary?"

"Let him go."

The sorcerer scoffed. "Unacceptable."

"If you lose, he dies," Carrick said, as if he thought he were the one giving orders.

Relief surged in Regulus. *I'd be free at least. No more pain. No watching Adelaide suffer and be corrupted by sorcery. Please. Kill me.* He shook his head to dislodge the invasive thought. He would never abandon her.

Adelaide gulped. "A compromise. If I die, you can kill him—only him, no one else. But if I lose but live, I'll remove the bond. Then you let him go."

"Hm." The sorcerer looked past her to Carrick. Regulus looked back at Carrick, not bothering to hide his rage—or his heartbreak.

Carrick glowered. "Fine. I can live with that."

Regulus was about to protest when Adelaide grabbed his hand. Her fear slammed into him. She would sacrifice herself with the hope she protected everyone else. But hope simmered under her desperation. She wanted to win and believed she had a chance. She was just preparing for the worst. It was a daring plan. The plan of a tigress. He squeezed her hand, and hoped she felt his admiration and belief she could win, and not just his fear. But he hated this plan didn't include him.

"I'm supposed to fight for you. I'm supposed to protect *you.*"

"We're supposed to fight for each other." Her fingertips lifted his chin. "And you already have fought for me and protected me. When you came for me after we separated. When you nearly died for me. When you came to my aid in the palace. And every time you pulled me out of a nightmare. Every time you didn't let me feel alone. You fought for me. It's my turn to fight for you." Her thumb rubbed his chin, flaking off bits of dried blood. "You've fought enough today, Regulus."

The surge of affection and gratitude from her wasn't enough to erase his anguish. Her fingers left his chin as she turned back to the sorcerer. Regulus' chin drifted downward.

"Do we have an agreement?" She held out her hand.

After a moment, the sorcerer took her hand. "We do."

The cold metal of the shackle pressed against Regulus' wrist as Adelaide closed it, her jaw clenched and apology in her eyes. He sat against the oak tree again. She wrapped the chain a few times around his forearm, then pulled back and chained his other hand. On the opposite side of the fire, Kirven used the other chain— which he had melded back together—to bind Carrick to a tree.

"I'm going to win," she said softly.

"I know you are." Regulus smiled. "You're a mage and a tigress. You can do anything."

She smiled, but her eyes were sad and harbored the same doubts he felt. "I love you."

"And I love you. After you win, I'm going to spend the rest of my life showing you just how much." She laughed, but it ended in a sob. "I believe in you, Adelaide."

Adelaide gripped his face and kissed him. Her tears wet his face. Regulus knew he was covered in blood and disgusting, but that thought faded as he kissed her. The chains held his hands back, preventing him from holding her like he longed to. He tried to push all other thoughts away and just be here, with her, alone in this moment. But tears slipped down his cheeks anyway, because he couldn't stop the thought—this might be the last time he kissed her.

"If you're quite done," the sorcerer said brusquely, "I have a fight to win."

Adelaide's mouth left his far too soon.

"Adelaide…"

She didn't meet his eyes as she stood and turned away.

Adelaide's insides felt scrambled, as if they had been rearranged and turned inside out. But she squared her shoulders and faced Kirven anyway, the memory of Regulus' kiss soothing some of the ache in her heart. *"Love,"* Father's voice echoed in her mind. *I'm not losing anyone else today.*

"I'd like to check you put those on properly." Kirven strode past.

"Fine. Then I'm checking you didn't cheat with Nolan's."

"Certainly." Kirven reached down to check the shackles on Regulus' wrists. She ground her teeth and stomped over to Nolan.

Nolan had stuck his sword in the ground a couple feet in front of him, and the sight of it tied her stomach in knots. Seemingly oblivious to her revulsion, he smiled.

"Comfortable?" she snapped. "I hope not."

"Not particularly." His smile took on a wolfish quality. "But it's not bad when I think about how comfortable I'll be tonight with you in my arms."

She shuddered as ice slid through her veins. *Focus. Only the fight matters.* She walked around the tree, tugging on the chain in various spots, then stopped in front of him again. The chain looped around him bound his arms against his sides. He shouldn't be able to move or break free. Hopefully.

"You killed my father." She stared at Nolan's hairline, unable to look in his eyes. "The thought of you touching me should be enough motivation to ensure I either win or don't survive this fight."

"Ouch." His voice softened. "I am sorry, Adelaide. I was focused on getting to the king. I didn't even realize it was your father until it was too late."

"Likely story."

"It's the truth."

She pressed the heel of her palm to her forehead. "If—when I win, I'm going to kill you."

"Love, I truly am sorry about your father." Carrick offered the sincerest expression of sorrow. Ever the convincing actor. "I didn't want to kill him. I had orders, kill anyone who got in my way. You know what happens if I disobey Kirven. I wasn't paying attention to who I was fighting. I wish he hadn't been there. Honest. I never wanted your family hurt. I wish I could change it."

Adelaide's chest tightened as her throat constricted. "Liar. You didn't kill the other guards."

"Hm, must have thought I did."

"You…" No. There was no time to force him to admit he was lying. She needed to forget about Nolan and the pain of Father's death and focus on winning this fight. And failing that, figure out how to make sure she died.

"Adelaide, love—"

"Don't call me that!" She clenched her hands and forced herself to meet his eyes. "I wish killing you would rid me of the memory of you. But at least you'll be dead."

"Oh, Adelaide." Nolan rested his head against the tree and stared up at the branches, like he hadn't a care in the world. "I admire your confidence. But I'm not going to die, because you're not going to win. And when you lose, you're going to marry me." He leered. "And then you're going to keep your promise."

She flushed and turned away, trembling so hard she feared she would start retching again. *Not now. Focus.*

"Don't worry, love." Nolan's honeyed tone was like sweets on an upset stomach. "I'll be gentle."

You don't know the meaning of the word. Adelaide straightened. She wouldn't cower before Father's killer. With her head held high, Adelaide strode back toward Kirven, who stood waiting for her halfway between Regulus and Nolan. Halfway between the man she loved and the man she loathed. Between the future she wanted and the future she dreaded. She looked at Regulus. She would focus on the future she wanted to give her strength to make it through this fight. Because if she thought about Nolan…she swallowed back the hopelessness that tried to drag her to the ground.

"You look tired." Kirven looked her up and down. "You should surrender now and save yourself the pain."

He was right. She was tired. But she smiled and forced all the confidence she didn't feel behind it. "Having second thoughts? I guess all that Prince of Shadow and Ash business was posturing to make up for your insecurities."

Kirven snorted. "You have a sharp tongue for a slave." He whipped his hand up so fast she barely had time to raise a shield before the line of razor-sharp shards of green light slammed into it. The impact pushed her back. She shoved her shield at Kirven. He sidestepped it and threw a fireball at her head.

Adelaide ducked. The heat of the fireball made her dizzy, but she threw her hand across as if throwing a knife to the side. A volley of small blue throwing knives rushed at Kirven from her fingertips. He put up a shield of his own before they reached him. Already she could feel herself tiring. Her eyes darted from Kirven over to

Regulus. He watched with wide eyes, his worry clear, but he caught her gaze and smiled encouragingly.

"Is that the best your sorcery can do?" she taunted. *Wear him out.*

Kirven responded with a wicked smile and held his hands out to his sides. Several spears of green light flashed into existence around him, then spread until they pointed at her from the front and sides. She surrounded herself with a barrier as they zipped through the air toward her. The spears sizzled out of existence as they rammed against her shield. Kirven paced back and forth, throwing attack after attack from every side and driving her back toward the trees while she struggled to keep up with his pace. She bent over, breathing hard with her hands on her knees, and sealed herself inside a dome of shimmering translucent blue.

Kirven laughed and stole some more energy from trees on both sides of her dome. "Out of power already? Taking energy from living things will have to be our first lesson. This is pathetic."

She didn't respond. She had convinced herself that somehow, someway, she would win. But her limbs wearied, and she couldn't bring Kirven down to the same level of mental, emotional, physical, and magical fatigue that plagued her. Not when he kept replenishing his energy when she couldn't.

She was going to lose.

Regulus strained to see around the sorcerer's back. Adelaide leaned forward under her barrier, like she was catching her breath. *Come on, Adelaide.* After a moment, the dome disappeared, and Adelaide straightened and threw a blast of blue light toward the sorcerer. The sorcerer leaned forward, arms crossed in front of him as he raised a shield, but Adelaide's blast still pushed the sorcerer backward. His feet slid across the grass.

That's right! Adelaide threw a blast of fire, but the sorcerer lifted into the air and away from her in a swirl of green. The fireball just missed the bottom edge of his robes. *Press your advantage, Ad! Don't let up now.* She walked forward, sending blasts of light and fireballs one after another. The sorcerer dodged or blocked each one, and the space between each of Adelaide's attacks lengthened. She was tiring.

Regulus couldn't help feeling that yet again, he was at fault. If he had been more level-headed when fighting Carrick, he might not have nearly died, and Adelaide wouldn't have needed to bind them. If he hadn't gotten captured, Adelaide wouldn't be here, and she wouldn't be weakened. She would doubtless disagree with him. The fact she didn't and wouldn't blame him was the only thing that kept him from completely breaking as he watched her switch to defense and give ground again against the sorcerer's aerial assault.

He had felt her sincerity when she refused to remove the bond. She wouldn't risk sacrificing him to save herself. Which made him feel guiltier that she would sacrifice herself to save him—even though he would do the same for her in a heartbeat if given the chance. If only he could give her back everything she had given him. If only he could give every ounce of energy and strength he had left to her, the way she had given her magic to heal him.

Come on! You're strong, Ad; stronger than you know. As she threw a reckless barrage of magic knives toward the sorcerer that went wide, Regulus wished he could get her to sense his thoughts without touching her. That she could understand how much he believed in her. One of the sorcerer's spears grazed her hip as she raised a barrier a moment too late. She yelped then glared at the sorcerer, but her posture betrayed her weariness.

Oh, Etiros. Give her strength! Why can't I help her? Why can't my strength be hers? What good is this bond if it helps only me and not her! He would give up the bond to give her back all the power his wounds had stolen. He would give his life if it gave her life. Blood stained the side of her dress as she held up a barrier against the sorcerer's attacks with one hand and healed her hip with the other. He might be chained and physically useless, but he wouldn't let her fight this battle alone.

"Adelaide! Who are you?"

She looked toward him, panting. Sweat gleamed on her brow. *If I could give you any strength I have, I would do it. But I'll give you my belief.* "Tell me who you are!"

Adelaide straightened behind her barrier. "I'm a mage."

"I can't hear you!"

The sorcerer glanced back at him and hovered closer to the ground as his focus wavered. "Shut up, Hargreaves!"

Regulus strained against the chains. *You're so strong. Any strength I have at this point is yours. All yours.* "Who are you!" He felt a strange draining sensation. Utter exhaustion hit him with the force of running straight into a stone wall. If he hadn't already been sitting and chained, he would have collapsed. He sagged against the tree but kept his eyes on Adelaide.

Adelaide lifted her chin. Her eyes shone with golden light. "I am a mage!"

Regulus realized then he had never understood what it meant to be in awe. But as flames arched up behind Adelaide and unfolded into the shape of gigantic wings and blue light swirled around her feet and lifted her into the air, as a sword as big as the one he had carried as the Black Knight flashed into existence in her hands, he knew what awe felt like. It felt like his heart leaping for joy and plummeting to the ground in shock, somehow at the same time. It felt like his jaw hanging down like it had come unhinged. Like his mind struggling to comprehend what he saw. And awe felt like an overwhelming flood of pride and love as Adelaide soared toward the sorcerer, her wings of flame trailing behind her.

366

Adelaide pulled the sword back over her head as she leapt, propelled by her magic and Regulus' faith in her. Kirven's face went white. He raised his hands, conjuring a barrier as he looked up, but he had misjudged where to place it. She passed over his barrier as she came back toward the ground. Kirven raised trembling hands. He created a shield just above his head right as she swung her sword down. The impact of the sword against the shield make a crack as loud as a thunderclap. Kirven's shield stopped her sword from cutting into his skull but couldn't stop her momentum. Shield and sword slammed into the top of his head. He crumpled and fell.

She landed on the ground next to Kirven's still form. Adelaide dropped the sword, her sudden burst of energy spent, then turned from Kirven's body toward Regulus. Regulus looked pale, but he grinned. Relief and joy bubbled up inside her as she ran to him.

"That's my *shiraa*!" Regulus sounded like he was cheering for the champion at a tournament. "That's my mage!"

She laughed and wiped a tear from the side of her nose as she dropped to her knees next to him. She hastened to remove the shackles. The moment his arms were free, he wrapped them around her and started kissing every inch of her face.

"You did it. You did it. I knew you would."

For the first time in what felt like forever, the tears that snuck down her cheeks were tears of joy.

He pulled her close. "My mage."

"My mercenary." She kissed his blood-covered scar. He brushed his fingers through her hair, but then his gaze darted away from her face and his eyes turned stormy. "What?"

"Carrick." Regulus scowled.

Oh. Right. Her heart sank. She didn't want to deal with him right now. But she stood anyway and held her hand out. Regulus took it, and she gasped.

"Reg!" As he stood, she gripped his forearm. It was still stained rust-red from smeared, dry blood, but… "The mark…it's gone."

CHAPTER 42

"WHAT?" REGULUS PULLED HIS ARM OUT OF ADELAIDE'S HANDS and looked closer. She was right. No black lines traced an intricate knot on his arm. The mark was gone.

"How…what—what does that mean?" Adelaide's voice trembled. "He…Kirven called it a lover's bond. Why…?"

"Hey, no." Regulus pulled her against his chest and cradled the back of her head in his hand. "It doesn't mean we stopped loving each other."

Carrick's laugh carried over the space between them from where he still stood chained to the tree. "How tragic. Guess that love wasn't as deep as Kirven or either of you thought."

Regulus' face heated. "No one asked the opinion of a dead man!"

That shut Carrick up. Regulus moved back to see Adelaide's face. "Don't listen to him." He ducked his head sheepishly. "I think…I may have—somehow—given it back?"

"Given it back?"

"I was praying I could give you my energy, my strength, the way you give me your power to heal me. Thinking I would give anything, even my life, so you could live and win." He scratched the back of his neck. "And then…I suddenly felt exhausted, like all of my energy had been sapped away. Honestly, I feel like I haven't slept in days."

Adelaide's lips parted. "And I got a sudden rush of energy. Oh, Etiros…" She pushed his hair off his temple. "I don't understand. But thank you."

The squeak of metal on wood and a grunt drew his attention back to Carrick. The villain strained as he tried to squirm out of the chains. Regulus walked around Adelaide, and she fell into step next to him. Carrick struggled more at their approach, his face red. Regulus pulled Carrick's sword out of the dirt as they passed it, anger overpowering his exhaustion.

Carrick stilled. "All right; let's talk about this. Is killing me necessary? We can just…go our separate ways."

"No, we can't," Adelaide said quietly. "Not after everything you've done."

Blue light flickered as Adelaide conjured a dagger of solid light in her hand and raised it toward Carrick's throat. But her hand shook, and her expression was strained. Regulus understood her hesitation. Killing an unarmed man felt different. Killing someone you knew…any decent person struggled with that. Unfortunately for Carrick, being a mercenary hammered a lot of decent out of a person. Regulus had no intention of letting him live.

Carrick paled, but quickly regained his irritatingly relaxed expression. "If I could go back and spare your father's life, I would. And I'm sorry you can't see how much I care for you. I'm sorry you won't accept that I just wanted to keep you out of the hands of this mercenary dog."

"You're the only dog here," Regulus growled.

Carrick ignored him. "I'm sorry you can't see that even when I was cruel, it was only because I didn't know how else to process that I love you, and you don't want me."

"You don't love me." Adelaide's hand bobbed, and the magic dagger softened on the edges. Regulus considered moving Adelaide out of the way and beheading the churl, but maybe she needed to confront him.

"Of course I do!" Carrick slammed his head back against the tree. "Love you, need you, crave you. You've made me mad with desire. You can't blame me for going to extreme lengths to make you mine. I'm willing to do whatever it takes to win you."

"To own me." Adelaide moved the tip of the dagger of light under Carrick's chin. "You killed…" She shuddered. "Part of me wants to kill you now. Part of me wants to drag you back to the palace so you can be hanged in front of everyone."

"An interesting idea," Carrick said. "Public execution is probably more just."

Regulus frowned. "He's just trying to buy time, think of ways to escape. We should kill him now. We're royal guards. We have the authority to deal with a threat to the crown with deadly force."

"I'm *so* threatening right now." Carrick rolled his eyes.

"You should hang." Adelaide lowered her hand and the dagger vanished. "A quick death is too good for you, anyway."

"I'll gladly do it slowly," Regulus growled.

"Slowly." Carrick smiled, cocky and self-assured. Regulus gripped the sword hilt so tight his fingers ached. "Slowly is how I plan on doing you, love."

Regulus raised the sword, but Adelaide had her dagger back at Carrick's throat.

"I don't know what the right thing is to do anymore. My father…" Her voice cracked. "He would say justice."

"Well…" Carrick smirked. "The thing is, justice doesn't rule. Power does."

Adelaide shook her head. "What does—"

Something curled around her neck and pulled. She reached toward her throat as Regulus cursed. Her fingers brushed against a rope at her neck. *No…* She'd killed him. *Never let your guard down until you are certain the fight is won.* She should have put her sword through his heart.

"First rule of combat," Nolan gloated. "Make sure your opponent is actually dead."

Adelaide choked as Kirven yanked on the rope. She stumbled backward and turned around, clawing at the suffocating rope around her neck. Kirven held his hands outstretched, a rope trailing from both hands. She traced the other to where Regulus had fallen to his knees, his face turning blue as he tried to free himself. She sent a blast of fire through the ropes.

The ropes vanished, and Regulus gasped and fell onto his hands, coughing and sputtering. Adelaide collapsed to her knees, dragging air down her raw windpipe. Glowing green ropes wrapped around her arms and bound them to her sides. She looked up as Kirven aimed a spear of sorcerous light at Regulus.

"No!" She pushed to her feet, arms still bound, and jumped in front of Regulus.

Kirven dropped the spear. "That close to being out of power are you, girl?" He strode forward and pulled on the ropes, tossing her onto her side.

"You were defeated." Regulus rubbed his throat as he looked up at Kirven. "You lost. It's over."

"It's over when I say it's over," Kirven snarled.

"Leave him alone!" Adelaide maneuvered onto her knees and blasted away the ropes. She raised a shield between Regulus and Kirven. Even such a small, simple barrier proved more difficult than it had in ages. Her head pounded. Her limbs weighed her down.

Regulus picked up Nolan's sword and rose unsteadily to his feet, his movements slow.

"Oh, very interesting." Kirven's gaze fixed on Regulus' arm. "You broke the bond to give her strength. I'm impressed, honestly. But," he smiled, "that technically counts as helping. That means you broke our agreement. According to the ancient and sacred rules of combat, cheating results in a forfeit."

"Mercenaries have never cared much for the rules of combat," Regulus snapped.

"Well, anything goes now, at the least," Kirven said with a wicked grin. He sent an arc of green light toward her. She raised a second shield, but the arc of solid light went right past the edge of the shield. She allowed herself a small smile. At least that blow to the head had weakened him and affected his aim. She had a chance, despite her exhaustion.

Regulus moved into a ready stance, the sword gripped in both hands, and looked toward her. She nodded at Regulus, but his eyes widened. "Adelaide!"

A strong arm wrapped around her as Nolan pulled her back against his chest. Kirven hadn't missed. He'd freed Nolan. The tip of a blade pressed against her side. She stiffened as Nolan pulled her away from Regulus.

"Drop the sword unless you want to see how well Adelaide handles the treatment I gave you earlier," Nolan said, his soft tone in glaring dissonance with his words.

Regulus dropped the sword, his face red. "You would torture the woman you claim to love? What sick kind of love is that?"

Kirven sent ropes around her shield. The ropes wrapped around Regulus' wrists and throat. Adelaide let the useless shield fall, conjured a dagger, and stabbed it into Nolan's thigh. He cursed, but didn't let go, so she stabbed again. Nolan released her and stumbled back.

"Let him go!" She burned through Kirven's ropes, the effort making her dizzy. Regulus coughed.

Kirven grunted. "Here's my offer, mage. Swear to serve me now, and I'll let the mercenary go. Otherwise, I'll have Carrick carve his heart out."

Adelaide glowered at Kirven, even though she didn't feel particularly defiant. "I beat you."

"Yet I'm still alive."

"She still won," Regulus protested.

"By cheating!" Kirven clenched his fists.

Nolan grabbed her arm, but Adelaide turned and sent a blast into his chest, knocking him to the ground. White spots sparked in her vision and she swayed. She shook her head then ran to Regulus, pulled him to the ground, and threw a dome over them. Her muscles twitched as magical energy leeched from her.

"Regulus." She had meant to sound more certain, but her voice came out small and weak "I...I'm going to surrender."

"Smart girl," Kirven said.

"What?" Regulus gripped her shoulders. "No!"

She lowered her head. "He's right. I would have lost without your help."

"That's ridiculous, and you know it." Regulus shook his head, his tone gentle. "It was your magic to start with, and what is some extra energy if you don't put it to good use? He stole energy from the trees! How is that different?"

"Because she can't repeat that trick, imbecile." Derision laced Kirven's voice. "I, on the other hand..." Green light covered the ground around the sorcerer and the grass withered and crumbled to dust.

Adelaide rubbed the heel of her hand over her eye, desperately trying not to cry. "I can't watch you die again. I can't." She bit back a sob.

"Ad—"

"I'm not strong, Reg." She let the tears come. Too much sorrow. Too much loss. Too much fear and failure. She had been so close and ruined it by one stupid mistake. "I'm scared, and I'm tired, and I don't want my family to die because of me. I—" A sob cut through her words. Kirven would make her do unforgivable things. But she pictured Minerva laughing with Gaius, her hands holding her swollen belly. "I have to save them."

Regulus pulled her close. She leaned into him. "Ad…" His cheek rested against her forehead, but his emotions didn't hit her.

The bond is gone, she reminded herself. Another whimpering sob burned at her throat.

"Hargreaves," Nolan said. "Kindly unhand my wife."

Adelaide shivered and clenched Regulus' shirt as his grip on her tightened. She wanted to fall asleep against him and wake up in a world where Father wasn't dead, where Regulus hadn't broken their bond, where she wasn't on the verge of collapse. She should fight. Fight until her last breath. She should die before she helped Kirven kill the king and subjugate Monparth and its neighbors. It was what Father would do. *But Father isn't here.*

"My mage," Regulus murmured. "Don't give up, *shiraa*. We'll fight—"

"I don't have any fight left." She wasn't the seasoned warrior he was, wasn't the tigress Father had thought her. Despair ate away at her heart. She could stop running, stop fearing. All it took to save her family, to save Regulus, to finally *rest*, was to give in and become a sorceress.

It would make her a monster. She would corrupt her soul until she enjoyed others' pain as much as Kirven did. But maybe the ache in her heart would go away. The people she loved would live.

And she'd be married to Nolan.

She couldn't surrender. She couldn't fight.

"Help me," Adelaide whispered. Whether she was asking Regulus or Etiros, she wasn't sure.

Kirven laughed. "Only I can help you now."

"I won't leave you." Regulus swallowed hard. "I'll serve him, too."

"No!" Adelaide pulled back to look him in the eyes. "Regu—"

"Forever, *piahre*." He held her gaze. "That's what you asked me. That's what I agreed to. Forever. No more splitting up."

She shook her head as her stomach twisted. "But—"

Regulus held her face in his hands. "We fight together, we die together, or we serve together. I'm not abandoning you."

"Not an option," Nolan spat. "Adelaide is mine."

"She's mine," Kirven said. "I'm just letting you borrow her. You can share."

Adelaide stared at Regulus and tried to block out Nolan and Kirven. They no longer shared their emotions with a touch, but she could read his face. His love and unwavering belief that she didn't deserve. But also pain and fear and anger. He didn't want to serve Kirven again. But he would. For her. For a woman who was too broken to keep going. How did he love her enough to give up the freedom he had worked so hard to earn? To go back to that life of pain?

"Love conquers fear," Father's voice whispered.

"Stop doubting yourself," Regulus murmured. "I love the woman I see."

She blinked. How could he know? Only one thing to do. "Together."

CHAPTER 43

CONFUSION WELLED IN REGULUS AS ADELAIDE'S BARRIER dissolved above them. She pulled away and took a shaky step toward the sorcerer.

"We surrender. You win. My family and Regulus' friends are safe."

Regulus' shoulders caved. For a moment, the spark in her eyes, the way she said together… He thought she had changed her mind. So that was it then. A lifetime spent serving the sorcerer. Spent watching Adelaide taint her soul with sorcery and suffer under Carrick's control. But the alternative of abandoning her to bear that alone was worse.

"Could have saved us both a lot of trouble and me a splitting headache if you'd given in earlier," the sorcerer grumbled.

"No harm will come to my family or Regulus' friends?" Adelaide pressed.

"So long as they don't interfere with me, no harm will come to them."

The sorcerer would provide himself a loophole.

But it must have been good enough for Adelaide, because she pushed her sleeve up over her elbow. "You'll take Regulus, too?"

The sorcerer huffed. "Fine. Give me your arm."

"What?" Carrick sounded offended. "You can't—"

"*I* can do whatever the hell I want," the sorcerer snapped. "Now stop whining before I change my mind about keeping my word."

Carrick grunted, but shut up.

This is wrong. Regulus gripped the hilt of Carrick's sword. If he could cut off Carrick's head…

"Drop it, mercenary." The sorcerer's voice was cold. "Now, mage. Your arm."

Adelaide hesitated, and hope sparked in Regulus. But then she held her arm out to the sorcerer. Regulus looked away. He couldn't watch.

"Do you know what *shiraa* means, Kirven?" Adelaide asked. Regulus frowned up at her.

The sorcerer shrugged. "It's Khast. Tigress." He placed his hand over her forearm.

"Tigers," Adelaide said softly, "don't like being caged." Her palm glowed a soft blue. A shaft of solid blue light appeared in her grip and extended into the sorcerer's stomach.

The sorcerer shrieked. A blast of green light knocked Adelaide to the ground. Regulus seized the sword and leapt up. The sorcerer was focused on healing the hole Adelaide had put through his abdomen, paying no attention as Regulus rushed him. Carrick shouted a warning, and the sorcerer's head whipped up.

Regulus swung with every ounce of energy he had for the sorcerer's neck. The sorcerer gaped and lifted his hands, his palms glowing green, but too late. Regulus screamed a battle cry, all his anger and heartbreak lending strength to his wearied arms. The sorcerer's head tumbled to the ground.

The sorcerer's body fell.

Regulus' chest heaved. It was over. Really, truly, over.

He lowered the sword. For the first time in two years, he felt free. He squared his shoulders as an immeasurable weight lifted off him. But then he looked for Adelaide, and his rage threatened to rip him apart.

Kirven's blast knocked Adelaide to the ground. Blackness crowded out her vision and her arms shook as she tried to push herself up. She lurched to her feet, but before she could turn to aid Regulus, Nolan wrested her to the ground and shouted a warning to Kirven.

Nolan rolled over on top of her, pinning her in place. She tried to send a blast of magic off her body, as she had done before to break free of Kirven's ropes, but was too drained. Nolan's legs trapped her hands against her thighs and his hands on her shoulders wouldn't let her shift enough to see what was happening with Regulus and Kirven.

"You won't want to see that, love." He pressed his forearm across her chest as she struggled.

Regulus bellowed a war cry. Adelaide slammed her head into Nolan's mouth. The impact hurt more than she had anticipated, and her eyes watered. Nolan cursed and pushed against her until she feared her sternum would crack. Regulus' shout stopped. Nolan gasped and pulled away, his brow furrowed.

"What..." He shook his head and shifted enough she could pull one hand free.

She blasted Nolan backward as Regulus shouted, "Get off her!"

Adelaide sat up, her body shaking and stomach roiling as her eyes fought to focus and her head ached. Regulus kicked the side of Nolan's head and held the point of the sword to Nolan's throat. Adelaide's gaze locked onto a mound of black and red robes.

Kirven's head was not attached to his body. She pressed her fist to her mouth, transfixed by the horror before her. Her stomach clenched. *Look away, look away...*

"Ad," Regulus said. She tore her eyes from Kirven's grotesque head to Regulus standing over Nolan. "I want to run him through." His voice was so low and gravelly she hardly recognized it. "I want to do more than that. But not if…" He grunted. "If you want him to hang."

She wanted to curl into a ball somewhere dark and cry until she fell asleep, then sleep until this was all a distant memory.

"Um…I vote hanging," Nolan said.

Adelaide stood, her legs shaking. "Why? So you can try to talk your way free?"

"To be honest, yes." Nolan's voice lacked its usual confidence. "I was tricked! And then he used me! He controlled me and tortured me and forced me—"

"Did he force you to kiss me?" Adelaide shouted. She conjured a throwing knife, even though the effort made her sway. "Did he compel you to assault me?" Her voice shook. She raised the throwing knife. This wasn't what Father would want. The king would appreciate a prisoner to make an example of. And it might help with her desertion problem. She sighed and let the throwing knife vanish. "I need a peace offering for the king."

Regulus shook his head. "What are you—"

"I…" She kicked at the grass. "I sort of deserted."

"What?" The rage vanished from Regulus' voice, replaced by fear. "To come find me?" She nodded. "You'll be hanged!"

Nolan laughed. "Fancy that."

"Shut up, or I'll run you through."

Adelaide raised her head and tried not to flinch at Regulus' appalled expression. "A prisoner the king can execute to remind his people he's in charge might help my case."

"Okay," Regulus sounded panicked. "Okay, that might work. Okay." His voice leveled as he calmed himself. "Looks like you're good for something, Carrick. Ad, can you get the chains with the shackles?"

Adelaide hurried to bring the shackles from the oak tree. She crouched next to Nolan, careful to avoid looking at his face. She closed a shackle around his wrist, then moved to his other side and closed the other shackle. Regulus used the chain to pull Nolan to his feet.

"Try to run," Regulus said. "And I'll slice open your ankles. Understood?"

Adelaide stepped next to Regulus and looked up at him as he stuck the sword in his belt. His stormy expression softened as he gazed at her.

"Are you okay?" he murmured.

She nodded, although her lower lip trembled. "You did it. We're…"

"Free." Regulus looked tired, despite his smile. "*We* did it, *mareh piahre*. We defeated him together."

She smiled, unsure what she was feeling in the wreckage of her emotions. Relieved, certainly. The echo of *failure* still resounded in the back of her mind. She doubted she deserved Regulus. But as she looked into his piercing gray eyes, she felt overwhelming love.

"Can we save the adoring looks for when I'm not around?" Nolan muttered.

"You should apologize, cad," Regulus growled.

Nolan glared at Adelaide. "I'm sorry." He pulled his lips back in a snarl, contorting his handsome features into the monster he really was. "I never should have let you leave that morning after I took you from Arrano. I'm sorry I didn't break into your room that night and make you my—"

Regulus' fist connected with Nolan's jaw with a sharp crack as Adelaide paled.

Nolan spit blood and grinned, his teeth smeared with red. "Too bad you can't kill me, since the wench got herself in a predicament."

Anger burned away Adelaide's exhaustion, mixing with her fear. She clenched her fists as she tried to stop shaking.

"Bet you can't make her tremble like that, mercenary."

Rage and humiliation knotted her insides and squeezed her throat. Regulus punched Nolan's stomach, and Nolan stumbled back, coughing. Nolan straightened and stepped back as far as the long chain would allow.

"Want another kiss, love?" He licked his bloodied lips as his eyes roamed over her. "Maybe a bit more?"

She shuddered. "Gag him."

Nolan gave her a mocking smirk as Regulus moved toward him. "I'll convince the king I was ensorcelled, and Hargreaves entrapped you. And when I marry you, I won't waste time—"

Adelaide screamed and threw a knife she didn't recall conjuring at Nolan. The glowing blade buried deep in his neck. His face went slack as he choked. *What did I just do?* The blade vanished and Nolan fell to his knees, pressing his hands against his throat. She stared in mute shock, rooted in place. *Your bargaining chip. You need him alive!* But she couldn't move as his face whitened. He fell forward with a clatter of chains.

Adelaide dropped to the ground. He might still be alive. But she didn't have the energy or desire to save Nolan's life. She stared at Nolan's body as tension built behind her forehead. Regulus knelt next to her and held her against his chest.

"He deserved it, Adelaide."

She sobbed and wrapped her arms around Regulus' neck.

"He was guilty and dangerous," Regulus whispered. "And he deserved so much worse."

"I murdered him." She buried her face in his shirt. "Justice…"

"This is justice." He rubbed her back. "Even your father told me Carrick deserved to die. Now or later, why does it matter? We're royal guards. We have the authority to kill a traitor to the crown."

"Well…you are," she mumbled. "Oh, Etiros, what have I done?"

CHAPTER 44

ETIROS, I DON'T KNOW HOW TO HELP HER. THIS WASN'T THE first life Adelaide had taken; Regulus knew that. But this wasn't a random bandit. And she wasn't a mercenary. The things he usually said to help a man struggling after his first battle didn't seem right. He wasn't even certain if she was more upset that she had killed Carrick, or worried about her desertion.

"You defeated the sorcerer," Regulus said tentatively. He rubbed her back. "And you saved the king's life at the masque. He would have to be an idiot not to see that you hunting down the sorcerer was a good thing." But a part of him worried, because in his opinion the king was an idiot. *But surely not that much of an idiot.*

"Is it wrong I'm relieved he's dead?" Adelaide whispered.

"To be honest, I'm happy he's gone."

They didn't say anything for several moments. Regulus wished he still had the ability to feel her emotions. He could ask her. But he didn't know if she wanted to talk about it, or if she could even be honest. He didn't want to pressure her. So he held her as exhaustion and relief pulled on his eyelids. He rested his head against hers and let his eyes close. But then he pictured Carrick straddling her.

"Ad?"

"Mm."

"Are you…" He knew she wasn't okay. And he didn't want to ask outright if Carrick had kissed her again. Part of him didn't want to know. But after last time…he didn't want to overstep when he no longer sensed her fear. "Is this okay? Me?"

She shifted, burrowing closer. "What do you mean?"

Regulus worked down the lump in his throat. At least she had moved closer. That was a good sign. "I don't want to… Carrick…" He bit his tongue. "Just… Tell me if I go too far?"

"Oh, Reg." Adelaide's voice cracked. She pulled away. The departure of her warmth left him hollow. Her deep, rich brown eyes were full of love and heartbreak.

He looked away. He had failed her; left her alone to mourn her father and almost caused her to become enslaved to the sorcerer and Carrick. He was supposed to protect her, and he had failed. Again.

"I'm sorry." He drew in a shuddering breath. "I'm sorry you were hurt because of me. I'm sorry I wasn't able to keep you from despairing—"

"Regulus Hargreaves, stop that." He looked up in surprise at the hardness of her tone. "If anyone should apologize, it's me." She looked down at her hands and twiddled her thumbs. "You wouldn't have been tortured if it wasn't for me."

"I—"

"But it wasn't our fault," she said softly. "And I would have given up without you. Any strength you see in me…it's from you."

Regulus couldn't stop the chuckle that escaped him. Adelaide looked up, her expression half offended and half confused. "And I was thinking my strength was all yours." He smiled and reached for her cheek, then hesitated.

"I'm not afraid of your touch, *piahre*." She laced her fingers behind his neck.

Regulus leaned forward, but didn't meet her lips, giving her a chance to pull back. She moved closer and pressed her lips to his. He kissed her, matching her gentleness at first, but then grabbed

384

her and pulled her close, holding nothing back. He poured all his love, his gratitude, all his passion into kissing her. She broke away. He opened his eyes to see her crying silently. A weight settled in his stomach and he released her, his heart heavy.

"I'm sorry—"

"Don't be. It's not..." She wiped tears from her cheeks. "Would you really have served Kirven?"

Oh. "I won't leave you alone." He rubbed her shoulders. "I love you."

She wiped at her tears. "But I failed—"

"No, you didn't." He stroked the top of her head as he tried to find the words to comfort her in the midst of his own aching heart. "And even if you did, I don't love you because you won or lost. I love you because you're kind and good and smart and independent and strong—"

"I wanted to surrender!" Her voice was thick with tears. "How is that good or strong?"

Regulus wanted to shout at her, to shake her until she understood, or kiss her until they both forgot her pain. He wanted to bring the sorcerer and Carrick back just to hurt them for what they had done to her. He wanted to slip into unconsciousness until the tension behind his forehead eased. Until the memory of Carrick's torture and his fear as he watched Adelaide surrender faded.

He recalled Adelaide's irritated rebuke as they made their way to retrieve the opal what seemed ages ago. *We don't always get what we want!* He lifted her chin so he could look into her eyes. *Give me wisdom, Etiros.*

"There are many kinds of strength. Love isn't weak. Surviving isn't weak. Wanting to surrender doesn't make you less worthy, it makes your final victory more impressive. You felt defeated, but you kept fighting anyway. You're amazing, and I wish you believed that." He stroked her messy hair. "I love you, Adelaide. More than you can know."

"Thank you." She looked more at peace, her face more relaxed. She touched the tips of her fingers to his arm where her mark had been. "I'm too weak now, but I'll put it back—"

"I don't need it." He took her hand in his. "I know you love me. No one's trying to kill us anymore. And I never want you in pain because of me again. But…" He grinned. "Estevan has been trying to talk me into getting a tattoo for years. I have a design in mind now."

She laughed, and even though her laugh was weak and broken, it was real. And it told him she was going to be okay. They both were. "Maybe I can get one, too. The horror on my half-siblings' faces would be priceless."

He chuckled. "They'll probably be shocked enough when you marry me."

Her gaze roamed over his face, and her expression saddened as she touched his scarred cheek. "I'm sorry they hurt you. But— maybe this is selfish of me… I'm glad my magic didn't erase your scar." She smiled. "It's a reminder. Scars mean we survived."

"I could kiss you for that."

"Then why don't you?" Her eyes danced, even though she looked exhausted.

He leaned forward to kiss her but glimpsed the sorcerer's severed head behind her. He grimaced. "The corpses are kind of killing the mood."

"Eugh." Adelaide winced. "We should probably get back to the palace, anyway. Let them know Kirven's dead."

"Agreed. I hope whoever's in charge lets you sleep before they start in with all the questioning." He picked up the sword and headed for Carrick's body.

"What are you doing?"

He looked over his shoulder. "We'll need to bring the heads back to the palace as proof of death. And then at least the king can display them if he wants."

Adelaide blanched. Her revulsion made his stomach twist. He lowered the point of the sword to the ground and turned toward her.

"Ad…"

"No, you're right." She still looked uncomfortable.

"Did you not realize this is what a mercenary did?" he blurted before he thought better of it. An irrational fear screamed in his mind as he watched her pinched expression. The fear she wouldn't want this side of him. He shouldn't make it worse, but cruel, taunting doubt pushed the words past his tongue. "I'm a killer, Adelaide, I've never pretended I'm not. Not to mention a bastard and social pariah. You're so worried you're not good enough, when I'm the one who can't ever deserve you."

Her face went stony. She stomped toward him. "Regulus, if you say anything like that ever again…" She clenched her fists, looking like she wanted to punch him. "I *love* you. And I'm too hungry and tired to tell you why you're amazing. So just…stop!"

"Okay." Regulus laughed. *Etiros, I love this woman.* "Easy, tigress. I think there's some food by the fire pit."

Regulus cut off Carrick's head while Adelaide consumed the last of the sorcerer's food. He could have eaten, too, but she ate like she had been starved. The least he could do was let her eat. He made a makeshift bag and padding for both heads out of the sorcerer's clothing, slung it over his shoulder, and they headed for the palace.

When they arrived at the palace gate, Regulus requested to see the officer on duty immediately. A guard ushered them straight to the royal guard barracks. Beale and Antar met them in the courtyard.

"Belanger," Beale snapped. "You—"

"Are a hero." Regulus dumped out the heads and they rolled across the dirt. He tossed down the sack and glared at Beale.

"The hell, Hargreaves?" Beale blanched and stepped back.

"The heads of the sorcerer Kirven and Nolan Carrick." Regulus nodded toward the heads. "Adelaide and I killed them. You're welcome."

Beale blinked. "The sorcerer is dead?"

"Unless he can survive as only a head," Adelaide said unsteadily. "I served my king and removed the threat to his crown. I—"

"You're still a deserter," Beale said curtly.

"Are you serious?" Regulus motioned to the heads. "She defeated the sorcerer! And killed his lackey! Who, I might remind you, killed a lord. And many royal guards, I understand."

"And Captain Matthews and Lieutenant Breck," Adelaide added. Beale glared at her.

"She disobeyed a direct order from a superior, abandoned her assigned post, and attacked fellow guards." Antar pushed at Kirven's head with the tip of his boot. "But she also saved my life. And, I'd say, the kingdom." He looked up. "Well done, Belanger."

"We don't have the authority to pardon her, Antar." Beale crossed his arms. "And I already sent a messenger to the king informing him of her desertion. The king will have to decide what to do when he returns. Until then, you're under arrest."

"That's ridiculous!" Regulus stepped forward, his fists clenched at his sides. He wanted to beat someone senseless, and as Breck was apparently dead, Beale would do almost as well. "You should be thanking her, not arresting her!"

"The king will likely pardon her," Antar said.

"But only the king *can* pardon her," Beale added. "Belanger. Are you going to come without any trouble this time?"

"Come *where?*" Regulus demanded.

388

"Yes, sir." Adelaide's voice was soft.

"Do I need cuffs or are you going to come along willingly?"

"No." Adelaide shook her head. "I'll come."

Beale motioned for her to follow him and headed out of the courtyard.

"You can't seriously be putting her in the dungeon?" Regulus stepped in front of Adelaide, panic squeezing him. He had promised not to leave her alone again.

"That's the law, Hargreaves," Beale said sullenly.

She patted his shoulder. "It's all right, Reg. It won't be for long." She kissed his cheek. "You said it yourself. I saved the king's life. He'll pardon me. Behave. Please?"

Regulus whirled toward Beale. "I want to stay with her."

Beale rolled his eyes. "Not protocol."

"Hang protocol! Look at her!" He pointed to Adelaide. "She was wounded, she's drained herself of her magic to kill the sorcerer, she nearly died, she's exhausted. She could have run, but she came back! If you were a decent person, you'd let her stay in her room! Post a guard if—"

"Enough!" Beale's expression darkened. "Your attitude grows old, Hargreaves. As does your inability to call me *sir*. Now back off, or you can spend the rest of the day in the stocks."

Regulus clenched his jaw. "Yes, sir." He stepped aside and watched Beale lead Adelaide to the dungeons with a heavy heart.

Regulus glared at the wall of the mess hall with enough intensity to burn a hole through the wood. He clutched his fork. Just when things seemed to have finally looked up, Adelaide was taken from him again. Most likely not permanently, but he didn't like it.

The other guards in the mess hall avoided him. Whether because he'd brought back the sorcerer's severed head, because he was the mage's betrothed, or because of the murderous look on his face, he wasn't sure. But he was thankful to be left alone. After lunch, he laid on their bed in the dark room, unable to sleep in the empty bed while Adelaide slept alone in a cell.

He wandered around the gardens until he was too tired to walk anymore. A spot under a willow tree, hidden by well-manicured bushes whose leaves were starting to show hints of red called to him. He hadn't meant to doze off, but it was early evening when he awoke to the rustle of willow branches and buzz of bees. His stomach drove him to the mess hall, and then his heart drove him to the dungeons. The guards wouldn't let him see Adelaide and threatened to throw him in a cell far from hers if he persisted. He left, muttering and cursing under his breath.

Their little room felt empty and harsh. He would have given anything to be lying in bed, sleep pulling at his eyes while Adelaide crouched over a formless blob of fabric, her brows drawn close together and absently biting her lower lip as she moved the needle and pulled out a staggering number of little pins. So help him Etiros, this was the last time they would be separated unnecessarily. He pulled off his boots and belt and tossed the dagger Carrick had stolen from Adelaide on the table before he blew out the lantern.

He'd only been lying on the bed a few minutes when someone knocked. *This can't be good.* He stumbled toward the door and slammed his foot into a bed post. Biting back a curse, he hopped on one foot. He survived mutilation and torture; he wouldn't be brought down by a couple stubbed toes. The person in the hall knocked again.

"You in there, Reg? Adelaide?" *Dresden.*

Regulus opened the door so quickly it banged against the wall. "Drez!"

"Oh, good." Drez peered inside the room. "Where's Adelaide?"

"In the dungeons." He stepped aside to allow Dresden to enter.

"What?" Dresden stared, rooted in place. "They're not still charging her with desertion, are they?"

"Wait, you *knew?*" Regulus crossed to the table and lit the lamp, filling the room with flickering orange light. "Drez, I swear—"

"Hey, you ever tried stopping her from doing something? She was throwing magic and fire and telling people off. Besides which, I was on her side. If she was doubling over in pain at what they were doing to you, I can't imagine…" Dresden gulped. "I was worried." He sat in one of the chairs by the table. "I like Adelaide's light better. Makes the corners less shadowy."

"What? How would you know that?"

"Come on, Reg." Drez leaned back in the chair. He looked worn; his beard considerably less well-kempt than usual. "She lost you; then her father died, and she couldn't save him. And she tried, Reg. It…was rough." He rubbed the side of his beard, his eyes distant. "I wasn't about to leave her alone."

Regulus sank onto the edge of the bed and a pang of sorrow went through his heart. "Thank you," he whispered.

"What are friends for if not to sleep on uncomfortable chairs and take care of your girl because you're too busy being captured?" Dresden gave a forced laugh. "Oh, also, if we ever run away to become mercenaries again, please take her with us. That mage healing is excellent."

"Wait, you were hurt?" If Dresden had been hurt, that meant he had fought Carrick, and that meant… *I could have lost him.* "How bad—"

Dresden snorted. "Compared to you? A scratch."

"Is that what Adelaide will tell me if I ask her?"

"I'm alive, you muscular nursemaid, relax. It was definitely nothing compared to Antar's leg." He straightened. "Which reminds me. As soon as I heard that you two had shown up at the palace with a couple of severed heads—nicely done, by the way, I heard you dumped them out and disgusted the guards, excellent style—I came straight to the palace with the aim of giving the staff to Adelaide. A pretentious Lieutenant Beale who's very concerned with protocol confiscated it."

Regulus plopped back on the bed. "Sounds about right. He insisted on locking up Adelaide until the king can decide if she should be charged with desertion."

Drez shook his head. "This is why I was on board when you decided to become a mercenary. No tradition and nonsense, just whoever fights best and whoever comes through when they need to. Justice is simple, effective, and fair."

Regulus laughed. "No nonsense, says the man who is still sore he lost his collection of lucky rabbit feet."

"And look where we are now." Dresden spread his hands. "Bet you we never would have met that sorcerer if I'd still had 'em."

"That is the definition of circumstantial and you know it."

"We both know I'm never wrong." Dresden laced his fingers behind his head. "And I bought those as a laugh, but we had the best luck for the month I had them."

Regulus rolled his eyes. It felt good to have this easy banter with Drez again. To laugh and have some normalcy. "I'm glad you're here." He laid back on the bed. "I just wish Adelaide was, too."

Another day and a half passed before the king arrived. Regulus tried several times to see Adelaide, but every time the answer was no. He watched the entrance to the dungeon and only ever saw servants enter with bags of bread and buckets of water. It infuriated him, and he told Beale off twice. The first time Regulus was denied dinner. Drez snuck in food from town. The second time Beale wanted to put Regulus in the stocks for two hours, but Antar convinced Beale to give Regulus a warning. Beale agreed, but told

Regulus his next offense of any kind would get him five lashes. Regulus kept his head down and grumbled only to Drez— particularly when the king didn't call them in for a hearing the moment he arrived back.

CHAPTER 45

ADELAIDE AWOKE FROM A NIGHTMARE, A SCREAM ON HER tongue and a pinch in her neck. Her body ached from lying on the hard stone. The cell was only around four feet deep and five feet wide. Bars separated her from empty cells on either side. The only item in the entire cell was a stained and odious wooden bucket shoved back in the darkest corner. Water dripped somewhere, and some other prisoner coughed in a distant cell.

She had naively hoped her incarceration would give her time to rest and process. Rest was difficult to come by on the cold stone floor with mice burrowing into her skirts. A few times she had caught herself wondering what Father would say or do when she saw him, how he would react to her being thrown in the dungeon. Then she would remember, and the pain in her heart would start all over again. But the nightmares were worse.

Once she dreamed of Nolan killing Father. She was stuck on the other side of one of Kirven's barriers, able to see but unable to help as Nolan ran his sword through Father's heart. In another nightmare, she stumbled past Father's corpse to where Nolan and Kirven were torturing Regulus. By the time she reached Regulus, she was so weak she couldn't even conjure a barrier. This time, she had awoken from a dream of Kirven burning his mark into her arm and handing her over to Nolan.

Every time, she woke to her screams echoing in the dungeons. No one checked on her. No one cared. She longed for Regulus' comforting arms around her. She curled up alone on the stone, surrounded by the unfeeling darkness and iron, and cried into her arm. *I'm safe,* she reminded herself. *They're dead. They can't touch me, or Regulus and my family. We're safe.* Except for Father. Father's words about her nightmares after her rescue seemed prescient.

"They'll fade. The memories. The dreams. And the pain. They won't last forever." When? *"I don't know. But they will. You will heal. You're so, so strong, my dear. Don't doubt that, all right?"*

She wished Nolan and Kirven's power over her life didn't feel like it extended past their deaths. But even with their shadow hanging over her, she was alive. *"Surviving isn't weak,"* Regulus' voice whispered in her mind. Still, Kirven and Nolan had changed her in a way she didn't quite understand yet. She felt like she had been broken and put back together a half dozen times over the last weeks, and she was different for it. More tender. Her heart more easily bruised. But also more resilient. A survivor.

Her empty stomach clenched. How long had it been since a servant had delivered a loaf of bread? Time was strange with no sunlight. She couldn't even hear the chime of the chapel bells under all this stone. It could be morning. Could be the middle of the night. Or the middle of the afternoon.

Her heart longed for sunlight, and she was on the verge of insanity from not knowing the time. Adelaide had tried to ask the guards a couple times, but they ignored her. The servants practically threw her bread at her, then hurried away without speaking.

And oh, what she wouldn't give for fresh air on her skin and dirt and grass under her feet. She might never wear sleeves again, Monparthian fashion sense be hanged. How did people live in dungeons for longer than a few days? It was torment.

And Regulus. Oh, Regulus. The only thing she wanted more than the open sky above her and nothing but trees, sunlight, and a misty morning all around her was Regulus. She wished he was with her. But she also didn't. Somehow, knowing he was free up there made a part of her free, too. Even though he wasn't there to comfort her, thinking about him helped.

As she watched the flicker of the torches stuck in the walls every few feet, Adelaide knew a few things for certain.

Father's death would always leave an ache in her heart. That pain might fade, but it would never disappear.

It was going to take her a long time not to become nauseous or afraid when she thought of Nolan, even with him gone. But Regulus was right—his actions were his own.

She wouldn't ever be separated from Regulus so far as she could help it again. And she was going to marry him at the earliest opportunity.

Heavy footsteps echoed down the hall and she sat up, even though it sounded like a guard, not a servant. A man carried a sputtering torch to her cell.

"Belanger." Antar smiled as he unlocked the cell door. "Time to go. The king would like to see you. You have an hour to get presentable and be back in this cell."

"In the cell?" Adelaide stood and brushed off her dress, only smearing the grime further. "The king is…coming to the dungeon?" That made no sense.

"Oh, heavens, no." Antar swung the cell door wide open. "It didn't seem right, you being…you know." He gestured at her bloodied and disheveled appearance. "Not after all you've done. Beale's out purchasing supplies in town." He winked. "What he doesn't know won't hurt him. Or at the least, he can't stop."

She stepped out of the cell and followed Antar down the hallway. "He doesn't seem to like me much."

"Yeah, well." Antar cleared his throat. "He was good friends with Breck. Some of the guards saw you with Carrick just before everything went to pieces. Saw Carrick kill Breck first and you not helping. He has this harebrained notion you wanted Carrick to kill Breck, since you two didn't get along." He shrugged. "I talked him out of thinking you were on Carrick's side, but he still thinks you didn't care if Carrick killed Breck."

"Oh." She didn't know what else to say. Just thinking about teaming up with Nolan for anything made her lightheaded. Even if she hadn't given Breck's death a second thought, she wouldn't have conspired to kill him.

It was morning—late morning. The sun was blinding, and she had to shield her eyes. Antar led her to her room. To Adelaide's extreme disappointment, Regulus wasn't there. Antar didn't know where he was. But there was a tub of water. "I'll be right outside the door when you're done. I mean, I know you won't run, but…"

"I understand." She locked the door nonetheless.

A bar of soap sat on the table, next to the lantern—and the ivory-accented dagger. She stared at it, frozen as she remembered the sensation of the steel pressed against her neck. She shuddered and pushed her fear away. Nolan was dead. But she still hated that dagger. She threw a dirty shirt Regulus had left on the floor over the dagger.

The water felt amazing, if only a little warm. She used her magic to heat it further, then sunk in and rested her chin on her knees. She healed the bruises from the night on the stone, then scrubbed off the filth and stench. Her hair was such a disaster she climbed out of the tub before cleaning it. She couldn't finish lacing her sky-blue dress on her own. The tangled knots in her hair fought her comb as she worked through her long thick hair. She was nearly finished when she heard voices in the hall.

"Lieutenant? What's wrong?"

Her heart rejoiced at the sound of Regulus' voice. She tossed the comb on the bed and made for the door.

"Ah, I can't let you open that door," Antar said. "For decency's sake."

"What?" Regulus sounded bewildered and flustered.

Adelaide unlocked the door and threw it open to a view of the back of Antar's head. Regulus stood across from Antar, arms crossed, his mouth curved down, pulling on his scar. Dresden stood at Regulus' side, a look on his face like he was sizing Antar up for a fight. Regulus looked past Antar as she opened the door. He broke into a wide grin. Etiros above, that smile made her heart dance.

Antar glanced over his shoulder and stepped out of the way. She barreled past him and slammed against Regulus' chest. Regulus grunted, then laughed as he wrapped his arms around her. She closed her eyes and breathed him in. He smelled like linen and pepper and leather. And like he had been training, but she didn't care. She held him like she might never get the chance again.

"Hey," he murmured. His breath tickled the top of her ear. "You okay?"

"Yes. I am now." She pulled back so she could kiss him and didn't stop until Antar cleared his throat—twice. Regulus looked dazed. She turned and pointed at her back. "Can you finish lacing me up?"

"Huh?" Regulus said. "Oh, yeah."

Deep red suffused Antar's face, and he turned and faced down the hallway. Regulus grabbed the laces, but the dress didn't tighten around the top of her torso. Instead, his lips pressed against her back between the laces. She blushed.

"I missed you, too."

"I'm standing right here," Dresden complained.

"Then turn around or something," Regulus grumbled. The dress pulled closer around her shoulders and down her torso as he finished tightening the laces. He tied off the bottom and her breath caught as his mouth brushed over the base of her neck. "Is this okay?" he whispered.

She nodded, her heart running away in the best way possible. "More than okay." His fingers stroked the side of her neck as he pulled her hair over her back.

"Marry me, Adelaide." He kissed her cheek and slipped his arms around her waist.

"Great," Dresden said. "In case you're wondering, he likes to be called Captain or My Lord when he gives orders."

"It's not an order, you idiot," Regulus said with a laugh.

Adelaide turned in his arms with a chuckle and curled a strand of his hair around her finger. His clear gray eyes were the most beautiful thing she had ever seen. "I thought we already agreed?" She leaned forward to kiss him again, but Antar cleared his throat like he was trying to get the attention of an entire courtyard.

"You should, ah, finish brushing your hair. I need to get you back to the dungeon before Beale gets back."

Regulus frowned. "What? Why?"

"Rules are rules to Beale. Rules are…bendable when Beale's away." Antar motioned her back into the room. "Compromise so she can look like a lady in front of the king."

With reluctance, she left Regulus' arms and returned to combing her hair.

"The king has asked for her?"

"And you," Antar confirmed. "Couldn't find you, but I figured you'd show up. I have a servant boy looking for you, though."

Regulus reddened. "I, um…"

"Snuck out?" Antar asked.

Adelaide froze with the comb in her hair. Surely he wouldn't have done something so reckless, not now.

"Oh, no! Drez and I maybe…kind of…practiced our swordplay in the king's private training yard." Regulus shrugged. "No one ever uses it."

Adelaide held her breath. Then Antar laughed. "This is selfish of me, Hargreaves, but I hope the king keeps you two around. You keep things interesting."

Adelaide finished combing her hair and braided it. She slipped on clean boots and tied a narrow navy cloth belt around her waist, then stepped out of the room. Antar led her back to the dungeon. Regulus accompanied them, holding her hand until they reached the guard room, at which point Antar wouldn't let him continue.

"I'll see you soon, *mareh piahre*." Regulus ran his fingertips around the edge of her face.

"And then no more splitting up. For real this time." She kissed his cheek and whispered in his ear. "The sooner I can call you my husband, the easier that should be."

She left Regulus staring after her with a ridiculous boyish smile as she followed Antar back to her cell. She paced back and forth to keep herself from sitting down or leaning against the bars and soiling her dress. Finally, footsteps echoed down the hall—but it was a servant bringing food. Nervousness about seeing the king reduced her appetite, but she managed to eat most of the bread before more footsteps approached.

Beale opened the cell door and wrinkled his nose as she stepped out. "How'd you get cleaned up?"

She smiled and waved a hand. "Magic."

He stared for a moment, then shrugged. "Come on. You've been called to an audience with the king." She followed him back to the guard room. Beale selected a pair of manacles off the wall and walked toward her.

"Seriously?" Adelaide stared at the shackles.

"It's protocol." He grabbed her hand and closed the cold manacle around her wrist. "You're not above the rules." He locked the other manacle in place. The round metal bars laid heavy on her wrists. "Let's go, Belanger."

Regulus stood waiting outside. His face clouded as he strode toward her, eyes flashing. "Manacles, sir? Really?"

"Protocol," grunted Beale.

Regulus ground his teeth and wrapped his arm around her shoulders.

"No touching the prisoners." Beale glowered at them.

But Regulus didn't let go. "What're you going to do? Shackle me? Fine, but we'll be late." Adelaide had to purse her lips to keep from smiling at the irritated look Beale gave Regulus.

"Fine." Beale motioned them forward. "Just keep walking."

CHAPTER 46

THE ENTIRE TIME THEY MADE THEIR WAY THROUGH THE palace, Adelaide stayed nestled against Regulus' side. Beale led them to a room a little bigger than where they had first met the king. The furnishings were ostentatious, with candelabras covered in gold leaf and black marble statues of rearing horses that framed a large fireplace. A wood throne with cushions covered in deep purple cloth sat unoccupied on a small dais under a stained-glass window of a white hart in the woods. The front legs of the throne were carved with a dragon on one side and a knight on the other.

The door to their right, next to the fireplace, opened. They all bowed as the king strode in, his crimson cape brushing the ground behind him. The dragon-hilt sword hung at his hip and a gold crown rested on his head. He did not look at them as he crossed to the throne. It made Adelaide feel small and nervous.

After he sat on the throne, the king finally looked at them. "Adelaide Belanger. Step forward."

Adelaide moved forward, Regulus' arm slipping off her shoulders and leaving her cold. She knelt before the king and lowered her head, the shackles on her wrists clinking a reminder of her tenuous position.

"Adelaide Belanger, you stand accused of desertion from the ranks of the royal guard, of disobeying a direct order from your commanding officer, of attacking other members of the royal guard, and abandoning your sacred oath to us, that you would protect us first and foremost. What defense do you give?"

The forbidding coldness in the king's tone wasn't promising. Adelaide took a moment to answer, praying for the right words.

"Your Excellency." She looked up at the king's hard expression and fought to keep her tone measured and even. "The night of the masque I did everything in my power to protect Your Excellency and your family. I gave my energy; I gave my strength. And against my will, I sacrificed my betrothed to capture and torture and I lost my father to the next life." Emotion gave her voice a slight tremor, and she had to push aside her heartache to continue.

"I did not disobey orders because I wanted to turn my back on Your Excellency or my duty," she continued. "I did not want to wait for Kirven to come. Nor could I. The bond between Regulus and I meant that the longer they tortured him, the weaker I became. If I had done as ordered, Kirven would have come and I would have been drained of power and Your Excellency's life would have been in danger. I set out to rescue Regulus and stop Kirven and Nolan Carrick before they hurt or killed anyone else, including Your Excellency. And that's what I did. I do not regret my choice." She lowered her head. "I humbly beg Your Excellency's pardon for my disobedience. I did it out of regard for my duty, not disdain."

The king sat silent while sweat beaded on her brow. "Sir Michael," the king called.

The side door opened. Sir Michael the steward scuttled in, the Staff of Nightfall in his hands. So Dresden had made it back to the palace, she realized with relief. Sir Michael held it out to Adelaide. She took it, confused why he had given it to her. The steward stepped away.

"What would you recommend we do with our brother's weapon?" The king rested his chin on his ring-laden fingers.

There was only one thing to do with it, but Adelaide doubted she had the strength. She lowered her head and gripped the Staff, letting her magic flow into it, exploring it. She flinched at the anger and destructive sorcery her magic brushed against in the Staff, but she also found weaknesses. Kirven had been right—the rebounded spell had caused fissures all along the Staff of Nightfall.

She closed her eyes and channeled her magic into the fissures, concentrating on hardening the magic into solid light, like driving a wedge into a crack. Light glowed in front of her closed lids. Then, with a sound like a crack of thunder, a flash of light, and a rush of her power, the staff shattered in her hands. Adelaide collapsed forward and pressed her trembling hands against the floor, panting, but allowed herself a slight smile. Gold and opal pieces littered the carpet.

"I would throw the pieces into the sea, Your Excellency," she said, breathless.

Several moments passed before the king spoke. "Sir Michael, please gather the pieces and have them thrown into the sea at three different points." Sir Michael gathered the pieces as the king continued. "Lieutenant Beale remove her shackles. Adelaide Belanger, you have asked for our pardon, and we freely—and gratefully—give it."

"Thank you, Your Excellency." Adelaide swayed as she stood and curtsied to the king, then drew back next to Regulus. Beale didn't look pleased as he removed her manacles, but she was too relieved to care.

"You are dismissed, Lieutenant Beale." The king waved a hand. Beale bowed to the king and departed with a quick glare at Adelaide.

Regulus placed his arm around her shoulders, and Adelaide slumped against his side, exhausted.

"We owe you both our life and our kingdom." The king inclined his head. "What reward would you ask of us?"

Could they ask to be released from the guard? She didn't want to appear dismissive of the king's generosity, but would asking be impertinent? Regulus also seemed unsure since he didn't speak. She had just been pardoned; maybe humility was best.

"Your Excellency," Adelaide said with a wobbly curtsy, "your continued rule is a reward in itself."

The king smiled. "A noble answer, but please. This is your chance to ask anything." His eyes danced. "We grant you two boons to show our gratitude. The first is our choice, the second is yours. First, in recognition of your service and your sacrifice, we release you, Lady Adelaide Belanger and Lord Regulus Hargreaves of Arrano, from our service. You are free to return to your former lives."

She curtsied and heard Regulus sigh with relief as he bowed.

"What would you ask of us?" the king pressed.

Before Adelaide thought of an answer, Regulus whispered in her ear. She smiled and nodded.

"Your Excellency, there is only one thing I want in this entire world." Regulus squeezed her hand. "Would Your Excellency perform our marriage rites?"

CHAPTER 47

"MARRIAGE? RIGHT NOW?" THE KING'S FOREHEAD WRINKLED. "Here?"

"If it pleases Your Excellency, yes." Adelaide tapped her toes, impatience restoring some of her drained energy. They could find a priest or lord or someone if the king said no, but she was ready now.

A slow smile spread over the king's face. He stood. "Very well." He looked around the room. "I shall send for a unity cord."

She untied the thin midnight blue cloth belt from her waist. "We can use this, Your Excellency."

The king took the belt. "Face each other and take each other's right hand."

They did as instructed, and Adelaide could no longer stop her wide smile. Regulus grinned until the skin wrinkled around his scar. She fixed her gaze on his sparkling gray eyes and her pulse quickened in eager anticipation.

"Lord Regulus Hargreaves, Lady Adelaide Belanger." The king began looping the belt over and around their clasped hands. "Today you declare before Etiros, before man, and before your king, that you shall henceforth be united. As we now bind your hands, may this cord symbolize that you shall be bound to each other, heart, mind, body, and soul." The king tied the ends of the cords together and rested the knot on top of their hands. "Let this knot never be undone, nor the bond between this man and woman severed."

The traditional Monparthian marriage blessing placed a dull ache in her heart. Her gaze drifted down to Regulus' right sleeve. He squeezed her hand. When she met his eyes again, they were brimming with joy and not a hint of doubt. The ache abated and she waited impatiently for the king to finish the blessing.

"May love and joy mark your days." The king clasped his hands. "When darkness falls, may you be each other's light. When light abounds, may you increase each other's joy. When storms come, may you be each other's strength. When you disagree, may you remember you started this journey hand in hand. And when tensions arise," the king tugged on the sides of the knot and tightened it further, "may they serve only to bring you closer together." He looked at Regulus. "Would you like to add your own vows?"

Regulus nodded. "I..." His voice broke and he cleared his throat. "I promise to respect you, honor you, love you, and protect you so long as I live. I will stand by your side as you stand by mine. I will love you and you only, wholly and completely. You are my home, my life—*mareh piahre*. I choose you to be mine and give myself to you. I would not change you, but I cherish you as you are, my mage, my *shiraa*." He rubbed her hand with his thumb, sending a spark dancing over her skin. "The bond that exists between us, connecting us heart to heart and soul to soul, shall never be broken."

The king looked to her, but she had to try several times to speak as she blinked away tears. *The bond that exists.* Not existed. Exists. They didn't need magic to bind them any more than her parents did. *I wish Father were here.* She swallowed back her sorrow as her mind drifted to the vows Mother had written for her wedding and framed in their cottage in the woods. A combination of Monparthian and Khastallander tradition. She adapted what she could remember of them now.

"From this day forward, I walk beside you." Her voice strengthened as she continued, echoing the resolve in her heart. "We will walk together, we will share our strength, our happiness, and our trials. I will walk beside you in love and sacrifice. What is mine is yours, and what is yours is mine." She paused, remembering his full acceptance of every part of her. "*Naem vishodah rohpe ahpek sanerpat hohn, aor haem ahp mareh kusheh.*" Regulus' brows drew together, but his smile didn't fade nor did the sparkle in his eyes. She repeated herself in Monparthian. "I am purely devoted to you, and you are my joy."

The king waited a moment to ensure she was done, then spoke. "Lord Hargreaves, do you take this woman to be your wedded wife, to serve and protect and cherish her, from this day until you breathe your last?"

"I do." Regulus responded almost before the king had finished speaking.

"Lady Adelaide, do you take this man to be your wedded husband, to serve and respect and cherish him, from this day until you breathe your last?"

"I do." She bounced on the balls of her feet.

"Then by the power we hold as king of Monparth, we solemnly charge you to keep these vows, and we pronounce you husband and wife. From this day forward, you will be known as Lord and Lady Hargreaves of Arrano. Lord Hargreaves, you may kiss your bride."

Adelaide grabbed the back of Regulus' head as he placed his hand on her waist and they kissed, their hands still clasped between them with her belt loosely tying them together. She could tell Regulus wanted to pull her closer, but instead he let his lips leave hers.

"May Etiros bless you and your marriage." The king gathered up the top of the belt and they slipped their hands out. He handed the tied belt to Regulus.

Regulus bowed and looped the belt over his arm. "Thank you, Your Excellency."

The king sat back down on his throne but did not dismiss them. Regulus slid his arm around her waist as they waited.

"We would recognize you in front of all our people," the king said. "Tomorrow night, we will host a banquet in your honor." He smiled. "After that, you are free to return to Arrano."

Adelaide curtsied and Regulus bowed as they murmured their thanks. The king rose and left the room. Regulus turned and swept her off her feet and kissed her with all the passion he had held back in front of the king. "My wife."

"My husband." She took his hand and they exited the way they had come in. A servant escorted them out of the palace, casting incredulous looks over his shoulder as they giggled like children and once nearly walked into a display of armor because they were too busy staring into each other's eyes. The servant left them in the rear courtyard in a hurry. They were so busy hanging onto each other, she didn't notice Dresden running toward them until he skidded to a stop in front of the entrance to the servant's wing.

"What did the king say?" Dresden demanded as they straightened and pulled apart slightly, heat rushing to Adelaide's face. "No shackles, so is everything…" His eyes narrowed at Regulus' arm and he pointed. "What—wait. Is that…a unity cord?" He staggered back, jaw hanging open and brow pinched over wounded eyes. "Regulus Daveth Hargreaves, did you get married without me?"

Adelaide blushed and looked away, hoping she looked less awkward than she felt.

"Ah… We, I mean…" Regulus cleared his throat. "The king released us from the guard and then he…we were…Drez—"

"Oh, I see." Dresden threw his hands up. "I get you two together and I'm not invited to the wedding!" He rolled his eyes.

410

"It's fine, I'm just waiting, mad with worry, while you're getting married without me, not even thinking about me, headed to your room clinging to each other like a couple of…" His eyes widened. "Oh great Etiros above and all the world below. I—I should go…" He edged away from the door into the courtyard. "Totally forgot, I need to…uh, see a man about, um…a goat?" He gave Regulus an exaggerated wink and left.

Regulus and Adelaide looked at each other, then doubled over laughing. Regulus looped his arm around her waist and drew her close as they made their way inside. At their door, Regulus stopped.

"Ah, wait. I've always wanted to do this." He pushed the door open then swept her into his arms. Her head bumped the door-frame and her boot caught on the wall. He stumbled into the room, both of them shaking with laughter.

"Well, that went differently in my head." He set her down on the bed and caressed her cheek. "How are you feeling? You looked drained after breaking the staff. Do you…need food? Water?" He hesitated. "Sleep?"

"Are you joking?" She grabbed his shirt and pulled him down to kiss him. Her heart danced as they tumbled onto the bed, tangled in each other's arms. "Right now?" she whispered, breathless. "I just need my husband."

CHAPTER 48

THE EARLY MORNING SUN WARMED REGULUS' BACK, AND HIS chest grazed Adelaide's back as they rode toward home. Her braided hair smelled of honey and flowers. A light breeze whispered through the yellowing leaves of the orchard to their right and the field of grain to their left. The horses' hooves kept a steady beat on the rutted dirt road. Dresden rode to their right, and a white mare from the king trailed along behind carrying their saddlebags.

"Zephyr was a gift from Father," Adelaide had murmured. "I'm sure I'll love her eventually. But not yet."

Regulus didn't mind riding together in the least. Since their marriage, he found he always wanted to touch her. Hold her hand, stroke her hair, put his arm around her waist or shoulders. Just to know she was there, and to let her know he was there. To reassure himself that she was his, and he was hers, and this bliss wasn't just a dream. Currently, he had his arms looped around her middle, Sieger's reins held loosely in his right hand.

They didn't have much to pack. Other than food, the saddlebags carried the gifts the king had given them at the banquet, in front of the court. Nobles had clapped and cheered and raised their glasses when the king toasted them and made certain to shake their hands and congratulate them. Many seemed genuine. Regulus pretended not to notice the others' occasional murmurs of *illegitimate*, *mercenary*, *non-noble*, and *foreign*. Their judgment hurt, but when Regulus looked at Adelaide, he knew they were stronger than any narrow-minded, insecure nobles.

The rich gifts made Regulus nervous to travel across Monparth alone. A sack of gold coins as a reward for killing the sorcerer. A small wooden box engraved with running deer with antlers carved from actual antlers that held their unity cord. A delicate sword, about a foot long and made of pure silver with a handle of gold as a gift for Lady Tamina Belanger in recognition of Alfred's sacrifice. Adelaide had cried when she accepted the sword.

The king had also given them the sword that hung at Regulus' side and a set of throwing knives and a dagger Adelaide had hidden in her boots. At least their riches were hidden in an average-looking saddlebag. Besides, between the three of them, any would-be bandits would regret targeting them.

"I still don't know how I'm going to tell Mother," Adelaide said, breaking the silence. "And Landon…he's going to blame me."

"It's not your fault. If he can't see that, if he doesn't see you as a hero like the king does, that's his problem." Regulus sighed and rubbed her upper arm through her soft sleeve. "And I'll be with you. You won't have to do it alone."

She shuddered against his chest and took a shaky breath. "Promise?"

"I already did." He kissed her cheek. "Forever and always. No more splitting up."

She laughed and wiped away a tear. "Thank you."

"Anything for my wife." He kissed the back of her neck. And then behind her ear, making her giggle.

"Again, I am right here," Drez said. "Save the newly-wed shenanigans for when you're alone. Gracious." But his complaining sounded a lot more like amusement than disgust.

"First on the agenda after we get to Arrano," Adelaide said. "Find Dresden a lady so we can get some peace."

"Now that," Drez said with a chuckle, "is an idea I can get behind; especially now that I have somebody to keep an eye on Regulus. Which is exhausting, I hope you realize. Say, you sure you're fresh out of unwed sisters?"

Adelaide laughed. The genuine, lighthearted laugh he loved so much, that reminded him no darkness was inescapable. "Quite sure." She leaned her head back on Regulus' shoulder and reached up to play with his hair. He had to fight the urge to close his eyes instead of paying attention to where Sieger was going.

Not that he cared much where they went. They needed to see Tamina, and he wanted to bring his wife home to Arrano. He could already imagine the congratulatory heckling the men would give him. But he was in no rush. He didn't care where they traveled or how long it took to get there.

Regulus was free to do what he wanted, not only what he was told. Free to face his men without worrying if he would hurt them. Free to love Adelaide and choose to fulfill her every wish. He rested his cheek against her temple and watched the sky turn from pink to brilliant blue.

He had everything he needed right here.

THE END

Author's Note

Many of the struggles Regulus and Adelaide face in this book—low self-worth, guilt, shame, depression, fear, self-doubt, assault, abuse, loss—are topics that are near and dear to my heart, all because I or people I know have experienced them.

Regulus and Adelaide spend a lot of this book learning to trust and draw strength from each other. While a relationship cannot magically heal anyone—and indeed, both Regulus and Adelaide are still healing and learning—I do believe in the importance of love and relationships of all kinds (familial, platonic, and romantic). I personally am so grateful to the people in my life who have supported me. And I am constantly striving to be a better friend to those close to me. I also find comfort in my Lord and Savior, even in the midst of brokenness.

I strive to write healthy relationships between people who make mistakes, are unsure of themselves, and sometimes do the wrong thing, but keep trying, keep listening and supporting and loving each other. My hope and prayer is that Regulus, Adelaide, Dresden, Alfred, Tamina, and the others encourage you to turn to loving friends and family if you are hurting, and to be that source of love and support for the people in your life. (And to know that you deserve friends who believe and encourage you, not who make you feel worse. ♥) I hope they remind you that whatever hurt you are facing—it will not last forever.

Thank you for following Adelaide and Regulus on their journey. Love,

Selina R. Gonzalez

SUPPORT RESOURCES

If you or someone you love are struggling with depression, suicidal thoughts, abuse, or with a difficult situation in your life, please ask for help. I know from experience how scary it can be to admit you're not all right, but you can get help. You are worth saving, worth loving, and your life is worth living. And if someone you know opens up to you about their struggles, listen, don't doubt or disparage or lecture, and seek to help.

You can find a list of a few resources on my website at: www.SelinaRGonzalez.com/Support

If you need help right now, the US National Suicide Prevention Hotline is: 1-800-273-8255

SELINA R. GONZALEZ

ACKNOWLEDGEMENTS

First, dear reader, thank you for reading! You are the reason I write, and the reason I can continue to write. And an extra thank you if you leave an honest review on your retailer of choice. ♥

Mom—thank you again for being my faithful reader, fan, and proofreader.

Thanks to Dad for always being proud of me, even when you're not quite sure what's going on.

Rebecca, Jessica, and Sylvia—thank you for your constant support and boosting me when I'm discouraged or overwhelmed.

Thank you, Alexis, for reading an early draft and for being an amazing, supportive friend and dealing with my randomness.

Mr. E, thank you for reading my drafts and always being excited to talk about writing, stories, and publishing over a cup of tea.

Becky, thank you so much for your feedback and encouragement and willingness to listen when publishing is confusing and hard.

Jenni, I appreciate your listening ear and constant readiness to chat, let me rant, or celebrate with me.

Rowan, THANK YOU for your incredible CP-ing of book one!

Janice, Claire, and Verity, thank you so much for beta reading!

To all my family who have bought copies, shared about it, and otherwise been so loving and supportive (and not just of publishing, but throughout my life), thank you. You've helped me so much.

Thank you to my reader group for all your excitement!

So much gratitude to the fun, amazing, encouraging, and supportive community on bookstragram.

To everyone who has helped or encouraged me on this journey, know that I'm thankful for you!

Finally, praise and thanks to God and Jesus Christ, with whom all things are possible.

ABOUT THE AUTHOR

Selina R. Gonzalez is a Colorado native with mountains in her blood and dreams that top 14,000 feet. She loves chocolate, fantasy, costumes, bread, history, superheroes, faux leather, things that sparkle, medieval Britain, snark, dogs, and Jesus—not in that order.

She loves to travel, and has driven coast-to-coast in the US, visited Britain three times (once for a semester at Oxford), and moved to Maine for four and half months. She has a list of places to go as long as Pikes Peak is tall, but always comes back home to Colorado.

You can find Selina raving about books she's enjoying (or adding to her bottomless pit of a to-be-read pile) on Facebook (Selina R. Gonzalez, Author) and Instagram (@NightTooIsBeautiful) and being generally goofy and snarky as well as talking about writing, life, and the antics of her siblings' dogs in her IG stories. Make sure you don't miss any of Selina's future books by subscribing to her newsletter on her website at SelinaRGonzalez.com.